Raising Elle

The Sweet Valley Series

Book One

S.E. Reichert

5 Prince Publishing

Published by 5 PRINCE PUBLISHING & BOOKS, LLC

PO Box 865, Arvada, CO 80001

www.5PrinceBooks.com

ISBN digital: 978-1-63112-307-8

ISBN print: 978-1-63112-308-5

Cover Credit: Marianne Nowicki

For my Grandma Emma, and all the strong women I know, who pull themselves up, stand tall, and keep fighting.

Domestic Violence Hotline

"Abusers repeatedly go to extremes to prevent their victim from leaving. In fact, leaving an abuser is the most dangerous time for a victim of domestic violence. One study found, in interviews with men who have killed their wives, that either threats of separation by their partner or actual separations were most often the precipitating events that lead to the murder."

—National Coalition Against Domestic Violence (NCADV)

For anonymous, confidential help available 24/7, call the National Domestic Violence Hotline at 1-800-799-7233 (SAFE) or 1-800-787-3224 (TTY) now.

Also by S.E. Reichert

RAISING ELLE

PROLOGUE

MEMORIES ARE FUNNY. FADED AND DISJOINTED. THE creak of the iron stair railing, the hard and quick pressure of his boot between her shoulder blades, the flashes of sunlight through the stairwell windows. The sickening crack of ulna and radius, as momentum overwhelmed their frailty. A jarring stair against her stomach, the metal clang before the world went black.

Breath—whisper.

Taste of blood, warm rush between legs. She tried to sit up but every limb felt a thousand miles away. She needed to change before he saw but her body was weighted to the earth. Yells funneled to whimpers, lost to a discord of light and noise, flutter of paper gowns, the even cadence of beeping machines.

Fight.

In and out of consciousness, while a disjointed reality played old movies just behind her eyelids. Sunlight and open hayfields. Her grandmother. Her sisters. Her mother. Power seeped through her anesthesia-addled brain, restrained for too long. The moment she knew she had to leave, by any means necessary, was the one she woke up in, still alive.

ONE

ELLE ARRIVED IN SWEET VALLEY WITH A LITTLE OVER A thousand dollars, a small bag of clothes, and face bruised to hell. Six years had not changed the town, save a new digital clock in front of the Valley Bank and Trust and a fresh coat of paint on the broken-up curb. The early spring wasn't immune to snowstorms, so the planters in front of the Thompson's Hardware store remained bowls of dirt, and the banners that flew during the summer events of the small town were still stored somewhere in the vaults of the Community Center. The town was sleepy, a slower-paced slice of Americana, tucked away from the world.

Elle grunted and shook her head. The quaintness was a double-edged sword. She parked her dilapidated truck and looked at the main street, showing the signs of wear and age without the income to repair it. Sweet Valley was always teetering on the brink of being another one of Wyoming's ghost towns. People here hated change. They didn't want big city life intruding. But that meant new businesses rarely made it, and the kids of the town moved away to where work could be found. The only people left were those that had no place else to go.

She guessed she was in the right spot.

She hadn't told her family she was coming. Shame seemed the most likely culprit. As if there wasn't enough of it in her crawling back home, but to see her parents' faces fall in disappointment at what she'd let herself become...

Elle swallowed the empty taste of bile when it rose to the back of her tongue.

Forewarning or not, they'd know soon enough. Some things in life change, but Elle was fairly certain Sweet Valley's gossip chain was not one of them. She imagined what they might say about her now, with a twist of anger in her belly, and all the ways she hadn't lived up to the girl she once was.

She was not at all the effervescent, small-town sweetheart that had won homecoming queen, science fairs; the fund-raiser extraordinaire. The years and the disastrous haircut she'd given herself in a truck-stop bathroom in Moapa erased the former beauty and her bouncing blonde curls. Mostly it was the years.

To be honest, she hadn't really known if she was going to make it this far. She didn't know what would catch her between L.A. County and here. She hadn't let herself think about anything but the next mile marker, the next rise of the sun. The next anything that was hell and far away from her past.

Elle's neck ached, her head throbbed, and the rumbling in her stomach turned to an angry discord of nerves and hunger. She sat in the seat of the truck, that still smelled slightly of the desperation of a gambler selling it for the next big chance, and listened to her body turn on itself. She felt the emptiness she'd come to associate with being Elle. She sniffed and wiped at her eyes. What was she doing here? She searched back through the memories. The why. The who.

There it was in shuddering waves behind the layers of so much dark. She locked on to the pictures. Seven miles outside of town, Warren and Melissa Sullivan were just getting done with the morning chores, feeding the horses, grooming, and taking temperatures. They'd be getting ready for breeding season and looking to figure how many they could manage with the budget that shrank every year. They would work beside each other, effortlessly, so attuned to the pattern and need of the other that they barely had to speak. But they would smile, often and sweetly, at each other.

Her father would head out on house calls or to his clinic in town. He'd be in his Wranglers and button-down shirt, a ball cap because his Stetson was too nice for a Wednesday, and definitely too nice for the blood and gore of veterinary work that came on any given day. Her mother would be in the garden, getting it ready for spring planting, feeding the chickens, maybe looking forward to an afternoon ride to check on the irrigation and fence lines. The memory chiseled away at the dark curtain and their lives froze in that perfect, cold morning of habitual work and peace. In Elle's mind, they had to.

She needed to believe that there was still something good in the world.

"Were you planning on telling us you were back, or were you just gonna sit here parked all catawampus in front of the hardware store until we heard it from Laura nose-up-your-business Pratt?"

The voice outside her window barked, and Elle jumped away. Her gut-reaction to throw all limbs out in defense was halted by the sight of the woman standing and scowling in at her. Elle's eyes grew wide in recognition, but paralyzed with disbelief.

"Katie?" A breath, a prayer. The freckled-nosed younger sister that she'd left behind at the age of twenty hadn't changed much but for a few extra curves and a keen look in her blue eyes. She'd just come from the hardware store with a new set of shears in her hand and an extra pair of gloves sticking from her back pocket. Katelyn stepped back and motioned for her to get out, and Elle scrabbled at the handle and unfolded herself from the truck. Tears that lay dormant for the last 1,800 miles bubbled up into her throat and broke out in a cruel sob.

"Katie," she whispered.

"Well, shit, Elle, I didn't mean to make you cry!" Katelyn
didn't let her fall into a crouch. Didn't let her run. Didn't let her
do any of the things that Elle did to stay safe. She rushed her,
pulled her into her arms, and held on tight. The muscle memory of
being held caused Elle to shudder and freeze. But Katelyn didn't
smell like cheap cologne and sweat. She smelled like sweet hay, and
barn dust, and dirt. Like the home that Elle wanted so badly to
remember. The home behind that dark curtain.

Katelyn looked around at the deserted street. "When'd ya
get in?"

"I just—just today. I didn't call or anything. I should have
called," she sniffed.

"Well, I'm headed that way. Let's go together. Whooee!
They're gonna love seeing you." Katelyn said. Elle wiped her nose
on her sleeve and left a streak of blood. Katelyn took an old
bandana out of her pocket and offered it. Then she pushed Elle's
shortened hair back from her face. Uncovered the fading bruises.
The still-pink scars.

"What the fuck happened?"

Elle looked away with a scowl.

"I don't want to talk about it."

"Fair enough, but if I see that son-of-a-bitch, I will kill him,
make no mistake about that." Katelyn scowled back.

"I'll follow you out," Elle said, aching to change the subject.

"Like hell, Eleanor Augusta. You look like you haven't slept in
a week, or eaten in a month. I'm driving."

"Do we gotta do this, right now?" Elle said, and tried to evoke
the big sister voice.

She knew she'd been too long away and lost her touch when
Katelyn responded by pulling her towards their dad's vet truck
with a simple, "Yep."

"Katelyn—"

"Six years, Elle! The last three, we haven't heard a word from you. I tried telling Dad we should go after you." She paused when tears threatened. "Goddamn it, I should have come for you."

"Katie, you were just a kid." Elle hung her head. Katelyn took her hand.

"So were you, Elle." She tried to look down into Elle's bowed head. "Get in, Slim." Katelyn nodded to the truck and Elle looked back to her own.

"What about my truck?"

"We'll send someone back to get it."

"Someone?"

"Sure, Dad probably forgot something *else*. I'll be running into town for later. Come on." Elle didn't follow and Katelyn looked back. "I swear to God, I'll hog tie you if you even think about leaving now."

"When did you get so pushy?"

"Well, Laney taught me a few things."

Elle swallowed. "How is the professor?" Sadness wrung her heart out for the older sister who had so often came to her rescue when they were kids.

"Well, she's divorced. I guess you might not know that with everything you got going on." Katelyn paused and huffed out a breath, clearly out of her emotional element.

"But her kids?"

"Yeah, well, apparently they weren't as important as the young piece of ass David found."

The sadness of it; of the time Elle had lost; the time taken from her made Elle heartsick. Her nieces were just babies when she'd left. Her older, steadfast sister, unbreakable, now broken. They were all broken. Except Katelyn, who seemed to be ornerier than hell.

"I—I'd really rather not go home right now."

"Girl, you're already home." Katelyn said. "Come on. Mom will tan my hide if she finds out I let you out of my sight." She paused, looked around the quiet street. "Speakin' of out of sight, where *is* Aaron, Elle?"

"I don't—I don't know." Elle swallowed. He could be anywhere. Around the next bend in the road, or still a thousand miles away. He could be standing behind her. She felt hot air touch her neck and turned around on instinct. Her little sister saw it all.

"Come on. Let's get you home." Katelyn yanked open the door to the truck and gave Elle's lanky frame a gentle shove inside.

The drive took forever and still not nearly long enough for Elle to collect her thoughts and gather the courage it would take. Her stomach tied itself in such tight knots that she was sure she was going to throw up. Luckily, there was nothing in it to come out. Katelyn watched her as they pulled into the drive.

"You look like you're about to be lined up for a firing squad."

Elle stared straight ahead, pale and unmoving.

"Hey," Katelyn reached out to touch her shoulder, and Elle jumped away, curling up against the door of the truck. Katelyn pulled her hand back.

"Jesus Christ, I will kill him." She grumbled, slammed the door, and came around to Elle's side. She opened the door, but Elle made no move to exit.

"I got you, Elle. I know it's been a while, but they got you, too. They always have. They always will. You just need to get out of the truck." Katelyn extended her hand and used a tone so soft and soothing it was no wonder she was a bona fide horse whisperer. From the house, a sudden squawk erupted, followed by the sound of a screen door slamming and hurried feet headed their way.

"Watch out now—" Katelyn tried to warn before Melissa Sullivan rushed in and pulled Elle from the truck into a tight hug.

"My baby! My girl!" she sobbed and buried her head of graying hair into Elle's chest. Elle tensed at the pressure and noise. Panic rose in her chest. Then...she breathed, and the smell stopped it. Dove soap. Fresh baked biscuits. Coffee. Home. Mom. Something deeper, cellular, caused Elle's panic to abate, and her lean arms went around her mom. She held on.

"Hey, Momma."

"Why, you aren't anything but skin and bones." she sobbed, pulling away to look at Elle.

"I can't argue with that," Katelyn said.

"Where are your things? Where's Aaron? Oh my God—" Melissa stopped her deluge when Elle's face caught her attention. "I'll kill him."

"Seems to be the general consensus," Katelyn muttered under her breath. Elle lowered her eyes. Her mother tilted her chin up.

"You look at me, you brave, beautiful girl. You are loved, and you are safe, and you're never going back there. You hear me?"

Elle didn't have time to respond. Her father was taking long strides towards them and when he saw Elle's face, his bright eyes turned stormy blue.

"I swear to God, I'm gonna k—"

"Kill him. We know, Dad. Get in line," Katelyn said.

"Slim," Warren said, voice cracking as he moved to hug her. Elle shook, every muscle tense. All of the years of being told she was worthless, unloved, unwanted, had built up a universe of disease in her heart. "Easy, Slim. Just take a breath." Her father's soothing voice was lilting and calm, his steady hands moving gently towards her as if he could sense the wounded animal in her.

Elle's heart quickened, heat rose in her chest, sweat sprung up in painful flashes, and the world tunneled into darkness.

TWO

She woke up startled, and sure that Aaron was at the foot of the bed, watching and waiting for her to regain consciousness. Every time she woke, it was the same. Things were still fuzzy; two concussions would do that. The first, he'd pushed her out of the car while it was still moving. The last one...Elle shuddered and a wave of nausea made her fall back into the bed. Stairs. So many fucking stairs, and she'd hit every single one of them on the way down. At least the bruises and breaks said so. She opened one eye to find her old bedroom dark and empty. She must have fainted, right there, in front of her parents, panic-attacked out, and lost it. A groan of embarrassment issued from under the blankets, tucked up to her nose.

Her skull pounded with the residual headache; a protest echoed from her empty belly. Everything felt hollow and dark. Why had she ever come home?

Then a heavenly smell floated up from downstairs. Pot roast with vegetables and homemade bread. And mashed potatoes. It had to be a dream. Elle flung the blankets from her legs and stood too fast. She sunk lamely back to the floor.

"Easy, Slim," she said, and heard Warren in her voice. She took the quilt from the bed, wrapped it around her shivering body, and made her way down the hall. She took each stair carefully and stopped short of the kitchen, listening to the timeless sounds of her family gathered. Pots clanking, boots scuffing as they were taken off by the door, and soft words being exchanged.

"Oh, she'll be so happy that you're here."

"My goodness, how big they've grown in a few months."

"Hey, Squirt!"

"How's the book coming, Laney?"

Elle sat on the steps, arms locked around her knees, and listened. Had she actually died in the last fall? She bit her lip hard to see what plane of reality she was in and split open the healing wound. Must be real, she thought, and dabbed at it with the sleeve of her shirt.

"When she gets more settled, we can talk about Gran's place. But she's been through a lot and I don't want to add to it." Warren said. Elle pictured him at the head of the table, all business, before the meal.

"We have to do what we have to do, but I'd rather we not sell it just the same." Katelyn responded.

"Last year's foaling was not quite enough to carry it, and the drought left us with no hay to sell last year. We could barely cover the property taxes last quarter. Nobody wants to sell it—"

"I wish I could get a signing contract on the next books—"

"It's not your job to save our land single-handedly, Laney June—"

"But it would be something."

"We'll get through it. Even if we have to sell it, Gran would understand—" Warren assuaged, even as the volume in the room rose.

Elle's foggy brain processed the new information. She was kept away from her family the last few years, so she hadn't known how hard it had been for them, financially. Her great grandparents had immigrated from Ireland in the 1930s and had settled a piece of land on the upper North Platte thirty years later. They'd built a life here. A thriving horse ranch; a name in the valley. But times were changing, and the only people who could afford land now were often the ones too rich to want to work it.

The family's land was in a deeded trust. All parties had to agree to the sale. What were the chances that she would stumble into town at the pinnacle of such a hard choice? She didn't believe in coincidences; she didn't know what she believed in anymore.

Elle sat back against the wall, stared at the homemade quilt under her fingers, and relived the memories in every checkered square of mismatched cloth. Some from old flannel shirts, some from old blankets. A couple of Gran's aprons. Too many losses settled in her heart and she didn't know how she'd ever lift herself from the weight. The thought of Gran's land being gone hurt her worse than her own troubles somehow.

Melissa peeked around the corner.

"Hey, baby. We didn't wake you, did we?"

"Don't sell the land," Elle's voice was loud when it echoed through her head.

"What?"

"Gran's land. Don't sell it. I mean, not yet. Maybe—maybe we —maybe *I* can help."

"Elle, honey." Elle got up and walked into the dining room, still wrapped in the quilt, pale and shaky, but on her own two feet.

"Elle," Laney cried and moved to hug her, but Warren held her back.

"Just ease up. Elle, honey, we're all going to talk about that as a family, later."

Elle looked around. Laney standing next to Katelyn. Neither one the taller and neither one less fiercely beautiful. To Laney's left, the two nieces she hadn't seen except in photos. Beautiful and unreserved, as they met her gaze, they rushed her. Little arms wrapped around her legs and nearly knocked her to the ground.

"Aunt Elle!" Charlotte squealed.

"We've missed you." Sylvia squeezed her hard until all breath left her body. Elle, unsure about what to do with such innocent affection, gently patted their backs and allowed herself to feel their warmth with hesitation.

"I want—I want to help. I want to help fix it up. Get the fields ready, clean up the house, the barn and stables. If we can make it a working ranch again, maybe it would sell easier."

"Eleanor—" Melissa interjected.

"It's free labor, Mom. Then you'll get more money from it when it is time to sell." The thoughts rushed around her tender head.

"Elle, you need to be worrying about getting better." Her mother gestured for her to sit down. Elle shook her head.

"I can't. I can't worry about me anymore, Momma. I can't keep reliving what he did to me and what I had to do to survive. I can't get better unless I can *do* something. Something real. Something on my own."

"Elle," Melissa's voice cracked. "Of course, you will, some day—"

"I mean today. I want to start today."

"Elle—" Laney started, but when their eyes met, she stopped and shifted her course, landing resolutely on her sister's side. "Elle's right. She needs something to do."

"Sometimes the best way to heal is to find purpose," Katelyn nodded and turned back to their mother, who screwed up her mouth disapprovingly. When faced with the, now three, sisters standing together, she knew there was no use to it.

"Well, all right."

"I want to see it. So we know what needs done."

"Yeah, that is a good point," Katelyn nodded and rubbed her chin in thought. "Those fields have been resting for years. There's an orchard and plenty of grazing land. The barn needs repairs, but the coop is still good. I think there's a lot of potential."

"Now hold on a minute," Warren held up his hands. The

women turned towards him, arms crossed in front of their chests, and he knew better than to argue. "Can't a fella eat a little something first?" He rubbed his belly. "'Fore we start thinking about fixing up a ranch in the middle of a tight year?"

Melissa smirked at him. "All right. Everybody, sit down."

Elle settled into a chair, a sister on each side, and stared at the steamy and tender roast, surrounded with bright orange carrots, and translucent onions, and gravy, the heaping bowl of mashed potatoes beside it, butter melting on the top as steam rose from it. The crack of the loaf of bread was as homey and familiar as the smell of it when Sylvia tore off a chunk to the dismay of her mother's sense of manners. Elle's mouth watered; her stomach churned. Her hands stayed firmly in her lap.

"What can I get you?" her mom asked.

"I don't...I don't think I need—"

Katelyn scowled and filled Elle's plate with big scoops of potatoes, a healthy serving of the roast, and a chunk of bread.

"Pass the butter?" she asked Sylvia.

"Katie, I don't—" Elle protested as Katelyn buttered her bread.

"Can't go making big plans unless you eat something. Those are the rules."

"Whose rules?" Elle scowled, still feeling Aaron's control in the pit of her soul.

"Gran's." Katelyn said. Elle looked at the plate. Laney put a fork in her hand.

"Go on now. You eat, then we'll plan."

ELLE'S BATTERED FORD F-150 BOUNCED ALONG AS Katelyn shifted it into a lower gear. They'd collected it from where Katelyn had made her leave it. Now Katelyn had insisted on driving it too.

Elle scowled and gripped her folded knees. She was too tall to be stuck in the middle, on the hump, but somehow they'd sandwiched her in. Her shoulders couldn't stay tense with the constant jostling of the road and every soft-shielded childhood memory shaken loose. Her sisters insisted on coming out with her to check out the land and house. They didn't seem to want to leave her alone at all. Elle wasn't sure she'd had a moment to herself since she'd been back. But it had kept the panic attacks at bay. Laney sat, notebook in hand, trying to scribble down a new chapter while the wash boarding in the road made it impossible.

"Jesus, Katie, are you aiming for every bump?" she growled.

"Can't you put it away for ten minutes, Shakespeare?" Katelyn teased and swerved dangerously in the gravel, causing Laney's pen to scratch off the page.

"I'm finally having a breakthrough on this chapter and I need to write it down before it's gone." Laney argued around Elle, who flinched. Laney dropped her pen and touched Elle's hand. "Sorry."

Katelyn righted the truck and slowed down. They both looked at Elle.

"Stop it, goddamn it, I'm not gonna break." Elle said to the both of them, surprising even herself. "Just stop hollering at each other through me. Wait until we get out in the open to push each other's buttons." The tension in the cab dissipated.

Elle relived every Thanksgiving in the ripples of washed-out gravel. Every Christmas morning, bouncing alongside her sisters in the back seat, anticipating hot rolls and presents at Gran's. Every late-summer crabapple picking in Grandpa's orchard resurfaced. When the smell of sagebrush and fresh-cut hay came through the open window, Elle was suddenly sixteen again, driving the combine, putting in hard days of work, watching sore muscles grow strong, and sleeping with well-earned rest. Dust billowed up in the rear-view mirror and covered the past. Elle touched her short hair self-consciously.

"Like the new 'do?" Katelyn said. She looked out of the corner of her observant gaze.

"Yeah?" Elle said and tugged at a curl.

"Me too, though I hate you for that long neck," Laney said, and bumped her shoulder into Elle.

"Well, I hate you for your huge boobs," Elle said unexpectedly and laughter sprung loud through the cab. The sound of it, light and airy, made Elle yearn to hear it again. "I'm like a carpenter's dream down there," Elle said and looked at her tiny front beneath the checkered shirt she'd borrowed from her dad. Katelyn snorted through another fit of giggles.

"No wonder Blake wanted to be a carpenter." she said and Elle's laughter stopped.

"Blake?"

The name felt foreign in her mouth. Like something she wasn't allowed to say; someone she wasn't allowed to think of. Scattered memories filtered in with the road dust. She was eighteen, just finished high school; the steamy windows of his old Jeep beneath a starlight sky. Blake O'Connor had broken her heart. Or did it happen the other way around?

"Blake, you know. O'Connor?" Katelyn said and nudged her. Elle's body swayed in the seat and her gut twisted. She hadn't been thinking about *their* past when she'd come back home.

"I know Blake," her throat felt sticky. "He's not still here, is he?"

Laney, who'd continued to write, despite the difficult conditions, nodded.

"Oh yeah, not really the same guy we grew up with. But he's here."

Elle's hands shook and the rising heat in her chest told her an attack was coming. She shoved her hands beneath her thighs and focused on breathing.

"I thought he was going to school to be a vet. I thought he couldn't wait to get out of this town." Elle gasped.

Laney looked through Elle to Katelyn. Katelyn took a deep breath.

"Yeah, I don't think he finished," she said quietly.

"What?" Elle swung her head to Katelyn.

"Yeah, he just sort of—well, I don't know the whole story. He was gone for a few years and came back." Katelyn said, and looked pointedly at Laney.

"And I'm supposed to believe that's all you know?" Elle scowled and then looked back at the oldest. "Laney, seriously? You write stories for a living; you can't tell me that's all there is."

Laney sighed and looked like she wished she could bury herself in a book.

"I write romances, Elle. I don't have a good grasp on reality."

"You guys are a pair of horrible liars, is what you are," Elle said and settled back into the seat as they drove past the open fields that had been bought up by the larger dude ranches. The same ones who would probably buy Gran's land.

While the open windows brought in the smells of early spring, Elle remembered the summer that Blake's father had come to help hay on the Sullivan ranch. Blake was seven at the time and made every effort to keep up with the girls. Elle was a year older and never let him forget it. She bossed him around and he argued back; rich, blue eyes peering at her from under dark brown curls, fingers hooked into belt loops and sneakered feet kicking at the dirt. Eventually, he lost the fights and had to go along with her plans. Blake and his dad moved off the ranch and into town after only a few seasons.

Things went on the same. They played during summers, swam in lakes, camped and hiked together. He'd been like a brother except—Elle sighed and closed her eyes. At the start of his junior year, he walked into high school two inches taller than her, filled out with the muscle of a hard-working young man, and something turned on inside that was not at all brotherly affection. Elle swallowed and smoothed her hair from her cheek and came back to the present as Katelyn skidded into the right-hand turn. They bumped across the cattle guard and bounded down the smaller lane. Laney's pen scribbled off the page again.

"Fuck's sake," Laney grouched, and Katelyn laughed.

Thoughts of Blake vanished when Elle looked down the cottonwood-lined road and saw the small white house nestled against the foothills, its familiar red barn sagging beside it. Her stomach rolled.

What was she thinking?

She'd never built a barn.

She'd never worked a ranch on her own.

In the last six years, she hadn't done anything on her own.

She felt the warmth of her sisters' shoulders on either side. The panic in her chest abated.

She wasn't alone.

THREE

PLEASE DON'T GO.

Blake O'Connor woke with a startled snort, unsure if her voice was in his head or in the room with him. The futon squeaked when he rolled over and reached his hand out to the emptiness. He was alone. In his mother's basement. He tried to focus on the angry numbers on the clock beside him.

"Shit." He staggered to the box of clothes he still hadn't unpacked. If he unpacked, it meant he was staying. And he didn't want to believe this was what his life had become. Waking up late, for a job he hated, hungover, in his mom's basement, hearing Eleanor Sullivan's voice in his head.

The dream came back in muffled waves. Strange, sad, and—naughty. She was there, running ahead of him, telling him not to let go. He'd caught up, and she wove her fingers into his hair, lips tasting like cherry and summers long gone. Blake groaned and put his fists to his head.

He didn't know why he'd started dreaming of her again; it probably didn't help that he'd heard at the bar last night she was back in town and staying with her parents. Seems he wasn't the only one that failed hard when they'd tried to get out of Sweet

Valley. The old barflies at the end of the room had whispered she was recovering. Blake didn't want to think too hard about what she might be recovering from. But his heart knew. It didn't take a genius to know where a relationship with Aaron Lowry would lead. He grunted and pushed Elle's battered face out of his brain.

Pulling a cap over his dirty curls, he stomped up the stairs and into the noon-bright kitchen. The smell of cigarette smoke settled above the mustard linoleum. His mother looked over her heavy-rimmed glasses.

"Blake," she said disapprovingly. He scowled.

"Mother."

"Aren't you late?"

He grumbled incoherently, opened the fridge, and stared at what remained.

"You'd better hope you still have that job, else you're not staying here anymore," she said. Blake slammed the fridge door.

"Thanks for the pep talk," he barked and walked out, banging the door behind him. His Jeep was parked lopsided in the driveway, with the mailbox wedged beneath the front bumper. "Shit." He'd have to fix it when he got back, there wasn't time now. By the time he got to Raymer's Lumberyard, he was nearly an hour late. Larry, the foreman, shook his head when he saw Blake sneaking through the front gates.

"You're late."

"I'm aware."

"How many warnings is that, O'Connor?"

"Two."

"It's three," said Larry, staring over his clipboard. Blake sighed. His head hurt like hell and every time he closed his eyes the sweeping wave of nausea hit him. Worse, he saw her face just behind the thin veil of morning-after sobriety, reminding him of all the good things in life he'd lost.

"I'm sure it's—" he stopped at the lack of patience in Larry's expression. "I'm sorry!"

"Are you? Sounds like maybe you're not."

"What do you want from me? I'm late. It's not the end of the goddamn—"

"Finish the day, Blake. Then collect your last paycheck."

"Shit, Larry. Come on."

"No, Blake. You can't just show up whenever your hangover lets you out of bed. You need to pull it together." Larry turned to head back to the office.

"I need this job!"

"I know!" Larry yelled. He turned back to Blake and lowered his voice. "Which is why I don't understand why you can't just buckle down and show up. It's not rocket science, Blake. I know you can be a hard worker. I know things haven't been easy on you the last few years and I've been lenient on that account. But at some point, you gotta sober up and get on to living again," Larry whispered. Blake took off his cap and slapped it on his thigh.

"Fine. End of day." He stormed into the mill. Sober up. Get on to living? What in the hell for? He would have left, but needed the paycheck if he was going to find a new place to stay.

THE TRUCK SKIDDED TO A HALT NEXT TO THE POLE fence, lined with deer antlers and secured by wire. It was just as Elle remembered. To the east of the yard was a giant rock pile that the family had spent years hunting for. The house nestled between the hill and a smaller creek which meandered through the land, alongside two fenced pastures. A sturdy but unloved apple orchard and an overgrown garden spread behind the house. Tall and gnarled cottonwood trees were beginning to bud and Elle knew they'd soon be drifting, the soft white snow of blooms that frothed up allergies and annoyance. She followed Laney out of the truck and slammed the door.

"Jesus, some things just don't change," Laney said and pushed her sunglasses up on her head, a habit that defined her just as the chalky white dust of the road defined the drive. Elle stuck her hands in her back pockets and rocked on her heels, while Katelyn and Laney stood on either side of her.

"Yep," Katelyn said, assuming the same position as Elle.

"Shall we?" Elle asked hesitantly and found the strength to step away from them and head up the walk. The gate creaked on its hinges as she stepped through. Laney followed, and Katelyn dawdled behind. Elle opened the screen door and her hand lit on the doorknob when Laney spoke.

"You sure you're ready for this? I mean, it could be a lot of work."

"I'm not afraid of work, Laney June," Elle scowled down at her.

"I know. It's just, Dad told us it would be rough. If we're getting it fixed up to sell, it's going to be a lot. Nobody's lived here since Gran passed away."

Elle remembered the morning in the snowy November of her senior year. Her heart had broken all to hell when their dad had come home from checking in on Gran with the news. Congregating at this very house, in the hours after finding her asleep, never to rise again, had been sad and unfathomable.

Days later, Elle had helped her mother and father clean out the cupboards and put the house to sleep. The empty quiet had been too much and she couldn't bear the pain of loss. She'd gone out for a ride on her favorite palomino, Kit. Bundled up, but for her long blonde curls over her shoulders, and puffing out clouds of steam across the field, is where she met Aaron. He was hunting with his father on the border between Gran's and the Bar Nunn, a large dude ranch whose guests were drawn in from all over the country to fish and hunt on their expansive lands. The day rushed back into her like a blistering wind and she lost her breath.

Elle twisted the knob in a panic to get inside, to the safety of what life was like before Aaron. If she'd never taken that ride. The door squeaked as it pulled from the warped wooden frame. The sound, unchanged from when the whole family had lived in this house, before her dad and mom had moved across town. When this was her kitchen too and afternoons were spent cooking and baking with Gran. When she was bright and beautiful and never spent a day without a smile.

Elle's panic fell to the floor of the kitchen and disappeared.

"Smells like home," she said, breathing in deeper than she had for months.

"Smells like dust," Laney said and stepped in behind her. "And, is that *eau de dead mouse*?" she said and went to check out the living room through the opposite doorway. Katelyn lingered outside the door and pried off the casing of the doorbell to fiddle with the wires. Elle stayed frozen in the memories of before. Dust covered the furniture and cabinets; the windows were rain-speckled and hung with cobwebs. Once-white walls had faded to cream. Gran's large farm sink sat below the window, looking out at the south pasture. It was different from Elle's tiny L.A. apartment, whose walls blocked the grim and noisy city from seeing what happened within.

Elle's heart, so artfully carved and scarred by Aaron, began to fear and fret.

I can't do this, beat her heart. *He said I could never come back home. He said no one wanted me here. He said I was alone...He said I couldn't do anything...he said...he said...*

The doorbell rang happily behind her.

"Ha! Fixed it!" Katelyn bragged jubilantly. She came up behind Elle and nudged her hip, short-circuiting the thoughts that had started to spiral out of control. Elle took a deep breath.

She was safe. She was here. She was with people who loved her. They were with her. They were in this together. She could do things. She could do hard things.

Elle closed her eyes and thought of the cunning it had taken to pick up small jobs around their apartment complex fixing things and babysitting. The fortitude to not look back once she'd left. The fear of this new beginning was nothing compared to the fear she'd left behind. She walked to the sink and looked at the gentle wave of overgrown hay in the far fields. Its hypnotic dance soothed her.

They spent the morning cleaning. Her dad and mom had kept it in good shape, but Elle started a list of necessary repairs to make the house livable again. She frowned at the sight of their heights and initials etched into the living room doorjamb. She'd been head-to-head with the others until the eighth grade and then shot up like a beanpole. A faded line just below her last mark stood out. Just one mark. Probably made on one of the many times he'd tagged along to play.

B. L. O.

"Blake Lee O'Connor," she said, remembering his middle name from the many times she'd heard it called across the field.

"Well, lookie there," Laney said from behind her. "Blake just seems to be springing up all over the place, huh?"

"You should save the kismet talk for the next novel, Laney." Elle said.

"Man, would I love to write a story about you and him," she said and snorted.

"Ew! Wouldn't that be weird?" Katelyn said from her perch on the ladder, changing out the light bulbs in the main hall.

"That story is long over." Elle frowned.

"Is it? I can't remember how it ended." Laney prodded her, applying just enough pushy-older-sister-force to bring out a counter nudge from Elle.

"Could we just not talk about Blake?" Elle grunted and went back to mopping the kitchen floor until it shone in the early afternoon light. After a clean out of the linen closets and a purging of anything moth- or mouse-eaten, they went back to the truck.

It was Sunday, which meant tomorrow, they would all go back to their normal lives. Laney would go back to teaching in Laramie and Katelyn to her latest contracted job in Casper, training therapy horses at a special needs school.

Elle loved them. But their parents' house seemed awfully small with all of them packed in. She needed to be alone. She looked back at Gran's house, its white face overgrown with lilacs and rose bushes.

The peace and quiet out here seemed to expose something tender in her chest. Just as they'd opened and aired out the closed-up house, she felt her own heart open and begin to clear. The breeze blew soft with a late-spring lightness that lifted the land after a long winter. Elle closed her eyes and took a deep breath. The smell of earth and early grass filled her with peace. She opened her eyes and tried to imagine a stranger walking through the door, tilling the garden, walking the fence line. The thought that came next terrified and elated her.

Gran's home was her home. It had always been.

"You guys should go ahead—" she said, voice choking. "I think I'll stay out here a bit."

"Uh, how we gonna get back to Mom and Dad's?" Laney asked.

"We can take the Dodge," Katelyn said and nodded toward the old beat-up truck next to the lesser beat-up sheep wagon parked beside the barn.

"Does that thing still run?" Laney asked.

"Dad takes it out to check the fields once in a while," Katelyn answered. "Keys are on the visor, I think."

Laney turned back to look at Elle.

"Are you sure?" she asked.

"Yep. I—I need some time alone," she said.

Katelyn gave her a sideways glance. "You're not gonna run, are you?"

"I'm not going anywhere." Elle said.

Laney smiled. "Listen, you don't need to explain it to me. I'm an anti-social introvert." She gave Elle a hug. Katelyn nudged her shoulder, and they both walked to the truck, exchanging worried glances. Elle's shoulders dropped as she watched them drive away.

For a moment she was paralyzed, unsure what to do with so little expectation and so little direction. She started walking until she crossed the sagging fence into the south pasture and bent down to inspect the soil. The irrigation ditches showed years of neglect. Piles of tumbleweeds and debris blocked the major intersections. The barn and stables were in disrepair. The pens needed fixed. The south pasture fence was all but on the ground. Gran had, at one point, raised some of the finest quarter horses in the state. When she'd passed away, the operation had moved to Elle's parents' land on a smaller scale. It wasn't lucrative to breed horses these days, and owning this much land was definitely more of a cost than a profit. Selling it to someone else seemed like the only way forward.

She sighed and leaned on the buck and rail fence overlooking the front yard. To the north of the house, a small chicken coop, in peeling red paint, looked charming and rustic. It made the possibilities butterflying through her head more interesting. Fix fields, plant fields, fix irrigation, fix barn, fix fence, fix coop, paint coop, find chickens. Clean out orchard, replant garden.

You're worthless. You're going to fail. You'll lose everything. Your family will hate you, Aaron stood behind her and whispered.

Elle turned around and caught sight of a doe crossing through the yard. She perked her ears up at Elle's movement but went unhurriedly about her search for tender spring growth. They were alone. She was alone.

The daylight faded. Elle went back inside and washed her hands and face in the kitchen sink. She didn't know how she would tell her parents that she wanted to move into Gran's or how they would react to the idea. Hemming and hawing wasn't going to make the situation better. She closed the door behind her and headed to the truck. The keys were just where Katelyn had left them. Elle's hands shook around the steering wheel as the old Ford rumbled to life.

She didn't know what she was so afraid of. Her parents would either tell her yes or no. She would either live with them and find some job in town, or she'd saddle herself with a shit ton of work she wasn't qualified to handle, and probably fail all over again.

Failing. Failing. Always failing, Aaron gasped. Her stomach turned. She'd already failed in so many ways. She'd already lost so much. The deer crossed in front of the truck, glancing Elle's way before bounding across the field and leaping over the sagging pasture fence. Elle watched her escape.

She wouldn't lose Gran's land.

FOUR

WHEN ELLE HIT THE MAIN STREET OF SWEET VALLEY, she slowed down. Small town cops didn't have much to do but find a reason to write you a ticket. The two gas stations, on either side of the highway from one another, were always changing the last digit on their per gallon signs to draw in the summer tourists. The volunteer fire department shared a building with the Odd Fellows Hall, and the City Clerk was next door to the one dentist in town. Most of Sweet Valley's businesses flanked the highway running through town. Small art galleries, outfitting businesses, auto repair shops and restaurants adapted to fill older buildings dating back to the 1800s when the town was settled.

Some had been there forever, like Julie Pratt's Flower Shoppe; half the town thought she'd misspelled the word, the other half thought she was being too 'big city'. Some businesses only lasted one summer and fizzled out when the winter turned brutal. Only the steadfast and hardest working were able to make it with such a small population and being cut off from most of the world. The only two things that could always be counted on to be open, Elle thought with a smirk, were the bars and churches.

As she made her twenty-mile-an-hour drive through the short

downtown, The Hotel Belle's lights brightened the street to her right. She hadn't gone out by herself since, well, ever. Starting a new life, surviving a death-trap marriage, and all the years before, hadn't offered her the time or freedom. She had both now; maybe a drink was in order. She parked the truck and walked inside the dimly lit hotel.

Swinging doors to the right led to the old brick bar and vaguely familiar faces looked up when she entered. Some of them she knew. Mary Collins had been in her class, an aspiring beauty queen who'd hated that Elle had snagged more attention at the county fair with her baked goods than she had for hers. Judy Prym had been the mayor's daughter once upon a time. Elle remembered her being far too popular to give any attention to the Sullivan sisters and their rough and tumble upbringing.

Elle kept her gaze straight ahead and nodded to Jim Travers who had been tending bar at the Hotel since probably the dawn of time. He nodded back with a genuine smile.

"Well, hey there, look who's come home! Good to see you back in town. Didja bring that rowdy sister of yours?"

"Which one?" Elle smiled and adjusted her hair over the faded bruises, thankful for the low light. She sat on an uneven stool and its legs tipped back and forth while she found her balance.

"Ha! You girls were never in short supply of trouble." he laughed.

"They've all gone back to their grown-up jobs. I'm afraid it's just me. I don't have a grown-up job yet."

"Well, I'm sure that'll come. Good to see you back, Elle," he said and put a bowl of peanuts and a cold beer on the bar before turning to attend to a group at the other end. A spark of warmth lit in Elle's chest. Something she couldn't quite replicate or explain. She listened to George Strait croon about Amarillo and sipped her beer. Years of being hyper aware triggered a shiver up her spine and she looked into the mirror behind the bar. A pair of beady eyes above a malicious smile had locked on to her.

Ty Brentwood.

Elle clutched her bottle, bit her sore lip, and wished she could melt into the peanut shell-strewn floor. Ty had never liked her family. Probably on account of their grandmother firing his father several years before due to his poor work ethic and distasteful behavior. Ty slugged back the rest of his whiskey, wiped his mouth on the back of his hand, hitched up his over-filled Wranglers, and came closer.

"Well, well, if it ain't Eleanor Sullivan!" His voice hit her between the shoulders and she flinched. "I thought that was you. What's the big city girl doing slumming in Belle's?"

Elle took a drink and didn't dignify him with a response. When he didn't take the hint and came closer, she sighed and looked at him.

"Hello, Ty."

"Aren't you too good to be mingling with us common folk? Eh? Miss Fancy L.A.?" Ty scooted out the stool beside her. His sweaty warmth seeped into the space between, smelling like hard, cheap liquor.

Elle looked around. The bar was noticeably quieter and the hushed voices heightened her discomfort. Judy leaned over the table to hear better, her eyes darted between them. Mary sat back and smirked; happy that Eleanor Sullivan, former goody two shoes, was finally getting put into her place. If only Mary knew the places Elle had already been put.

"I lost my high horse a while ago," Elle choked out. Ty's tongue darted across his lips, oblivious to her broken demeanor.

"Well shit, sweetheart, you can ride me home." He reached down to touch her thigh. Elle knocked his hand away ferociously.

"Don't touch me."

"Wassa matter, princess? Doncha want a proper welcome home?" Ty put his arms around her and panicked flashbacks hit Elle. Her body responded.

"Let me go!" She stomped down on Ty's foot and threw her head back into his nose. His grip loosened.

"Ouch! Goddamn it, you little b—"

"That's enough, Ty." The deep voice interrupted him and made them both turn. Elle stumbled and looked up to the sweet, blue-eyed boy from so long ago, now a grown and scowling man before her.

"Blake?" Elle whispered. Her heart rose like a confused mess in her throat. His hair was long and shaggy over his shirt collar. His eyes blazed as he focused on Ty.

"Oh—uh—hey—hey, Blake." Ty stuttered. "I was just welcoming Miss Snoot back into town. Doesn't it surprise the shit outta you that she'd come back here? I mean, especially *you*!"

Ty, having neither the brains nor the internal governor to choose his words more carefully, laughed at the immediate tension that crackled between Elle and Blake. Mary snorted from her corner. Judy cleared her throat.

"Why don't you just go home, Ty," Judy said suddenly, garnering a look from Mary.

"I think that's a fine idea, Ty," Blake agreed.

"Fuck you! You don't get to tell me what to do, Blake. The two of you always was too good for everyone else. Now look atcha both. Nothing but broken-down has-beens."

Elle did look at Blake, her eyes thirsty for him, her heart hungry. He fell into her gaze just as hard. Best friends, before so much hurt had come between. His dark, arched brows fell, and he studied her as though she were a problem he thought he'd already solved. When his eyes met her battered face, they softened.

Ty took advantage of the distraction and hit Blake with a nasty right hook across the jaw. Blake's head snapped back. He stumbled two steps, tripped over a chair, and fell.

"Hey!" Elle shouted as a rush of protective anger filled her. She grabbed the bar stool next to her and swung it across Ty's back, sending him sprawling across the bar floor, mid-victory dance.

Blake looked up at her in shock.

"Jesus, SoCal, you're a handy fella in a fight," he grumbled, embarrassed. Elle dropped the stool at Ty's feet and tried to calm the rising urge to vomit.

"All right you three, that's enough! Ty, get the hell outta here! Blake, you too. You know you've run your tab up and I ain't givin' you another goddamn ounce until you pay it. Elle...you okay, honey?" Jim said from behind the bar. Elle peeled her eyes away from Blake and nodded.

"I'm okay." Her shaky voice contradicted her words.

Ty got up, shot them both a vile look, and hobbled out the back door. Whispers flew through the room. Mary snorted "serves her right," under her breath.

Judy looked at Elle. "You really okay?" she asked softly.

Elle could only nod as she offered a shaking hand to Blake, still on the floor. He looked at it as though it were a thorn bush and backed away to stand on his own. Elle couldn't help the way her eyes fell into his, like puzzle pieces snapping into place. Like coming home. Warmth spread through her body and shone in her smile.

"It's good to see you," she said. Blake seemed mesmerized for only a second before he frowned.

"Wish I could say the same," he muttered. "Looks like you've —Somebody—How are—" he stopped and shook his head. He wiped his bloodied lip on the cuff of his sleeve and smiled cruelly. "You know what? You're not mine to worry over, so I suppose it doesn't matter how you are."

"Blake, I should have—"

"Save it, Elle. I don't care anymore," he said, and she watched him disappear through the swinging door. Their unexpected meeting, him standing up for her, and the cold distaste he left with, were loops on a rollercoaster that left her dizzy. Jim cleared his throat.

"That was a hell of a shot, kid. Haven't seen a swing like that since your softball days."

"I'm working on my average." She laughed unexpectedly and Jim returned a deep, gruff laugh. Elle watched Blake pull away in the same beat-up Jeep he'd once driven her through town in. The windows they'd once fogged up. She paid her tab and left, with the low timbre of his voice still rattling through her head.

Elle's thoughts were so jumbled as she drove that she nearly missed the turn into her parents' place. She hadn't predicted what seeing Blake again would do to her heart. Her memories of his hands on her body, his lips on hers, the unwavering love in his eyes in the delicate and brief moments they shared felt like sunshine breaking through the years of darkness.

The way he looked at her now sure was different.

A family on the brink of loss. A rock-bottom self-esteem. A former first love hating every once-broken bone in her body. By the time she got out of the truck and walked to the front gate, she was convinced that coming back to Sweet Valley was the stupidest idea she'd ever had. She had half a mind to turn around, and drive straight out of town and find some big city where no one knew her.

"Hey, Slim." Warren's voice cut through the escape plans. "How was Gran's house?"

Elle looked up at him, standing on the porch by the kitchen door, and wasn't sure if she'd just stepped back in time. She walked in slow, methodical steps to the house.

"Hey, honey." Elle's mom walked out of the kitchen with a dishcloth on her shoulder and hands still bubbly. "Oh, was it so bad?" She asked when she saw Elle's face. Melissa pulled her into her arms and the sudden warmth made Elle jump. Indecisive tears, that had settled at the edges of her control all day, sprung loose.

"Oh, Momma," Elle sniffed.

"Now baby," Melissa fussed. "Don't you worry. It's okay if it's too much work. We'll find someone to buy it as is."

"No Momma, that's just it. I—I—" she paused. She wasn't ready to tell them her impossible dream of saving it all. She swallowed back the whole of her new and tender truth. "I'd like to live there. While I work on it. On my...on my own." she stuttered. She hadn't been allowed to be alone for years and asking for it felt like Aaron was standing behind her with his fist raised. She shrunk into herself.

"Slim," her dad started.

"I'm sorry." Elle's voice shook.

"Stop." Melissa cut her off. "You don't have anything to be sorry for. Not one damn thing!" The unusual curse on her mother's lips interrupted Elle's rising panic. "Wanting to have some space? Wanting to figure things out and be yourself again? No, you don't *ever* be sorry for that."

"I—" Elle's foot slipped off the step, but her mother held her in strong and unfailing arms. "I don't know if I'll ever be myself again, Momma."

"You will," Melissa argued, and tipped up a proud chin to Elle's sorrow. "You may not be the same girl you once were, but you'll find out what kind of woman you are."

"Melissa," Warren started softly.

"Warren, don't interrupt me. This is girl talk." She looked deep into Elle's brown eyes. "We spend most of our lives being who everyone else wants us to be—"

"Now, hang on, I don't—"

"Warren, go check on the pot," Melissa pointed into the kitchen.

"But you aren't cooking anything."

"Now!"

Elle flinched and Warren smiled at his wife lovingly.

"All right, all right, don't get your feathers frazzled," he chuckled, and kissed her forehead before heading in. "But for the record, your mom is right. Sometimes you can't be yourself until you get a little space to do it." Melissa gave him a gentle swat on his narrow ass and he whooped with a laugh. Elle watched, bewildered that their short argument ended in smiles, and kisses and gooses to the backside.

"Mom, what if? What if I can't do all the work? I couldn't—I didn't make it work. I failed at my marriage."

"You did not fail, Eleanor Augusta!" Melissa gasped. "You survived. What Aaron did to you was not your fault. Do you hear me?"

"Momma, I—" Elle felt the desperation swell, but the strong warmth of her mother's voice made the dark fog recede.

"None of that was your fault. He did that to you. It's *his* fault. All of it. He's the one to blame."

Elle fell into her mom's arms and words. She squeezed her tight, and Elle inhaled, forging the memory of the safety she felt, dropping the memories of all the fear and pain he'd laid down over the years. Home rolled through her soul; a warm arc over the shuddering world.

"It's gonna take time to heal up and hair over. It's gonna take love and patience from us, but from yourself too," she sighed and kissed Elle on the top of the head. "It will help you to have some purpose and some space. You can do what you want out there, whatever it is you need to do. Just make sure you keep us in the loop. Don't—" Melissa's voice filled with tears. "Don't leave us out of your life again, OK?" She lifted her chin and tried to be stoic.

"In the loop, ha!" Warren chuckled from the kitchen where he stood at the stove, not stirring a pot. "The loopy coop, with all of these wild hens clucking around." Melissa scowled in his direction with mock disgust. He sauntered to the screen door, sensing the sacred female talk was winding down.

"You know," Warren scratched his head. "The south field has had a long rest and may put up a nice hay crop this year. If we can work out the irrigation, you can have the profit from that. It's at least two rounds of good hay. It sure would help if the barn and stable were in better shape. Then you could store some of it for winter. And whoever buys it will need a sturdier place to put livestock in." Warren looked at her and cleared his throat. "That is, if that's the direction you want to go with it. That's where I'd start."

"I think that's a fine place to start," Elle agreed with a sniff. The clouds in her mind cleared.

"For all these big plans you two are making, it won't mean anything if you aren't taking care of yourself too." Melissa looked at Elle. "You're coming over every Sunday for dinner, so I know you're getting enough to eat," Melissa said. Elle nodded and kissed her mother's cheek.

"Yes ma'am."

Of all the lies Aaron had rooted in her head over the years, the one that hurt the worst was that her family didn't love her. Elle ate a hearty dinner, with no concern for a mandatory weigh-in the next morning or fitting into clothes someone else picked out. They laughed over Warren's veterinary stories from the day. Her mother heaped two big pieces of homemade pie on her plate afterwards and sat with her until she'd eaten nearly all of it.

The warmth of food and family left her in a daze. Her body and brain tried to compensate for the cycle of stress and relief that had roller-coaster'd through the last few days. She climbed the stairs, knowing that she'd be in her grandmother's house the next night.

She would be on her own for the first time in her life.

Snuggled into her old bed, she listened to the owls hooting solemnly to one another outside. It reminded her of summer nights as a teenager, listening for the sound of Blake's Jeep tires in the drive, there to sneak her out for some late-night shenanigans or just to hang out in the old cottonwood tree by the window to talk. Like best friends did.

She took an uneven breath and stared through the darkness. Blake had never bothered to hide how he'd felt about Aaron. But where Blake had pulled away after Gran died, Aaron had come to gather her floundering heart and offered promises of a bigger, better life. How could she have been so naïve and stupid? How could she have ignored so many warning signs?

If only she'd made that one different choice. Where would she be today?

"There's no way of knowing. Every road is a long set of scattering tracks," she said softly to the silence. A phrase Gran had used often. A balm for regret. A reminder to do the best for the moment. Elle sighed.

She'd just have to do her best in this moment.

FIVE

BEING ALONE LEFT A LOT OF QUIET TIME TO THINK, AND thinking led to ghosts sneaking around the edges of her brain, hiding in the mottled gray of her peripheral vision. Loud noises, the barn doors slamming in the wind or the creak of the old house's bones settling, made her jump. She took the stairs in the old house carefully, often clinging to the banister when waves of nausea would roll over her and her temple throbbed. Elle had to learn how to breathe again, how to eat, how to walk, how to sleep. She had to teach herself how to face the fears lurking at the edge of her consciousness, how to open her eyes to the truth of this new and untainted start.

Well, almost untainted. Just as she had to let go of her fear of Aaron, she had to battle the hope of getting back on Blake's good side. The memories that the old house brought up, of their childhood, made it hard to reconcile the people they were now. Maybe some wounds were just too deep.

She paused, mid-clothespin, as she hung out the sheets to dry on the backyard line. She'd seen those same soft moments catch in his eyes at the bar. Moments when he remembered, when longing and need overpowered his angry distrust. Or at least she wanted to believe that's what she saw.

Elle busied herself with cleaning out the closets that afternoon and found three of Gran's old aprons in good repair. They were patterned sweetly from material she was sure must have come from flour sacks or feed bags, from back in the time when everything had a dual purpose and the world didn't have much to waste. She washed them on a delicate cycle and went through the old photo albums. So many faces lost to time. So many memories before she'd even been born. She found one photo of her grandparents, before her grandfather had been shipped off to the war that took his life, and hung it in an old wooden frame above the mantel. Gran was younger then, and had the same deep brown eyes as Elle. The eyes that could be tender and forgiving, or slice through bullshit in a heartbeat.

Elle came from sturdy stock. She sat back on her heels, looked down at the old sepia photos spread out on the floor and realized that no matter what she'd gone through with Aaron, what she'd done to survive it, she was never meant to be on that path to begin with. In a way, she'd corrected her course, and just like she knew she didn't belong in L.A., she felt equally certain that this place would be her home for the rest of her life.

That afternoon, she moved the furniture around to suit her, washed the rest of the linens, and made minor repairs to the cabinets, moldings, and window casements. She set up the small, cozy bedrooms, and made plans to paint them cheery colors from extra, unused paint her parents had.

She kept the secret hope in her heart that those bedrooms would be where her own kids might sleep someday. The thought hit her in the busy work of the afternoon and she had to sit at the base of the stairs, fighting tears. When she collected herself, she went out to the old barn and found a few pieces of furniture. An art deco vanity from sometime in the thirties with a hazy oval mirror. A rolltop desk that she was sure Laney had taken the matching chair for to her office at UW. An antique iron bed frame, painted in white, stood untouched against the back stall, and she wrangled it up the stairs on her own. Setting it up in Gran's old room, and moving the mattress she'd been using onto it, solidified the feeling of it being her space. That night, as she collapsed into bed, her body and heart felt stronger. She was even too damn tired to dream, which meant no nightmares.

The next day, in the budding warmth of spring, Elle walked the irrigation lines in her grandmother's old waders, clearing debris and testing the water system. With the snowmelt coming soon, she would be able to see if her father's suggestion of running the ditches on a sharper angle would help spread what little water there was further. In the quiet evenings, after days of hard work, in a place that was more home to her than she'd ever had with Aaron, she began to find her way back to who she was. She opened the windows and let the cool breezes blow through her bedroom.

Her favorite thing to do in the moments she wasn't fixing or painting something was, by far, sitting with her grandmother's old recipe book. Each formula, scrawled out in shaky cursive, was a memory and a mouthfeel, and Elle could taste the flavors even as she read. Gran could have made millions with her biscuits alone. Never mind her fried chicken. Or pies, or cookies. If she had had the time, Gran could have run her own restaurant.

Elle stopped; hand frozen on the hodge-podge page of taped-on index cards.

A hushed memory; a recipe that changed everything, the one her grandmother told her about in a dream as she lay in the hospital bed, recovering. It faded in and out again. Food was a powerful thing. It could bring comfort. It could change people. It could change lives.

Elle tucked the recipes away, feeling a rising tide of something strange in her belly. She looked at the old clock above the kitchen door and despite it only being 8pm, she turned off the lights and headed up to bed. She wasn't really running from the ideas playing merry-go-round in her head, but she wasn't ready to slow down and get a good look at them either. She pulled the covers over her head and willed the pinprick of truth to stop needling her. She reached a hand out from underneath the flowered bedspread, shut off the light, and listened to the world settling.

The solitary thought that remained was Gran, her cooking, how she could have made a living feeding people. Her recipes were comforting and sturdy, basic and timeless. Elle's brain rolled the thought over and over like a marble in a tin can. She'd loved to cook with Gran. She loved to be in the warmth of the kitchen, helping with the meals, and the joy that came with feeding people. Was it something she could make money at? What if she failed?

Aaron's voice was silent on this question, in undeniable knowledge that she made at least one recipe work. Elle buried herself in the safety of bed and let the day's hard work ease her to sleep.

WARREN AND ELLE AGREED THAT GETTING THE irrigation up and running, fixing the barn, and rebuilding the fence was essential for the sale. The barn only needed minor structural and cosmetic work, but they couldn't do it alone if they wanted it finished before haying season. Warren said not to worry, that he'd find the extra hands, but Elle needed to do something on her own without having to ask her parents for more help. She printed out fliers at the town library and delivered them to businesses, promised homemade goodies, iced tea, and good company to anyone willing to come and help.

She'd talk to the local lumberyards and had gotten rough-cut boards delivered out to Gran's for next to nothing. She pored over the recipe box and picked out the best ones to use for a crowd. The first round of biscuits came out hard and burnt, and Elle had to feed them to the gathering songbirds who were getting used to the idea of someone inhabiting the quiet farmhouse again. The deer wouldn't touch them and much preferred to nip the tender buds off her crabapple trees; Elle responded by chasing them away with a broom.

She didn't touch the shotgun in her grandfather's safe, though she always knew where it was. She may have stopped looking over her shoulder, but she hadn't lost the hard lessons of her past. They were like armor covering her body.

Elle did a lot to reintroduce herself to the town in small and wary ways. She sat in on morning coffee with her dad and his old ranching friends. She went to her mother's knitting group, but her fingers didn't seem to purl or chain like they used to as they shook in moments of quiet and delicate work. But the women were gentle and kind and no one brought up where she'd come from or why she was back, only that they were happy to have her, no matter how long it took her to knit a scarf.

She had plenty of support from people who cared and wanted to help out the family. The only person she hadn't asked was the one she was sure would say no. But he was also the one with carpentry experience, and she'd heard he might be in need of the work.

So, when Elle found herself in the parking lot of Sweet Valley's shadiest motel, she told herself it was for the barn. Because he was qualified. Because it would be rude and maybe even weird to invite everyone *but* him. Because maybe she was looking for atonement. Because maybe she was looking for a piece of happiness in his memory.

Then again, maybe she was just looking for trouble.

She'd gone to Blake's mother's house first and found that Lori O'Connor still had a panache for giving disapproving looks over the top of her glasses.

"What are you doin' back in town?" Lori asked.

"Well, I," Elle shuffled back and forth. "I'm looking for Blake."

"'Course you are," Lori said, sizing Elle up. "But he ain't here."

"Do you know where I can find him?"

"I don't. And I can't say I care. I kicked him out after he lost his job at the mill. I ain't puttin' up with his bullshit anymore."

"Right." Elle turned to leave with anger in her belly. Neither of his parents had ever given him the love and support he needed. Lori called after her.

"You might try the Silver Lake Motel. I heard he's got a job at the bar there. Though who knows how long that will last."

"Thank you."

"Elle," Lori's voice turned soft.

"Yeah?"

"It would just be best to leave him be."

"Yeah," Elle sighed. "You're probably right. Thanks Lori."

Despite the warning, Elle found herself outside of the Silver Lake Motel, staring at its dilapidated green siding and waiting for some greater force to stop her from going up to Blake O'Connor's motel room. Maybe an inner voice of reason would intervene. Maybe the universe would send a sign, like "hey asshat, don't do that, you've already caused each other enough trouble." But nothing happened. No voice. No sassy comeback. Just the lazy buzzing of grasshoppers zipping around the sunny, dirt parking lot.

Elle killed the engine, got out, and stepped over the concrete parking curb that was probably meant to keep drunk drivers from running into the rooms. She let out a deep sigh and knocked. The television inside blared in response. She knocked again, harder.

"What?" he yelled. Elle's throat constricted at the sound. She raised her hand to knock again as Blake ripped open the door, shirtless. His eyes dropped as if he'd been expecting someone taller, the hotel manager perhaps.

"Uh...hey, Blake."

"What the hell are you doing here, SoCal?" he said. She looked around his shoulder into the room, littered with takeout containers, bags of clothing, stacks of bills, over-stuffed boxes of books, and a sagging bag of tools.

"I came to see what you knew about barn building," she said.

"You came to see if I'd build your barn," he corrected. His once-beautiful smile seemed twisted. Elle scowled; fighting with Blake had the uncanny effect of straightening her spine as if they were still kids arguing over who got to ride shotgun in the pickup.

"I don't need you to build my barn. I'd just need some extra people. I remember you being pretty good with your hands—" his eyes lit up, and he smirked. "Ugh, I mean with building."

"Go ask your daddy, SoCal." Blake tried to close the door but she stopped it.

"It's a big job and I want to finish it before haying starts."

"Then you'd better find some help quick, I guess." He tried to close the door again, but she pushed it open and stared at him pointedly. He frowned. "Some *other* help."

"Blake, come on." Elle shoved at the door and stepped in, crowding him back with an exasperated sigh. "You could use the work."

"Oh, really? Is that what this is? Charity?" He looked down at her. "You sure you're not here to play a game of catch-up on the last few years?"

"What? What are you talking about?"

"I'm sure you're just biting at the bit to tell me about all the wonderful adventures you and Aaron had, living the dreamy, southern Californian life."

Elle blanched, but he didn't stop.

"Or maybe you're gonna tell me how you came to my motel room to play the helpless female. Maybe Aaron's away on another trophy hunt and poor little bored Elle wanted to go slumming." He nudged her backwards and slammed the door closed behind her. His eyes stayed on hers, and she felt the strange urgency of being alone with him.

"Blake," she breathed in a panic. "That's not what this is."

"Oh, come on, SoCal. Don't you want to?" He soothed while his heavy-lidded gaze fell to her lips. He stepped forward, and she stepped back. The smell of liquor drifted off of him.

"Have you been drinking? It's ten in the morning!"

"Aw, that's cute, you all indignant and surprised." His hand moved to his mouth, wiping away the sweat above his lip. "Funny that a worldly woman like you would be shocked by anything."

"I'm not worldly." She argued and circled around him.

"It's also funny, SoCal—"

"Stop calling me that!"

"Oh, I'm sorry...Aren't you a big city girl now? Aaron's real housewife of L.A.?"

Elle's desire to cry was superseded by the desire to give him a good walloping. Her fists clenched.

"I don't like being called that. That's not who I am." she asserted.

"Oh? How about Eleanor Augusta? It's funny, Eleanor Augusta."

"What's funny?" She stuttered, thrown by the use of her far too fancy name and the fact that he remembered it at all.

"It's funny that you're making such big plans. I thought you were just visiting and now what? You're building barns? What are you, actually moving back?" He grunted a laugh. "What's Aaron think about that? I know he and his dad enjoyed coming out here to shoot our best game at the Bar Nunn, but do you think he'd honestly move here?"

"I couldn't care less what Aaron thought about anything and it wouldn't matter anyway. He's not here."

"Oh? Lovers' spat, huh?" he smirked. "So, you're here to make him jealous, is that it? Didn't we play that game before?"

Red-cheeked with anger and embarrassment, Elle's brown eyes misted over. Blake's self-assuredness fell to his feet at the sight. When she didn't respond, he shook his head and went on remorsefully.

"When are you going to remember you're too big for this town, Elle? When are you going to high-tail it out again? As soon as he says he wants you back? As soon as small-town living gets too small? Leaving a half-finished barn and God knows how many more broken promises behind you? When are you going to give up?"

Blake's eyes fell, dark lashes on his cheek bones, the blue depths hidden, so she couldn't tell if his heartache was real or if he was just feeling guilty for being an ass. She wasn't in a mood to baby his too-late feelings of regret.

"I'm not giving up," she said, "and you have very little talking room about quitting, Blake O'Connor. Laney told me you dropped out of school. What in the hell is that about?" She put a finger to his bare and solid chest.

He stepped back, hands in the air, and a false smile on his lips. She didn't know whether to slap his stubbled cheek or pull him in and kiss him. She took the smart option and crossed the room to the door.

"Oh, so you *don't* want my help now?" He chuckled behind her.

"Now that I think about it, no, I don't. I guess I don't really need you anymore. Maybe I gave up on you just in time." Elle slammed the door behind her and drove away in a heat of anger that could have lit the whole town on fire.

SIX

THE DAY OF THE BARN BUILDING BROUGHT A WIDE-OPEN Wyoming sky. The morning wind was edged with a cold bite, reminding Elle that winter wasn't ever truly over on the high plains. She was up before dawn, cooking, baking, making pots of coffee, and filling every basket, bowl and thermos she could find. With sweaty palms and a racing heart, she checked the front windows every few minutes. After all the years away, a number of people Elle didn't know were eager to meet her. The ones who had known her were curious to hear just how and why she was back.

Judy Prym and her family were coming, and Elle worried what they'd say; what they'd think. Judy used to be the judgmental type, especially when it came to the Sullivans and their non-feminine behavior. Still, after the bar incident with Ty, it seemed she'd done some growing up herself since high school. Judy looked at Elle in a way that said she was ready to put the past behind them.

The older people in town, the gossips and the hard-noses, may not be so forgiving.

Aaron's voice simmered in its dark way that *they'd see right through her*, to how *worthless* she was. Elle swallowed back the stomach acid rising in her throat.

"Shut up, you prick. You don't own me anymore," she grumbled, and the whisper faded.

Her dad arrived just as a second round of the colossal buttermilk biscuits came out of the oven. He buttered one and slathered it with jam. Elle paced in the kitchen, checking and rechecking her gravy, bacon, and scrambled eggs.

"I don't know. Do you think it'll be enough?"

"Sadly, only for a couple of infantries." Warren shook his head over the warm biscuit and Elle added bacon and a side of gravy to his plate absentmindedly.

"Your mom already fed me breakfast this morning," he said and inhaled the heavenly smells.

"Well, we both know you don't mind a second breakfast." Elle stopped mid-pace and felt, for a small moment, that she was a beloved daughter again, and not someone's worthless wife.

"Did you even get a first?" He asked, and eyed her. "You're going to need your strength today." Elle looked back at him on her way to the sink, her memory flashed to a long, dark walk, a heavy weight, and the strength it took.

"I'm plenty strong."

Her dad smiled. "I know you are. I also know you used to eat us out of house and home, Slim." Elle stared at the delicious food, the smells of it surrounding her like a warm blanket that she'd meant to cover everyone else with. She was tired of being small.

Elle grabbed a biscuit, slathered it with butter and jam, and took a healthy bite.

"That's my girl," Warren's eyes twinkled. "Looks like the first ones are showing up." He nodded towards the front drive. Elle wiped her hands off on the towel resting on her shoulder and, still with crumbs on her chin, rushed to the door.

Ranching families from around the valley came. They brought tools, warm smiles, and enthusiasm for the excuse to gather. The women brought coolers of food and tea for later in the day and some of the men wandered around the outside of the structure, nodding and shaking their heads. Elle felt an odd sensation in the center of her chest. It took her a moment to recognize gratitude and the sense that everything would be all right.

Valley's residents proved their willingness to lend hands and hearts, despite what gossip may have flown before. She knew she'd heard more than one person, including Mary Collins and Ty, say that she'd turned her back on the town, that she'd left willingly and without even looking back, so why should they do anything for her? Even Blake had accused her of abandoning them for bigger and better things. But if the people here felt that way, none of them showed it when they greeted her. She joined her father in the inspection, falling behind him after helping the others set up the tables of food.

"Did you leave anything for us to do, Warren?" asked Derek Morrison, the town's general contractor, as he walked into the nearly empty barn.

"Talk to Elle. She's been doing all the work so far," Warren said and nodded back to Elle. Derek raised his eyebrows and smiled.

"Well, I'd expect nothing less of a Sullivan," Derek said. Being called Sullivan again sent a flutter through Elle's chest.

One group got to work stripping away the old paint on the still-good boards; another peeled away the warped and rotted planks and piled them by the fence. The others measured and cut the needed replacement planks, and planed the rough-cut wood as best as they could. With breakfast spread out on the picnic tables, every belly full of warm food, and every heart full of laughter, the work buzzed along.

That afternoon Elle stood on the tallest ladder, her hair covered in a kerchief, painting the trim of the hayloft a bright white. Every time the wind blew, the ladder swayed. She gripped on and tried not to look down. Feigning bravery was getting easier in everything she did.

She climbed down carefully to refill her paint cup at the supply table where Warren was putting more nails in his old tin cup. She nearly dropped her paint at sight of the beat-up Jeep swinging into her drive. Warren followed her line of sight and arched one crazy, gray eyebrow.

"Well, I'll be," he said, pleased.

"What the hell is he doing here?" Elle huffed. Warren looked at her quizzically.

"I suspect he's come to help."

"He's no help."

"Well, he's here and looking relatively sober. Maybe you oughta tuck that anger away for another time," Warren said and went back to work. Elle didn't respond. Blake got out of the Jeep, strapped a well-worn tool belt across his lean hips, and adjusted his sunglasses. He ran a hand through his wayward hair and walked, head hanging low, to the barn.

"Relatively sober," Elle muttered and did her best to avoid him as she climbed back up the ladder. People shouted questions and encouragement up to her. She smiled and took the time to talk to each of them, reacquainting herself with friends and faces from long ago. It was difficult for her to come out of her shell; hard to not shy away. But Elle made herself be brave in the warmth of their generosity.

She just finished the trim when the wind picked up and the ladder tipped. Elle grabbed onto the sides but before she could scream, it suddenly steadied and she looked down to see Blake, hands on either side of the rickety metal legs below her.

"I thought you had better things to do than help me," she said, scowling down at him.

"Oh, I'm sorry. Did ya want me to let go?" He grinned and took his hands away. The ladder shifted dangerously to the right and Elle shrieked.

"No!"

He steadied the ladder again.

"Don't let go," she breathed and shimmied down. She stepped off of the last rung, but his strong arms stayed on either side, around her shoulders, close enough that she could feel his breath on her neck; smell that he'd showered.

"What are you doing?" she said as his warmth spread across her back.

"You told me not to let go," he whispered in her ear. "Maybe you didn't realize how good I am at holding on to things, Elle." His lips grazed her earlobe when she turned into the sound. Elle's belly warmed and her heartbeat sang in her chest. When had she last been touched without hatred or to control? She leaned into him and let the protective warmth sink in. He chuckled and whispered, "Yeah, some things just don't change do they, Elle?" Her body stiffened, and she turned sharply, sloshing paint down his arm.

"Hey!" He stepped back and avoided getting it on his jeans.

"Oops," she said without a hint of remorse.

"I think you did that on purpose."

"I was just so surprised that you showed up sober, I could hardly hold on to my paint," she countered. Blake scowled and Elle immediately felt the wrenching fear of retaliation. She stumbled backwards and stuttered.

"Blake, I—I'm sorry, that wasn't fair, I—"

"Of course, it was fair." He looked to the terror in her eyes, saw one hand trembling around the cup, the other guarding her throat. Protecting it. Her bruised face from the night at the bar flashed in his memory. He backed away, hands up.

"You're just saying what everyone else is thinking. At least you're still honest," he said. When she looked down, he continued quietly. "You shouldn't be afraid—" he sighed and tried to meet her gaze. "You shouldn't be afraid to say what's on your mind, Elle. Ever."

She turned and walked back to the barn. Blake left to help haul the new planks to the north side. His words hung in her mind and suffocated the flash of fear. In that moment, he was her friend again. The boy she'd loved. Elle sighed; that world was so far gone, and the girl she was then, gone with it. She didn't know why she let herself kindle any hope.

She threw herself into the work and by four that afternoon, the group was finishing up. Elle was covered in red paint splotches, but the kerchief kept most of the spatter from getting to her hair. Her shoulders ached in ways she hadn't known they could. She offered cookies and lemonade to the volunteers, but didn't see Blake anywhere.

Her heart fell; she'd been trying all day to ignore the itch in her heart that he'd irritated by being gruff and sweet. She was too long gone from any kind of healthy relationship to know how to read him, or what a normal reaction from a man should be. Even her own father walked around her as if she was perched on broken glass and any sudden movement or word might cut her.

Elle took the cookies and pitchers of lemonade into the barn. The flooring had been repaired, sanded down smooth, and sealed against the wind that would blow through on the cold winter nights to come. Five stalls lined the east facing side; each with its gate repaired and hooks for ropes and harnesses. The upper loft, which surprisingly hadn't been rotted, was repaired. The Episcopalian deacon, a former mechanical engineer, was working on the mechanism for the hay slide and directed the group around her with the technical aspects of the pulley system.

The west wall had two larger stalls and a third space where the gate had been removed. Loud voices came from the corner and Elle walked over to see what the problem was. Her eyes fell first to Blake.

"Everything OK?"

Blake sighed, got up from his squatting position in the corner, and tried to contain the anger written on his face when the other man started in.

"This kid's messing up the whole stall. You won't be able to use it." Derek complained.

"I'm not a kid anymore, Derek, and I didn't mess it up. It's a workstation, for vaccinations, records, that kind of thing. There's space for a small fridge, a heater, a chair," Blake's voice died away as he looked at Elle. He hooked his thumbs into the tool belt. Long fingers fanned out against his hips, knuckles bumped and cut, hair curling over one eye. She repressed the desire that sprung up and made her skin warm.

Two new windows shed light on the built-in desk he'd crafted out of the prettiest planks of Lodgepole Pine he could find. It was sturdy, with small shelves beneath. In the corner, he'd hung several hooks for extra tack, coats, hats, and reserved a space for two small chairs. She quirked her head and looked at Blake.

"In case your nieces wanted to help you," he blushed. Her fingers trailed over the smoothed and polished desk and chairs. Blake's hands, blistered and covered in a fine dust, tucked back into his pockets.

"It's beautiful. It's wonderful. Thank you, Blake."

Blake nodded curtly and left. She watched him go and looked back to the work that he'd spent his whole day doing. Why would he have put in all that work when he hadn't even wanted to help her to begin with?

When the barn was done and the cleanup finished, it was nearly seven in the evening. Elle handed a basket to each of the families with her biscuits and jars of honey that she'd found in Gran's storage cellar. She thanked them all individually with hugs and smiles.

Judy Prym and her husband, who'd just opened an outfitting business in town beside the river, asked if she'd considered selling her baked goods. The thought mirrored her own from the previous week, and the words busted out of her before she could think to censor herself.

"I've been thinking about it," the small seed planted itself snugly in Elle's heart. "But I don't know. Don't I need some sort of license?"

Judy, her mouse-brown hair back in a ponytail and her tanned skin warmed by the sun, smiled broadly and looked as though they had crossed a barrier that had been arbitrary and ridiculous.

"I can have my brother come by. He works for the county inspection board and makes sure everything meets the standards and whatnot."

"That'd be, well, that would be great, Judy. Thank you."

"It's us that should be thanking you. Those biscuits and cookies are the best thing I've tasted in a long while! My husband's been trying to throw together picnic baskets for the people we take down river, but he's failing pretty miserably at the whole food thing. Don't tell him I said so," she laughed conspiratorially to her with a wink.

Elle laughed so brightly that it surprised even her. Judy gave her a quick hug.

"I'm glad you're back, Elle. Really." She turned to catch up with her family. Elle was still getting used to the difference in Judy's demeanor compared to high school. It was true that time changed people.

The cars wound their way out of the gate and down the road. Warren stood beside her as they waved to the last set of taillights. Though her body was tired, her brain still buzzed with the overwhelming task of starting a business while fixing up Gran's place. She looked back at the barn and saw Blake's Jeep still parked in her drive. Warren saw it too and nodded.

"Well, reckon I should get on home. Your mom is cooking dinner. Will you be over?"

Elle shook her head distractedly and peeled her eyes from the Jeep.

"Oh, dad that sounds wonderful, but I'm—" she looked over her shoulder but saw no sign of Blake. "I'm tuckered out. I think I might just get to all those dishes, have a hot bath, and go to bed." Warren put his hand on her shoulder.

"That sounds like a good idea. Though I think that you might get to skip the dishes." He nodded to the house. Elle heard the clinking of plates coming from the kitchen. Her father drove away with a wave and a smile. Elle watched until he disappeared down behind the bend in the road. Her legs felt like jelly and she could barely stand. She wasn't sure if she'd actually sat down once all day. The full day, and the knowledge that she and Blake were the only people left on the ranch, made her feel heady and light, like she might blow away with the next strong breeze.

She didn't have the strength for much of anything, let alone another argument, so she decided to take a moment outside in the cool evening air. She crumpled onto the porch step and collected her thoughts in the silence. The pretty picture the barn made in the fading light encouraged her.

"Bet you're thinking of running away now," Blake's voice held a hint of laughter as he came out, smelling like dish soap. Elle smiled and scratched the back of her head where the sweat and sawdust were still caked in her curls.

"What? Over this? This is nothing," she said with mock assurance. "Just a little major construction. You know, I thought I should start with something completely unmanageable." Blake sat down beside her on the step with a groan and stared at the rickety old fence falling down around the pasture next to the much-improved barn in the middle of the field.

"Yeah, with all of this *minor* stuff, there's no way you'll burn out," he agreed, his mouth skewed into an almost honest smile. She nudged him with her shoulder. The familiarity of sitting next to him with the scent of fresh dirt and early dusk warmed Elle in an all-too-comforting way, and youthful exuberance rose in her heart.

"Thanks for coming to help out today. I know you didn't have to, and it means a lot, especially after how I behaved at the motel. I'm sorry." Blake stiffened and pulled away.

"You sure do apologize a lot these days," he shook his head. "You shouldn't apologize for standing up for yourself when a guy is being an asshole," he said. Elle looked down, too afraid to face the truth of his words directly.

"What you did in the barn," she paused to swallow. "Really amazing. I wouldn't have thought to do that." Blake looked uncomfortable and scooted away. "And I never thanked you for standing up for me at the bar the other day, with Ty and all."

"You kinda saved yourself on that one, SoCal, I mean—" He chuckled suddenly. "A fucking barstool! Jesus." He folded his hands in front of him and smiled.

"Yeah." Elle dropped her head and laughed. "Well, I guess I didn't take well to him hitting you." Blake stared out into the fields and the bright red barn. He shook his head with a tired sigh.

"You sure know how to pick the losing side of a fight."

"I know," she said and looked at him. Her eyes fell to his lips as the thought of kissing him drowned out all else. The corners of his mouth turned down, and the past slipped into his eyes.

"I'd better leave," he said. Elle looked away.

"Yep, I suppose so. I'll see you around?"

"I think I've met my Elle quota for the decade."

"Blake," Elle's voice shook. He stood up and let the coldness settled between them. His aloof, non-caring set jaw; eyes indifferent to her, felt like a punch to her gut.

"I—" she faltered. What could she say? No words seemed enough; just a rickety bridge over an endless chasm. What would ever heal the wounds they'd suffered or the time she'd left it to fester?

"Have a good night," she said lamely and dropped her eyes.

"Yeah, thanks," he grumbled and left.

Elle went back inside. Her breath was caged in her throat by the way he'd swung from good to jerk yet again. He'd washed and dried all the dishes. But then he looked at her like his heart had slipped onto his sleeve and it hurt him. Their old wounds hadn't healed much in the time she'd been gone.

Elle reached for a bottle of wine someone had brought. She

poured some into a clean mason jar and sipped it as she stared out at the barn, bathed in the falling light, its hue turned orange. The grass waved beyond it in the open space. Space and peace. Something she'd been lacking in the bustle of metropolitan living. Something her soul had missed more than she'd realized. The fence sagged sadly beside the road.

Space and peace...and work. Work, and work, and more work to go along with it. Blake was right. A hell of a lot of work lay ahead of her. He didn't think she was up to the task. She continued to stare at the empty pastures and rich grass that had grown tall from years of being left alone. She closed her eyes.

What could she do to help her family? What could she give to a town that, today, had given her so much? What was she good at that could also make money? She opened her eyes when the thoughts became too complicated and the years of doubt threatened to settle on her tired shoulders.

Elle wandered into the living room. With its cozy fireplace, worn second-hand furniture, and tattered rugs, it was a sharp contrast to the apartment she had shared with Aaron. He'd insisted on hard lines and sterile modernity. Gran's house was creaky and worn. It was antique sideboards, whose legs had suffered stick horses scuffing them. It was antique mirrors and reclaimed barn wood signs with 'Fresh Eggs' painted in faded white. It was sunny yellow rooms and the smell of her grandfather's pipe.

It was her memories of being a little girl. A remnant of a happier and carefree time. Elle sat on the floor with her back against the brown flowered couch and closed her eyes. This was the exact spot where she'd sat while her grandmother combed and braided her tangled curls. With her eyes closed, Elle could almost feel the strong fingers pulling across her scalp.

Her grandmother had never had a girl of her own and had adored her three granddaughters. Though she doted, Gran hadn't coddled, and she'd expected the same hard work and good behavior she'd raised her own kids with. She worked harder than any man; never differentiating roles by gender. Whatever needed done got done, by whoever was there to do it.

Elle opened her eyes.

She was the only one here now and things needed doing. The land was ripe with potential. It was asking for something to happen. She no longer had to wait around for Aaron's approval and she didn't want to wait for any other man to help her. Not even Blake.

Sexy, demi-god, brooding and broken Blake, who carried his heart in his eyes but built high walls to keep her out. She looked back to the kitchen, and the neatly stacked dishes. If he hated her, why'd he bother doing thoughtful things? Like the desk in the barn. Like the dishes. Things that made her life better in ways he might not have even understood. She sighed.

"What in the hell happened to you, Blake?" she whispered.

BLAKE'S HEART CONSTRICTED WHEN HE DROVE AWAY from Elle. He felt it begging him to go back, to stay for a bit. He denied it. Dust billowed up behind him as he drove away. She was in his rearview mirror, watching him go. He nearly hit the post at the cattle guard and had to swerve, throwing gravel into the ditch with his tires.

Goddamn all of this! And damn Elle too. What in the hell was she thinking, moving back here, leaning on him for help? And what in the hell was he doing giving it to her?

He may have seen what Aaron was back then, but he never tried talking her out of it. It should have made him gloat, being right, except for the broken way she cowered. And those bruises she came into town with. And the way she apologized and looked scared when he'd gotten loud.

Goddamn it, he hated this.

He hated that he'd never been able to get over her. He hated how her smile made his heart leap and her laughter made his neck feel warm. He hated that he wanted to kiss her every time she bit her lip. He hated that he loved her new haircut and how it made her neck all the more tempting.

Beyond the ever-present physical attraction, what really needled him was the way she had changed. She was always kind, but the quiet and shy came from the high price of being hurt and something behind that quietness built heavy walls between her and trusting others. She didn't seem to have a problem spontaneously correcting or insulting him, but the fear that rushed in afterwards was new.

Blake returned to his hotel room, threw the tool belt in the corner, and flopped down on the worn, red vinyl chair with a brown bag in one hand and a basket in the other. Warren had put the basket in his Jeep while he'd been otherwise busy. He scowled at it. He didn't want the Sullivans taking care of him. He wasn't an eleven-year-old boy with a deadbeat dad and a strapped-thin mom anymore. He didn't need home cooking, or reassurance, or someone feeling sorry for him.

His stomach grumbled. He opened the forty in the bag and threw the bottle cap across the room while still staring at the basket. Sweet, simple, and tied with a red ribbon. Pretty quaint for a girl who spent time in the glitz and glamor of L.A. She was really playing up her short-lived move back home.

The beer bubbled and burned in his empty stomach.

Maybe food wouldn't hurt; he *had* built her a nice desk.

He reached in and found half a dozen biscuits, along with jam, honey and her raisin oatmeal cookies. He grimaced; his favorite, and Elle knew it. He looked around, as if someone might catch him with his mouth watering, before plucking one out of the basket and taking a huge, angry bite. It tasted like a warm, cinnamon hug to his soul, even better for having been so long since his last home-cooked anything. He closed his eyes. God, his body was tired. His knuckles were bleeding from the sanding and carving tools, and the blisters on his palms hurt.

What in the hell had he even gone for? People were surprised to see him, if they were kind; others only afforded him angry scowls. A few of the women found reasons to give him a shove or hit him with a random board. Judy Prym had 'accidentally' kicked him in the shin after the incident with Elle on the ladder. It was no secret that he wasn't the most liked man in the Valley. He'd been breaking hearts and burning bridges since the day he'd quit college and come back.

He finished the cookie, brushed the crumbs onto the green shag carpet, and reached for a biscuit. His legs protested as he stood to search the room for the plastic knife from the takeout of two days ago. The mirror over the bathroom counter top showed that a day in the sun had given him color, but his eyes were still glassy. A hunger inside them that no food could reach. The feeling of her close against him, the clean scent of her, her backside against his hips. The way she had softened into his arms before pulling away. He held onto the memory long enough to get a reaction that made his jeans uncomfortably tight.

"Damn it, Elle," he whispered and wished she could have just been another easy one-night. That she could be nameless, and faceless, and not invade his every thought. The worst part of the day had been the end, sitting with her on the porch, wanting to stay when he knew he had no right to. He hated the vulnerability he felt around her. He rubbed his blistered hands together, looked back up at the mirror. He wouldn't see Elle Sullivan again. The town was small, but it wasn't so small that he couldn't stay out of her life.

SEVEN

THE NIGHTMARE BLED INTO THE REALITY OF THE DARK predawn and woke Elle with a start. The noise had been real, even if the cause was unlikely to be Aaron sneaking around her property. Still, Elle took the baseball bat beside her bed down the stairs with her. She slung it over her shoulder, loaded and ready. A flick of the switch by the door illuminated the yard and the flash of at least a dozen eyes lit up inside her fence line. Elle screamed in surprise. Three pairs of eyes immediately went out, and she heard bodies hit the ground.

"What in the—"?

The soft bleating and startled hoof beats drew her out of the house, in nothing more than an oversized shirt and her rubber waders, a baseball bat still poised for action. There, on her lawn, or what was left of it, stood a herd of goats, all mismatched and contentedly chewing on her spring buds just emerging from the ground.

"What in the hell is this?" she said, but her tone had gone from frightened to delighted and she watched as the three goats who had fainted in response to her interruption of their midnight feeding, came back to their feet and continued alongside the rest. If she didn't do something, they'd destroy her yard and the flower beds she'd just gotten ready last week.

"For the love of—OK, that's enough!" she grumbled, and with the bat and an old rope that was hanging on the fence, herded them into the barn. "Since when did wild goats roam Sweet Valley?" she griped and nestled them into the largest stall for the night. Before leaving them, and still in her underwear, she fed them what little hay she had and gave them fresh water.

"I don't know who you belong to, but that'll be a problem for the morning to fix. Until there's more light and we can figure it out, that'll have to do." She shook her head and couldn't help but stay and watch them settle in. Two looked large enough to be carrying babies, three had long and beautiful wool. Two pygmies bounded around the others, as if springs were buried in their legs beneath gray and black mottled fur. The larger male, some kind of godawful mutt, only had one leg and the brightest blue eyes Elle had ever seen.

"I don't know what they call you, but I bet you're the leader of this mangy pack," she said, and the goat bleated in agreement. "I'm torn between calling you 'Lucky' or 'Frank'. What do you think?" The goat bleated softer and turned to the food. "My dad would say I shouldn't name any of you, that my heart is too soft for ranching —" she swallowed as her voice died away in the dimly lit barn.

"I'm talking to a goat, in the middle of the night, in my underwear," she said and shook her head. "Still, not the strangest thing I've done." She nodded to the unexpected visitors as if it were one of the better conversations she'd had all week, and went back to bed.

The next morning, Elle called her father.

"You mean to tell me that my daughter is the only one who could charm that rangy pack of goats into a pen?" he said with a chuckle.

"You know who they belong to?"

"No, I don't. I honestly don't think they belong to anyone.

They've been roaming the valley for probably the last year. I think they must be ones people left behind or let loose when they moved or sold their land. Probably why it's such an odd mix."

"Well, what do I do with them? How do I give them back if I don't know whose they are?"

Warren sighed and she could tell he was scratching his head. "Well, Slim, nobody's claimed 'em yet. Hell, nobody, including the game warden and animal control, have been able to catch them so, I guess they're yours."

Elle scowled out the window at the barn. "Well, what the hell am I going to do with a ragged bunch of mismatched goats? You know one of them doesn't even have all his legs?"

"Well, I suppose you could turn them into animal control. They'd probably be put down. Seems they've been quite a nuisance in the valley, eating up people's gardens and crops."

"Put down?"

"Elle, now you know how these things work."

"Well," she paused as their bleating floated across the lawn, filling the empty space with a strange feeling of companionship. "Don't call anybody, just yet. Let me think about it."

"Uh huh," Warren said, understanding just as Elle did, that she was now the proud, if reluctant, owner of a roving band of trouble-making ungulates.

Later that morning, after shoveling in some of her hay supply, changing their water, and carting out their piles of fertilizer, she sat at the kitchen table and used her newly acquired internet service and laptop, thanks to Laney and her own selfish need for the connection during visits, to research what she might need to do for the pack of miscreants who'd shown up and now resided in her barn.

It didn't matter, they shouldn't be staying. She could change her mind.

"And send them to their death? For what? Being set free?" she said to herself at the kitchen table alone. She'd been lost and hungry once. She found a home. Tears filled her eyes, and she sniffed, wiped her nose on her sleeve, and went to work. There had to be a way she could make them earn their keep. She typed in her search and started humming *Strangers In the Night,* then giggled and the sound both startled and delighted her.

Warren and Melissa were taking Elle to the Morris' auction and then out to lunch. She was in no mind to argue. She'd been working so hard out in the middle of her own private nowhere that she was actually excited to see people and have an afternoon away from her honey-do list. The Morris family, now just May and Donald since their kids were grown, had sold their small plot of land to the Bar Nunn and along with it the river rights below Gran's place. While Elle was happy for their ability to retire and enjoy a good profit, she felt like the wolf was one more step closer to her own door.

The reality of what Gran's property was worth, to her family and the future of her parent's retirement, gave her a heavy stone of regret in her belly. While she'd found that three of her goats were angora wool producers and most likely pregnant, the others in the group didn't seem to be good at much but eating her one fenced pasture down to nubs. But even that could be a bonus. She knew that the Bar Nunn was putting in its own solar panel field in the middle of sage and high grass country. She also knew that the panels were too close to get a mower in. But pygmies were small. She had made a call that very morning to the property manager with a proposal for an eco-friendly and quaint solution to their over-grown patch of panels.

She almost didn't want to leave the phone in case he called back, but she was also curious to see what the Morris' would be selling. Her bank account was getting pretty low, and she wasn't scheduled to drop off her first round of 'test' baked goods until mid-week. The practical part of her said she had no right to be even daydreaming about adding more debt to her ledger.

THEY STOOD IN THE YARD, STUDYING THE FEW GOATS and horses and the coop full of good-looking chickens, Elle's brain ran a ticker tape of cost on a constant reel, that felt like it was spilling out her ears and down to the ground. God, she'd take them all if she had the money. In the first round, they were auctioning off two more angoras and three pygmies. Elle had enough goats to be sure, but when the rowdy man next to her raised his fist and made a comment about the good hundred pounds of meat he'd be getting. Elle's head swung to watch the goats pouncing around the pen, butting into one another.

"Meat?" she said in a hushed voice to her dad.

"Elle—" he warned.

"Well, what else are they good for? I don't raise pets. That's just more mouths to feed," the man barked back at her.

"Well, I'll be happy to take them then," she grouched back and raised her hand. "May, you just give them to me; I'll look after them."

"Elle—" her dad began.

May's round, bright face lit up, and she nodded. "Sold!"

"Now wait just a goddamn—" the man started.

"Now, don't get upset, Chuck, she's looking to start a business." Warren said with a kind glint in his eye. The rancher looked at Elle, who stared back at him, shoving down the fear of confrontation that welled up in her throat. She was getting better at looking people in the eye. Chuck's face softened.

"All right, young Eleanor. I remember when you took my girl out for her first driving lesson," he nodded.

"How is Holly?" Elle brightened, partly ashamed that she hadn't recognized Chuck Hayes.

"Well, she's good and said she'd like to see you more often, but she's working so much these days."

"Well, I'll try to stop by The Trap sometime." Elle's smile melted the older man's weathered scowl, and he nodded.

"You see that you do, 'n tell her how well you're treating my stew meat." He chuckled. Elle laughed brightly. The bidding started all over again and Elle bit at her thumb nail as tractors, equipment, feeding troughs, and stock pen railings were sold. What in the hell had she been thinking, bringing on more mouths to feed?

The last thing on the docket were the horses. Elle studied the large gelding, a draft horse mix, lazily grazing beside the stocky American Quarter mare prancing along the fence line. She was a red and white pinto, beautiful and sturdy. Elle sighed and could nearly feel their warm and steady breath of ribs against her legs. How long had it been? Not since Aaron. The mare crowded closer to the gelding as the noise of the people rose. But when Ty Brentwood's voice cut through the din, she startled across the pen.

"How much you startin' for them two?" he yelled to May and pointed his stubby finger.

Elle looked over at him and her whole body tensed up. Warren tsked his tongue and met her scowl with a matching one.

"What's that son-of-a-bitch know about horses?" she growled.

"Elle, careful." Warren warned.

"Yeah, I don't see any barstools handy," Blake said from behind her, and Elle turned around.

"Well, hey kid," Warren said and extended his hand. Blake blushed and awkwardly accepted the handshake. Elle faced forward again; arms crossed in front of her chest.

"What in the hell are you doing here?" she grumbled.

"Donald said he had a nice set of hand tools—"

"With what money?" she grouched back over her shoulder.

"You're a fine one to talk. You've already committed yourself to some expensive pets, SoCal."

"Don't call me that." she said.

"I'll give you five-hundred for the pair!" Ty yelled over their fight and threw Elle a vicious smile. "That mare looks like she enjoys a good ride, eh Blake?" he licked his lips and Blake's mouth twisted into a frown.

"Eight!" Elle suddenly shouted.

"Eleanor Augusta," Warren breathed in her ear. "Do not let your temper get the best of you."

"I'm not going to let that abusive asshole—"

"$900 for the pair," Blake shouted from behind her.

"And just where in the hell do you think you'll keep horses? In the parking lot of the Silver Lake Motel? Are you insane?"

"How are you going to feed them, Elle? You don't have any hay yet. And do you even remember what to do with a horse? This isn't some Californian petting zoo—"

"Blake O'Connor you—ugh! When was the last time you even rode a horse, let alone treated one? You quit vet school."

"You ran away."

"You stopped talking to me!"

May's voice dimmed as people silenced to the verbal scuffle at their center. Blake's breath was hard and his eyes fell as if she'd just cut him across the gut.

"Do I hear a thousand?" May asked timidly.

"Here!" Ty raised his hand and leaned closer to Elle. "Imma enjoy whipping that mare's hide," he chuckled. Still locked in Blake's gaze, she tightened her fists at her side. Warren put a gentle and firm hand on Elle's shoulder.

"I'll give you $2000 for them right now," Warren said.

"Dad," the spell broke and Elle shook her head.

"Not now, Eleanor."

"Sold!" May said quickly to cut Ty's next offer off. Blake's jaw clenched. He nodded to Warren.

"Well, at least someone got what they wanted." he said, looking at Elle.

"Did I?" Warren shook his head and watched as both Blake and Ty huffed off through the crowd. Elle watched Blake's backside. Damn it, if he didn't still have the nicest ass she'd ever seen.

"Dad, I'm sorry. I got a little—"

"Don't apologize. We couldn't let Ty have them and Blake's good of heart, but poor in pocket."

"Aren't we, too?" she sighed. Warren tipped up his hat and scratched his head.

"We'll get along ok. Still, your mother's gonna have a fit."

"About what exactly?" Melissa's voice tugged his attention away, and he watched her sauntering up with some quilts of May's in her arms. Warren blushed, took off his hat, and bowed his head.

"Oh Lord, you bought more horses, didn't you?" she scolded.

"It was my fault." Elle stepped in.

"It was the right thing to do," Warren said at the same time.

"You two—I can't leave you alone! You big, old, dumb soft-hearts." She exhaled quickly through her nose and looked at the pair of horses. Brown eyes softened. "Oh my god, she's beautiful. And look at him. Damn it." She sighed again. "Guess this means we're not going out for lunch for the rest of the summer."

Elle broke into a smile and pulled her mom into her arms. The world shifted, and for a brief moment, she forgot about the fight with Blake, and the financial burden she'd just committed to, and the ugly way Ty had behaved. Later, as they were talking with May, Elle took out her checkbook and bit her lip. If she could make a couple of payments, it would be better, she said. May looked at her with a thoughtful scowl.

"You know, I remember your Gran. She drove me all the way to Louisville in a snowstorm when Tiffany came two weeks early and Donald was gone in the oil fields. She came back and watched the stock for us while I was in the hospital. Can't count how many times your dad has come over in the middle of the night to help with a bum calf or a stupid, garbage-gut goat."

Elle smiled and dropped her head. "We're a family of dumb soft-hearts."

"Thank God for that," May replied. "The world's hard enough. Lots of hate and pain. Having neighbors that care, people there to offer a hand—well, soft-hearts are a rare blessing Elle Sullivan." May said and looked over the crates of chickens, the pen of goats, the horses. She saw the cost adding up in Elle's brain.

"I'll throw in the chickens for free, since you and your dad saved Goliath and Lottie from getting taken by Ty. Both of them are decent workers. Goliath can pull the door off a tank and Lottie is maybe the best cutting horse I've ever had. You just—just pay me what you can, an' we'll figure the rest out later." May said. Elle looked at her dad, who nodded.

"Deal," Elle said.

On the drive back to Gran's, where Lottie and Goliath would be staying, Warren sighed beside his wife. The cab was heavy with each in their own thoughts.

"You know, we ought to be careful not to take on much more."

Elle leaned against the door frame; the sweet, clean air ruffled through her hair. "Yeah, I know. I'll figure something out," she grumbled. Warren drove in silence, blue eyes fixed on the road ahead.

"You always were our soft-hearted one, Elle. Are you sure you have the heart this is going to take? I mean, taking on all these animals. You gotta be prepared to do what needs doing. The hard and dirty parts. Sometimes it's a lot of blood and gore." Melissa said.

A sudden and strong memory flashed in her belly and Elle and turned away.

"I grew up the same way Katie and Laney did."

"We know, but things hit your heart harder." Warren said.

Elle thought about all the hits her heart had taken over the last six years. Being able to wring a chicken's neck for dinner wasn't something she'd enjoy, but it was a hell of a lot easier than some things she'd done. The sound of shoes scraping over rocky ground, mumbled threats, silence. Bile rose in Elle's throat and she swallowed it down.

"I'll figure something out."

At the end of the day, Elle Sullivan settled into her ranch with twenty mixed-aged chickens, four pygmy goats, three angoras, whatever the hell Frank was, and two horses. She tucked them into their respective pens for the night, gave them fresh food and water, and walked her parents back to their truck.

"You're going to need to fix that fence around your south pasture, young lady."

"Yessir, I know," she said tiredly.

Warren smiled down at her, pulled her in for a hug, and kissed her forehead. Elle didn't shudder this time. Her spine felt straight and strong. She'd faced down a lot of different conflict today, and didn't back down. It felt good. It felt like coming back stronger than before her fall.

"I'm crazy, aren't I?"

"Little bit, honey. But that's how we get through the world without failing. Keep a little bit of crazy on your side. I think you got a fine start here." Melissa said and smoothed Elle's hair from her face.

"I got a broke start," she said.

"Well, the best of us started out broke. You'll do all right. Your sister Katie will be just beside herself with joy. I bet she'll love to help you out with Goliath and Lottie when she gets back from Casper."

Elle hugged them and watched them go. She spent the next two hours watching the goats and the horses. It was a world she'd been away from for too long. She studied how the animals moved. While she watched them, they watched her. Lottie, in particular, seemed to take interest. As Elle leaned against the pole fence, Lottie walked calmly up, snuffled, and bowed her head. Elle looked at the strange map of spotting and the beautiful, intelligent eyes that seemed to stare into her soul.

"Hello Lottie," she said and caressed the horse's long nose. Lottie pressed into her hand. Goliath, not wanting to be left out, trotted over to see what treats or attention he could garner.

"You too?" Elle laughed and gave both of them attention. She smiled and felt, for the first time in months, safe. "Alright, you two, I'll call Katie and see what we can do about getting you what you need." She gave them each affection before putting them to bed.

Elle had horses.

Calm and collected ones that made her feel safe and somehow stronger. The sudden loud bleating made her jump. She also had goats. She sighed and shook her head. Before the light was gone, she walked to the chicken coop and checked on the hens. The fencing was secure, and the foundation was solid, even if the paint was still sticky.

She counted nineteen and searched the coop until she heard the low and self-satisfied sound of a hen settling in somewhere below her. Peeking through a loose board on the foundation skirting, she found the youngest and fattest hen snuggled in the tight spaces below the floorboards.

"Well, what are you doing in there?" Elle grunted and shimmied beneath the coop in the confining darkness to pluck the protesting chicken out.

"Henrietta, that's what I'll call you." The chicken cooed as Elle put her back on the perch and secured a board over the gap where she'd escaped. "But don't tell my dad I named you."

Elle turned on a small heating bulb for the cool evening and locked up her new investment before going inside and collapsing, still dressed, into bed.

EIGHT

"You stopped talking to me," Blake grumbled to himself as he drove away from Creekside and the Morris' auction. Of course, he hadn't been there to buy tools. He'd been there because he knew Warren and Melissa would be there to support their friends. He'd been there because he'd hoped Elle would be there too. He hadn't been disappointed.

For all the years of daydreams, picturing her in some short, tight dress and heels, tanned by the southern California sun and soaking in the L.A. vibe, nothing did justice to standing, unnoticed, behind her and studying her lanky frame in jeans and the button-down shirt. It hung off her shoulders more than he liked, and her shorter hair made her neck seem longer, pale but for a few freckles that he remembered pressed beneath his lips in a different life. The fire in her brown eyes as she stared down Ty, a heart as big as the world driving her need to protect the animals from that man. When she'd gotten mad—Blake ran his hands through his hair, God she was beautiful when she was mad. But it was the cutting, truthful words that laid him down for the count and caused him to turn tail and run.

You stopped talking to me.

He had. He'd cut her out of his life when she'd left with Aaron. No, it was before that even. He'd cut her out of his life the night after they'd made love.

"It was too big," he whispered to the wind blowing through his open window. "It was too big, and I was just a kid. So was she." His mouth felt dry, needy. Something that could only be solved by getting a drink.

THE NEXT MORNING, ELLE ROSE EARLY. SHE'D HAD leftover biscuits and fresh coffee for breakfast, and couldn't wait until she had eggs from her hens. She fed the goats and grimaced at the emptying cart of hay. It wouldn't take long to get through that. She let the herd out in the two paddocks that were still properly fenced. She needed to get the other six up and secure. She needed to fix the south pasture so she wouldn't go poor, feeding them off bought hay. She needed help with the irrigation and the care of the overnight ranch she'd saddled herself to. The worries looped endlessly while she mucked out the stable.

She didn't want to call her dad for help with the fence. Laney and Katelyn were busy with their own lives. And after all the work that the people of the small community did for her with the barn, she didn't feel like asking for more favors any time soon.

She needed a hired hand. A cheap one.

Elle took her grandfather's small notebook from the rolltop desk and went out to walk the property lines. If she'd had a saddle, she might have taken Lottie, but as it stood, she wasn't quite ready to get back on a horse, and she couldn't afford to go spending more money on equipment besides.

Her body was getting used to the physical labor. She was growing resilient muscle where there had only been skin and bones before. Strength that had always been there, reemerged. She mapped out the fence that needed fixed, estimated time and materials, and worried over the cost while she walked the irrigation ditches in Gran's old wader boots and took her preoccupied brain back to the house. She came around the corner of the barn and nearly ran into the sheep wagon.

Their dad had fixed it up for Katelyn to use while she was a camp counselor in Jackson Hole two summers ago. Elle pocketed the notebook and opened the unlocked door. A nice bit of space, a little dusty but not drafty. Maybe Laney's girls would like to camp in it when they came to visit. Maybe she could rent it out. Maybe she could sell it to help pay for the dwindling feed stores.

Elle settled back into her busy mind, which had driven her so ambitiously in her youth and spent the rest of the morning cleaning out the wagon, finding fresh bedding for it, and fiddling with the oven in the small kitchenette. Her father's truck pulled up later in the afternoon and she came out from the improved camper, cleaning bucket in hand.

"Just thought I'd check in with your herd," he said.

"I'm a lucky girl to have a vet for a dad."

He stepped into the barn and looked over their teeth, eyes, and hooves. He confirmed his suspicions of the previous day. Two of the angoras were pregnant and would give birth sometime in the late summer.

"Not an ideal time, heading into the winter and all, but I guess it's more milk."

"How many do you reckon?"

"Well, I can get my ultrasound machine down here next week and we can get a rough count."

"Sounds good." Elle nodded. "Are you getting much help at the clinic?"

"Not enough. I'm running myself a little ragged. Your mom keeps asking when I'll be retiring."

"I know it's probably hard to think about when there's so much debt—" Elle stopped and looked at the barn that was worth more sold than housing goats. Warren put a hand on her shoulder, sensing her worry.

"We're all right, Slim," Warren said. "Your mom and I planned ahead and I suppose I could retire, but the closest vet to Sweet Valley is forty miles away. What would people in town do without me?" He leaned against the rail and looked at the three-legged goat butting one of the smaller pygmy goats into the far corner.

"Too bad Blake O'Connor never finished school. He could have taken over for you." Elle said from the thoughts in the back of her head.

Warren nodded sadly.

"He would have been a good vet. Way I hear, all he needed to do to finish, was take his NAVLE. I think that kid could be good at anything if he'd just buckle down. He had so much potential to do whatever he wanted. Just boils my blood," Warren said and shook his head.

"Mine too," Elle sighed. "Well, at least he's got a job at the bar," she tried to sound positive. Warren looked away and grunted.

"Yeah, well, maybe not." Warren picked at a scab on this arthritic knuckle.

"What do you mean?" Warren shook his head. "Dad?"

"I heard over coffee this morning that he lost that job too. I heard he took his last paycheck straight to another bar this afternoon."

Elle dropped the bucket.

"Which bar?" she growled.

"Elle, he's a grown man." Warren warned.

"Is he?" Elle huffed and paced back and forth along the fence. She looked at her dad, and away again.

"You can't control his life, Slim. He's making his own decisions, and you're not responsible for what comes of them. You're better off not getting involved." Warren said.

"That's what people keep saying," Elle seethed.

"Well, then maybe you oughta listen."

Elle leaned against the fence. Blake was smart, but his parents never encouraged him. He was talented, but no one ever pushed him. She had. She helped him get into school, she encouraged him to sign up for classes and clubs, and helped him study for placement tests. He always listened to her. The past and present contradictions of their situation muddled in her brain.

"Blake's been one of my best friends since I was eight years old, Dad. I can't stand by and just watch him do this kinda thing and *hope* he'll make better choices later on. He's got to know that it hurts more than just him."

"Who else is it hurting, Elle?" her dad asked softly.

"Well I—" she sighed and came out of her mad long enough to see him studying her. "People who care about him."

Warren sighed.

"Give him a night at least. Let him sleep it off before you go ballsing in to yell at him."

"Ballsing, Dad?" Elle said distractedly, and her eyes fell to the sheep wagon she'd just cleaned out that morning. The chaotic thoughts bumbling through her brain fell into line.

"You know what I mean. Let him get it out of his system before you go self-righteousing in his face."

"OK," she mumbled, biting her lip and looking back to the south pasture and its fence, the irrigation, the field she needed for food. She looked back at the sheep wagon.

"You're gonna go do something anyway, aren't you?" Warren sighed.

"You better head on home before Mom worries. Bring the ultrasound machine out next week if you have a minute," Elle said, very businesslike, as she picked up the bucket.

Warren sighed. "All right, Slim. Be careful, whatever it is you're thinking of doing."

Elle went inside and took a shower. She put on clean clothes, straightened up the kitchen, ate leftovers from the fridge, and then stared out at the field from the kitchen window and took in a breath for bravery.

"Gonna do something anyway," she whispered to herself.

"Hell yeah, I am. I get to do whatever I want now." Elle picked up her keys and headed to town.

THE BEAVER TRAP WAS THE LAST BAR IN TOWN SHE hadn't been to. Elle hoped Blake wasn't there either, because she was losing her nerve. When she pulled in, his tumbled-around Jeep sat two cars away, parked crookedly. Like he'd not been entirely sober when he'd arrived. Elle killed the engine and sighed. She rubbed her sweaty palms against her skirt and picked a stubborn patch of white paint on her knee. She worked up all kinds of excuses to not go in.

Why should she even care? Why couldn't she just let him make his own mistakes?

"I'm not responsible for his life." she said angrily to the dashboard. "But I'm not going to let him hurt himself either," she answered back. A couple passed by and gave her a wide berth and a strange look. Self-conversations were easier to justify in the barn when it looked like she was talking to the goats. Now, sitting alone in the parking lot of the bar, having a full-fledged discussion about how to save her drunk, ex-best friend, seemed like she'd crossed the line over to crazy.

Her ex-best friend. Her ex. Elle inhaled suddenly as the memory of Aaron pulling her up by her hair flooded her mind. Her heart beat painfully and sweat broke out on her forehead. The world seemed to close in around her. She gasped and fought the memory back with her newfound strength. Aaron never knew how strong she really was.

"You don't know her, Ty! You don't get to say shit about her!" Blake's voice drifted from the open bar door and broke her out of the flashback. She pulled the door of the truck open and stalked inside. The muffled music became blaring noise as she opened the door, and the rainbow speckled dance floor surged with rowdy couples. No one looked familiar in this light and she searched for Blake's height, his hair, anything recognizable.

When she heard his angry voice again, she zeroed in.

"You don't know what the fuck you're talking about." and then, "No, you're out of line. Fuck you!"

"Blake Lee O'Connor!" Elle's voice cut through the crowd with icy disapproval. Blake turned on her with his anger still raging. Behind him, Ty backed away. He glared at the both of them.

"Y'all deserve each other." he said and pushed his way through the crowd. Elle watched him go with a sudden cold dread dropping into the pit of her belly.

"And what the hell are you doing here? Looking for trouble, I 'spose. You're always getting me in fucking trouble." Blake slurred.

"You watch your mouth." she berated as though he were still a child. "It seems like you're doing a fine job of finding trouble all on your own. What is it with you and Ty getting into bar fights?" She gestured to where Ty had left.

"Go home, SoCal." Blake spat and turned away. Her scowl deepened. She did not cower, like she'd done so well with Aaron. She wasn't that girl anymore.

"Holly, it's time to cut him off," Elle said as Blake finished his double whiskey in one gulp. He smiled out of the corner of his moist lips. The bartender, Holly Hayes, whose dad Chuck had been at the auction, smiled at Elle and raised her eyebrows in agreement.

"Oh, you're good at that, aren't you? Cutting me off? Eh, SoCal? When I don't fit into your little life plan?" He stood up, lost his balance, tripped over a chair leg, and fell on his back with his head between Elle's legs. He looked up the flowery sundress she'd borrowed from her mother. A goofy smile spread on his face.

"Nice panties," he chuckled. "Think I'd like to try my hand at shimmying those off later."

Elle stepped back and nudged him with her foot.

"Get up. You're making an idiot of yourself."

"Or am I'm making an idiot out of you, Elle?" He stood unsteady as a new colt. The crowd hushed to watch. Blake continued. "Pretty high school darling comes crawling back to a man who doesn't want her anymore." He inhaled sharply and grasped his shirt front. "That must hurt."

Elle's heart stopped. She could tell, despite her naïve fear, that most of them already knew. But the new Elle wasn't running. She didn't whimper, and she didn't shrink. She wasn't going to be beholden to any man by marriage or by nostalgia. Elle reached her hand up to Blake's cheek, grazed his chin with her fingers before she grabbed on to his hair and yanked him down to her height. Blake howled.

"Ouch! Jesus!"

"I bet that hurts worse," she growled.

Blake staggered behind her as she led him through the bar and to her truck. "Go on. Get in." She opened the door and shoved him.

"I'm not going anywhere with you, Elle. Not ever again. How do I know you aren't going to take me out on some deserted road?" He yelled out the open door even as he let her push him inside. "Like that one night,'" he continued and leaned across the seat of the truck. He didn't fight when she shoved his legs in.

Elle stayed quiet and avoided looking back at the small crowd that had followed them. At her silence, Blake stopped, his breath heavy in his chest. He looked into her eyes and felt the memory of their night creep up. His brow fell, his stomach churned. The world spun around them.

"Elle, I—"

"I wouldn't sleep with you if you were the last man left on the planet." she growled and slammed his door. "But I'm not going to let you kill someone when you drive your drunk carcass home." She marched to her side and got in with a huff.

"Well, I wasn't planning on *going* home!" He snapped back, regaining the lost ground from sympathy that stopped him before.

"You were about two seconds from getting kicked out. Where were you planning on going after that, exactly? Stumble down the highway to the next bar? And the next? And the next after that?" She turned to face him. "When are you going to pull your life together? Before you lose everything? Or are you just gonna aim for ending up in jail or dead?" Elle's frustration made her voice shake.

"I've already lost everything. What does it matter where I end up?" he yelled.

"It matters to me." Elle yelled back.

"Ha! I don't believe you. You don't give two shits about me, and why should you?" His blue eyes stared at her through a red haze of fury. Her face drained of color. Blake quieted. He sat still and put his hands up.

"Elle, just because I'm yelling doesn't mean I'd—" he stuttered and a strange, fuzzy understanding began to dawn on his face. "I'm sorry I yelled. You know that I'd never raise a hand—"

"Please, just stop," she interrupted. Did she know that he wouldn't hurt her? She wasn't sure. The pause sat heavy between them.

"What is this?" He stole a glance at the crowded porch. "What do you want with me? Where are we going?"

"Take him home, Elle!" A rowdy man in the crowd yelled. Elle shut her mouth against all the things she wanted to say. She swung the truck around and out onto the highway. Blake burped deep in his throat and held on to the dashboard with both hands. His head hung down, and he coughed expectantly.

"Don't you dare throw up in my truck," she seethed at him.

"Well, if you wouldn't drive like a fucking maniac—"

"Can you *please* stop using that word?"

"Maniac?" he teased.

"You know which word I mean." She looked over at him in the

dark cab. He slung an arm over the back of the seat and leaned in close. His breath was hot with whiskey and his nose gently touched the skin behind her ear.

"Fucking?" He whispered seductively. Elle drifted over the yellow line. "Whoa, keep it between the lines, SoCal!" he chuckled.

"Put your seat belt on and stay on your side," she growled and nudged his ribs with her elbow. Blake sat back with a smile. It took less than two minutes to get from one side of the town to the other and they were pulling into the motel parking lot before he could figure out the complexity of the seat belt.

"What the hell are we doing here?" he said as if he were insulted and abandoned the fight with the belt.

"Isn't this where you're staying?"

"Not anymore." He hiccuped and shook his head. He wavered in his seat and his eyes widened.

"Oh God," Elle said and shoved him over just in time for him to open the door and vomit. Elle's stomach turned at the garish sound.

"Evicted," he coughed out the last bits. "I ran out of money, so they kicked me out two days ago."

"Where have you been staying?" she asked.

"You left my new place in the parking lot of the Beaver Trap," he said, and leaned out again for another round of vomiting.

"Jesus," Elle groaned and took a moment to think. "I can't take you to your mother's. She'd be—"

"Disappointed?" He coughed and sat back up, slamming the door. "Don't worry, Elle. She's way past disappointment. I think we all know she never really cared where I ended up anyway."

"Oh, Blake," Elle rested her forehead on the steering wheel.

He was quiet, stomach and heart empty, in the seat next to her. She looked at the rundown brick building that would have saved her the next decision if only he'd been able to stay there. But he couldn't stay, and she couldn't let him go back to his Jeep.

"Fine." She started the truck. They drove down the street, back to the highway, and turned south. She rolled down her window and sighed with the fresh air that helped ease the smell.

"You're not perfect yourself, you know? You came back home too. You failed out there just the same as me," he grumbled, crossed his arms over his chest and sat back against her silence.

"I did come back." She shifted up to a higher gear as they gained speed out of the city limits. Her voice was laced with a hollowness. "But I wouldn't say I failed so much as I survived."

Blake's head swung over to look at her; the pale profile illuminated in the dashboard lights, and saw a history play out in the twitch of her cheek and the glassy stare of her eyes. They stayed quiet for most of the drive until they turned down the small county road.

"Hey, look at that," he burped again as they jostled down the dirt road. "You *are* taking me home." He smiled into her glowering face.

"I'm not sure where home is for you," she said. "Or if you even have one." It hurt to say it, and probably hurt him to hear it. He sunk into the seat. Elle pulled into the drive, but Blake remained still with his arms crossed.

"Should I just sleep in the truck then?"

"You're not sleeping in my truck, for God's sakes." She sighed and tried to think. The bed in the wagon wasn't made yet and it would be too easy for him to sneak out in the morning.

"How 'bout in your bed?" he said.

"In your dreams," she returned with thinly veiled anger.

"I haven't dreamed about you in a long time," he lied. Elle's heart fluttered knowing that he used to.

"You can sleep on the couch," she said.

She got out and Blake staggered behind. He fell against the gate and tumbled into her grandmother's lilacs. The branches cracked and broke beneath his weight and when she looked back all she saw was his long legs sticking out beneath the bent and tattered bush.

"Oopsies!" he laughed. "Little help here?"

Elle was beyond her limit, pissed off, tired, and unforgiving. But as he lay, scratched and bleeding, laughing in her lilacs, completely oblivious to the pit his life had become, her greatest anger came from how much she still loved him.

"Get the fuck up," she growled at him.

"Ooo, can you please not use that word? It upsets my delicate sensibilities." He surrendered to another fit of giggles, and Elle made a disgusted sound as she offered him her hands and braced her legs for his weight. He pulled himself up and lurched into her. His hot skin pressed everywhere as they fell backwards. Blake's arms wound around her and they landed on the grass.

"Well, hey now," he laughed. "Here on the lawn? I didn't know you were so adventurous."

Elle felt his body respond against her bare leg and his hand trailed gently under her skirt. She stared at his lips, his jaw, his smile and felt the past come crashing down all around her. She was seventeen again. The silk-light touch from hands she knew curved up the delicate skin of her thigh.

"Elle," His voice caught in his throat as his eyes fell to her lips.

"Blake, please." Her voice was like a dream in the delicate moment of indulgent, grass-pressing and the cool, summer air on heated skin.

"Is that a please yes, or please don't?" he whispered. His eyelids fell as his lips touched hers. She trembled beneath him, and Blake froze.

"D...don't Blake, please," she said. Blake pulled back, the hurt in his eyes turned to something else, and Elle wasn't sure if it was anger or disgust.

"Do you think I'd—" he rolled off of her and staggered to his feet. "You think I'd force myself on you, Elle? Is that what you're used to? Is that what Aaron does—"

"Please, stop," she cried and scrambled away. She righted her dress and wiped at her eyes.

"What in the hell did he do to you?" Blake's words were strained and angry.

"I don't want to talk about it, Blake. I'm not gonna talk about this with you." She shook her head, and Blake wanted to take her trembling fingers into his own. He wanted to hold her hand like they had, as kids, as teenagers; in that lifetime ago, before they'd both been so wrecked and ruined. Blake's brow fell. He took her hand gently in his.

"You used to tell me everything, Elle."

"You stopped listening," she sobbed and tore her hand from his. He followed her to the door. Elle turned back and took in a deep breath.

"If you come inside this house, *my* house—" she corrected. "Then you're staying on the couch, Blake O'Connor. And tomorrow morning you and I will be having words."

"Ugh," he said. "That sounds awful. I think I'd rather sleep in your lilacs," he answered.

"Get inside!"

"OK, OK." he said, shocked but proud of her regained composure. He stumbled behind her into her house.

Elle switched on the light above the kitchen sink and motioned for him to sit. She left him in the dimly lit kitchen, sitting at the old wooden table where they'd shared countless meals as kids. She came back downstairs with fresh sheets, a pillow, and a blanket. As she made up his bed on the couch, she stole glances over her shoulder at him. He leaned his head into his hands to stop the world from spinning. She turned on a small lamp by his temporary bed and straightened the pillow.

"You look like an angel in that light," he said. Elle looked back at him and tried to shield her heart from the soft words.

"Little late for sweet talk, O'Connor. Are you going to throw up again?" she asked.

"No," he whispered. She came back to the kitchen and poured him a glass of water from the sink.

"Go sleep it off. We'll sort it out tomorrow."

"OK," he said contritely and watched her walk past him and up the stairs.

"Elle," he called.

"Yes?"

"When you do want to talk about it, I—"

"Goodnight, Blake," she interrupted, and left him for the safety of her room.

She wasn't sure if she could ever talk to him about what happened, and right now, with unclear minds and hurt hearts, it wasn't the time to go digging into the past. She closed her bedroom door behind her and listened until she heard the familiar creak of the couch's springs and the soft groan of a man settling in. She sighed.

"Goddamn it, Blake." She pressed her back to the door and looked skyward. "What am I doing, Gran?"

Second chances sometimes make for better people. She heard her grandmother whisper through her brain. Elle undressed, put on a light chemise to sleep in, scrubbed her face, brushed her teeth, and ignored how tired her reflection looked. Then, setting her dad's old Louisville Slugger against the dainty white nightstand, she slid beneath the sheets and listened to the house creak and Blake's snore drifting up the stairway.

NINE

Please don't, Blake. Please...

Blake's hands clutched at the blankets as he tossed in circles on the couch. He panted as his brain relived the soft smell of her skin and the way his rough hands slid beneath her skirt. The smallness of her beneath him and her heart beating against his ribs. Her breathy plea.

The erotic waves that began his dreams faded to the memory of the inevitable pain of watching her fear him. They faded into the day, years ago, when she'd driven away from Sweet Valley. He'd loved her so much. What they had and lost, tore a chasm in his soul so wide and deep that nothing ever seemed to fill it up.

The morning came, muted behind the living room curtains, and Blake stirred. He buried his face away from the light while the world rocked outside his aching head. The world was Elle Sullivan's house, her little ranch, and the foolish, youthful dreams he'd left eons ago. She'd gotten to him again; she always did.

"Shit," he grunted into the pillow. He'd been such an asshole last night. The things he'd said, in front of all of those people. Being disgusting towards her, belittling her, vomiting, falling, pressing her into the soft grass only to have her body stiffen with traumatic memories.

"Shit," he mumbled again and wished he could sneak out and go find a quiet, dark place to die. He listened for her footsteps above him. The only sound was the old house settling and some goddamn bird outside who was too happy for its own good.

His temples throbbed.

Maybe she wasn't up yet and he still had a chance to leave without having to rehash the night before. He sat up, naked but for his boxers. His mouth was dry, and it tasted like the ass end of a badger. He staggered into the bright kitchen and shielded his eyes. The aroma of coffee hit him first, and then homemade biscuits and bacon. But the room was empty of her. The dishes were done, neatly stacked, and drying in the sunshine. She'd left a note on the coffee pot.

Breakfast is in the oven if you want it.

He found a clean mug and a bottle of Advil on the counter. The coffee was hot and perfect, and he drank two cups before pulling out the warm plate of bacon, eggs, and biscuits.

Sitting half-naked in her kitchen, Blake quieted his disgruntled belly. At least she hadn't lost her talent for cooking. He looked around at the clean kitchen with its flowery curtains, white cupboards, old farm sink, and warm wooden floors scattered with woven rugs. Flowers decorated the table, daffodils and some of the lilacs he had broken off in his fall. He stopped mid-bite.

She *should* have turned him out on his ass. He looked at the empty plate; instead, she had taken him in like that pitiful three-legged goat and babied him. Picked another lost cause while she was on a roll. He wished she had left him on the lawn or made him sleep in the barn with the rest of the animals. What she did instead made him feel more guilty. Not just from his behavior last night, but from what he'd become.

Blake finished breakfast, licked his fingers, and washed the dishes. He looked out the window and saw Elle turning her herd into the small, gated pasture by the barn. With sweet and smiling calls, the flock followed her, just as pleased as punch, and the self-satisfaction in her smile melted him.

"Well, look at that, Elle Sullivan, goat-charmer," he allowed a smile before he looked away. He went back to the living room for his clothes, but they were gone, replaced by a note.

They're in the dryer. Take a shower.

He grimaced at her curved handwriting and crumpled it up.

"Stop telling me what to do, Elle." The house had heard those same words many times before. Her telling him what to do was practically written in the bones of the place. Still, a shower would feel good, and it wasn't like he had anywhere burning to be, except gone. Blake trudged up the narrow staircase off of the kitchen. The scratches on its well-worn banister brought back memories of racing after the girls or away from them. The stairs squeaked in the same places and the banister swayed slightly on loose nails.

The same flowered wallpaper went the whole way to the hallway. He reached the top of the stairs and peeked in each door as he walked past. Four bedrooms, the first three small but cozy, were bare of anything but beds and side-tables. One had a sewing machine and a desk where he could see invoices and bills stacked neatly.

His brow creased, and he wondered how far in debt the Sullivans were. The barn raising was supposed to help get the ranch up and running again, but everyone knew that ranching didn't make money. It lost it. Still, even with the size of that stack, there was food to eat, and the house was warm. Elle had been raised to live simply, even though Aaron's family had been rich. He'd always thought that had been, in part, why she'd left. To get out of the small, poor town and live a different kind of life. At least that's what he'd thought until last night. Blake leaned on the doorway of the bedroom that used to be hers.

The old cottonwood tree swayed outside the window. He used to climb up it to get to her. Some nights they'd sneak out. Some nights they'd just talk. She used to tell him everything. She'd never been the kind of girl who cared about money. Maybe he really had stopped listening. He pressed his fingers into his eyes and felt the hangover claim his reasoning even as his brain jumbled through their past. Whatever had happened to her, it had changed her. She was—harder. And even though flashes of her broken came through at times, she was standing up, taller than she had before.

She'd stood up to him. Maybe newly alone was something that was good for her. Blake walked to the last bedroom. He found her touch and smell everywhere, from the fluffy down bedding to the baseball bat beside her bed. Library books about farming, ranching, goat herding, and chickens were stacked on the bedside table. She had her own small bathroom, and while Blake could have used the one down the hall, he chose Elle's instead.

He started the water in the old, cast-iron tub and took off his days-old underwear. Looking at the sorry mess of them, and slightly embarrassed, he tossed them into the trashcan. The bathroom filled with steam as Blake stepped into the tub and sorted through the various bottles of soaps, and God knew what else.

Women were strange creatures. He sniffed the shampoo and quickly put it down. Clean was one thing; he didn't need to smell like a goddamn garden. He found a plain bar of soap, the basic white kind. That clean, no frills smell that he remembered about her. He soaped up, hair and all, and rinsed off. The warm water eased his headache and made him feel almost human again.

When he stepped out, all he could find were her flowery towels and begrudgingly wrapped one around his waist. He wiped steam from the mirror above the sink and stared at the frightening sight of his ashen cheeks, dark with stubble. He hadn't eaten a real meal in days.

Blake had always been lean, but the recent years of hardship had left him hollow. His dark and angrily arched brows seemed menacing over the new pallor of his face. The left one seemed particularly malicious, with a scar running through it where the hair never grew back, a souvenir from a car wreck three years ago and the eight stitches it gifted him. He didn't remember much about that night except the strange sensation of flying as the car turned over and over across the median of the highway, and the disappointment of being alive when it was all over.

Why had she ever let him stay? Why'd she bother hauling him home from the bar last night? Couldn't she just let him sit in his comfortable rock bottom? He was nothing but a mess; a broken and useless failure. Blake's stomach dropped, and he hurried from the bathroom.

His clothes were in the dryer, warm and smelling clean for the first time in weeks. He put on the hot denim without underwear and breathed in sharply where the rivets stung. Fuming as he pulled his t-shirt on and cranky from the resurgence of the headache, he marched with fists balled up tight, straight to the barn. Her ridiculous red barn with its bright white trim, looking like something out of a Country Living magazine; neat as a pin and built to last. He didn't want her lasting, not here. Not so close to him and his rock bottom.

Elle was shoveling manure into a wheelbarrow. She wore jeans and a button-down shirt. The curve of her backside stole his attention and made him forget why he was mad. She turned, with the pitchfork still in her hand.

"Oh good, you're up."

"I guess," he grumbled.

"Did you eat?"

"Yes," he said. "You're probably eager to get me back to town."

Elle sighed, wiped the sweat from her forehead, and put the pitchfork down. She took off her gloves, tucked them into her back pocket, and cleared her throat. He could tell she was about to launch into a talk, and he rolled his eyes with a preemptive sigh.

"Chuck and Holly brought your Jeep out this morning,"

"Oh?" He crossed his arms in front of his chest. Between the anger and the headache, he hadn't noticed it in the drive.

"It was awfully nice of them, considering the ruckus you were making last night."

"I suppose so. See you around, Elle." He muttered and turned to leave.

"Slow down there, cowboy," she said, and Blake heard her jingle his keys. "I'm afraid you're all out of favors."

"What in the hell does that mean?" He scowled down at her with his arms still crossed. She slipped the keys into her shirt pocket.

"Means Chuck has a porch that needs fixed, and I think you could get that done in about an afternoon. Also, they need someone to help vaccinate their horses."

"I'm not a vet, Elle. Or didn't you get the memo about me dropping out of school?"

Elle continued without batting an eye. "You didn't drop out; you just didn't take the test. Dad has the vaccines and will meet you there tomorrow."

"Well, what if I don't want to?"

She looked at him sternly and stepped closer. "You've been floundering for too long, Blake."

"Don't know why that's your business or why in the hell you even care," he said.

"You have no job. No place to live."

"Thanks for reminding me." He turned to leave. He'd rather walk the six miles back into town than listen to her lecture.

"So, you're going to live here and you're going to work for me," she said firmly to his back.

Blake stopped, one foot out the barn door, and turned. "Are you crazy?"

"I need help with the goats and the ranch. And you need a place to start."

"And where would I stay, Elle? With you?" He smiled cruelly and walked towards her. She looked away with red cheeks.

"No."

"Then where, genius? There's only one house."

"Well, I've thought of that too." She walked past him.

"'Course you have," he grumbled and followed her with heavy footsteps.

Behind the barn was the old sheep wagon, left over from the beginning days on the ranch when Gran would summer her flock further down the valley. Elle looked at it with a sense of pride at the new bright white coat of paint she must have done herself. The trim was red, and she'd even planted flowers in its outside window boxes.

"What the hell is that?" Blake said and pointed at the quaint camper.

"It's your new start." She opened the door and gestured for him to go inside.

He looked at her warily and stepped up into the wagon. A loft bed below the back window was neatly made with thick and cozy blankets. There were storage drawers beneath it. A small pot-bellied stove sat on the left side with a kettle for tea or coffee, cups and plates, and a small table. One wall had shelves of worn paperbacks. Elle had put in a small fridge in the corner beneath the bed.

"You'll get three meals a day and all the work you probably can stand."

"That's all? You're not going to pay me?" He scoffed. "Who in the hell would sign up for that?"

"A man who's lost every other job in town, I reckon."

He looked down at her angrily.

"You won't get paid," she admitted. "At least not at first—not until I start making a profit, but you'll get to work with my dad, and he'll count every hour you spend helping him towards internship hours."

"What?" Blake's heart hammered in his chest.

"So, you can take your NAVLE's."

Blake was silent. He looked away and his fists tightened.

"So that's it, huh? You're just deciding what I'm gonna do with my life?"

Elle shrugged as if it weren't the worst option he'd been given.

"I don't want your charity, Elle, and I sure as hell don't want you making my choices for me." he said. Elle's cheeks flushed, and she clenched her jaw. She even put her hands on her hips, just like when they were kids.

"Well, what else are you going to do, Blake? Waste away in the bar? Be nothing but a useless drunk? Stagger around the streets of Sweet Valley for the rest of your life? Don't you think you deserve better than that?"

"No, I don't!" he replied. "It's my life, Elle. If drinking myself to death is what I want to do, you don't get a say in it."

"You're right. You make your own choices, Blake. You have two of them now. You can either stay in a warm and safe place with three meals a day and good work that'll give you a chance for something better, or you can go back to where you were and keep spiraling down into nothing. That's up to you. But you know that this is *it*." She gestured back to the ranch. "This is all you have left. You've reached everyone else's limit, and no one is gonna take you back!"

She tossed his car keys to him and stomped away. Blake watched her go. He was so angry and confused that he couldn't breathe. He clenched his fist around the keys until they bit into his hand. He looked out of the wagon's window to the green and uncut fields; the potential and the sunshine warming the earth around him. The thirst for a drink that was still heavy in his mouth, but the small part of his soul that knew that's not really what he was craving. The rusty wheels in his brain cranked to life.

ELLE WILLED HERSELF TO NOT LOOK BACK. SHE couldn't bear to watch him drive away. The offer was her Hail Mary, and she was scared to death that he wouldn't take it.

She was scared to death he would.

It wasn't going to be easy either way. While she needed the help, she also knew inviting him into her life could cause trouble. She had enough fixing to do in her own life, without worrying about fixing a man too. A man, Elle snorted. Blake wasn't a man; he was just the boy she'd loved a lifetime ago. Trouble was keeping that lifetime from interfering with the current one.

She paced the kitchen floor and gnawed her thumbnail down to the quick. The pain shot up through her finger and Elle remembered Gran used to pay her a dollar for every week she didn't chew them. She closed her eyes and lean against the sink.

"What am I doing, Gran?" she asked the stillness. "Blake O'Connor? What the hell am I doing?"

A soft voice whispered in the back of her head.

Second chances sometimes make for better people.

Elle opened her eyes and looked out the window. She hadn't realized she was holding her breath until she saw him marching to his Jeep with the angry gait she was getting accustomed to. He yanked open the door and pulled two trash bags and a box from the passenger seat, slammed the door, and walked back to the camper. Elle blew out the breath and her stomach filled with butterflies.

"Well, OK then. OK," she said and went to get her tools from the hall closet.

TEN

THE MAY SUN WAS RELENTLESS IN THE SOUTH PASTURE. Waves of hot air rose and cooked away the small amount of moisture left in the earth. Sweat dripped down between Blake's shoulder blades and soaked the underarms of his shirt. He wanted a goddamn drink, and they were just getting into week one of what Blake thought of as "Elle's Torture Camp".

They'd spent the first day of his indentured servitude fixing the porch of The Beaver Trap for Chuck and Mary Hoyle. The shame of having to apologize was terrible, but the forgiveness he was given seemed worse. They'd moved on to helping Elle's father with vaccinations. Blake couldn't even meet Warren's eyes as they worked with Chuck's horses.

Warren hadn't said much to him since he'd graduated and moved back. Then again, Warren rarely said much to anyone. He was as quiet and patient as ever, and he handed over most of the work to Blake. But when Blake's hands shook too hard to finish the delicate job, Warren stepped in. It hurt Blake's floundering pride, but he wasn't given time to dwell. Elle just kept him plugging along from task to task. He hated the smug expression on her face whenever he finished one thing, no matter how small. The way she'd nod and then toss her head towards the truck.

On to the next repair. On to the next job, the next lesson, the next hopeless cause. But never on to a cold beer or the reprieve of a shady bar and the numbing liquid it served. In the course of the week, they'd put in a garden, helped build a gazebo at the community center, repaired the window casings of the upstairs bedrooms, and laid new flooring at the Head Start school. He suspected she was using him to help pay back the barn raising.

He also suspected she was avoiding her own problems by focusing on repairing the bridges he'd been burning. He watched her from the corner of his eye and how she shied away from being too physically close to any person, including him. Loud and sudden sounds sometimes made her cringe. She protected herself from life while she forced him back into it.

Now, they were out working on the south pasture's fence and he was exhausted. The haze of heat, hard labor, and quiet dinners together where neither of them said much, left him spent. Blake's body was suffering. It was aching for booze and respite, and he resented Elle for keeping him out of town with long days that left him too tired for anything else.

"Hand me the pliers," she said, rousing him from his stupor.

"Huh?" Blake said as he sagged against an old stump.

"Pliers," she said more forcefully and knocked him on the chest. He flinched with annoyance and flung them at her feet. "Thanks a lot." She took them and tried to grip the poorly hammered u-nail, but the gloves made it impossible.

"Dang," she said as the pliers slipped and she scraped her wrist on the edge of the post. Blake tipped his cap up and squinted.

"You all right?"

"Fine," she grunted. "How are you?"

"You know how I am, goddamn it," he growled.

"The withdrawal is probably pretty rough."

"I can live through the withdrawal. It's my *boss* that makes me miserable," he said snidely. She scowled.

"Your *boss* is liable to fire you if you don't get back to work. You're fully grown and capable, so stop whining," she said without a glimmer of pity. Blake stood up and watched a bead of sweat caress her neck and fall over her collarbone down the v of her shirt.

"Maybe my boss keeps me around hoping I'll use my fully grown and capable self to work on her."

Elle reached out and pinched him hard on the arm with the pliers.

"Ouch, Elle! Shit!" Blake yelped, dropped back and massaged the bruised skin. The stern pucker on her lips was the same one she'd had as a bossy eight-year-old. The same beautiful pout that made him realize he'd probably love her his whole wretched life.

He wasn't much better now than the stupid kid he'd once been.

"I'd like this fence built sometime this century. I don't want to have to keep coming back to fix your mistakes," she said. "And I don't want to share my bed with a man who lives in a bottle." Elle turned away. Blake rubbed his arm and scowled at her back.

"Well, I don't want to share your bed *at all*. I don't want to share anything with you, period, Elle. You've been nothing but trouble to me since you walked back into town."

Elle spun around, fiery eyed, and wielding the pliers.

"Well, then why don't you just leave, you sorry son-of-a-bitch." He staggered back at her uncustomary curse and bumped into the truck. She kept coming. "If you hate me so goddamn much, then quit. Just like you always do! Walk away when things get hard. Isn't that how you roll? It's worked *so* well for you this far."

Blake's dark brows drew together over angry blue eyes that stunned her silent. He was torn between the way his heart skipped at her returning swagger and the painful truth of her words.

"You walk back into town thinking you know me, Elle? Huh? Thinking you know a goddamn thing about what I've been through? You never looked back once after you left with your pretty golden boy. And how'd *that* work out for *you*?"

Elle looked like he'd sucker-punched her in the gut.

"I made a bad choice." she yelled back. "But I'm not running from my mistakes or trying to drown them in booze."

"Really?" he stepped closer, close enough that the sweat and heat of their bodies co-mingled. "Because you're here now. So, if you weren't, running then why didn't you stay in California? If you're not running, why aren't you still with him?" he yelled.

"There's a difference between leaving because you don't want to work for it and leaving because—he hurt me," she admitted. Blake leaned back and his biting reply died. He felt sick. Sick with anger at a man who was not there to punish. Elle took in a shaky breath, and he changed the subject as much for himself as for her.

"Why should I bother to work for anything, Elle?"

"I can't give you a reason. But I *know* you can do better...*be* better. You're just afraid to trust in yourself."

Blake flushed, and he felt like throwing up. She persisted.

"You don't like that people remember who you were. Kind and good-hearted, and smart. Holy cow, you were smart! I think you don't like believing that you still are those things." She swallowed. "You think it makes you vulnerable, and it's—it's hard to be vulnerable." Blake's chest tightened; the truth sat like a hot coal between his lungs.

"Maybe I'm not those things anymore." He paced in a circle around her and backed her closer against the truck. "I don't even remember that boy." Elle held her hands out, brushed his chest. She looked at his mouth.

"I remember him."

Blake's eyes turned hard as he looked down at her. "He left the day you did."

"So, suddenly, all your failures are my fault?"

"Well, you leaving sure as hell didn't help me," he said, and studied her lips hungrily. She leaned in and her eyes fell to his mouth; his wall rose to the painful truth she'd made him face and fought back. "Didn't you ever stop to think that breaking my heart would set me up to fail?"

Elle's eyes snapped back to his. Her mother's words came back to her suddenly, swirling in questions of blame and responsibility. She stood up straighter and stronger.

"Don't you dare put that on me, Blake. Don't you dare." She shoved his chest. He stepped away with his hands up. "You were just as much to blame for how it ended. You never returned any of my calls. The only one responsible for your behavior is you. Blaming me or anyone else isn't going to make your mistakes right or justify how you're living."

He glowered.

"Well, I guess we'll have to pick up this discussion later. My boss doesn't like me fraternizing on the job."

"Frater—" Elle's cheeks burned and her words stumbled as he picked up another bundle of poles and carried them over to the next section.

She went back to the other side of the pasture to continue her own work, but had a hard time keeping his angry words from rolling over and over in her head. She looked back at him, the sweat soaking his shirt, plastering it over the muscles of his back as he worked. He had been strong and healthy, but now he was nothing more than skin stretched over bones. The work would do some of his healing; the home cooking would do more. If he could stand being around her that long. Beyond that, she didn't know how she could repair the damage of their past.

At the end of the long and hot day, where nothing much more was said, Elle loaded the tools into her truck and closed the tailgate. She took off her gloves and knocked the dirt from them on the side of her thigh before tucking them into her back pocket. Blake dried his face on the tattered tail of his shirt. His flat stomach peeked through and the dusting of hair trailed down below the waist of his jeans.

Elle stared, frozen in the beauty of it; her body tingled, flashing a spark so long ago lost that she almost didn't recognize it. When Blake took the shirt off and doused his head with water from the canteen, the spark ignited and she imagined her nails down his chest, sweat and water moist on the pads of her fingers.

"Why, Eleanor Sullivan, are you ogling me?" Blake chuckled. Elle jumped and turned away.

"What? No, I was just—put your shirt on!" She opened the door to the truck and scrambled inside.

"Why? Are you afraid you may not be able to keep your hands off me and you'll have to take back that whole not sharing your bed with a man in a bottle speech?"

"Shut up, Blake," she said and started the engine. Blake leaned into her open window.

"Don't I get a ride?" he said. The sparkle in his eyes was magnified by the water still clinging to his lashes.

"Why don't you walk back and cool off," she grumbled and sped away.

"Yes, boss lady," he yelled after her.

THE DUST CLOUD SHE LEFT WAFTED PAST HIM AND coated him in filth. His temples banged from dehydration and the poison that was still working itself out. He'd sweat today. Not just from being sick, but from working hard. She'd kept up, right beside him, and together they'd put up a good portion of the new fence. He turned back to look at the straight and narrow line of it, beautiful in its simplicity. A small seed of pride sprouted in a back corner of his heart. His shoulders were sore, his back ached, and he was dirty, tired, and hot. While he walked to the white farmhouse in the distance, the sun started to descend.

He paused to take in a deep breath of the cooling summer air, clean and fresh, and stared out to the green and lush pasture. He rubbed his chin and felt the stirring of vigor inside of his chest. Even with the soreness and fatigue, he still felt better than he had in months.

And Elle had looked at him.

Not like usual. Not with regret or pity. But like a hungry man looks at food; he smiled crookedly, even if she was too embarrassed to admit it. It was the first time he'd seen something besides fear in her eyes at the thought of intimacy. He turned off the two-track to his camper beside the barn. When he got there, he refilled his canteen and washed his face. The odor of his own sweat and body made him recoil.

Blake looked at the clock. She'd probably yell at him if he were late for dinner. He sorted through his clothes. Some were cleaner than today's, but all of them were stiff with sweat. He didn't have much left after being evicted. Blake sat down, deflated. He looked towards the house. Why did it matter what he smelled like?

It mattered because she'd be clean, smelling like sunshine and soap, pink cheeked and perfect across the dinner table. His pride reared its ugly head, but his heart cowed it back down. He gathered all of his dirty laundry into a trash bag and crossed the drive in the dusky light. He knocked on the kitchen screen door. He shuffled from foot to foot, his dirty shirt half-buttoned and his hands in his back pockets. She answered with a dishtowel on her shoulder, a smudge of flour on her cheek, and smelling like fresh bread and cream.

"Dinner's not ready yet," she said, worried.

Blake cleared his throat.

"It's OK, I didn't—" he sighed. "I was wondering if I could use your shower? And maybe the washer?" he asked. The breeze blew in from behind him and she leaned back from the sweat, traces of smoke, and souring whiskey. He looked away, and her gaze softened.

"Course you can," she said and stepped back to let him in.

"Take off your boots before you come inside," she said, and he complied with a slow and sweet 'yes ma'am'.

"Give me your clothes," she said and reached out for the garbage bag.

"Huh?"

"Your dirty clothes," she pointed to the bag that he'd shoved behind his back. He handed it over with a frown. "Go on now," she nodded to the stairs, and Blake did as he was told. Elle checked on dinner and went to empty half of the bag into the washer in the back mudroom. He glimpsed her checking for stains and holes before starting a heavy-duty load with an extra scoop of soap on his way up the stairs. The shower felt like heaven and Blake wished he could stay under the warm spray forever, but the smells from downstairs made his stomach grumble and his mouth water. Living with Elle wasn't so bad after all.

His brain stumbled on itself.

Of course, it was awful. She'd broken his heart. She'd left. When she did come back, she bullied him into straightening up, picking him up from rock bottom, and trying to force him to take responsibility for his mistakes. Blake clenched his fists at his sides and the water ran in rivulets around them. He shook his head, dropped his gaze to her bar of soap and thought that it'd be easier to have a fifth of whiskey and go lick his wounds. The clatter of dishes in the sink downstairs startled him out of his daze. At least he would get as many home-cooked dinners out of this fucked up deal as he could. It wasn't like he was staying forever.

This was just a waypoint.

He toweled off and when he stepped out of the shower, he saw clean clothes on the sink. She must have stepped in while he was showering and left some of her father's old clothes. He hadn't even heard her. He wondered, with a smile, if she'd taken a peek.

Probably not. Elle wasn't one to take advantage of anyone or cross her good-girl line. Which made it even more surprising that she'd left her husband. Blake felt heated anger rise in his throat. He could have told her that Aaron was bad for her six years ago. He'd tried to...hadn't he? Hadn't he asked her not to go? She said he hadn't returned her calls. That he stopped listening. Is that how it had ended? Blake couldn't remember.

"Got what we deserved," he mumbled. "Didn't we?" Warren's shirt was tight across his shoulders and the jeans were narrow in the hips. But they were clean. His stomach rumbled as he descended and found the table set with enough food for ten men.

"What's all this?"

"It's dinner. I didn't know how hungry you were and, well, I thought we'd just use up the leftovers." She reached up and brushed a blonde curl from her sweat-glowing brow. He studied the way her shoulders and face fell with the weight of exhaustion and the guard she carried. Blake shook his head.

"What?" she said, spine straight.

"I wish you would have let me help. You worked just as hard as I did today."

She looked at him as if he were an undiscovered species.

"You can help eat it," she said, her voice lightened. Blake hated how much he loved to see her happy. He sat across from her and tucked into the food like he hadn't eaten in a month. Between the hunger and the exhaustion, neither spoke except to ask to pass a plate or the pepper. After she'd cleared the dishes, she turned to face him her eyes fell to the open buttons on his shirt.

"Well, have a good night," Elle said, her palms braced against the sink behind her. Blake looked at her tense shoulders curiously.

"Don't you want help cleaning up?"

"Nope, I think I'm all good here. You go on and get a good night's rest."

"Well, maybe I'll go into town," he said off handedly.

Elle straightened and crossed her arms in front of her chest. "For what?"

"A drink."

"No."

"No?" Blake stared down at her.

"No, you're not going into town for a drink or you're done here."

"You can't tell me—"

"That's right, I can't. You do what you want. And if you want a hot breakfast in the morning and a warm roof over your head for the next week, you'll stay in that wagon and get a good night's rest," she said defiantly.

"Listen, Elle you—"

"Blake. This isn't rocket science. Aren't you tired?"

"Yeah, I am."

"Then stay here. Stay here and just rest," she said. "Please don't go," she sighed. Blake's head snapped up to look at her. Something strange passed in his features, pale and surprised, until the surliness came back.

"Fine. I'll stay here. But not because you said so." he argued.

"OK, fine."

"I'll see you in the morning."

"Great." she said. She watched him stalk to the wagon and slam the door before she moved from the window. The week had been hard and awkward, but they'd survived it without quitting or killing each other. Elle took that as a win.

ELEVEN

WITH HIS BODY ACHING AND HIS BELLY FULL, BLAKE fell into bed and groaned. She was going to be the death of him. She was going to systematically kill him with hard work and good food. Yet, somehow, he felt better now than he did from the binges he'd been on before. He rested a hand on his stomach and fell back into the pillows. The moon was muted through the dusty window of the wagon, lending a soft gray glow to everything it touched.

Something about the way the light threw itself across the bed, about knowing it was shining in her bedroom window too, stirred up memories. The night of their first and only time together.

He closed his eyes and began the memory of their argument out on that dirt road. He knew it was foolish to relive it, but there she was, sitting next to him. Arguing. She'd thrown up her hands in frustration after he'd said no man was ever gonna be good enough for her. The way she looked at his lips when he smiled in the face of her anger. Her hand on the door handle, seconds away from making good on her threat to walk home.

The desperation of loving her, wanting her, needing her above all else, drove him to leap off of the seat and stop her. His hand slipped around her shoulders and pulled her close, whispering, *sorry*, and *please don't go, Elle.* Her sweet, cherry-kissed lips, the warmth of her, the way she sighed and held on to his shirt, pulling him in closer in equal need. Their fumbling and heated hands seeking the warm flesh beneath clothes. The youthful curves of her breasts, the responsiveness that shocked them both. The gentle and fervent lovemaking that was as perfect as any first time could have been.

Blake's groin tightened; his body straining against his jeans. He loosened the zipper and undid the button. His eyes opened languidly to stare at the moon while he fell again into the memory of her small, frustrated cries and her desperation as she climbed on top of him, her skirt pulled up and her heart open. Blake closed his eyes; his body throbbed. He hadn't known what it would be like to be inside the first and last woman he'd ever truly loved. It had ended him.

Even now, his body reacted with a soul-deep intensity and he came with a shuddering swiftness that surprised him. He groaned as the rolling waves of it shivered through his skin and his hips rose and fell. He buried his face into the pillow and muffled the sound of his frustration and release. He wanted to cry, and laugh, and kick himself for being so stupid over her after so many years. Breathless and spent, he rolled back over and watched the lights in her room go out. He put his hands up to his hair and tugged at it.

Did she ever think about their first time? Or was it all just a regretful past? He'd been so confused, so in love. So worried that if he told her, she'd do what everyone he loved did; leave. He worried that if he told her, she would stay and regret picking him. Regret being tied down to this little town when she had so many bigger plans. He thought he'd been doing the right thing, letting her go. She'd tried to talk to him but he was convinced he was doing her a favor by not responding. When she'd left with Aaron, he was sure she'd never really cared for him at all.

So he'd let her go.

And she'd never looked back.

He stripped down in the hot night and threw his clothes into the hamper beneath the bed, and lay naked on top of the covers. Throwing his arm over his eyes, he tried to shield himself from the moon and the memory. She was here now. Safe. Home. She'd come back. The shimmering echo of words rolled through him.

Please don't go.

Blake drifted off into the deepest sleep he'd had in a long while.

He woke abruptly from dreams of her lying in the sweet hay beneath him. Her breathy sighs as he thrust into her were still loud in his mind when a knock shocked him back into reality. He stumbled to the door and tore it open.

"Hey Blake, I—oh!" Elle stopped and turned away.

Blake, hands on his eyes shielding the new dawn, came slowly to the realization that he was naked and fully aroused.

"Sorry," he grunted, shut the door, and grabbed his hat from the table. "What?" he asked roughly as he opened the door again. Elle looked back only for a moment, seeing that he was still naked but for the old Stetson held over his groin.

"Just, I...I have your laundry so you can put some—clothes on?" She set the pile of clean and folded clothes at his bare feet and stepped back. "I was...I also...wondered if you wanted to go for a hike today," she said and put her hands in her back pockets. She blushed and bit her lip. He watched the way her teeth tugged it, holding back laugher and something more.

"It's my day off," he grouched.

"Right, I know. I just thought it would give you something else to do."

"Something 'else' to do, Elle?" Blake's mind flashed back to the dream she'd interrupted. "Who says I don't have plans already?"

Her eyes traveled over his broad shoulders, her cheeks turned pink, and he heard her sigh before she looked back up into his face. She looked like she wanted something other than a hike. She looked, Blake thought with a small fire of fear building in his belly, hungry. Fantasy was one thing. Touching Elle in reality was a whole different mess of trouble. A mess he couldn't afford.

"Well, that's—" she stuttered. "That's fine. I just didn't—"

"Didn't want me to be drinking," he finished.

"I just thought it might be nice for us both to have a day off from everything. From the ranch, and the work, and just go be... someplace else."

"I really don't feel like spending the day talking to you," he said. The memory of the back-to-back fantasies made him feel weak and longing erupted in his heart.

"We don't have to talk, just hike. No conversation necessary."

Blake, not thinking about anything but his frustration and the unsettling desire addling his brain, tugged at his hair with both hands. Her eyes fell down to where the hat remained. She mischievously raised one eyebrow and giggled.

"What?" he grumbled and looked down at her.

"Nothing," she chuckled. "That's a nice hat."

Blake looked down and turned away, flashing his perfect backside. "Jesus, Elle!"

"Well, that side's fun too."

Blake grabbed a jacket off the hook by the door and wrapped it around his waist. "Not going to let me say no to this hike, are you?"

"Well, it is your day off," she said. The blush in her cheeks started to fade. "You can do what you want."

"Do what I want—" he mumbled. He wanted to pull her into his bed, fuck until they were absolutely breathless, down a fifth of Jack, and fall back to sleep. In exactly that order, and repeatedly, until his day off was over.

"Well?"

"Yes," he said, his thoughts still on what he wanted.

"OK, great." she nodded and turned to leave.

"What? Wait!" Blake backpedalled, but couldn't find a way out of it. "Where are we going?"

"Mitchell Peak."

"Mitchell—shit Elle! That's an eight-mile hike. It's twelve thousand feet!"

"Yeah, but the trailhead is at nine, so really it's only three thousand feet."

"Ugh, God." He protested.

Elle smiled. "You can say no. You always have a choice."

"I can't let you do that alone." He argued.

"The hell I can't. I'm not some delicate princess, Blake. I can do it without your big, strong manly help," she bristled.

"Shit."

"Fine, stay here, but I swear to God, Blake O'Connor if I find out that you've so much as touched a drink today I will—"

"Yeah, I know." He glowered down at her. She was so goddamn cute when she was trying to care. And the truth was, he didn't want the drink as much as he wanted to hike. With her. It made him crazy, and angry, and hated himself for it.

"Fine. Give me ten minutes."

"Only ten?" she said, her eyes caressing him brazenly.

"Quicker if you're offering to help," he said. Elle flashed him a smile he hadn't seen on her lips in years. She leaned closer; he did too.

"Well, you don't get a girl to help by promising it'll be quick," she whispered and walked back to the house. He gathered up the clean pile of clothes and closed the door with a smile.

A hike. He took a deep breath. He hadn't hiked in years. Truth be told, the last time he'd gone up to Mitchell Peak, had probably been with Elle and her sisters. That was before they'd all grown up. Before life beat them up and sent them running. Before Elle left. A whole lifetime ago. Blake stood up and searched through the clean pile of laundry.

He pulled on socks and thought about the hikes they used to go on. Being outside, in the wild and untamed beauty of the Rocky Mountains, seemed frightening. It was too free, too remote.

Too quiet and away from everyone. Blake swallowed a lump in his throat. While he preferred being away from people, being alone with Elle, without work to do, was another matter entirely.

When he pulled a shirt out of the pile, it smelled like her detergent. He buried his nose in it and sighed. It smelled like home, like a real home, with someone who cared if your clothes were clean and if your belly was full. Like family; like love. Blake stared out the window and something twitched anxiously in his chest.

"It'll never work, asshole," he grumbled. He'd sustained too much damage, and she hid all of hers. Whatever had happened with Aaron, Elle had come back with broken pieces in place of her heart and he was in no position to try to fix that. Blake sighed and resolved to keep his hands and his heart to himself, no matter what this day brought.

Elle kept her promise and stayed silent as she drove. But he found that the silence let his mind wander farther than he liked. Despite his resolution, dreams and memories played on repeat in his mind all the way up the two-track road to the trailhead. He hated getting his hopes up about anything. Blake's hand tightened on the armrest and he looked over at her. She was concentrating on the winding road and lost in her own thoughts.

They pulled into the trailhead and the slam of her door snapped him out of his daze. She put on a pack and tightened the straps before he even got out. It seemed to swallow her narrow frame, and remind him of the weight she carried in the smallness of her.

"What in the hell's in there?" He grumbled as he smoothed back his hair to put on a baseball cap.

"Lunch," she said with a shrug. "And water, of course." She tightened the pack's waist belt across her hips and closed the pick up's tailgate. "There's a blanket in there too," she said before turning to start up the trail.

"Blanket? What in the hell do we need a blanket for?" he

grumbled behind her. He looked up and she'd already gained a good lead. She was prepared in a white tank top, a zip up powder-blue hoodie and her khaki cargo pants, her trail shoes and her hair held out of her eyes by a silver butterfly clip. She looked pink-cheeked and young when she smiled back at him.

"You OK?"

"I guess, as OK as a man can be, up at the ass-crack of dawn to go hiking."

Her nose crinkled when she smiled, and he couldn't help the stupid grin that answered her back.

Damn it, don't, he told his heart as it flip-flopped. They began a steady pace up the mountain. True to her word, she didn't offer any conversation, except to point out loose rock, tricky roots, and sharp outcroppings.

"I'm not five," he grumbled. "I know how to walk up a—" he tripped on a root and fell towards her. Blake reached out, his hands steadying on her hips. His face inches from her chest, the smell of her clean skin warm in his senses. His left ankle throbbed, but he pushed away from her as quickly as he could.

"Are you OK?" she said, out of breath.

"I'm fine." Blake's cheeks burned with the thought of touching her and what it did to his brain. Elle took out a bottle of iced water and handed it to him. She took a drink from her Camelbak and nodded at his feet.

"Did you hurt your ankle?

"Will you stop worrying about me?" he grouched, took a drink, and nodded to the trail.

"I don't think I'll ever stop worrying about you," she said and continued on.

ELLE WASN'T SURE WHAT SHE HAD BEEN THINKING, asking him to come along out in the wilderness, and away from the safety of their work. Just that she wanted to spend time with him. See if there was anything left of the man she once loved. The smell of pine needles and dirt, the rush of wind through aspen leaves, caused a tickle in the back of her mind. A memory. A different night. A different forest. For a moment, all thoughts of Blake were pushed aside and her heart rate climbed. Elle took a deep breath. She stopped to look back, where Blake was catching up. She focused on him. No ghosts walked among these trees.

This place, this trail, was safe. Being with Blake was safe. She told herself over and over.

Nature healed. Nature found balance. She'd been so long gone from it, that it felt like a giant hole carved into the middle of her soul. Getting out in the woods, in her small human body, made her feel like she was part of something bigger.

She turned her eyes back to the trail ahead. Blake's heavy breathing and footsteps followed her. His warmth and smell just paces away. When she looked back, he was staring at her ass with a smile on his face. She blushed and felt warmth spread in her body. The sweet and unfamiliar feeling of being desired without fear tingled in her veins. She gasped.

"OK?" he asked.

"Yeah, I just—" she refused to turn back even though her heart seemed to hammer harshly against her ribs. "Just lost my breath for a second."

"Too much sea level living," he grumbled.

"I wouldn't say I did much living," she said.

Sudden, terrifying memories came at her like a tidal wave, intensified by bird cries and broken twigs beneath her feet. The air turned heavy and suffocating; Elle quickened the pace and Blake stumbled to catch up.

"Hey! Elle!" he yelled, but it only seemed to drive her on. She stumbled and fell to the side of the trail. Blake rushed to her side. She turned over and scrambled back with hands outstretched. The feel of stones and dirt beneath her back, pain digging into her skin, palms scraped, and the smell of blood caused her to tense at his approach.

"Hey," Blake said, softer. "Hey, Elle, baby. It's me. It's Blake. Just me," he whispered, gently took her hands and made her meet his gaze. "Easy, Elle. It's only me. You're OK."

The blanket of fear lifted slowly, like waking up from a dream. She felt her heartbeat in her ears calming, slowing, her breath following.

"I'm OK," she said, surfacing to the present. Blake stared at her. Her heart slowed as his hands gently caressed her palms. She didn't like the way his brow was crinkled with worry. She didn't like how quickly it had hit her or that she'd broken down in front of him.

"Are you?"

"Let's just keep going." She stumbled to her feet and turned away from him to continue.

"Elle, maybe you should take a break!" His words were lost to her retreating back. She felt stiff, embarrassed by whatever had just happened. She shied away from calling it what it was; a panic attack.

"Elle, what the hell is going on?" he huffed from behind her.

"Nothing! I'm fine." Heat swarmed her, and she wavered. The trees on either side of the trail swayed into her and she felt the world spin.

"Damn it," Blake caught her and pulled her to a fallen log to sit.

"Have *you* been drinking any water?" he asked.

"A little—" she stuttered and felt his hands through her sweatshirt, the pressure of touch confusing her embattled and recovering neurons. "Not as much as I should be."

"Goddamn it, you are just like Gran. Always taking care of others before you look after yourself. That shit has to stop, Elle," he grumbled and brought water to her mouth. She drank the cool liquid and he tucked a sweaty curl back behind her ear. "Slow down," His voice was tender, as though he could read the upheaval just behind her carefully placed wall. Elle felt the world come back into focus and was annoyed. He wasn't supposed to be taking care of her.

"I'm fine," she said.

"Oh yeah? Panic attacking on top of heat stroke? I'm glad you weren't up here alone. Just sit." His nimble fingers unclasped the pack and eased it off her shoulders. The lack of its weight made her feel untethered, like she would float away. His words. What he saw and understood all made her feel ashamed and weak. He grunted as he put it on the ground. "This goddamn thing weighs a ton."

Blake unzipped her jacket, slipped it from her shoulders, and bunched it up into one of the outer pockets of the pack. He slid his hands down her shoulders to her hands. The caring and light caress felt strange and warm and her body arched into it, thirsty just as much for him as she was for water.

"I'm fine," she whispered.

He looked at her and his hand grazed her forehead and felt the dry heat of her. He took her hand and led her a few meters off the path to a shady glade. Elle stumbled behind him and took small sips from the pack he had slung over one broad shoulder.

"Here?" he asked. She nodded. He dug into the pack, took out the blanket and spread it on the ground, then took her by the hand and pulled her gently to sit.

"Why are you worrying over me? I think I'm OK now."

"When did you eat last?" he asked, as if she was an animal being examined. He took out the containers she'd carefully packed.

"I had some coffee this morning."

He scowled at her. "That's not food, Elle."

"I had to get the lunch packed and all the chores done so we could leave early."

"Eleanor Augusta, you have no right to mother-hen me unless you're willing to take some nagging yourself."

"Oh? And what would you nag me about?" She managed a

weak smile. Her fingers were steadier as she took out the small plastic dishes and forks. She opened the containers, and the smell made his stomach growl. He'd skipped breakfast too.

"You need to sleep more. You definitely need to eat more. Slow down just a goddamn bit. You need—" he paused and clenched his teeth shut.

"What?" she said.

"You need to take care of yourself. Or find somebody who will."

"What?" she laughed. "What do you mean by that?"

"I saw what happened back there. I don't know what triggered it, but I think I know where it's coming from. Elle, you gotta talk to someone. Whatever it was that happened with Aaron. You should find someone you can talk to about it." He looked down between his hands. Elle didn't like where the conversation was headed.

"And did you find someone to talk to? When you were fired? When you quit school?" she snapped back.

"No, I didn't, goddamn it."

"Because you didn't want people to think you were weak."

Blake looked at her and sighed.

"Because I was too weak to admit that I needed help." Elle's eyes fell to the blanket. "And I didn't have a Sullivan looking out for me."

"I don't need help. I'm strong. Stronger than I was before."

"You are strong but that doesn't mean you don't have things to sort out." he sighed and picked at the bark of a fallen log while she avoided the truth of his words by getting a plate ready. "I've been through some shit. You don't have to worry about judgment from me, if you want to talk about it." Blake said. Elle wasn't sure he could handle all the things she had buried in the past.

She sighed. "I don't want to," she shook her head. "You've got your own problems. You don't need to shoulder mine too."

"Isn't that what friends do?"

"Are we friends?"

"I'd like to think so." Blake said.

"Here," she said, and held out a full plate. He didn't reach for it. He was staring at her breasts. "Aren't you hungry?" she asked.

"Yes," his voice raw with a hint of desperation. She felt it too. In the desire in his eyes, in the solitude they had. Memories of him, shirtless and wet.

"Well, then? Come on," she nudged the plate at him until he took it. He sighed and tucked into the food, scooting as far away on the blanket as he could.

"You'd better eat too."

"OK, Blake."

"And more than a bird does, for God's sake." He took another large thigh from the container and put it on her plate.

"I eat!"

"Yeah, when you sit down. But you never sit down." She wanted to argue, but nibbled on the chicken leg instead. "There, was that so hard?"

She scowled at him.

"Better. Good." He nodded approvingly.

He went to work on his own lunch, grunting with delight. Elle stared at the thigh on her plate, felt the hangover of the panic attack in her shoulders and a growing headache. He hadn't shied away. He'd stayed with her. Taken care of her, when she refused to believe she needed care. Blake pinched her knee lightly and motioned back to her plate.

"Eat, Elle. Please."

She didn't answer, but took a huge bite. Her stomach growled in agreement.

"Only about a mile and a half to the lake," Elle said, looking up at the granite peak in the distance.

"Shouldn't we head down? I mean, you being the fainting damsel and all?"

"Shut up." She nudged his thigh with her knee. She took a big drink from the tea jug and handed it to him.

"Just got a little hot that's all."

"You're hot all right," he said, taking a swig.

"Oh?" Elle smiled at him.

"Yeah, a hot mess. A hot, beautiful mess," he said. She looked off into the forest and its quiet, calm emptiness.

"Beautiful, huh?" She looked back at him. The silence fell hard, and they both felt the pressure of being alone in the woods, on a blanket, in the dappled shade, grasshoppers clicking by and the pattering rush of the aspens quaking like rain drops in the breeze.

Elle leaned in to where he was propped against the tree, legs outstretched and long. Her mouth watered. God, she wanted him. His eyes fell to her lips.

"We should get going," he whispered and got up before she could get too close. Elle watched as he put the ice into her Camelbak and threw the chicken bones out into the woods. She rose, finished her last few bites, and repacked their trash. She hitched the pack up on her shoulders, confused and frustrated at why he pulled away so quickly.

"Why don't you let me carry that?" Blake said to her back.

"Why don't you just shut up and hike," she argued over her shoulder. He must have known she'd wanted to kiss him. He'd been teasing her since she got home about how much she probably still wanted him. And yet, when the opportunity came, Blake had turned awfully pious. She kept walking, feeling much better at least for the food, and set her mind on future plans for the ranch, instead of on the past.

The sun hadn't let up and as they approached mid-afternoon, their sweat-slicked skin, coated in dust from the trail, began to itch. Mosquitos bit, deer flies stung, and neither of them said another word until they were just a quarter mile from the lake.

"The town street dance is in a few weeks," Elle suddenly said, the thought crossing her mind just before it crossed her lips.

"So?" Blake answered, dodging a pine branch and swatting a mosquito on his neck.

"So Judy and some other people are going."

"So what?" he grunted.

"So, let's go."

"Why?" he grouched.

"I just thought it might be something fun to do," she grouched back.

Blake snorted. "Oh yeah, there's no wilder time than at the Sweet Valley street dance."

"Why don't you want to go?" Elle paused on the trail, turned back and leveled her eyes on him. Blake swallowed and looked her over. It occurred to Elle that perhaps he was afraid to be alone with her.

"Nobody in town likes me."

"I like you."

"You don't count. They'll just gossip, and probably about us. I don't want to ruin your reputation."

"My reputation? Ha, that's funny. You don't think they're already talking with you 'helping me out'." She leaned in.

"Just keep walking." He turned her by the shoulders to face up the mountain, and gave her a gentle shove. She wished he'd patted her backside. He said nothing more, and they fell into mutual silence until they reached the narrow path that led to Silver Lake. The hundred-meter-wide pond was deserted and quiet.

"Huh. No one else?" She looked around the edges of the crystal-clear water.

"No one else in their right mind goes hiking in 90-degree weather up miles of trail." he answered.

Elle smiled and struggled out of her pack.

"Well, their loss then. Look at that view," she said and gazed at the granite peaks beyond and into the evergreen-lined edge of the lake. Blake stopped to look too. She watched his face, the calm way it settled into features she knew. So much of the anger gone for a moment. So much the calm and confident young man she used to know. He'd said that he'd been through some hard things, that he would understand hers. Her heart wanted to believe that. She leaned closer to him.

"Looks cold," he said.

"Yeah, it does," she said wantonly and removed the pack and her shoes. She un-tucked her shirt and unzipped her pants.

"What are you doing?" Panic rose in Blake's voice.

"What we always do." she said.

"What? I don't remember this." He protested.

"Sure you do. Katie, Lane and I always went for a swim, and you always flipped out and blushed, like you're doing now." She laughed and kicked off her socks.

"We were ten!"

"Better turn away, Blake. Wouldn't want to upset your delicate sensibilities."

"Damn it, Elle," he shook his head, and she felt like a kid again. "I shouldn't have to look away, because you're not ten anymore, and you shouldn't be taking your clothes off in public."

"Public?" She opened her arms to the deserted shores. She felt knots untying in her chest, as though her past was starting to unravel with every piece of clothing she shed. "I can do what I want. It's my body," she said, and pulled her shirt over her head defiantly and threw it down on the rocks. He stared in wonder and she let him. A beautiful sense of power and confidence filled her when she watched the way his body language responded. A power she'd lost for so long.

"It is—all yours," he said huskily and his eyes fell to her bra, lacy and white that held the soft creamy flesh. "That's your body," he stuttered and tried to look away, but his eyes came back as she shimmied out of her pants and kicked them to the side. He shifted uncomfortably, and she turned back to wink at him.

"Shit," he said, and looked skyward.

"My, how far you've come as a gentleman," she teased before taking a deep breath, channeling her inner youth and running into the water with abandon. The freezing cold hitting her hot skin felt all at once shocking and delightful. She shrieked when it reached her chest and she felt her breasts tighten and her whole body shiver at once. Elle came up, sputtering and laughing breathlessly. Blake stood on the banks, eyes fixed on her.

He'd watched her the whole way in, and now there was a hunger in his eyes that he couldn't hide.

"Well?" she yelled at him.

"Well, what?"

"Come on, chickenshit!"

"What?" he said.

"Get in here. Or are you scared?" she spit water at him.

"I'm not eight, you can't goad me." Blake yelled back.

Elle responded with an impressively accurate chicken call and laughed.

"Don't be such a baby, O'Connor." Her laughter and playfulness must have reached him, because he smiled suddenly and rakishly, giving into her dare with very little provocation.

"Fine, but avert your eyes," he said. Her giggle echoed against the granite peaks.

"Oh, it takes a lot to get me excited. At least enough to hang a ten-gallon hat on."

"Hey! That's *my* body you're objectifying," he countered with a grin and threw his cap on the ground next to the pack. He stripped off his shirt and everything else.

Elle watched with rapt fascination, barely breathing, as he stood naked on the water's edge. Obviously watching her undress had affected him and she found for the second time today she was seeing him naked and aroused. This time she didn't look away. Neck deep in the cold water, she stared unabashed at him, her eyes turned languid and dark.

"Enjoying the view?" he asked.

"Yep," she said.

"Well, don't get your hopes up."

"Oh, why not?" she said.

"Once I get in that cold water it won't be nearly so impressive."

She laughed and tumbled back, swimming farther off into the lake. She shivered and closed her eyes as she swam in circles and dived underneath. She hadn't remembered him being so blessed. But she had been nervous and excited back then, and it had been dark, and new. And he'd been so gentle.

The sudden splash and yelp behind her let her know it was safe to look back. He came up sputtering and cursing.

"Holy shit, that's cold!"

"Course it is. What kind of moron jumps into a snow-fed lake?" She shook her head and looked up to the streaks of white that still nestled in the cracks and crannies of the granite above them. He swam towards her and his eyes narrowed.

"What are you doing?" she giggled as he paddled closer.

"Lookin' for a warm spot," he said with a lift of his eyebrow. Elle squealed and splashed him, before swimming out of reach. He followed her and they swam around the lake, her feet always just out of reach from his hands until they were both breathless.

"What would you do if you caught me?" she laughed. Blake stopped.

"I'm sorry. I must be delusional from the cold."

"It happens to us, pretty easily, huh?"

"Probably because we're not good for one another," he said and the sadness that came over the both of them made the water seem grayer. He started back to shore but she caught up to him, grabbed his feet, and pulled him under. He came up coughing.

"Damn it, Elle."

"No one else is here, Blake."

"And I'm starting to see that as a giant problem." He scowled as she came closer. Elle felt bold, and for the first time in years, sensual. He hadn't left the lake, she could sense he was hesitant. Not thinking of consequence or tomorrow, she swam to him, wrapped her arms around his shoulders and her legs around his naked waist. "Elle," he shook his head. "Please, don't. Please don't do this." His hands went around her waist, caressed her back. His breath quickened against her neck.

"Catch me, Blake." She said in a broken and soft voice. "You can catch me," her lips met his. Her breasts pressed against his chest and she sighed into his lips, wet and cold.

"No," he shook his head, and he gently pushed her away. "Not like this. I'm not—" he sighed and closed his eyes. "I'm not ready."

"You seemed ready," her voice shook. Elle wanted to cry.

"God, Elle, yes, my body is. It's my he...my head." he shivered trying to explain the battle inside of him. "I can't do this. Not with you. Not with everything," he whispered and waded for the shore. He got dressed and slung the pack on.

"I'll wait further down," he said from the edge of the lake.

Elle's heart was in her feet. Her eyes blurred with tears.

Not with you, he'd said. Anyone else but her. The crazy girl who had panic attacks and carried dark secrets in her heart. Elle got out, dried off with her jacket, and pulled on her clothing. She met him on the trail but couldn't look into his eyes. For the rest of the hike down the mountain, they didn't speak a single word. The sun was fading as they reached the truck.

"What do you want for dinner?" she asked as she started the engine.

"Nothing, I'm going out for dinner," he said and took off his cap to run his hands through his hair.

"Oh," she nodded in defeat. "Of course."

"Not at the bar," he assured.

"You can eat where you want," she said. "You don't have to answer to me, Blake. I know you can make up your own mind. I'm sorry if I made you think otherwise."

"I'm going to my mom's."

"Oh," her voice was quiet. "That's good. I made some pies yesterday. Do you want to take one over?" she asked.

"No, thank you. That's OK." They drove in silence until they reached the turn off. Elle pulled in next to his Jeep.

"I may take a shower."

"Yes, of course," she nodded. "I'll stay out of the house."

"You don't have to—" he started to say, but Elle had already slammed the door behind her. She walked into the barn with her shoulders straight.

She busied herself in the barn, feeding and checking on everyone. She felt the weight of the day, the exhaustion from not just the hike but the emotional trip her brain had taken. From panicking to feeling safe. From wanting to being rejected. Blake was probably right. Neither of them were in a steady heart place to be making decisions concerning one another. She stopped at the desk he'd made and ran her fingers over it. She could see from the window as he came out of the sheep wagon, clean clothes in hand, and ran into the house.

When he came out, refreshed and dirt-free, she was just getting done feeding the chickens and had grabbed the pack out of the back of the truck.

"You'll be OK?" he asked as they passed on the walkway to the house. She glowered.

"Of course, I will."

"Eat something." He pointed at her.

"I'm not hungry."

Blake shook his head. "I don't care. You need to eat." He nudged her, but she didn't smile.

"What day is the dance?"

"Why does it matter?" she countered.

"What day?" he asked again.

"Three weeks next Friday," she answered. "Why do you care so much? Aren't you afraid people will think we're sleeping together?"

"Fuck what other people think. I'll need that Friday night off though, if that's OK with you, boss."

Her eyes shot up to his.

"Fine."

"Good. Eat," he reminded her.

"Stop nagging me. Get out of here."

"If you promise you'll eat."

"OK, Jackass!" she said, stamping her foot on the ground. The self-assured response, not cowering, made them both stop.

"OK." He smiled back. He nodded goodnight.

TWELVE

ELLE WATCHED HIM GET INTO HIS JEEP AND LEAVE WITH a strange self-assurance in his gait that hadn't been there before. Maybe the hike had been a deeper sort of healing for both of them.

It had hurt when he'd refused her. But it was also a sign that he was thinking of his future and not just his immediate gratification. Elle stared for a long time down the road. What would her future look like? Would he even be a part of it once he was back on his feet?

For so long, she hadn't felt desire. She hadn't enjoyed sex or felt that kind of want in years. Then life had thrown Blake into her orbit again. A heart she once trusted so deeply, locked inside walls, surrounded in a body she couldn't stop thinking about. She felt like a horny teenager.

Elle rolled her eyes. Was she any better than him when he'd made a pass at her? The chemistry was there, but she had no right to assume he'd want her now; sober. Maybe she shouldn't have kissed him; shouldn't have been so forward. She felt stupid and ridiculous.

Her body was tired and, despite not wanting to, she went to the kitchen, made herself a sandwich and walked outside, eating as she strolled through the barn. Everyone was bedded down and ready for the night. She went back to the house and took a shower. He'd left his razor on her sink. Two dark whiskers stuck in the blade and the smell of the shaving cream lingered. She sighed. The regret of inviting him to stay hit hard. She'd only wanted to help them both stand on their own again.

Elle crawled into bed and lay awake and listened to the clock tick. At exactly 9:15, the Jeep pulled in, his door slammed, and the crunch of his boots on the ground trailed to the wagon. She closed her eyes and took a deep breath. She didn't know how she'd face him the next day, let alone for the rest of however long this whole thing would last. How could she act like nothing had happened after wrapping her naked body around his? After he'd told her she could talk to him, without judgement...but that he couldn't be with her.

Outside, the distant yip of a coyote over the ridge, followed by the delighted calls of its friends, drifted into her window. Elle closed her eyes and her mind fell back to a different night, beneath the stars so many years before. The summer before she'd left. Half an hour from curfew, out on a dusty road not far from where she lived now, Blake had taken her out for a drive in the country like so many times before. To talk about their dreams, to vent frustrations, to decompress with someone who understood. He pulled over when their conversation turned from laughable to sensitive.

"I never have," he confessed. Elle didn't believe it.

"Shut up, don't lie," she teased. Blake shook his head and looked out the windshield.

"Well, have you?"

"No," she interrupted. "I haven't."

"What?" he asked, disbelieving.

"It's just too new, with Aaron. I don't know if I—" she stopped and stared at her fingers, threaded in her lap, seeped in conflict by the way the moonlight lit the depths of Blake's eyes. She shifted and looked out her window.

"Well, you shouldn't trust him." He finished her thought. "That guy's a jerk. He's not good enough for you. Nobody is good enough for you, Elle." Blake had said.

Then the argument had begun. Hands in the air and voices raised, and she threatened to walk all five miles home. Blake pulled her in, begged her not to go, gave her the sweetest, most passionate kiss she'd ever had. And she couldn't stop at one, because he tasted so good and so much like home, and she didn't have to be afraid or nervous around Blake because he was always her guy. Breaths came fast and clothing was pushed away and she wanted it so much, she climbed into his lap. It had been her in control, maybe for the last time since. They'd barely had time to think. Afterwards, when the sweat and the heat had fallen away in the quiet night, and her hands were shaking against his chest, he changed. He dropped his eyes from hers even before their breathing could still.

"Damn it, Elle," he said and gently lifted her back to her own side of the Jeep. He ran his hands through his hair and dropped his head in his hands. "What the hell did we do?"

She yelled at him that they didn't need to feel bad about it. That she had wanted it to be him. All along. He didn't say a word, but drove her home in silence and barely waited for her to close the door before skidding out of her drive. He hadn't returned her calls and refused to see her when she came looking for him.

Two weeks later, broken hearted, she moved to L.A. with Aaron and he trampled her budding ideas of culinary school and convinced her that he'd 'take care of everything'. Being hurt and confused made it easy to fall into his overzealous attentions. She'd tried writing Blake but he never responded. She'd even sent a wedding invitation, hoping that if he loved her, he'd show up and say something.

But he never did, and she hadn't been strong enough to run. Not until many years later.

Elle sighed and wished that one night had ended differently.

"If wishes were fishes, we'd all stink," she whispered Gran's words. Of all the ways she was healing, trying to not blame herself for how things had happened was one of the deepest wounds. Maybe Blake had been right today. That one night set in motion a chain of events that broke them both wide open. She couldn't help but think, even when it made no matter in the grand scheme of things, of all the heartache they could have saved each other if she'd never gotten in his Jeep that night.

Thirteen

Outside of Prym and Proper Eatery on Monday morning, Judy and Elle chatted for fifteen minutes while Blake sat, irritable in the truck. The high school rivals were now laughing and smiling like old friends. Elle had that effect on people. At the post office, Old Ed from the hardware store had talked their ears off, all about how proud he was of the barn and happy the store had been able to help. He smiled at Elle like a daughter that'd come home. And Elle opened up to it, a blossom in the sun of the small town's affection. But at the same time, she'd pulled away from him after the lake.

He regretted telling her no and wondered if what was broken between them was just destined to stay that way. Blake hunched down with his hat tipped low and crossed his arms over his chest. When the door suddenly opened, he startled.

"All of them, Blake! I sold them all! Judy said she wanted double orders for next week. She's sending her brother over to make an official inspection, but I think we'll be OK, right? Can you believe I sold every single one of them?" Elle was breathless as she jumped lithely into the seat next to him.

"'Course you sold them all, and of course they want more.

Your baked goods are better than crack." Blake grumbled. "And the kitchen's clean enough to pass a medical exam, so I don't think you should worry," he finished. The paper check shook in her hands and Elle stared at it with glassy eyes.

"You better sign that and get it into your account," he said quietly.

"My account," she whispered. "I can have my own account." She turned to him and Blake watched her bite her lip.

"Yes, you can."

"I will. It'll be mine."

"Yep," he said, and the moment was a harsh reminder that she'd been denied the simplest of rights for too long. He thought of the lake, of how much it probably took for her to come to him, to trust someone physically. It swelled the worsening sadness in his chest.

"Whatcha going to do with all that cold hard cash?" he asked. Elle got a funny look on her face. It was the same look she had when she started making big plans.

"Probably nothing special," she shook her head. "But if I can keep it up, I might start paying my indentured servant," she said and smiled out of the corner of her mouth. Blake shook his head and threw the truck into reverse. He backed out of the parking lot and on to the street.

"Don't go getting his hopes up. He'd really be unbearable to live with then."

Elle laughed out the open window and the wind blew through her hair. It seemed like the whole two blocks of downtown Sweet Valley laughed with her. The sun shone brighter, the red-bricked buildings seemed a deeper shade, and the roses blooming wore their colors in happy rainbow waves of yellow, and red, and pink. Elle made the town come alive around them and Blake fell all over again.

THE NEXT WEEK WAS LESS AWKWARD, THOUGH ELLE
still danced out of Blake's way at every opportunity and kept
conversation strictly to the ranch. He arrived for breakfast every
morning early, said very little that didn't pertain to the goats or the
chickens, then set about helping her with whatever the project of
the day was. They finished the south pasture's fence, including a
new gate, and started removing dead cottonwood stumps from
behind the house in order to clear space for a green house and a
larger garden.

It was hard and tiring labor and they both barely made it
through dinner at night without falling asleep. Elle used the
nervous energy she had left over to prepare meals that kept his
mouth so full there was no obligation to talk. His strength grew
and a healthy glow returned to his cheeks. They didn't talk about
what had happened at the lake, but since the moment they'd stood
on its banks, surrounded in the quiet beauty, feeling the potential
for something more, Blake had developed a sense of clarity and
euphoria. His desire to drink waned and faded the more he
remembered how good it felt to be present in the moments with
Elle. Though they hadn't talked about what happened in the cold
water, their companionable silence and simple conversations were
healing, nonetheless.

Blake got dressed one morning and noticed that his t-shirt fit
tighter in his shoulders. He paused in front of the small antique
mirror, took off his shirt, and stared. He turned around and looked
at his back, now strong and broad. His muscles were more defined
and larger from the work and the hearty meals she set in front of
him. Homemade bread, chicken, steak, and always some vegetable
that she insisted he eat. Milk, fresh from her dad's cow, the first
small eggs from her hens that grew each week, pancakes and
muffins. Bacon, pan-fried potatoes, and squash. Her homemade
pies and cookies were a treat at the end of each day, and she met
him with coffee and a plateful of the heavenly food every morning
at the door.

"You cook too much," he'd muttered that morning between bites. She stared at him over her coffee cup and smiled. It warmed his heart and he let it.

"I love to cook, especially for someone who eats it. Aaron—" she paused and looked away.

"It's OK to talk about him, Elle. I mean, it's OK with me if you need to talk about him." Blake said. The gentleness in his words was unexpected.

"He didn't—doesn't like this kind of food. It's too—" she looked to the ceiling and searched for the right word.

"Fattening?" Blake said around a bite and stared hard at her. "You know, you're not fat. You never have been. You're practically perf—"

"I like cooking," she interrupted. "It calms me down." She got up and filled her coffee cup. He put a muffin in front of her when she sat down.

"Where is he these days?" Blake took a chance. Elle stopped mid pat of butter on her muffin. He watched her hand shake around the knife.

"I don't know."

"He hasn't tried to call you or—"

"No," she interrupted sharply.

"I'm sorry, Elle," Blake stopped himself before he could ask what was really on his mind. He wanted to know if he should worry. If he should start sleeping on the couch with a shot gun. If Aaron was coming back for her, just when she was getting her life back together again, and if she needed help curtailing that sorry son-of-a-bitch.

"I don't want to—"

"I know. You don't want to talk about him. With me." Blake said.

"It's not that. I do, and I will, talk to you. Someday."

"Someday?"

"Right now, all you need to know is, he's—far away."

"And you're safe?" he asked, leaned over and finished buttering her muffin.

"I've never been safer," she said softly and watched him with liquid brown eyes that made his heart shackle itself to hers. "It makes me feel safe, sitting here, like this. With you," she said. He cleared his throat, and they went back to silence.

The nights brought well-earned exhaustion and the warmth of food and home lowered their walls. In equal parts, they left behind prickly comments and focused on the business of the ranch, the start-up of her new baking business, the hiring out of her herd to people looking for natural and nimble weed control. The few angoras she had were ripe for a shearing and both Blake and she agreed, in order to not cause them undue stress, once a year shearing during the hot months of the year would be the best option. The local knitting group was very interested in buying the mohair to dye and use.

"If the Bar Nunn is serious about the contract for their solar field, we could easily pull in an extra $500 a month. I think the angoras might give us fifteen kilos of mohair—that's about $400 extra for the summer," Elle said over dinner one night, over the ledger she'd bought at the country dollar store last week.

"They might as well earn some of their keep," Blake said and smiled at her shift of confidence. Maybe she would be sticking around after all, he thought, but this time with more hope than dread.

While they washed the dishes together, they mentioned the funny things they'd seen or heard that day. Blake told her about outcalls he'd gone on with her dad as he leaned against the sink with a towel over his shoulder. Elle laughed her beautiful, heart-lighting laugh when he told her about how an animal or owner behaved. He liked to watch her long fingers dry the glasses as she engaged him with questions and prompted him to indulge in the excitement and joy he found in the work.

He was less and less willing to leave each night. They sat in the living room for longer to play a game of cribbage or Scrabble, and he'd watch her yawn and snuggle into the couch. That was his right mind's signal to leave, before he could slip an arm around her and let her head nestle under his chin. Before either of them could let the quiet intimacy lead anywhere else.

She hadn't made physical contact since the lake, but Blake could tell she was still aware of the chemistry and the changes in him. It was in the way her eyes lingered on his arm. The way she would bite her lip as he lifted the bales of hay with ease. The time he caught her staring at his Wrangler-clad backside. The way his calm manner brought out her smile. The way she laughed at his jokes. The way she stopped flinching at loud noises and hadn't panicked, that he knew of, since the hike. Small and slow, a change sparked in Blake's brain, and took root. Her faith in him was a tender sprout and he tiptoed around it with fear and reluctance, while the dawning glow of hope rose in him.

He reluctantly accepted the new dynamic. The changes he was making were challenging enough without having to account for a romantic relationship. But having a friend at his side helped him feel up to those challenges. So, he let the strange and new way of them be, just as it was.

Fourteen

Today was the big day. Judy Prym's brother, Ben, was coming to complete their health inspection. Elle carefully cleaned the kitchen the night before, and again in morning, much to the bemusement of Blake, who stood in his socks, in the center of the room with his boots safely on the rug and arms crossed over his chest.

"I don't know what you're freaking out about—"

"Did you clean the pens and all the tools outside like I asked?" she interrupted.

"Yes, Elle," he answered tiredly. "Twice, since you did it yourself."

"And the chicken coop, you've made sure the cords and the water troughs are all—"

"Yes, Elle." He rolled his eyes and inched forward towards the cookies on the counter.

"Don't even think about it." She snapped the cleaning rag at his hand.

"Ow!" he laughed and shook the sting from his finger. "Come on! We've done everything. It's gonna be fine. Besides, you ought to let me test one. What if you give him subpar cookies?"

"Oh my God, do you think they're bad?" she asked, worried.

"No! Jesus, no, they're fine." He laughed outright, and Elle wished he'd pull her into his arms.

"The pens are all secure? Frankie got out last week."

"It's all fit as a fiddle, Elle. Take a breath, baby."

She looked up at the endearment, and their eyes met. The moment, tender and small, was interrupted when the car pulled up outside and Ben Prym stepped out with a case in hand. He squinted into the sun and waved. Elle pushed past Blake and ran out, brushing the curls from her face and plastering on a smile.

"Hi Ben! Good to see you. It's been so long."

"Good to be seen, Elle." The muscular ex-wrestler smiled with dimples and pulled her in for a hug. "You look just as pretty as ever!" His eyes twinkled, and Elle remembered how popular he had been with the girls in his class. She smiled back. Blake cleared his throat.

"Ah, you're too sweet! Should we get on with the boring business part?" Elle said.

"Yeah, we should," Blake said and stepped between them. "If you'll just follow me," he lowered his voice. Ben raised his eyebrows at Elle.

"What have you been feeding that guy? He looks like a broodier Hemsworth," Ben asked Elle behind Blake's back.

"Oh, he's not that charming," she teased and winked at Ben.

"I'm sure Ben has lots to get on with, Elle," Blake said as he led them to the coop. They walked around the newly repaired building, the egg collection practices, the feed, water and cleaning procedures. Ben made notes and checked off boxes, taking samples from the collected eggs she'd gotten that morning.

Next, they walked into the new barn.

"Judy told me about all the work you put into it. This place is beautiful!" Ben said, looking over the structure. He stepped into the corner office, inspected the fridge with vitamins and medicines, and took samples. "Nice space for work. I can tell someone thought this through. Your dad's idea?"

"Actually—" Elle began.

"It was mine," Blake said and leaned against the wooden beam. Ben looked up at him and smiled at Elle.

"Nice work, Blake. You've really changed." Blake scowled at him. "In a good way." Ben held up his hands and smiled at Elle. "You'd think a guy eating your cooking all the time would be happier. I know I'd be," he said.

"Ben Prym, you're just as sweet as you ever were. I'm too old for you and we know it," she laughed, unaccustomed to light flirtation.

"A few years don't really matter, Elle."

"Follow me. I'll show you to the herd." Blake interjected. "We've got a small processing machine and only use pasteurized milk for public consumption, of course. Elle doesn't use much of the milk in her baking, but we wanted to cover all the areas."

"Of course." Ben stepped ahead of Blake to walk the length of the barn. All the goats were in their freshly cleaned stalls, or out in the paddock, secured and feeding. Elle talked him through the process, showed him the milk producers, gave their histories, ages, and all the health information she could give. She even told Ben their names and personality quirks, which elicited a smile from him. Her love and devotion to the herd couldn't fill any box on his form, but he noticed all the same.

The last stall was empty; its latch hung lamely to one side.

"Who's supposed to be here?" Ben asked.

Elle's mouth hung as open as the pen.

"Ah, that's—well, that's just a clear stall. We don't put any of them here, since its latch needs fixed." She looked pointedly at Blake. Ben nodded and made some comments in his notes before walking outside.

"Last bit is the kitchen," he said over his shoulder. Elle smiled and waved him ahead. She turned back to Blake.

"Where in the hell is Frankie?" she whispered.

"I don't know."

"Coming?" Ben yelled from the front porch steps.

"Yep, it should be unlocked!" she said while Blake looked back and forth across the paddock, the road, the lawn, and garden. Elle stepped gingerly up the stairs behind Ben.

"Now Gran's house is a little older, but I think you'll find that everything's running well. Oven, refrigerator, power outlets, and a new—"

"Disposal?" Ben asked when they came face-to-face with the three-legged goat on the counter, leisurely enjoying the plate of cookies.

Blake came in behind Elle.

"Shit."

"Ben, I swear, I—he doesn't—this isn't—" Elle sputtered with cheeks flushed. Blake looked for a lead, but Elle had already removed her belt and secured it around the goat's neck, leading him gently down and to her side. "This is Frankie. He's an asshole. I'm sorry he ate your cookies, and that we wasted your morning. If you'd just give us a couple more weeks, we can get it all squared away and try again."

"Elle." Ben smiled out of the corner of his mouth as he looked at the stubborn set of her chin. "Don't fret, honey. I know that this kitchen is probably cleaner than any of the restaurants in town." He took a swab from his kit, ran it over the kitchen table, and secured it in a bag.

"I don't want to get you in trouble, or make anyone sick." Elle felt like she might cry. She held the belt tightly. Frankie bleated and Blake stepped up to unwind the noose-like grip of the leather around Elle's hand.

"I'll just go put this little asshole back. In a more secure pen," he said and led Frankie out the back door where he'd snuck in. When he'd gone, Ben turned back to Elle.

"I came out here expecting a much worse situation."

"What could be worse than a goat on a counter top?" Elle sobbed. Ben laughed and handed her a tissue from his shirt pocket.

"Honey, you should see some of the places I inspect in Sweet Valley. Don't worry," he said again and had her lead him through her processes, checked her freezer and refrigerator temperatures, oven, water and the safety of the outlets, and where she kept her very organized cleaning products.

"So," she said, more composed but still worrying over her bottom lip with her teeth. "When will I know?" she asked.

"I'll run all this stuff through the lab and get it back to you by Friday, but I don't anticipate any problems."

"But if there are problems?" she asked. Blake came back into the kitchen and stood quietly by the door. Ben looked at the worry in his face and smiled. Blake O'Connor hadn't cared about anything in a long while. Not enough to protect it; to think of it before himself. Ben turned back to her.

"Let's just cross that bridge if we have to." He leaned in and gave her a quick hug and turned to shake Blake's hand.

"Good to see you, Bruce Banner," he teased. "I'll let you know as soon as I do," he said to Elle.

"Thanks, Ben." Elle said, and she and Blake watched him drive away.

"Well, shit. I guess it's a good thing you didn't get your hopes up about a paycheck," she said, waving at Ben as he left.

"Elle, it's gonna be fine— "

"What if it isn't, Blake?" She responded with a different shade of worry in her voice. Like she was pinning more than just her own hopes on this business.

"You heard Ben. Let's not worry about that bridge until we have to cross it."

· · ·

BLAKE WAS ON CALL WITH WARREN THAT AFTERNOON and told Elle's father about the mishap with Frankie that had caused Elle to affix three extra locks on his pen. Warren hooted with laughter and shook his head.

"Sounds like she kept her head," Warren said as they turned the corner.

"She sure did," Blake said. "You know a month ago, I'm not sure she could have. I don't know what happened back in California." Blake stopped and looked down. He really had no right to ask, but the question surged out anyway. "What did happen, Warren? Exactly?"

Warren's smile fell and his long fingers, so much like Elle's, tightened around the steering wheel. "I don't know if I'm the one to be telling you. And I can't say that I know exactly," he said quietly.

"I don't mean to push, she won't tell me anything and I—I can't help thinking that if I'd just been there." Blake stopped when he remembered the useless state he'd been in at the time she needed him most.

"I think we all feel that way." Warren stopped him. "Elle blames herself, and we blame ourselves, when really, there's only one person to blame." Warren swallowed. "Jesus, I think it was bad." he said and choked up. Blake watched his calm demeanor shift to tears.

"Warren—"

Warren sniffed and composed himself. "She's here now. She's here, and she's safe," he said and pulled into the drive. He blew his nose on an old handkerchief.

"Do we know that for sure?" Blake looked out the window at the faded street sign. "Has he tried to contact her? Have you heard anything from him?"

"No, not that I know of. I would like to think she'd say something."

"Just seems a man like that, with that kind of—" Blake

swallowed a darkness in his soul. "Control over someone, wouldn't just let her walk away."

"Do you think he'll come looking for her?" Warren asked.

"I don't know. But if he does, he's not gonna get anywhere near her."

"No," Warren nodded to Blake. "He sure as hell won't."

Blake nodded, and they got out of the truck. His heart raced as he walked up to greet the owner. He'd never cared about his reputation in town until he showed up somewhere with Warren. The pressure to not embarrass or disappoint the man he'd so long looked up to was intense, and so he kept quiet as much as possible.

This particular morning, they were in town to see a terrier who'd been hurt digging through a trash pile, and Blake was met with a nasty glare from its owner. His newly clear mind remembered a heated one-night stand, followed by sneaking out the next morning, but not the woman's name. He thought she might be a teller at the bank. She huffed and steamed behind them as they wrapped the dog's cut paw and administered antibiotics. Blake kept his eyes down and tried to survive without dying from shame.

When they got back in the truck, Warren whistled.

"Whew, I never saw a woman give a man so many daggers. What in the hell did you do to Sandra?"

"Sandra," Blake said, the name clicking. "I think we—I mean, I think." He flushed and looked down at his hands. Warren waited.

"You *think* you might have what?"

"I—dunno." Blake shook his head.

"Don't you remember?" Warren's quiet reprimand made Blake's heart fall.

"I wasn't always sober in the past. Sometimes not with women." Warren started the truck and they drove in silence until the edge of town.

"And now?" Warren said; no doubt his mind worrying about Blake living with his daughter.

"I haven't been with a woman in a long while. And I haven't had a drink in over a month. I'm trying to figure things out and—" Blake stopped in frustration. "I'm working on getting better. Being better."

When Warren finally spoke, Blake had to lean in to hear him.

"It takes a strong person to change, Blake. Getting up from the bottom of a pit feels like a long haul in muddy water. You're doing all right, son. Just keep on with it." Warren gave him a smile as they got on the highway. The compliment from his childhood hero and being called 'son',made it all feel worth it.

"Want to stay for dinner? Elle always makes enough to feed ten." Blake asked as they pulled into the drive and he got out.

"Well, that would be nice, but I think Melissa's got something planned already. Plus, the dance is coming up and I've gotta get to bed early if I'm going to make it past nine." Warren smiled. Blake's face blanched.

"The dance is this week? Already?"

"Yep. Friday."

"Shit, I forgot. I don't have anything to wear—" he stopped.

"Poor Cinderella," Warren said with a twinkle in his eye and reached into his back pocket. Blake looked back at the lit kitchen windows. Warren handed him a few neatly folded bills through the truck window.

"No, sir," Blake said, and handed it back. "You can't, I'm interning; you don't pay me."

Warren shook his head. "You take it, and don't argue with me. You've been working hard, and I don't want Elle to browbeat you for showing up in grubby work clothes. Wouldn't be fair." Warren winked. Blake looked down at the money.

"It's too much."

"Well, now, get a haircut too, and put a little away. Maybe don't tell Elle I gave it to you, just the same." Warren said and put the truck in reverse.

Blake flipped through the bills. He hadn't had money to spend in months. The bar was a short six miles away; the liquor store only five. The dust from the departing truck billowed up, tracing the long road out to the highway. Blake's chest filled with the uncomfortable warmth of gratitude at Warren's words. When enough people believe in you, he thought, it gets harder not to start believing in yourself.

"You coming in or just gonna to stand out there staring at the road? The stew's getting cold! We need to make it an early night. Katie said she's coming over with a surprise tomorrow." He heard her call from the kitchen. As he came up the walk, she leaned back from the sink to smile at him through the screen door.

Elle, beautiful Elle, who, despite all of his harsh words, piss-poor attitude, gruff nature, crude come-ons, and snarky comments, didn't give up on him. Hearing her voice in the falling dusk, calling him to dinner, felt like coming home. He pocketed the money as she came to the door.

"Stop bossin' me around, lady!" he teased from the bottom step. She looked down at him through the screen door.

"Who you callin' lady?" she said, an affectionate smile on her face.

"Is it OK if I take Friday afternoon off?" he asked.

"Friday?" Elle said and searched his eyes. "This Friday?"

"I'll be back in time for the dance. I just have a few things I need to take care of before."

Elle nodded. "Sure. Of course. Everything go OK at Sandy's?"

"As good as it could," he shook his head. She didn't push, despite noticing his discomfort, and they had a quiet dinner. Afterwards, they played a game of Scrabble, which turned heated when he argued that "aerogun" was indeed a word.

She contested with her chin raised and a "prove it!" The argument caused his heart rate to spike, and he wanted to reach across the table, pull her into his lap and kiss her. He must have been staring at her lips because she bit them and sat back.

"Well," she cleared her throat. "I'll—take your word for it. We should call it a night."

"Don't be too eager," Blake said softly to himself.

"What?"

Blake's eyes were on her lips before he snapped out of the daze. He cleared his throat.

"I mean, tomorrow. Tomorrow don't be too eager about Katelyn's surprise." he back pedaled.

"Why? What do you know?" Her eyes lit up.

"Nothing much—but it might be—horse sized."

Elle squealed suddenly and reached out to grab his hands before pulling away. She sat back, still vibrating with excitement.

"Do you think it's something for the horses?"

"I might have heard a rumor that Kenny, the stable manager at The Kicking Post, has a lot of extra gear and equipment. Katelyn's been talking to him, working out a trade. I'm sure Kenny would like to trade her in dates."

Elle looked sideways at him with a snort. "Katelyn would clean his clock."

"Yeah, she would. You Sullivans are scary." He chuckled as she slapped him with the folded-up Scrabble board. Her bright pink cheeks and laughter drew him in closer.

"I'm not scary. I'm a big ol' soft heart." she giggled. God, he wanted to kiss her.

"You are," he smiled. "Elle, patron-saint-of-homeless-orphans." He leaned closer.

"*And* lost causes."

"Those too," he whispered. He studied her lips and his hand inched towards hers.

Elle cleared her throat and her hands gripped the game board.

She bit her lip, and he lost his breath. The heat burgeoned between them. Elle leaned away and stood up. "Goodnight, Blake."

He snapped out of his desire.

"Good night? Don't you wanna play another round?" he asked.

"No, I'm not ready. I mean I'm tired."

Blake noticed the way she'd pulled back. He must have really hurt her feelings at the lake. He stood up and checked his pockets absentmindedly. He felt the cash, felt the warmth of home, but most of all, he felt the desire to kiss her more acutely than ever before. Elle gathered up the game and her face fell into sadness.

"You OK?" he breathed.

She barely looked over her shoulder.

"I'll be fine. Have a good night." She stored the game in the old wooden chest by the wall. He watched as she turned off the lights in the living room and hall; her way of saying that nothing else would happen tonight.

"G'night," he said and left. As the screen door closed gently behind him, he wondered what he could do to cross the line he'd drawn between them. He'd been awfully obvious about wanting to kiss her, and she'd withdrawn. Which is what he'd asked her to do at the lake. Blake sighed and looked back as all lights went out in the farmhouse except for her bedroom at the top. He stared at it.

"How do I get back to you, Elle?" he said, and shook his head.

ELLE TOOK DEEP, SLOW BREATHS, WITH HER HANDS ON either side of the bathroom sink. Aaron had killed her once-healthy sex drive in subtle ways. Sex was power to him. It assured him that she wasn't wandering, it relieved *his* stress, it was to remind her who she belonged to. For the last two years, she hadn't engaged in it willingly. She knew if she didn't cater to his needs immediately, the price psychologically and physically would be much worse. It only lasted a few minutes anyway.

But with Blake. The way he looked at her lips, the way he'd leaned in. The lake, the blossoming of her own desire, was something she wanted for herself and it raged like a storm inside her head. She didn't belong to Aaron anymore. She was a free woman. But the only man she wanted had said he didn't want her. So, why was he looking at her like that now?

Elle looked down; her hands were calloused and cracked with wear, her body now curved and muscular to a degree that her pants hardly fit and the buttons on her shirt were starting to strain. If Blake was taking the afternoon off, maybe she would as well. Maybe she'd get a manicure. Maybe even a new dress. She didn't even own a dress. She'd left her L.A. apartment in the dead of the night, with nothing.

She hadn't shopped for herself in years and she had no idea even what the style was these days. Who could she call to help? Her sisters came to mind. Laney tended to dress more fashionably, for Wyoming's standards. Katelyn couldn't care less about clothes, or anything girly for that matter. Elle picked up her phone from the bedside table and sent out emergency texts to Laney, Holly, and Judy.

They all responded, with a "don't worry yourself, we got you" and it was settled that they'd meet Friday afternoon for a girl's spa day, downtown. Elle's heart flip-flopped. She hadn't had a girlfriend, let alone three, in a long time. Her heart warmed with a sudden and full feeling of being accepted.

For a moment, she was distracted away from Blake and his hungry stare. She brushed her teeth and got into bed. Maybe at the dance, when they were relaxed. Maybe if she looked and felt like more than just a worn-out, near-failing, goat-herder. Maybe when Blake had a night off, and was clear in his head. Maybe with music and starlight. Maybe they might both find out the truth about how they felt.

Fifteen

"You remember when Grandpa used to go into town and trade horses after he'd tied a few on?" Laney leaned over the fence.

"Are you saying they'd be better off with Ty?" Elle said, one eye squinting to the late morning sun. "And I wasn't drunk!"

"Did you talk to Dad first?"

"I don't need to ask dad about everything, Laney June," Elle said defiantly. "I know my way around a horse."

"Sure, her swayback will help the saddle stay on." Laney's mischievous smile flashed.

"That's a perfectly fine quarter. She's not sway—" Elle stopped when she saw Laney double over with a hoot of laughter. "You're such a shit sometimes."

"Whoa! When did you start cursing?" Laney came up with happy tears in her eyes. Elle looked down at her with a disbelieving huff. She knew exactly where she'd gotten that phrase. Blake was in town getting feed for the chickens, cake for the horses, and udder cream for the goats.

Elle looked down at her scuffed boots and kicked a stray pebble into the corral. She watched Lottie snuffle the fresh hay in the tire feeder. She wasn't a large horse, but she was bright as hell and already had shown interest in the goats and played with them from the other side of the fence. Goliath, who was still edgy around anyone who wasn't Lottie, had taken to Elle just fine. He knew she needed stability. She hadn't ridden either yet, but had walked them, bridled, through the fields with Blake. How long had it been since he'd ridden a horse?

"Uh oh, from that look on your face, I take it you're having some inner turmoil. Is it the horses or that curly-haired boy?" Laney asked. She put her foot up on the buck rail next to Elle's as they watched the horses snuffle their food, swat the flies on their flanks, and shake their manes.

"Elle?" Laney asked again.

"Huh?" Elle looked at her sister. "Fine. No, I'm not...turmoiled."

"Have you had sex?" Laney asked. "I mean in the present day?"

"What?" Elle's head swung around. "No, why? Why would you ask that? Are people saying that?"

"Well, now—" Laney quirked a knowing eyebrow. "Someone might mistake that kind of reaction for a guilty conscience. Do you have a guilty conscience, Eleanor?" Laney smiled.

"No! We haven't. Well, just that once in high school, but that was a whole lifetime ago. We're not anything. He's just working here until he gets back on his feet."

"Come on," Laney protested. "There's gotta be more than that."

"We don't all live in romantic fantasies, Laney June."

"Ugh, I'd rather you call me a little shit." Laney laughed. "You know what I think?"

"I don't, but I imagine you're gonna tell me anyway—"

"I think that either you *are* sleeping together and you don't want me to know, or you both *want* to, but you're pretending you don't, and that, my dear Eleanor Augusta, is the start of a fantastical romance."

"He's not interested." The words came out sharp, exposing the vein of hurt she'd been trying hard to hide since the lake.

"Come on. There's no way—"

"He had a chance. I tried to start something and he didn't want me." Elle huffed out a pained breath. "He and I aren't anything. We probably won't ever be. So, can we just drop it, please?" Elle said. The rattling of tires on the wash boarded road made them turn and a dust cloud wafted through the pen as Blake's Jeep came to a halt near the fence.

He came out of the Jeep and reached into the back seat for a large box.

"Your order came in." He held up the box but his excited smile dropped from his face. "Oh—hey, Laney," he said.

"Blake." Laney nodded, with just enough of a protective sister glare to make him hang his head. Elle rushed over to open the package of bags, jars, and pie boxes she'd designed and custom ordered.

"They're perfect. Look at them!" she gushed and held them up to Blake's face. He reacted in kind to the light of her smile.

"I can't wait to fill them up." Elle said, and turned back to Laney. "Give me a sec, I just want to run these inside." The urge to kiss him hit her hard, and Elle backed away. "Thanks for picking them up," she mumbled.

"Yep," he croaked as she took the box and went to the house. "I'll be out in the south pasture, checking the lines," he called after her.

"OK!" she called back.

BLAKE'S EYES FOLLOWED ELLE LONG AFTER THE BANG OF the screen door. He turned back to Laney's scrutinizing glance.

"What?" he asked.

"Nothing," Laney smiled. "It's just good to see you, Blake. You look healthy," she said.

"Thanks."

"Living with Elle must be treating you pretty good," she led.

Blake looked back at her. "Better than I thought."

"I'm glad you're here, Blake."

"Oh? Why's that?"

Laney sauntered closer and looked at the house, causing him to look too.

"Because she's been through hell, and she needs you in her corner."

"In her corner for what? Has she talked to you about him?"

"She hasn't talked to any of us, not since coming home all bruised to hell. I think every single one of us wants to murder that son-of-a-bitch—" Laney said, not taking her eyes away from the screen door. "But none of us know where he is."

"I asked her, and she didn't say much." Blake confided.

"Do you think she doesn't know, or is it more than that?"

"How in the hell should I know?" Blake grunted. "She hasn't said anymore to me about it than to you."

"She's always loved you, you know."

"What?"

"Since she was about eight, I think."

"How in the hell do you know that?" Blake's voice caught in his throat.

"She told me, before she left with Aaron. Couldn't live in the same town, loving a man who didn't love her back." Blake turned away.

"I can't change what happened, Laney. I couldn't—I couldn't be what she needed." Blake's face turned red.

"I'm not asking you to change what happened." She stopped him from storming off with a hand on his arm. "But maybe you both could do better this time around."

Blake looked at Laney, and the pressure to be some kind of savior to Elle was too much. He was barely healed himself.

"Well, who's to say she still loves me?" he shook his head,

trying to not think about all the quiet nights and hard days of work. "And even if she did, what if I don't deserve it?"

"Well, I never took you for a damn coward, Blake O'Connor." Laney said.

"What do you want from me, Laney?"

"The only person she's ever really trusted, really loved, and he won't let her decide what's best for her?"

Blake blanched. "What in the hell does that even mean?" he asked.

"It means that you're stupid, and stubborn, and you're gonna lose her again, Blake. All. Over. Again." Laney turned on her heel, got in her car, and shouted out the window; "Let her know I'll pick her up with Holly and Judy later." Then, she drove away in a Sullivan-like fury.

"I am not, and I will not!" he yelled at the departing car while confusion and pain flooded through him until all he wanted to do was get away from the whole lot of them. He forgot about the lines in the south pasture and climbed back in his Jeep and rushed off to town to buy clothes for a dance he regretted ever saying he'd go to.

ELLE MUCKED OUT THE STALLS WHILE SHE WAITED FOR Katelyn to come by. Elle feared that the halting way she was trying to run Gran's ranch would come under scrutiny. Of the three girls, Katelyn was the lifer. She wouldn't ever not be a ranch girl, one way or another. Elle worried how she would react to the work she'd done. While she was breaking even, she wasn't saving anything. She came out of the barn reluctantly and watched Katelyn pull in.

The truck skidded to a halt, throwing gravel and dust into the air, and Katelyn hopped out as though rage itself were driving her. Elle's heart hit her throat. The younger sister launched herself at Elle and her warm and strong arms surrounded her and pulled her close. The soft laughing cry she made turned Elle's fear into relief.

"Oh, Elle," Katelyn said softly into her neck. "I'm so, so, so happy you decided to keep it. Look at what you've done already! I'm sorry I wasn't around to help more. Oh, I've missed you something awful." Her voice broke with tears and Elle pulled away, unexpectedly crying as well.

"Oh, Katie, don't cry," she admonished and brushed her hair from her face. Katelyn wiped her nose on her shirtsleeve as she stepped back. She cleared her throat and regained her composure. "I appreciate you coming out. I know you aren't home for long, but Laney said I should have the 'expert' of the family take a look at the new crew." Elle smiled at her and nodded towards the paddock. "Plus, I heard you might have something for me?" she cleared her throat, trying not to sound too eager, as Blake suggested.

Katelyn's face lit up. "I might. I had it sent in for repairs as soon as Dad told me you got the horses." She rushed to the bed of the truck, hopped up and bent over to lift the refurbished and shiny saddle.

"Gran's saddle?"

"Circle-Y's will last you forever if you take care of them. Dad had it in storage. I think it's gonna fit you perfectly." Tears stung the corner of Elle's eyes, and she took the heavy leather saddle from Katelyn. It was beautiful and liberated a flood of memory and emotion.

"It's perfect, Katie. I can't even thank you enough." She set it down and pulled Katelyn in for another hug.

"Oh, and I brought one of dad's old ones for Blake. I hope it fits. I hear from Ben he's big as a brick shit house." Katelyn unloaded the other saddle and looked around to the empty yard. "Where is the brick shit house, right now?"

"Uh, I dunno—" Elle stuttered. She'd heard him and Laney arguing while she'd been in the kitchen, and then he'd left. She hoped he'd come back before the dance. Katelyn shrugged.

"So? Where are your new babies?"

"I can't help but feel like you should be the one out here, running Gran's place," she said.

"I'll help where I can, but you know, I've got a bit of a travel bug lately."

It was true. Katelyn was a vet tech and an equine massage therapist. She liked traveling to different parts of the country to work on and with injured horses. She had a wanderlust that kept her moving. Elle was perfectly happy to stay and set down some roots. Maybe she was the real lifer.

"Well, maybe someday you could come back and manage it so I can spend my days baking." Elle suggested with a smile.

"Yeah, but then I'd have to settle down," Katelyn chuckled. They walked, bumping shoulders together as they did. After storing the saddles in the tack area of the barn, they headed out to the paddock. Both of the horses were out, tracing the edge of the fence line and nipping at each other playfully.

"Laney said they're swaybacked."

"Laney's an ass hat." Katelyn laughed and leaned against the fence to watch the horses swish their tails. The wind gently teased the straight honey brown wisps of hair around her face as she squinted at the horses before ducking under the fence.

"They seem bonded. These the ones you got from the Morrises?"

"Yep," Elle nodded. Her booted foot was propped on the lowest rung of fencing and she watched with sisterly pride as Katelyn approached the two horses in her relaxed, laid-back swagger, Wranglers and well-worn boots. Katelyn scratched her own slightly crooked nose, before gently placing a hand on the mare. Lottie nickered without shying away.

"That's a good lady," Katelyn cooed. Her strong hands ran the length of her, stopping to run over the red and white paint. She inspected various muscles and common problem spots. Lottie gave her a gentle nudge and ruffled her hair with hay-scented breath.

Katelyn moved on to Goliath. He was a bit jumpy, and shied to the side as Katelyn approached.

"Easy," Katelyn clucked. "Sheesh, why do boys have to make a big deal out of everything?" she teased in measured tones that calmed him.

"Is that why you're still single?" Elle said from her perch on the fence.

"Prolly," Katelyn twanged.

"Surely there's been someone since I was gone?" Elle asked. Katelyn smiled as her hand stroked Goliath's forelock.

"You know how shallow the pool is here," she scoffed.

"Yeah, but you travel. You're around some interesting and adventurous guys. You're telling me not one of them has made an impression?" Elle asked with disbelief.

"There have been some interesting characters," she paused, sighed, and scratched Goliath's neck. "But nobody that seemed worth the trouble."

"Trouble? Katie, come on." Elle said and smiled.

"Well? When my two amazing, beautiful sisters get their hearts broken by men who didn't deserve them? Kind of makes a me boy-shy," Katelyn said and looked back at Elle. She frowned at the truth. "Elle, I'm sorry, I—"

"No," Elle stopped her. "You're right." She climbed up the fence and hopped over it. "We haven't been the best examples."

"That's not true."

"Well, it's kinda true. But that doesn't mean that you shouldn't try at all. Look at Mom and Dad, Gran and Grandpa. Sometimes love works."

"Is love going to work for you, Elle?" Katelyn asked, genuine concern in her face. Elle looked down at the youngest, not yet as jaded as her older sisters.

"I don't know," she said. "I'd like to think so."

"What about Blake?" she asked with a sly eyebrow quirking.

Elle scowled. "You and Laney both need to stop."

"She might have mentioned something in passing about what's there," Katelyn said and nodded to the quiet sheep wagon.

"Nothing's there! Blake doesn't want me. At least, I'm pretty sure."

"That's the thing about Blake, Elle. Ever since we were little, when you'd yell at him or wallop on him, he always forgave you. Especially you. He loved you."

"He did not." Elle argued.

"You don't know Blake like I do," Katelyn said and Goliath twitched his mane.

"Oh? And what do you know?" Elle asked.

"I know that when you left, he did nothing but mope over you *for months*. I think he knew he'd made a mistake, though I don't know the exact details," she stopped to look at Elle who gave nothing away. "When you got engaged, Blake just sort of fell off the map. I know he went to school. I know he graduated. But he didn't take his test. It was like his heart died inside of his chest and he went on trying to kill the rest. I think he broke inside." Katie's voice turned soft and Elle saw tears in her eyes.

"He's already told me that I ruined his life—" Elle began.

"Oh, bullshit, you didn't ruin his life." Katelyn stopped her. "He did that all on his own. I'm saying he loved you so much that he wouldn't save himself when you left."

"Well, if he loved me so much, why didn't he tell me so?" Elle said hotly. "Why did he make love to me and then not ever talk to me again? He—" she choked on the pain in her chest and Katelyn reached across the horse and took her hand.

"Elle, I didn't know."

"There's a lot you don't know," Elle said. When she didn't say more, Katelyn sighed.

"Look, all the choices Blake made were his own. And he made some stupid ones. Sounds like maybe he hated himself just as much as he hated you leaving. All I know is that he was anchored so tight to your memory, that life without you made him crazy with longing, and that's not something a few years can just erase. That kind of love—"

"Katie—"

"I know! I'm not giving you advice. I'm just getting back to you asking me if there'd been anyone. Well, no. Because *that's* what I'm waiting for. A love *that* strong. A love so deep and slow, that time, and distance, and life won't sway it. If I had a man that loved me that way? Hell, Elle, I'd hitch my wagon to him." Katelyn finished. "That'd be a man worth loving."

Katelyn patted both horses and sighed. Elle stayed quiet while her sister's words dug trenches in her brain.

"Looks like a good investment. They're both healthy, seem to be even tempered. You said they're broke?" Katelyn asked, switching the subject as if they hadn't just pared through the complexities of everlasting love.

"Lottie is experienced. Goliath is newly broke. I figured with Blake's help, I'll get him fit to ride."

"Blake or the horse?" Katelyn asked with an evil grin and stuck out her tongue. Elle kicked a rock at her.

"Shut up, Katie May," she responded, and they broke into laughter.

Sixteen

THE MORNING DRIFTED AWAY WITH KATELYN AROUND. They saddled the horses and took them for a short ride around the paddock. Katelyn, the far more experienced rider, took Goliath with an ease and grace that made Elle believe he might be broke over the summer with Katelyn's help. Before they knew it, it was time to meet Laney and Elle's friends in town.

It seemed decadent to go into the small downtown with its quaint coffee shop and ice cream parlor. They were going to all three of Sweet Valley's clothing shops, which also sold local jam and honey and bear spray. Sure was a change from L.A. The passing thought faded with Judy's voice to her right.

"You look like you haven't bathed in a week," she teased. Elle looked over at her freckled face in the shop's front windows. Aaron had often commented on how she should stay out of the sun to keep her skin from aging. Elle turned her head to the side and admired the small crow's feet and the line between her eyebrows. She'd take them, and the sunshine.

"Three days, give or take," she laughed and Holly wrinkled her nose.

"Nice! If I didn't have to work around all those smoking drunks, I'd probably skip it too."

"How are things at the Trap?" Elle asked as they headed into the first shop.

"Good and busy, like usual. Not much else to do in a small town, you know." Holly said and started sorting through the flower print dresses on the first rack. She held one up to Elle's tall frame, made a face at the red hue, and put it back.

"Been a little *less* busy lately though," she added easily over her shoulder as Elle looked at a pale blue skirt in the corner.

"Oh?"

"Since Blake's not been around," she said, leading. "Sure are a lot fewer fights."

"Oh well, that's good?" Elle said and bit her lip. Holly and Judy both studied her blush and smiled knowingly back at her.

"Probably a lot of broken-hearted girls, too," Judy said and nodded at the skirt Elle held, "now that he's spoken for."

Laney choked on her own spit and started coughing.

"Oh, we're not—" Elle's face erupted with warmth. "We're not dating."

"Right, just living together. Totally different," Judy chuckled. "My brother said he looks like a goddamn titan or something, guarding over you, all stoic and shit."

"He's not guarding—stop laughing, Laney June!" Elle said and tried not to fall into a fit of giggles herself.

"Ben wanted to ask you out, but he was afraid Blake might deck him."

"He did? I would never let Blake do that," she said and blushed.

"Wouldn't *let* him, huh?" Laney teased. Elle rolled her eyes and turned back to Judy.

"Blake doesn't—we're not dating. I'm just helping him out until he can—" Elle stopped.

"He can get back on his feet?" Laney asked and slapped a

pretty, cornflower blue dress against Elle's shoulder. "Try this one, Leggy McLeggerstein." The women chuckled with knowing smiles and had the kindness to drop the conversation for the rest of the afternoon.

They grabbed a cup of coffee after their three-store spree and laughed and talked about Judy's kids and Holly's feet-dragging fiancé. Laney didn't say much, but when asked if she was seeing any hot professor in the big city of Laramie, her face fell.

"Oh, you young kids. I'm just an old spinster. I'm off the market."

"But those books you write." Holly argued. "I keep them next to my bed with the good parts dog-eared! You've got to have some muse back there, keeping things nice and hot in your bedroom."

"The only thing that makes me hot in bed are night sweats," Laney laughed, and they all joined in, except Elle. She saw the sadness behind Laney's eyes. Despite her harsh self-deprecation, Elle knew she was lonely in a deep way.

"Laney, you're not old." Elle said.

"Well, I'm old enough. We should get you cleaned up, Cinderella, before the ball. Three day's stink is no way to win a titan's affections."

The resounding laughter that filled the coffee shop made Elle's heart feel like a bird taking flight. When she opened her teary eyes, she saw Ty scowling at her from the corner table. She hadn't noticed, as happy as she was to be out with friends, that he was in the coffee shop. He got up abruptly and stormed out, whipping his car out of the lot and nearly hitting a truck full of hay on his way down main.

Elle watched him go, and her momentary happiness was lost to the chill that ran up her spine.

THE REFLECTION IN THE CLOUDY ANTIQUE MIRROR IN the living room stopped her. She hadn't worn makeup in a long while. Holly had helped her shape her eyebrows and Judy had helped her arrange her hair in cute, pinned curls around her face. Laney had been right about the dress. Its low-cut bodice made her neck look long and graceful. Elle smirked and the pink, shiny lips in the mirror smiled back. She could hear the tickle of Aaron's voice in the back of her mind.

Whoring up to go out?

Elle smoothed her hands down the mid-thigh length dress and felt her pulse quicken.

"I'm not a whore. And you don't get to talk to me like that anymore." she whispered.

Before the memory could argue, the screen door slammed and Blake's heavy footsteps crossed the kitchen. She wasn't sure how he'd chosen to spend his Friday afternoon, but she knew he'd showered from the wet towel he'd left hanging behind her door. She looked back up to her glassy eyes in the mirror.

"We doing this thing or what?" he grumbled. She thought about running upstairs to wash the makeup off her face when he came into the living room.

"Well? Are we? 'Cause—" he stopped in the doorway.

They both stared at one another, speechless. He was dressed in new Wranglers, a crisp, white button-down shirt, and new boots. His strong legs and tapered waist showed the weeks of hard work, and the shirt hugged his broad chest. His hair was trimmed but still unruly enough to not betray his aging sense of rebellion. She wanted to push him down on the couch and forget all about the dance.

"I—" she faltered.

"What's that?" His voice wasn't accusing, it was pained. He stepped closer. His skin and freshly-shaved cheeks smelled clean, and it made her feel heady and dumb.

She looked down at the low neckline of the dress and beat back the residual sense of needing to justify herself. "A dress? I found it on sale."

"No, on your face." He pointed.

Elle bristled. "Well, that's called make-up, genius."

"Well, what for?" he countered. Elle's face felt hot.

"Because I want to look nice."

"Well, you don't need it." he yelled back. "You're perfect without it."

"I—" she started, but faltered at the compliment.

"Christ, Elle. I'm having a hard enough time."

"Hard enough time with what, Blake?" she asked.

Blake shoved his hands in his pockets and leaned back.

"I did it for me," she said quietly. "Aaron always told me what to wear, how to look. But now I get to look how *I* want to. And *you* don't get to tell me I can't wear a little makeup."

Blake looked up from his boots, his jaw clenched and his blazing eyes searched hers.

"I'm wearing make-up tonight, because *I* wanted to feel pretty, for me. Because I spend most of my day ankle deep in manure and over hot ovens, and I wanted to feel, I dunno, different, for a night."

Blake stared at her without saying a word.

Elle sighed and grabbed her purse. "Never mind, let's just go." She skirted around him.

"Elle?"

"What?"

"I just meant that you don't need anything to be beautiful. You're beautiful every day. In jeans, knee deep in manure. Even when you're yelling at me—" he stopped to swallow, ran his hand through his hair and closed his eyes.

"Then why are you angry?" she said as he passed by to open the kitchen door for her.

"I'm not angry. I'm just—" he stopped and looked away as she came closer.

"What?" she whispered and reached up to refasten one of his buttons that had come undone. Their body heat radiated in the tight doorway. He sighed as he studied her face.

"Frustrated," he said softly. "You're too good, and I don't—"

"Don't what?" she said and looked up at him. The light was fading on the horizon and cast a beautiful orange glow over them. He glanced down at the swell of her breasts and closed his eyes.

"Well, I don't want to just play Scrabble with you." He blushed.

"Because you know I can still kick your tail at Scrabble, even in a skirt?" she said with a smile and felt a flutter in her chest at his confession. She bumped him out of the way so she could lock the door.

"And so we're clear, I'd never tell you what to wear. It's your body. I just...I have a hard time seeing you like this," he confessed quietly.

"In a dress? Why? What's wrong with it?" she asked as he opened the gate for her.

"You know nothing is wrong with it—" he stuttered with frustration. She walked to him and Blake put his hands back in his pockets and leaned away. His eyes fell to her legs.

"Why do you do that?" she said, noticing his hungry stare.

"What?" he grumbled and looked back up to her eyes.

"Stop yourself from saying what you mean?" she asked.

"I'm not. I just don't have the right to—" He grunted in frustration.

"Don't have the right to what?"

"To want you, Elle." He stood still, ashamed of the confession.

"You—you want me? But I thought that you—"

"The clearer I feel, the more I want you. And I can't want you." His nostrils flared and his breath quickened.

"Why not?"

"Because I don't deserve you." He turned and walked to the truck.

"You don't get to decide who deserves me." she said angrily to his back.

"Just get in the truck, will you?" he grunted and got in the driver's side.

"Blake, you deserve so much."

"Elle, please shut up and get in the truck." When his eyes met hers, she saw his tears.

She sighed and relented. Tonight was not the night to solve their underlying and mutual grief. She was lucky to have him here at all, so she backed down. When she climbed in next to him the words burst out of her.

"I want you, too, Blake." she paused and blushed.

"Elle—"

"But I don't deserve you either," she said as he turned the engine over.

"Dammit, Elle." Blake sighed and knocked his head on the steering wheel. "Aren't we a terrible pair?" He shook his head and sped out of the drive.

THE DANCE WAS JUST AS LAME AS HE EXPECTED IT TO BE, Blake thought as he stood at the edge of the crowd and gripped the solo cup of iced tea. Elle gave it to him when he'd approached the keg. The butterflies in his stomach made it impossible to enjoy any of this. He hadn't meant to confess his feelings to Elle. He watched the older couples dance and the high school kids duck between buildings to sneak a smoke or a make-out session. He couldn't remember the last time he'd been to one of these sober. Usually, he'd stumble out of the bar into the middle of all the nonsense and quickly stumble back inside.

He leaned on the railing of The Belle, beside the wild rose bushes growing up between the old wooden porch's planks. His eyes darted from face to face, searching for Elle. She'd been pulled away by Judy Prym at the food tables, and he hadn't seen her since.

Blake took stock of everyone and was glad that Ty was not among them. Ty had always hated the Sullivans. Blake suspected it was because Elle had rejected him in high school. He'd carried anger over it for a long time. Blake grimaced; was he any better? He poured the iced tea down his dry throat.

Last week, when he'd been in line at the feed store and Elle was making deliveries, he had to keep from beating Ty to a pulp when he'd made crude comments about Elle and their working arrangement.

"Where's your little Californian bitch, Blake? I still owe her one from the other night. You best hope she's not alone out there for too long by herself," Ty had said. Blake turned on him, anger pushing the adrenaline through his veins.

"You stay the hell away from her," Blake growled and left before he could pulverize the little man's face. More than once, Ty drove past them when they were in town; his beady eyes narrowing on her. Blake re-checked the crowd. Ty was either home or in a bar this evening and Blake thanked his lucky stars for one less fight. Because he would fight for her. Now. Though she wasn't his to fight for and he had no responsibility to protect Elle. He was a day late and a dollar short for any white knight dreams. He hadn't been there for her when she needed him. He wasn't even sure he deserved to be her hired hand.

Blake threw his cup away in a trashcan and shoved his hands in the pockets of his stiff jeans. The door to the bar swung open and the comforting smell and noise drifted down. Blake thought of ducking into the bar just as he heard Elle's voice.

His head swung around to find her laughing with Elva Miller, the town museum's curator. Elle's perfect white teeth that had tugged so sweetly on his lip in the middle of an ice-cold lake and made him lose his brain, spread wide in a smile. He looked down the length of her, slender fingers curled around her solo cup, skirt delicately blowing in the night breeze.

As if she could feel his eyes on her, she turned her smile to him.

Elva turned to see what had taken her attention, and her papery lips pursed disapprovingly at the sight of Blake. She whispered in Elle's ear. Elle frowned, shook her head, and Elva excused herself. Blake's collar felt tight and his neck erupted in heat. He turned and walked up the last step to the bar. Elle's hand clamped around his wrist.

"Hey cowboy," she said. "Where you headed?"

"For a drink," he growled.

"How about a dance instead?" she smiled and tugged at him. Blake didn't budge.

"Why would you want to dance with someone like me with my reputation?" He pulled his hand away and grabbed the door handle. Elle stepped in between him and the door. He ran into her with a grunt. "Damn it, Elle."

"Dance with me," she said lowly into his chest.

"No. What did Elva say?" he asked. She backed him down the stairs, never letting her eyes leave him, until they stood at the edge of the street.

"She told me that I shouldn't trust you. That you broke hearts. That you slept your way through half of the women in town."

"Well," he said and swallowed a lump in his throat. "I guess she's right. You shouldn't trust me." The same sense of failure and lowness hit him, and Elle followed his eyes down to the ground between them. She took his hands in hers.

"I've broken hearts too," she said. "Good ones. Ones that didn't deserve to be broken. Ones that I should have taken better care with."

"Elle—" Blake's voice caught.

"I've done bad things, Blake. Worse than you could even imagine."

"Oh, really?" he scoffed. "What did you do? Tear a mattress tag off? Seriously, Elle." People stopped to watch. Elle wiped tears from her cheek.

"Jesus, don't cry." He pressed her to his chest so her cheek was against his heart and her tears soaked into his shirt. "The town already hates me. If they think I made you cry, they'll probably tar and feather me."

Elle stayed silent but for a sniffle.

"You haven't done anything wrong," he said, softly.

"That's not true," she shook her head, but he held her too close to pull away. "I have."

"All right, Elle. You big, law-breaking rebel. Someday you can tell me all about your life of crime, but for now, let's just dance." He slipped his hand around her waist and took her hand with the other. The music swelled around them, the voices of the crowd muted, and Blake closed his eyes. He inhaled the sweet clean smell from her hair and his hand clung to hers tighter.

God, what he wouldn't give to have things be different, to go back in time and be the man he should have been. But he couldn't go back to fix the mistakes he'd made with Elle. Their history would always have a dividing chasm. When the song was over, he drew away, left the close warmth of her body but held on, momentarily, to her fingers. He didn't know what to say, except that he was sorry. Sorry things weren't different. That they'd both been through hell. But sorry wasn't enough for the years they'd wasted or the damage that had been done. Elle looked away at the downturn of his face.

"Well, I'm beat," she said. "Can we just call it a night?" Blake breathed a sigh of relief and nodded.

"Thank God. Please." He followed her to the truck. People waved as they passed, some not bothering to hide their curious glances. The arched eyebrows, the assumptions being made all over town that Blake and Elle were probably sleeping together. That he was still a no-good troublemaker who was about to ruin her new start. Blake felt the dramatic energy as the hushed whispers followed them. His shoulders pulled up; his fists clenched. He turned on the gossipers.

"What are you looking at?" he said.

Elle placed a hand on his forearm and redirected his path.

"Let's just go home. It's nothing to get riled up about."

"They're talking about us."

"There's not much else to do in Sweet Valley, but talk."

"Well, it shouldn't be about us," he seethed. "There's nothing going on! I'm just working for her!" He yelled over his shoulder.

"You're just gonna make it worse," she shushed him. "The more you deny it, the more they'll think you're lying about it." Blake turned back towards the onlookers, but Elle handed him the keys he'd put in her purse earlier that evening and distracted him from continuing his tirade.

"Thanks for driving. I'm tired," she said. Blake nodded, pulled away from annoyance at the busybodies and focused on the warm feeling of being needed. He opened her door for her, then walked around to the driver's side.

"I'm not going to let your reputation suffer because of me," he grumbled as he settled into the front seat. Elle burst out in a hearty laugh that surprised him.

"Well, don't worry your pretty little head about my reputation, O'Connor. That was ruined a long time ago," she said as he pulled out of the parking spot and into the street.

"Oh, right, we're circling back to that deviant, criminal mind of yours?"

Elle looked out the window at the darkening night. She looked like she wanted to say something. Something that seemed like a heavy weight in her mouth. Something that couldn't come to the surface yet.

"Elle, what is it? What's on your mind?"

"It's exhausting, isn't it? Worrying about what everyone thinks of you all the time? Trying to please someone else?" she said and scooted across the seat to rest her head on his shoulder, in a comfortable and soft way that melted his anger and his guard.

"Yeah, it is," he answered.

When they turned down the dark road toward the soft,

glowing lights of the house, Elle's head was heavy on his shoulder. He leaned close and smelled her hair and she smiled and made a pleased sound in her throat.

"Missed you," she said. Blake kissed her forehead, acknowledging that he'd missed her too.

Elle sat up suddenly, nearly knocking Blake in the face with her head.

"What?" he asked. The pasture gate was hanging off of one broken hinge. Standing in the gray side glow of the headlights was Goliath, blood on his foreleg. Blake pulled in quickly and cut the engine. They both came out slowly so as not to startle him. At the sound of Blake's voice, the large horse neighed and reared, but settled down when he took his bridle in hand. Elle bolted into the darkness.

"Elle!" Blake called after her. "Elle, dammit, wait!" he followed, pulling a defiant Goliath behind. Blake pulled out the flashlight on his phone. The light barely shone far enough ahead to see her. She stopped, fallen and sobbing into the grass. Her arms tightly holding on to something. "Oh no...oh no, oh no...no," she cried, and Blake shone the light on Frankie's crumpled and bloody body.

"Shit," he breathed. He searched around, looking for the predator, but the meadow was quiet. He knelt next to her and took the goat's limp head in his hands. Despite the blood, he could feel small puffs of air struggling through its nose. "He's still breathing."

Elle's bloodied hand went to cover Blake's, and she felt the delicate and fading breath.

"Call Dad," she said desperately. Blake's brow creased.

"Elle, I don't think—"

"Call him, Blake, now!"

Blake looked into her tear-filled eyes and thought he'd probably call the president at this point if it would make her stop crying.

"OK, OK." He dialed the number.

SEVENTEEN

ELLE PACED THE KITCHEN FLOOR AND BIT AT THE STUBS of her nails. Her inability to help was infuriating. She wanted to peek her head around the corner of the living room, but the reprimand she'd received from Blake last time kept her away.

She closed her eyes, leaned against the sink, and tried clearing the image of helping Blake put the bodies of one of the pygmies and one of her pregnant angoras in the back of the truck from her mind. He'd tried to keep her from seeing them, but she pushed him aside and took in the damage. The horror of the blood and their torn throats flashed memories in and out of her vision.

She took a deep breath. She straightened her spine and focused.

Loss was part of life, and she wasn't going to shy away from it. While Blake walked Goliath back to the barn and secured him inside, she put Frankie on her lap and drove the short distance home, whispering reassurances while his blood soaked through her dress. She reached the drive and Blake opened the door and took him from her lap.

"Take him into the kitchen," Elle said.

"Elle, I didn't see Lottie."

"When dad gets here, one of us can go looking. She knows where home is. I hope she does." Elle cleared her throat and kept her tone even, but Blake caught the desperation in her eyes. He took Frankie in. Elle kept herself busy boiling water, tearing up strips of old cotton shirts, and bringing him the first aid kit. The ragged old goat's eyes were wild with pain and fear. His throat had been bitten, his chest gashed open.

Elle's flustered and nervous energy in the room with Blake had earned her a one-way ticket to 'go do something else'. He had already begun to treat the wounds himself, using Elle's sewing kit and administering care with a steady hand.

Warren rushed through the door of the kitchen ten minutes later with his vet bag and the painkillers that Blake had requested. Now, Frankie's bleating had calmed down at least. Warren sat beside Blake, only offering help or advice as needed.

"I'm going out to look for Lottie," she said, as she walked into the living room and tried not to gauge how much blood the goat had lost. It sure smelled like a lot.

"The hell you will," Blake said, from his knees on the floor where he'd had the sense to lay down a shower curtain. She looked down at him, tying up the fine stitches, both hands steady. Warren was simply observing.

"She's out there with a predator." Elle pointed into the darkness beyond the screen door.

"Yeah? And she can run a hell of a lot faster than you, Elle. What happens if what did this finds you first?"

"Well, I need to do something!"

Warren brought the tone of the argument down. "We can all go out. I can get my .38 from the truck when we're all done here."

"I should have never left them." Elle whispered, and tears welled in her eyes.

"Hey," Blake's deep voice soothed and Warren nodded to him, taking over his last bit of cleanup. Blake's eyes softened as he rose. "Ranchers don't cry."

"I'm not. I'm not crying," she argued as her hands tightened at her sides. "I'm just—I'm just so mad!"

"I know you are. And you have a right to be mad, Elle. So, be mad."

"I don't need you to tell me to be mad! I get to be mad all on my own." she yelled back. The feeling of power in her chest was so strong and fierce that she felt the overwhelming emotion nearly choke her. Blake smiled.

"All right." Blake washed his hands in the kitchen sink and looked down at his bloodied shirt with a disgusted grunt. Warren gently took Frankie into the laundry room, where he made up a softer bed of old blankets and put out water for him. Blake moved out of the way to let him wash. Warren looked at Blake and Elle's ruined clothes and shook his head.

"Well, I 'spose that's just why ranchers can't have nice things." He cleared his throat. He turned to Elle. Even a man with the calm countenance of a saint couldn't look at her distress without being affected.

"I'm sorry, Slim," he said. "Blake did a fine job in there. He did what he could and the meds will keep him comfortable, but I don't think Frankie's much longer for the world." Elle put her hand to her mouth and nodded. She turned to go check on Frankie, but her father's words stopped her.

"Have you checked your coop?" He asked.

"No, I haven't." She rushed past both of them. Across the yard, the pretty white door swung open on its hinges. Blake and Warren's calls echoed behind her, but she did not hear.

Blake arrived alongside her to a scene of rampant and cruel destruction. In the dim light, darkness splattered the walls and feathers and gore clung to the perches. Eggs were pummeled in their nesting boxes and turned the hay sticky with blood and loss.

"Oh my God," Elle fell to her knees and her hands reached out to the broken and eviscerated bodies of her hens. "No!" she screamed and felt the carnage all around on the floor of the coop.

Warren came with a flashlight. The beam did nothing to improve the scene. Something had torn the birds to pieces. Elle was crying now, screaming in anger, as she searched for life among the bodies. Blake pulled her up.

"Elle, you okay?" He squeezed her shoulders. She put her bloody hands against his chest. Her cries softened and her eyes grew wide. She broke away and pushed past him, outside and around the back. In the faded glow from the porch light, she scrambled beneath the coop. Blake and Warren followed and watched her shimmy half underneath.

"Elle, what the hell are you doing? Come out of there," Blake said.

Then they heard what she had; the soft cooing.

Elle wriggled back out with Henrietta tucked safely under her arm, unharmed.

"Well, I'll be," Warren said.

"Blake," Elle said and cleared the emotion from her voice. "Can you take Henrietta to the barn, put her in the small stall, fresh water and food. And check to see if Lottie's found her way back?" she paused to swallow.

"Sure," he said and nodded at the calm coming down after her storm. He took the hen gently in his arms and walked to the barn. Elle looked at her father.

"It's too big for a coyote and we don't get wolves this far south. Why would a predator do this? Not even eat them?" she asked. Warren looked at his newly stoic daughter with pride.

"You're right about the marks. They're too wide for a coyote. The carnage in the chicken coop isn't something you'd see with a fox or raccoon, maybe a skunk, but you'd sure know it from the smell. It's more likely the work of an aggressive dog." Warren finished. Elle looked down and nodded.

"Somebody let the horses out too. Somebody with guts enough to sic a dog on a herd but not do the dirty work themselves."

Warren looked at her for a tense second before he spoke. "Do you—" he paused, sucked in a breath. "Do you think this was Aaron? Do we need to call the cops?"

Elle's head snapped up.

"It's not Aaron."

"Honey, are you sure? I know it's scary to think he might be in town but—"

She walked back to the house without acknowledging the idea. Frankie was balled up by the heater in the laundry room. She knelt down at his side and stroked his ears. He'd been sedated and stitched up in six different places. His breath was shallow.

"I'm sorry," she whispered, and the goat's legs twitched as she ran her fingers over his tattered body. She stood, pulled a jacket over her bloodied clothes, went to the locked cabinet, in the far corner of the room, and stretched up for the key, hidden on top. Blake came in behind her.

"Are you all right?" he asked. She didn't answer as she took the Winchester twelve-gauge shotgun from the safe and a box of shells. "Whoa, now. What are you doing?" Blake said with a concerned voice. "What's going on, SoCal?"

"Don't call me that, please," she said calmly. "And it's probably better if you don't know what I'm doing." She straightened the collar of her jacket and grabbed the keys from the sideboard.

"Damnit, Elle, where are you going?" he yelled and followed her out to the truck.

"Stay here, Blake." she yelled back.

"No."

"That's an order from your boss." She huffed as she got in.

"Well, then I quit." he said. She looked at him through the window and frowned.

"You can't quit."

"What are you doing, Elle?" He held on to the doorframe. "What *are* you doing?" he asked more softly. "Look if this—if this could be Aaron, you shouldn't go anywhere. You should stay here with your dad."

"It's not—" she began tensely, closed her eyes, took a deep breath, and went on. "Did you notice who wasn't at the dance tonight?" she asked. "You know who got arrested last fall for dog fighting? Baiting dogs?" Blake's eyes narrowed; her deduction slowly dawned on him. "The gossip mill is good for some things."

"I wish you wouldn't do this."

"Stay here and out of trouble," she said, ignoring his plea.

"Fine advice, SoCal. Why don't you take it for yourself? You shouldn't do anything when you're hot headed and emotional." he insisted.

"I'm not emotional! And *don't* call me SoCal!" she yelled. Blake reached through the window in desperation and cupped her cheek, gently making her face him. His touch made her heart slow down.

"Elle, please don't. We don't know he did it. *Someone* took something from you; something you loved. You have the right to your anger. I know that anger. I know what it's like to watch something you love suffer because of someone else." His eyes were sad as he touched her face. "You need some cooling off time."

Elle's hand came up to his at the shift in conversation. She narrowed her eyes on him.

"Sometimes you should fight for what you love. Sometimes you shouldn't wait so long. Sometimes you shouldn't cool off. Sometimes you should act when the pain is sharp, and new, and damn the consequences." She turned the key in the ignition and pulled out of the drive, leaving him to stare at her retreating taillights.

Elle's words twisted like a knife in his gut.

"Shit," he breathed.

"I'll say," Warren's voice came from behind. "Son, you'd better go after her, 'fore she does something she can't take back," Warren said, looking down the lane where she drove off and handed him the keys to the Jeep. "I'll check on Goliath, and see if Lottie came back. You keep her out of trouble."

WHEN ELLE ARRIVED AT TY'S SMALL LOT ON THE outskirts of town, she was still reeling from the anger and adrenaline pulsing in her system. She grabbed the shotgun, got out, and slammed the door. She wasn't prepared to see Blake, baseball bat in hand, facing Ty, who stood in a sweaty tank top and underwear, his hands up in fear. Blake must have taken the shorter route through the country roads in his Jeep. Elle clenched her teeth. She'd be damned if she'd let him take away her revenge.

"Blake, goddamn it!" she yelled and walked up the driveway with single-minded determination.

"Call off your hired pig, princess, before he gets thrown in jail, *again*," Ty spat.

"If anyone is getting thrown in jail, Ty, it's going to be you," she said, and put her hand on Blake's arm. The bat lowered at her touch. Ty's dogs, caged in dilapidated metal kennels, frothed and bit from their massive jaws while barking and scratching at the ground. Elle walked to them even as Blake whispered at her to stop.

"Go ahead and reach in, princess. They'll eat your pretty little hand off." Ty sneered as she knelt beside the cage. Blood splattered their coats and small white feathers stuck between their paws.

"Looks like they may have already had enough for one night," she said.

"Now you—you get away from them, you hear?" Ty yelled. Elle stood tall and turned to face him. Blake moved to get in between, but she stopped him with a withering look.

"The law says I have a right to shoot any predator I find attacking my herd," she said, lifted the shotgun in her right hand, and cocked it. The sliding metal resounded, and she pointed the barrel towards the kennels. Blake tensed beside her. The dogs whined. Elle's face went eerily calm. She swung the barrel away from the dogs and to Ty.

"Since these dogs only do what they're told, I reckon that predator is you."

The gun went off and the ground at Ty's bare feet exploded with clumps of dirt, grass and ricocheted pellets. Ty yelped, fell backwards, and scurried across the dirt yard to his porch. With surprising efficiency, she loaded the shotgun and cocked it again, drowning out the sound of Blake's warning. The next shot blew past Ty's ear, spraying the side of the trailer and nicking his shoulder. He screamed and held his head between his hands.

"You know, Ty, Gran taught me to shoot when I was just seven?"

Ty whimpered and pleaded as he soiled himself. Elle walked closer.

"I don't *have to* miss." She lifted the barrel a third time. She aimed it at his groin.

"Elle! Now, damn it, that's enough!" Blake's angry voice cut between them. Elle's eyes stayed on Ty.

"You or your dogs step one nasty foot on my property again, and I'll blow your goddamn nuts off."

Ty mumbled incoherently, and a sob escaped his throat.

"What's that, *princess*?" Elle asked.

"So—so—sorry. I'm sorry." The smell of urine came from the puddle beneath him.

"Elle," Blake said from behind. "Eleanor, honey—"

The soft sound of her name on Blake's lips was the only thing that reached through Elle's anger. His hand came over her shoulder and she let him take the gun.

"I'm calling animal control tomorrow, Ty. They're gonna take those dogs and you'll be getting a bill for the stock you destroyed. I suggest you pay it." Elle said calmly.

Ty wouldn't meet her eyes as he sat, shaking on the ground, in his own filth.

"Ty?" Blake asked firmly. "Answer the lady."

"Yes...Yes, ma'am," Ty managed and backed up closer to the house.

"Come on." Blake took her arm in his grasp. She shook him off, got in her truck, and drove away. Two miles from home, she realized the vice-like grip on the wheel was putting her fingers to sleep. She checked her rear-view mirror and saw the familiar grille of Blake's Jeep not far behind. She had to pull it together before they got back. He was sure to have words for her.

When she got home, the night had settled. Her father had taken the dead chickens from the coop and the lost goats and loaded them into his own truck. She would have to ask him what the requirement for disposal was in the county. That could wait for the morning. She slammed the truck door and strolled as calmly as she could up to the house. Her dad met her on the walkway. She expected the Jeep to swing into the drive at any moment.

"Blake didn't do anything stupid, did he?" Warren asked, peering over his glasses.

"No, he didn't," she mumbled as headlights illuminated the dust floating between them. The Jeep's engine cut.

"Hey, goddamn it!" Came the bold reprimand from the dark. Blake slammed his door. "What in the hell was that? You want to get arrested? You coulda killed him!"

Elle turned to glare at Blake, who bustled up the walk, temper tearing through him. She stiffened her spine.

"I *coulda* killed him, but I *didn't*! I'd say that constitutes great restraint on my part," she said and walked away, slamming the screen door behind her. Warren shrugged his shoulders in defeat when Blake looked to him for a level-headed ally.

"Don't know what to tell you, kid. I raised them to be a bit too bull-headed." Warren clapped him on the shoulder before getting into his truck.

"I'll be by tomorrow to check on the rest of the goats and take Frankie's body. The ones that made it seem shaken but not hurt. I checked over Goliath. He's not hurt. I think the blood came from Frankie, when he was trying to chase the dogs off. When it's light, we'll put the word out about Lottie, but I'll take a pass 'round with Melissa tonight to see if we can find her." Warren paused to look at the house where they could hear pans banging melodically. "Maybe keep your distance tonight, huh? Until she comes down off the gale she's riding?" Warren advised before he drove away.

"She's gonna ride a gale all right," Blake growled and stormed up the walk. He nearly ripped the screen door from its hinges.

"You," he started, coming into the kitchen.

"Don't you, 'you' me!" she yelled back.

"Well, you can't go around shooting people." he said as she stormed away from him and into the living room.

"I didn't shoot him!" Elle yelled. "I shot *at* him."

Blake burst into an unexpected laugh as the emotions he'd put on hold flooded through him. The stress of seeing her charge into danger and the pride at watching her hold her own all came out in an uncontrollable fit of laughter. Elle fell into giggles too as her own stress bubbled to the surface.

"The look on his face when he wet himself—" she hooted.

"Well? You sounded scary as shit! I nearly wet myself too."

"Do you really think I'll go to jail?" she said. The laughter faded, and Blake wiped his forehead and shook his head.

"I think Ty would be an idiot to go to the cops. He'd have to admit his part in it," Blake said. He grabbed at his chest, where his heartbeat felt irregular and frantic. "You really scared me back there," he said. She didn't respond. "I mean it, Elle. My heart—" Blake turned to look at her, and she met his eyes.

"Blake." His name on her lips was soft and small. She took his hand in her cool fingers. It was too close, it was too warm; she looked too good, and they'd been through too much. Her eyes turned dreamy, the way she'd looked so many years ago when they'd lost each other. When he'd let her go. When he didn't fight for her.

Blake's heartbeat quickened. The pain seized him anew.

"I'm not going to be here to watch out for you forever, you know," he scolded.

"Who says I need you to look out for me?" she returned angrily and stomped to her grandfather's desk and pulled out the bottle of whiskey that had been there for more than twenty years. If ever there was a night, if ever there was a time, when her heart and body were so on edge and hurt, this was it. She poured a glass and emptied it with a healthy swig before collapsing into a coughing fit.

"I'll be fine," she croaked. "With or without you." Her throat was raw, her eyes teary.

"Elle, come on, that's enough—" he moved to take the glass before she could pour another. She stepped away and pulled it out of reach.

"No, I get it, Blake. I do. You've moved on. You said you wanted me, but now that you've seen what I'm capable of, I understand that's changed. I'm a little thick, but I think I finally get it."

Blake scowled. "Listen, sweetheart, *you* were the one who left *me*."

"*You* stopped talking to *me* the night we—"

"Don't." he interrupted.

"Why not, Blake? Because you wished we hadn't? Because you didn't want to?"

"Of course I wanted to!" he roared.

"Then why wouldn't you talk to me after? Why didn't you stop me from leaving with him?"

"You knew how I felt about you and you went with him anyway."

"I didn't know!"

"How could you not know?" he yelled back. "How could you not know how much I—" he stopped, threw his hands in the air, and turned away.

"Why can't you just say it?" she growled at him. When he didn't respond, she poured another drink.

"Put that down, goddamn it!" He took the glass from her.

"Hey!" Elle jerked it back and whiskey sloshed over their fingers. "I'm a big girl now, Blake. You can't boss me around!"

"You can't handle your liquor and you know it!" he countered.

"Maybe you don't know me so well anymore!" she turned away from him. "Maybe you never did."

Blake swallowed the biting and hurtful words on the tip of his tongue. They were best friends once. Now she stood, shaking and teary in front of him, choking down whiskey that she'd normally refuse. He thought about how she'd changed. Tougher and jaded. Hauling him out of bars and setting him up to change despite his resistance. Shooting people who took what she loved. Holding in so much of her own history of abuse, it made him sick.

The real problem, the one he'd denied from the moment they'd sat on her front porch together after the barn raising, was that he was falling harder for the woman she was now than he ever did for the girl she used to be.

"Maybe I don't know you anymore." His voice was strangled as the word love bounced around in his head and scared him silent. The air inside was so thick and painful that he couldn't breathe. He took his keys from the table and stomped out. The screen door slammed behind him.

Eighteen

ELLE CRINGED AT THE BANG OF THE SCREEN DOOR. Blake's heavy footfalls down the steps mirrored the sound of her heart ripping out of her chest. The Jeep reversed and grated gravel as it swung out of the drive. When she couldn't hear the engine anymore, she broke down. The glass fell from her fingers and shattered on the tiles beside the fireplace. She dropped to her knees in the sharp fragments, seized with pitiful weeping and the deep remorse. All of life's weight, heavy on her for too long, kept her on the floor.

She crawled to the bottle and took it to the laundry room to sit with Frankie. Her back pressed to the dryer, her knees bloody and stinging, her vagabond, half-wild, dying goat, wedged himself closer to the heat of her legs. She wiped her nose on the sleeve of her jacket and swigged from the bottle. Elle closed her eyes.

A quarter of her flock dead. Her chickens slaughtered. Her only employee quit; the one man she ever truly loved, gone to the wind. More tears fell and with them more sips from the bottle, until she couldn't feel the pain from her cuts, lost count of her losses, and the banging of the screen door was silent.

Sometime after midnight she startled awake and looked down at the sleeping goat, still hanging on somehow, with deeper breaths. She stroked his head, his long and ragged ears. The wind whistled outside between the barn and the sheep wagon. She stumbled to her feet and kicked the half-empty bottle across the floor, weaved her way through the kitchen, fell against the screen door, tumbled down the porch steps and came to rest on the grass, belly up to the sky. She remembered the night, not so long ago, when he lay on top of her in this very spot, warm hands on her skin. She wished she could feel his weight pressing her into the cold, damp lawn now. The stars above spun wildly until she curled up, turned over, and vomited.

Elle pulled herself up on the shabby fence post and scoured splinters into her palms before staggering to the empty sheep wagon. She yanked open the door and was rewarded with a rush of warm air that smelled like him. She clambered up to the bed, threw her arms around his pillow and snuggled in.

"Blake," she sighed over and over in the empty bunk until she fell asleep wrapped in the smell of the only man who'd ever felt like home.

BLAKE WAS AT THE BAR, NURSING THE SAME DRINK IN front of him the whole time, with its ice melting. Holly looked him over as if he was a giant, possibly dangerous, question mark. From his blood-stained shirt to the glossy stare he couldn't break out of, it was obvious that he'd been through some shit tonight.

"You...uh, you OK? Are you hurt? That's a lot of blood."

Blake scowled at her; having forgotten he was in the same bloody clothes. He looked down and sighed.

"Ty sic'ed his dogs on Elle's flock tonight, killed two, including one of the pregnant does, took out all her chickens and let her horses loose. We still haven't found the mare." The words were rough in his throat.

"Shit, is she okay? Is she alone out there? Should we call the cops?" Holly fired off the questions. Blake spun the glass against the wooden bar top and stared at it. He shook his head.

"She handled it." The words were final, and Holly raised her eyebrows.

"I bet she did. I think our Elle has turned into a badass." She winked at Blake and moved on to help another patron.

"Our Elle, the badass—" he swallowed, remembering the sounds of her cries when he left. His brain was troubled and his thoughts tumbled, but he found, even with the drink so close, he didn't want to deaden the feelings rushing in and out. He wanted to feel them all. Regret, ache, love, and hate jumbled up behind the steady gaze he held on his drink.

"Blake? Shit dude, are you sure you're all right?" Holly asked again five minutes later. "Does Elle know you're here?"

When he grunted and responded that there was a lot of things Elle Sullivan didn't know, Holly reached for the phone. Blake stopped her.

"Don't," he said. "Just—I just need a little time to think. I promise, I won't get stupid."

"Sounds like maybe you already got stupid. I heard you yelled at people at the street dance," Holly said. "Not your best night, huh? What else is the matter? Didn't like the dress?"

"Why are you so chatty?"

"Maybe because you're sober for a change, and bar top therapy is kinda my job. Maybe because I like Elle and I'm watching out for you."

Blake rubbed his forehead and heaved a sigh. "I loved the dress."

"Well, then, what the hell are you doing here?"

Blake looked up at her, the hurt and sting of impossible hope in his eyes.

"We both know I don't deserve to be anywhere near Elle." Holly gave him a curious once over, noting his reserve, the clarity in his eyes, the way he wasn't throwing them back and flirting with all the young ladies in the crowd.

"I'm not saying I disagree," she smiled and tossed her brunette ponytail over her shoulder before leaning across the bar to whisper, "but, ain't that for Elle to decide?"

"She shouldn't be making any decisions right now—"

Holly slapped his shoulder with her bar towel. "Bullshit. That girl is on fire with choices and decisions, and you best be letting her make them."

"I don't want her to get hurt." Blake yelled back.

"Well, then don't hurt her." Holly argued.

"Well, I can't help it. I'm a shitty guy."

"You are not." Holly said and slammed a bottle down beside his still untouched drink. "If you were a bad guy, you would be halfway through this bottle by now and a third of the way through the women. But instead, you're here and moping over her... worrying over her. And I bet my right arm she's probably doing the same for you this very minute. So, stop being so goddamn stupid."

Blake watched the liquid in the bottle settle as Holly walked away and his gut twisted. Elle was worrying over him. She said she'd never stop. But she also said that he should have fought for her all those years ago. Goddamn it, she was hardheaded and foolish. She was wrong about how things had happened. She was also right. Neither of them had done well by the other. Neither of them had done enough.

Losing her goats and chickens had hurt her; it may even drive her to quit and leave Sweet Valley. Isn't that what he wanted all along? His hand stopped turning the glass.

Elle could leave again.

If he turned his back on her like he had before, she'd be gone, and who knew where she'd end up. Maybe back with Aaron.

The thought boiled his blood, and even if he wasn't ready yet to admit it, he loved her too much to let that happen. Blake stood and put a ten on the bar for the untouched drink. Holly smiled and gave him a "go get her" nod. He got in his Jeep, sped down the hill, out of town and towards the ranch. The lights were still on downstairs. He parked, shut off the engine, and wondered what in the hell he could possibly say that would make up for the asshole he'd been.

Start with the truth, Blake.

Blake could almost see Gran's bright blue eyes leveling him.

"Right, the truth," he sighed. Painful butterflies sprung up in his stomach at the thought of telling Elle he loved her. Caught in the fight between his heart and head, he was pulled to the present at the sight of the screen door torn off and hanging to the side.

"What in the hell?" he whispered and walked with measured steps into the house where the lights still blazed. Droplets of blood scattered and smeared on the floor and table. He went back further, careful to avoid the trail, his ears tuning into the slightest noise in the house. He wondered, with a deep drop in his gut, if Ty had come for her. Or worse, what if Aaron had? His heart stopped beating, and he raced into the living room.

He found the room empty, but for the broken glass littering the floor and a pool of blood formed around the crystalline pieces of it. He found another swipe of blood against the dryer next to the goat, who was snoring soundly. He traced the blood spots into the kitchen, down the steps, and down the stone walkway where she'd lost one of her shoes. Blood on the gatepost led him on the most likely path to the sheep wagon, where her other shoe perched precariously on the step. He yanked open the door, and cursed while he fumbled for the lantern on the table and illuminated her silhouetted form, curled up safe in his bed.

"Thank God, Elle," he whispered, relieved. "Two heart attacks from you in one day's about all I can take." He climbed into the bed and nudged her. "Hey, Elle, wake up—" he caressed her forehead, and she hummed.

"Blake," she murmured, lost to dreams. "I love you so, so much." She nestled into his chest.

Blake stilled next to her. His heart thudded and yearned and he warned it not to believe that her unconscious and inebriated thoughts were real. But hearts pay no mind to reason.

"Make that three heart attacks." He kissed her forehead. He checked her over with gentle caresses and found the cuts on her knees. He could feel the hard points of glass that were still stuck in her tender flesh and she gasped with breathy, pleased noises as his hands touched her, checking for others. She arched into him.

"Easy, Elle. We gotta get you fixed up," he said, but she only mumbled incoherently. He carefully lifted her from the bed and carried her inside. She slung one arm over his shoulder and nuzzled her face into his neck. The smell of whiskey, blood and vomit mixed with her clean scent. He hated himself for leaving her alone; for every night he'd ever left her alone.

He took her upstairs and laid her on the bed, slid the jacket from her shoulders, and pushed her dress up past her knees to see the damage. Dexterous fingers stopped to trace the delicate skin of her calves as he squinted at the blood-covered cuts. His fingers traced up her thigh as he reached for the light beside the bed. She moaned and arched her hips.

"Lord in heaven, Elle. This isn't exactly how I pictured undressing you," he sighed.

"Yes, please," she mumbled. He shook his head with a sideways glance and hurried to the bathroom. In the medicine chest, he found bandages, tweezers and antiseptic. He filled a cup with warm water and took a washcloth with him. When he got back into the dimly lit room, she had rolled over on her side, the skirt hitched up to past her waist and her curvy bottom framed in lace. With a deep breath to strengthen his will, he used his shaking hands to turn her back over.

Her skin was impossibly smooth, pale and perfect. The panties had a little pink bow in the center, right above where he wanted to be. Like a present waiting to be opened. Blake sighed and closed his eyes. He knelt at the edge of the bed between her knees, and with excruciating care, plucked the pieces of glass from each knee and deposited them on the gauze. Blood pooled beneath the shards.

"It's lucky you're drunk, Elle," he said and struggled with a particularly small-ended shard. It was difficult to grasp, but when he finally grasped it and pulled, Elle sat up, clenched her legs together, and struck him in the head.

"Ouch!" they both exclaimed before she focused on him, between her naked thighs, looking startled and his cheek pink.

"Blake?" she breathed.

"It's not what you think." He fumbled and held up the sharp, needle-like piece of bloodied glass with the tweezers. She closed one eye to focus on it, then looked down at her bloodied knees and promptly passed out. Blake blew out a breath.

"Well, now we know whiskey and the sight of your own blood are two things that knock you the hell out."

Blake cleaned the wounds. It was more intimate than he'd thought it could be. Touching her so cautiously, watching the water dilute her blood and clear away the caked-on gore. The cuts weren't so bad; the deepest was still not wide enough for stitches. He gently smeared antibiotic over them. She sighed his name. He applied the bandages and moved up to take off her bloodied dress. He lifted it up over her head and she responded to his movements by shifting her shoulders to help. He washed her hands with another warm washcloth and found small cuts and a few splinters that he removed easily. He kept his eyes on her hands and not on the gentle rise and fall of her breasts.

Every curve of her body, a body that had been so badly treated for so long, seemed to ache to be held, touched, caressed, and kissed. He wanted to bury himself in her heartbeat; inside of her. He wanted to taste the hard tips of her breasts, and every delicious inch from them downward. She rolled over, slung a hand around his neck, and pulled his frustrated body to hers. He held on to her hips as her lips found his. He met her kiss with a sigh of surrender, accepted her tongue as it gently tested his own. She grew more fervent. Her heart pounded against his chest as she tasted him, in the thin edge between consciousness and dream.

"Blake," she whispered again. He kissed her cheek, her neck, moved to her collarbone and the hollow of her throat.

"This isn't how we should do this," he whispered as she wrapped her long legs around his strong thigh and pressed against him. He groaned. "No, honey. No—" he muttered as she bit his earlobe and brought his hand to her breast. His fingers found her hard nipple, and he brushed against it, despite the chivalrous stance he tried to take. She clung to him and threw her head back. He pushed her into the mattress, put his full weight on top of her and his body grew harder. He wanted so much. He needed...

"God, Elle, please," he begged, using his weight to still her body. "Stop," he whispered. "Stop. Not like this. Not like this, baby."

Elle moaned and turned her head away, frustrated and hurt.

"I know," he soothed. "I know," he untangled her legs and turned her in his arms. Held her closely from behind. "Me too. It hurts me too," he whispered into her hair. He wouldn't take advantage of her, but he wasn't going to leave her either. The fear of what could have happened still rattled him and he needed, more than anything, to not leave. Elle curled into his warmth and fell off the world into the darkness beside him.

Blake listened to her quiet and even breaths. He tightened his arms around her, buried his face into the soft curls at her neck. He let his mind wander, in this stolen moment, to what it would be like to lay with Elle every night. To hold her safe in his arms, wake next to her, have coffee and talk about their day. Be partners in the ranch...in life. To work alongside one another, laugh and sweat, and come back home tired and happy. What it would be like to have her every night in his bed? Without the pain of their past intruding?

The pain of the past was the least of it, Blake thought to himself. What had happened after, the abuse she'd suffered, the abuse he'd put himself through, had shaped them into broken souls. But when she'd gotten thrown from her horse, she'd dusted herself off and got back on. He would have died happily in a downward spiral without her intervention. He didn't deserve her. She fought; he gave up. He had no right to be here in her bed. He moved to leave, but Elle slung her naked leg over his hips.

"He took my baby," she mumbled into his chest. His hand found her smooth thigh and his caresses stopped.

"What baby?" the question whispered to the darkness.

"When...the stairs, and he pushed...and I landed...my baby—my head." She touched the scar above her eyebrow and snuggled into his warmth, away from the memory.

"Shit, Elle," he whispered, and felt his throat close with sudden tears.

"But he's—he's—sorry. I'll make him—stew." She yawned and snuggled in close, and a soft chuckle came to her throat that sent a chill up Blake's spine. "These parsnips taste funny." Then she fell silent to sleep. Blake leaned up to look at her, but she was gone.

"Elle," he sighed and kissed her forehead. She'd been pregnant. Aaron had pushed her down a flight of stairs and she'd lost the baby. Blake closed his eyes. He held her tighter. He cried in the darkness where no one would see. He stayed.

NINETEEN

ELLE WAS CERTAIN SOMEONE HAD SPLIT HER HEAD OPEN with an ax. She moaned and curled into the warmth behind her. Her knees and hands hurt. She was afraid to look at what she'd done to them, but she vaguely remembered the broken glass. A heavy arm weighted her down, across her shoulders, but she felt no panic. She knew Blake's smell. Something else, hard and long, pressed against her back. Elle slid against it and the blossoming heat distracted her from the pain.

"Hold still," he grumbled into her neck, "you're not helping."

Elle smiled despite the way her head throbbed and held his arm tight around her.

"You came back," she said. Blake was quiet. She could tell from his warm and heavy limbs, and the sexual electricity between them, that he was weighing his options.

"I did."

"I'm glad," she said.

"I wouldn't think you'd be glad about much of anything this morning," he said with his eyes closed. "How's your head?"

"Awful," she moaned and scooted away from the light coming

in from the windows. His erection slid against her bottom. Blake took a sharp breath. Elle arched her back closer.

"Did you kiss me last night?"

"You kissed me," Blake corrected and moved to get out of the bed, but she held him still. Her other hand traced up his thigh.

"What else?" she asked. Blake moved his head to look at her profile.

"What else did you do?" he asked.

"Yes," she said, looking up at him.

He paused as the memory of her confession came back.

"You know what? It doesn't matter." He moved again, but she held his arm.

"Sorry. I'm sorry."

"You don't have to be sorry, Elle. You didn't do anything wrong."

"I said things, mean things and I drank—" she paused to swallow, "too much."

"It's my fault. I got angry, and I provoked you when you were already hurting. I should get up," he said.

"I think you're already up," she whispered with a smile.

"Yeah, well, you shouldn't listen to that *guy*. He's a single-minded jerk," he grumbled.

"A man with purpose," she said huskily, and pushed her hips back against Blake. He held her still.

"Goddamn it, Elle. Please stop."

"Oh, you don't like it?" she teased, with a new sense of power.

"I—" he stopped at her smile. "You know I like it," his voice broke with a laugh.

"Blake," she breathed. He groaned and buried his face in her neck and kissed the sensitive skin. Maybe it was just time to stop fighting it. His hand trailed down her thigh and back up.

"Elle, I know that you've been through a lot, so I don't know what you need," he said. She turned to face him, his body pressing into her soft, warm skin. She nudged his chin with her nose, kissed his jawline and he closed his eyes with the sweetness.

"I don't know either," she said, understanding. "Let's just take it slow and see." Her words were lost in his kiss, fervent, as though Blake wasn't sure how to stop even if she wanted him to. His mouth was warm and firm as he kissed his way down her neck, to the swell of her breasts. His hands were calloused with a sure touch as he rolled her over to sit on top of him. In the morning light, the warmth and softness of her thighs on his hips was more than he could stand. He reached up, fingers sliding beneath the lace of her panties to feel her.

The tires crunching on her gravel drive made Elle swing her head towards the window.

"No," Blake whispered and brought her down to his chest, his fingers still delicately stroking the sweet wetness. Elle shivered and smiled. "Shh...just pretend we're not home," he said, voice hushed like a teenager in the back seat. She hungrily took his mouth in a kiss and put her hand over the large bulge between them.

"Elle? Eleanor Sullivan?" the voice from outside shouted. Blake sat up, his hands disengaging suddenly. Elle looked to the window and felt his heart start to beat faster under her fingertips.

"I thought we weren't home," she whispered and tugged on his earlobe with her teeth.

"We're gonna have to be," he sighed, dipped his head to kiss her and gently moved her off of him. "That's Stan."

News spreads fast in a small town.

Tales of Ty's cowardly attack on Elle's herd ran straight from Holly at the bar to the gossip mill. Everyone talked about how he'd unleashed his dogs on her goats, killed a pregnant doe, maimed Frankie, and killed her entire flock of chickens. Whispers about Ty's house being shot up soon followed. The humane society had come for his dogs. He'd soiled himself. Elle Sullivan went from being the sweet-natured, good girl to a woman not to be crossed. There was talk of pressing charges on both sides of the argument.

"You can't take away someone's livelihood."

"Damn shame, all the work she's been putting in."

"Serves him right, that dumb son-of-a-bitch."

"I woulda paid to see the look he gave when she shoved that twelve-gauge into his face."

"I heard she shoved it a bit lower than his face!"

These were the things passed over cups of coffee in diners and across counters in the shops around town that morning. It didn't even take 'til ten before Stan Townsend, the county sheriff, was paying Elle a visit. Blake had gathered up a clean spare shirt from the closet and ran down the stairs. Elle quickly dressed, brushed her teeth and watched as he walked down the drive to head off the sheriff.

"Oh no, you don't," she growled, hopped into her jeans, and bounded down the stairs to intervene. Blake stood in front of Stan with his hands in his back pockets and his head hung. He nodded to the questions Stan asked him.

"Blake, even with it being warranted, you can't just go shooting at people." Stan said regretfully. "Damn shame with— well, all you've been doing in town lately and how hard you've been working."

Blake nodded into his humility. "I understand, Stan. Do we gotta do cuffs?" he asked, embarrassed.

"Won't be necessary, it's just a few questions."

"Won't be necessary at all, because he's not going anywhere with you," Elle said and came between them.

"Hello, Elle. How are you? Man, I had some of them biscuits at Prym's this morning, and they were amazing." Stan said and tipped his hat. "'Fraid I gotta ask Blake some questions. Discharging a firearm in city limits and all."

"Well, he can't answer them," Elle shook her head.

"Elle, don't—" Blake interjected. She put a finger on his chest.

"You don't tell me what to do, O'Connor." She looked back at Stan. "He can't answer your questions because he didn't do anything. I did it. It was me that shot up Ty's place. And if Blake hadn't been there, I might have killed that little son-of-a-bitch too."

"She's lying! Look at her. She couldn't shoot someone." Blake said and put his hand on her arm. Elle shook it away and glared at him.

"Screw you, Blake, you know I can so shoot and that little troll was asking for it. If anyone is going in, Stan, it's me. Ask Ty, he'll tell you. I'm the one who shot at him."

"Elle, goddamn it! Shut your mouth." Blake pleaded. Stan stepped between them and held up his large and gnarled hands.

"Easy now, you two just take it easy! I'll ask you *both* the questions right here and now," he paused to take off his hat and wipe his brow while shaking his head. "Shit, you two always did have a way of fighting," Stan chuckled. "Why did you shoot *at* Ty, Elle?"

Huffing, cheeks pink, she tore her eyes from Blake and looked at Stan.

"He sent his dogs after my goats while we were gone. Killed a pregnant doe. That's milk and more wool I won't have next season. He maimed my buck and killed twenty of my hens. He let both my horses out and we've—" she paused, suddenly worried about Lottie, who she hadn't gotten a chance to go after last night. "We still haven't found the mare."

"So, you decided it would be best to take the law into your own hands?" Stan reprimanded.

"Well—I didn't want to ruin your Friday night."

Stan tipped his hat up and looked down at Elle with an amused smile, then he burst into laughter. Blake threw his hands up, muttering 'stupid' and 'stubborn' under his breath.

"Did you have intentions of actually hitting Ty?"

"I'd be lying if I said I didn't," she said.

"Elle, for God's sakes! Shut. Up!" Blake said and came at her, but Stan held him back.

"Easy, now, son, calm yourself. She needs to finish tellin' her side."

"I know what I did was wrong, but I just couldn't let him get away with it, sir," she said, and avoided Blake's glaring eyes. "He's been hassling me ever since I came back home, and this was just the final straw."

"You're going to go to prison, you know that?" Blake seethed. "You're admitting to pre-meditation."

Elle looked into Blake's eyes and it wasn't the anger on the surface she saw, but the worry underneath. The cutting worry that seemed to make his whole body shake. Blake turned to Stan and his voice and eyes leveled on the sheriff.

"She didn't do anything. I got the gun. I went after Ty. You know how hot headed I am. You know I'm nothing but trouble," Blake said.

"What in the hell, Blake? You can't lie to an officer of the law!" Elle rounded on him. "Stan! It was me. We both know it. Blake's just being—"

"All right, all right! Jesus, you two!" Stan said more forcefully and with his patient but giant strength, put a hand on each of their shoulders. "Ty's not pressing any charges. No complaints have been lodged here, except yours," Stan sighed and shook his head. "Lord, you two. Gran would have a fit. She'd tan both your hides. Elle, you're getting a ticket for discharging a firearm within city limits. You can contest it in court, but if you pay the fine, nothing will go on your permanent record. In the meantime, you two need to work your shit out. 'Cause this kind of fighting either ends in marriage or murder," he said with a serious frown below laughing eyes.

"Marriage or murder—?" Elle choked.

Blake saw her face drain of color and wondered which part of the phrase bothered her more. He started breathing harder and looked down at her with Stan's hand still on his chest.

"Elle, do you understand everything that I've just told you?"

"Yes, sir," she said, but her eyes never left Blake's until he turned away and stormed off to his camper. Stan stared off after him. Elle flinched as Blake slammed the camper door.

"Honestly, honey. The whole town wondered what kind of crazy got into you when you hired him."

"I wonder that myself sometimes," she grumbled. "Must be that stubborn Sullivan thing."

Stan looked down at her with a smile. "I think you're doing good by that boy," he nodded to the wagon. "I reckon your Gran would be proud of you."

Elle looked back at him. "Really? I did shoot *at* a man."

"No blood, no foul, Gran'd say," Stan nodded. "Ain't news that Ty's had it comin' for a long while. But next time, young lady, you call me. Don't worry about ruining my day. And exercise a little more control with that pump action. I won't be so easy next time."

"Yes sir," she nodded. "What about Ty? What about all the damage he did?" she said.

Stan tipped up his hat.

"Well, given that his dogs had blood all over them and so did his truck, I think the judge won't need much convincing. I can see if Ty would be amiable to settling out of court."

Elle's palms erupted with sweat when she thought about standing in a courtroom.

"Out of court, yeah, I'd prefer that," she nodded.

Stan got into his Suburban and drove away. Elle went to work with a busy brain and a worried heart. The warmth of the morning's near love making was a complete one-eighty to having to talk with the sheriff about bloodshed and assault. Elle clenched her eyes shut tight and focused on what she needed to do in the now.

She started by going back inside and calling Katelyn, Laney, Holly, and the neighbors down the road, asking if they had time or resources to help find Lottie. Katelyn said she would take the day off from the clinic and drive the property lines. Laney, who was heading up later that day anyway, said she and her girls would check the nearby ranches on their way through.

She could leave too, but there was so much to clean up here and the longer the gore and blood sat in the hot sun, the harder it would be to get rid of. She hung up the phone after her last call and rushed into the laundry room, expecting to find a dead goat in need of burying. But the room was empty. The door cracked open; its handle misaligned.

"What the—motherfu—" she seethed, her head aching with tension and dehydration. Elle stormed through the unlatched door and found the bandaged goat contentedly gnawing on her lettuces and tomatoes.

"Well, good to see you're up and being an asshole so early," she reprimanded, took a rope off the fencing from the last time he'd gotten loose and contained him back into his own pen in the barn. Too well fed, hyped up on pain meds, and pleased with himself to fight, he settled down into a fresh bed of hay.

"Made it, huh?" Blake said from behind her and startled her to yelp.

"Yeah, I guess some things are too damn tough to die," she said.

"I called your dad. He's coming over and we'll go out to look for Lottie. That is, if you'll be okay here?"

"I'm fine." She secured an extra lock on Frankie's stall and let her shoulders drop in disappointment. She didn't want to be fighting with him again. She wanted to be naked in bed. "You'll let me know? And I'll call if she shows up here?"

Blake nodded with a sigh, hard to read and harder to not want in his tight shirt and jeans, barely disguising the body she'd straddled not an hour before. She bit her lip and looked down and quickly back up.

"Or maybe I can stay for a few minutes?" he said, inching closer. "That is if you're not too mad at me for trying to take your place in the county jail," he smiled.

"Don't go to jail for me," she whispered. A horn honked outside the barn. Blake jumped.

"Shit," he grumbled.

"Later, O'Connor—I've got a hot date with some dead goats and a chicken massacre." She sighed and walked out, continuing on with the chores and ignoring the way he watched her with hungry longing.

Elle watched Blake get into her dad's truck. Warren waved at her through the open window and they were off. Elle wanted to cry. And throw up. And go back to bed. But she took a deep breath and set about every single chore, one by one, until later in the afternoon.

After most of the work was done, her head was still in a cottony haze. Her stomach growled, and she thought she should eat, but still had the coop to clean up. Hangovers were a bitch, and worse, she hadn't seen or heard from anyone about Lottie. She hadn't even spoken to Blake. He did come back around dusk while she was getting ready to finally start on the coop. Her father stopped to ask if she needed anything, rehash that he'd talked to most of the people in the Valley and Lottie hadn't been spotted yet.

Elle's guts twisted. What if she'd been attacked? What if someone had taken her? What if she went rogue and was now running with the wild herd near Laramie? She checked in on Goliath, who hadn't touched his food, and shied away from contact. She nodded to her dad.

"Maybe I can go out tomorrow and see if I can check the river down to the boundary fence. She's really liked the area when we've gone out."

"Just hope she didn't fall in," Warren nodded. "The water's still pretty high this summer."

"Thanks a lot, Dad." Elle glowered.

"Now, easy, I'm sorry. I'm just trying to prepare you for—"

"The hard life of ranching, Dad? I think I've got that lesson learned," she said. Warren sighed.

"That boy is awful worried about you," he said.

"Worried? Why, what did he say?"

"Well, not a damn thing, and that's not like him. Just kept staring out the window, tugging on his hair. Truth be told, I think he's more frustrated than a bull in heat." Warren's eyes twinkled.

"Dad!"

"Well—happens to us men when the women we love get upended. We just wanna rush in there and protect ya'll, and fix things."

"What in the hell do you mean, love? And I don't need that. I don't want to be protected and have things fixed for me."

"I know. Blake knows that too. And you know he loves you, he always has."

"Always?" Elle tried not to think about the times they'd failed each other. "Well, it's been a long rollercoaster for both of us."

"I know it has," Warren nodded once and stared at her. "And he's still here. He showed up. He stood up. Sober and all." There was a pride in her father's words. "You don't have to let him help you. You don't need anyone to fix anything for you. But he's worrying and feeling useless. He needs things to do."

Elle stared at her dad. Blake felt useless? When he'd been helping her stay afloat for months? When he'd stopped her from killing a man? She bit her lip; he did still have something to do, something that had been very decidedly *undone* since that morning.

"Thanks for your help, Dad," she said, distracted, and pecked him on the cheek before he left. She filled two ten-gallon buckets with water and squirted soap in one before carrying them to the coop. The water slopped on her jeans as she went. She was too distracted to care. She was too distracted, wanting him, loving him, to notice the burning in her arms and the tired way her shoulders sagged. After the awful night, the bloodshed, the anger, the stress and heartache, he was still there. He came back.

With a hard wire brush and no flinch of mercy, she scrubbed down the walls, dunking the bloodied and feathered brush into the water only to begin again. In the temporary coop to the south, she looked up to see Henrietta watching her with beady, brown eyes and her head cocked to the side. She went through hell, watched unspeakable horrors, and made it through. Elle sat up and sighed. Henrietta cooed at her and went back to the food pan. Crazy bird was still clucking and scratching while Elle scrubbed the intestines of the other hens from the perches of the coop.

"I'm cooking tonight," Blake's voice startled her. Elle leaned back on her heels and looked at him through the mesh with disbelief.

"What?" she asked angrily. "It's only—" she paused to check a watch that wasn't there.

"It's already six, Elle. We slept in and you've been busy with chores for hours now. I helped your dad while we were out with the bodies. I checked back in on Goliath. I think he's calming down, but I don't think he'll be the same until Lottie's back. I fed him, took him for a few paces around the paddock, and checked all the locks. Their pen doesn't have any damage, so he should be safe in there tonight." He stood with his arms crossed over his broad chest. Elle thought of her father's words.

"Thank you for all of that. I can cook, just let me—" she began to rise. Blake shook his head, a small smile playing on his lips. He took out his phone.

"I found a recipe on that damn pin-ter-est site you're always talking about and I'm cooking. Not a discussion, so don't even start arguing, 'sides I already started."

"Uh, OK...s...sure," Elle stuttered.

"OK," he said, relieved. "Thirty minutes. Think you'll be done by then?" he asked.

"Yep," she said softly, still looking up at him through the wire, the smell of blood everywhere, her hands stained with red, tired, and feeling like giving in.

"Good," he said and headed for the house.

"Yep," she said to herself, and watched his butt as he walked away. Her heart softened and fell as she tumbled, head first, in love with him.

"Shoot," she said and felt like crying. She wiped her nose and recommenced her fury with the brush. "Love in the time of chicken guts," she sniffed.

INSIDE, BLAKE STOOD AT THE SINK AND WATCHED Elle's shoulders as they bobbed up and down with the work. The grimace on her face, the tired way her back rounded, and how she kept wiping her nose and eyes. All day, watching her work, knowing she was tired and sick. Knowing her nerves were shot. Knowing, he sighed with tears in his own eyes, that she'd lost a baby, and the weight she carried every single day because of it. Knowing there was more to her coming home than just a jilted husband. The oven beeped and interrupted his thoughts. He put the flank steak he'd carefully stuffed with spinach and cheese and herbs in, and started making a salad and mashing the potatoes.

Blake's heart tore at his chest as he relived the previous night's events. Thoughts of sharing this life with her. The playful morning in a sunlit bed that should have led to more. Holy Christ, the world was working against his efforts to keep from loving Elle. He swallowed hard and chopped the carrots so fervently that he missed and cut his finger open. He hissed, put it in his mouth, and stared out the window at the fading light.

"I don't want life to be hard for her...not anymore. I want to make her life easier. I want to see her happy. Because I love her." The words dripped from his mouth like the blood dripped from his finger as he held it over the sink. He wrapped his hand in a paper towel and continued.

He turned back to the recipe and tried to remember if he'd added the right amount of rosemary. Did he forget the garlic cloves too?

ELLE CAME IN FROM OUTSIDE, FEATHERS IN HER HAIR, blood up to her elbows, sweaty and tired. She studied him, from the dishtowel on his shoulder to the way he ducked to read the splattered screen of his phone that he had propped up on a bag of potatoes. One hand was wrapped in paper towels. He was concentrating with a scowl and mumbling to himself.

"Hi," she said dumbly. He swung his head around and smiled. Not a response she expected, given that she looked like the Texas Chicken Coop Massacre.

"Go wash up, chicken little."

She nodded, kicked off her rubber boots on the rug, and tried to not touch anything. She noticed the blood soaking through the towel around his hand and gasped.

"Are you ok?" She pulled the ratted paper away to reveal a deep gash in his pointer finger.

"I'm fine. Don't worry about it. It's just a little cut."

"You should get that checked—"

"You should stop momma-henning me and go take a shower," he said with finality and plucked a feather out of her hair. "Though, you do kinda look like a hen." His tone was soft, and she wished he wouldn't be so sweet when she was balanced on the knife-edge of loving him.

"OK," she said and turned to the stairs, but he caught her by the wrist, pulled her in, and kissed her. She gasped in surprise and pulled back to look at his smile.

"I smell," she said.

"I know," he whispered and gently swatted her backside, sending her up to the shower.

A new sense of urgency drove her to scrub away the blood and gore from her body. She scoured beneath her fingernails and the smell of blood faded. When she came out, much calmer, she slathered on lotion to help clear her nose of the lingering smell. Blake whistling downstairs was punctuated occasionally by a curse and mutterings of whatever wasn't turning out like he wanted. Lord, she loved him. She sighed, rolled her tired shoulders, put on her pajamas, and went downstairs.

He pulled the smoking pan out of the oven with an expletive. The hot metal burnt the edges of his fingers where the potholder didn't quite reach, and he dropped the pan on the stovetop. He put his hands on his hips, stared at the charred piece of meat.

"Shit," he said and covered his eyes. Elle walked to him, took his hand in hers, and led him to the sink where she immersed his hand in cold water. Their fingers caressed. She looked over the burn and the cut.

"I don't have workman's comp, you know?" she teased.

"How do you make it look so easy?" he said with a mock scowl. "I messed it all up."

"It's OK. It's going to be fine."

"It's burnt," he grumbled and stared at the pads of her fingers tracing over his thumb.

"It's just—browned. It's going to taste great. You know, I burnt everything I ever cooked the first year I was learning," she said and smiled up at him.

"I don't believe that."

"You mean to tell me that you don't remember the snicker doodle cookies? I added too much cream of tartar and they were like little, blond hockey pucks?"

Blake smiled. "I think I chipped a tooth." She bumped him with her hip. "What were you, fifteen?"

"Or fourteen, I think. That's the summer you left the ranch.

Your dad had just gotten the job at the mill and you moved into town."

"I'm sorry," he croaked.

"Don't worry about dinner. It's fine."

"No, Elle. I'm sorry."

"For what?" she asked, dried her hands and took out the silverware. She set the table quietly behind him.

"Last night," he said. Elle's hands stilled.

"I'm the one who owes you an apology. I went too far."

"You didn't—"

"With Ty and—," she paused to close her eyes. "And the whiskey—"

"I'm sorry I let you leave!" he blurted out, and the forks clattered to the table.

"What?"

"I'm sorry that after we had sex, I shut you out. I felt guilty and worried, but most of all I felt like—" he paused to put his hand over his mouth. "Like if I cared about you that much, that if you knew how much I did, you'd leave me. So I left first. It's stupid, and it was childish and I didn't understand, and I'm sorry—"

His words were cut off when she rushed him, threw her arms around his neck, and kissed him with tears and gasps. She whispered his name and held on to him, crying into his shirt.

"I should have tried harder."

"You couldn't have, Elle. I was so messed up. I'm still so messed up. I don't deserve to be with you now any more than I did then."

"Shut up you idiot." she sniffed and looked into his deep blue eyes through her tears. "We've all made mistakes. Lost things that we shouldn't have." Her tears were renewed, and Blake pulled away. He framed her face with his hands.

"It isn't your fault."

"What's not my fault?"

Blake sighed. "That you lost the baby."

Elle pulled away. Her eyebrows drew down. "How did you know?"

Blake leveled his gaze on her. "You mentioned it, last night, in your sleep."

"What did I say?" Fear pounded in her heart and shone wild in her eyes.

"Just that Aaron pushed you down the stairs. You hit your head and you lost a baby." Blake couldn't be sure but he thought she looked almost relieved. "That wasn't your fault, Elle."

"It was," she nodded, and the tears began fresh. "I told him I wanted a divorce. That I wanted to go back home. I made him mad. He pushed me, because I made him mad."

"He pushed you because he's a goddamn psychopath who had no right to be with you in the first place!" Blake yelled. "And he wouldn't have gotten to you except—except I never called you back." Broken edges cut through his words and he looked at her.

The screen door banged open and startled them both. Laney and her daughters came through into the kitchen, carrying a load of grocery bags and flowers. Elle dried her eyes and tried to smile.

"Jesus, are you two fighting again? You know, I think that'd stop if you'd just sleep together."

"L—Laney what are you doing here?" Elle stuttered.

"Well, I was going to stay at Mom's but it turns out that Katelyn is over there and has taken up two bedrooms with saddles she's refurbishing and—well I thought you might need a hand around here," Laney replied with a heavy breath, and shoved the bags of groceries into Blake's hands. "Cool off, stud, and go take care of these."

"Right," Blake grumbled and went to put away the pantry goods and vegetables.

"Oh, honey, I'm so sorry." Laney pulled her in for a hug and Elle returned it.

"Thank you," she said, her voice muffled in Laney's neck.

Charlotte and Sylvia came up too and put their tiny arms around Elle's long legs and slim waist.

"Don't worry, Auntie Elle, we'll help," Charlotte said.

"That's right, we'll get you set back on your feet," Laney said.

Blake scowled and his stomach dropped as he listened from the small room off of the kitchen. Here was her cavalry rallying together when things got rough. She probably didn't need to have his emotional rollercoaster in the mix. He made for the door in the midst of the chaos.

"O'Connor," Laney said, and pulled him back. "Get back here. You look exhausted. You need to eat. You both do." Laney made them both sit and turned back to the roast.

"Elle, uh, I get you had a rough day but, I think your skills are slipping—"

"I made that." Blake said indignantly. Laney smiled.

"You are a good man, Blake." She kissed the top of his head. "Shitty cook, but a good man." She set to work cutting up the good bits and serving dinner. "I'm glad you were around." She put her hand on his shoulder when he rose to leave and pushed him back down. "I hear you kept her from a murder charge last night."

"I tried to," Blake said, while sneaking glances at Elle over the heads of her nieces who sat on either side of her. He watched the way her gaze softened when she looked at them; felt the heartsickness of her own loss.

"Not easy with a Sullivan on the warpath," Laney said. They sat down and ate, laughing and talking with Blake barely saying a word. Laney regaled them with stories about her students' snafus and the girls filled them in on their summer exploits. Charlotte and Sylvia went upstairs to put their bags in the small guest room with double beds.

Blake shifted uncomfortably at being injected into the middle of the sisters' conversation and felt, once again, like the outsider he always would be. He stood quietly. Elle's eyes followed him while Laney continued to talk. He cleared his throat at the door.

"I think I'll turn in," he said. Elle swallowed and hung her head.

Laney stopped and looked at him.

"OK. Except, you're going the wrong way." She turned back to where Elle was biting her lip. "You two are both tired. Head on up and I'll finish the dishes."

"Uh—"

"Laney don't—"

"Argue with me—go on. I've got this. I could use a quiet moment."

They both stood statue still. Laney put her hands on her hips, channeling their mother to a degree that both Elle and Blake leaned back in shock.

"Elle, go!"

"Fine—god you're pushy." Elle yelled back, turning to leave the kitchen.

"I'm going to go out to the wagon," Blake reiterated as Elle trudged up the stairs and closed her bedroom door behind her.

"The hell you are." Laney whispered.

"What?"

"I saw the way you were looking at her, and the way she's looking back. If you haven't already—"

"That's not any of your business, Laney."

"She's been through hell the last few days and she shouldn't be alone."

"She *has* been through hell, the last six years as a matter of fact, and she's *not* alone. You're here. All of you. You're all here. And I'll be damned if I share a bed and a lifetime of wanting her with a couple of kids just down the hall." he said in a strained voice.

Laney sat back. Her big brain thinking. "You're right."

"I don't think those words have ever come from your mouth."

"Girls!" Laney shouted. They came bounding down the stairs.

"Yeah, Mom?" Charlotte said.

"Plan change. Grab your pillows, we're having a camp out in

the sheep wagon." The girls squealed with delight and rushed to get their stuff. Blake stared at Laney; fire still in his eyes but now his nerves were set alight as well.

"Laney—I—"

"A lifetime of wanting is too long a time, Blake." She said softly and kissed him on the cheek, before leading the exuberant girls out for a camping adventure.

TWENTY

AFTER BRUSHING HER TEETH ANGRILY, ELLE CRAWLED
into bed. She was exhausted and disappointed. She heard Blake say
he was going out to the wagon. Probably for the best, as they had
no privacy with the thin walls. The dishes clinked downstairs, and
she yawned so hard her tired eyes watered and she closed them
with immediate relief.

Her dreams came fast and painful. Dreams of running towards
Blake only to have the distance grow. Dreams of tumbling into a
pit, dark and deep, where Aaron's shadow loomed from above. She
dreamed of her grandmother holding a swaddled bundle, but
when Elle reached out, Gran pulled it away with a stern look. No,
she shook her head. This one's not for you.

Elle thrashed and fought the world that crashed down. She
startled awake when the mattress sank beside her. Blake's strong
arm went across her shoulders and pulled her back down next to
him. Her heart thudded in her chest and her breathing came in
gasps.

"Easy," he said lowly, his lips close to her ear. "It's just me."

Elle turned and threw her arms around his middle. She buried
her face in his chest.

"What are you doing here?" she asked.

"I had to finish the dishes," he said. "And collect my thoughts." Elle sighed and held tighter.

"Blake, the girls are—"

"Sleeping with their mom in the wagon," he whispered.

"Damn that romance writer," she said with a smile.

"Once in a while she has a good idea," he said, and his hands ran down the length of her bare thigh. He traced his nose along the graceful line of her neck and made shivers roll through her body.

"You don't have to be here—" she began.

"I don't want to be anywhere else," he whispered. Elle nuzzled her nose into his neck and started unbuttoning his shirt. Blake's hands loosened on her back and he rolled over to let her.

"I don't know how to do this."

"I think we probably remember," she reassured, with a smile.

"I—" he chuckled when her nails tickled down his ribs. "I don't know if this is a good idea," he said, in stumbled words, distracted by her warm fingers tracing down his chest and stomach.

"What do you mean?"

"I mean, what if I'm not the kind of man you need for this time? I'm afraid—what if I don't know how to—to be gentle? You need gentle. What if I lose control? What if I hurt you? What if it's too much?" he was breathless as her hand caressed his hard stomach while she gently kissed her way down his chest. The slight taste of salt, and the scent that was Blake, made her heady and weak as she bit the edge of his rib cage and her nails scratched over the brown sprinkle of curls above his belly button. His stomach was velvet-covered steel. A shivering wave cascaded through his body and his hips rose from the mattress.

"I'll tell you, if it's too much," she whispered. "You won't hurt me."

He strained against his jeans, throbbing in painful ache.

"I'm not so sure—God, I want you," he groaned. She slowly

pulled his zipper down and his hands threaded into her short curls. "Elle," he begged, and captured her mouth with his. She slid up the length of his body, straddled his hips, and bit his neck. He seethed, hands reaching under her nightshirt to discover her bare bottom. Blake smiled wolfishly.

"Eleanor Augusta! Where are your panties?" he tsked, his tongue and she smiled into his lips.

"Must have misplaced them, sorry," she gasped.

"I'm not," he grunted as he pulled her down against his hard cock and the rough fabric of his jeans pressed against her sensitive core.

Elle gasped, sat up, and felt pressure sing up the insides of her thighs and tighten into a curl in her belly. Blake closed his eyes and sighed. She leaned down and her teeth tugged on his bottom lip. He captured her mouth with his, kissing her with the relentless thirst of a man searching for salvation. He pulled away with a deep breath.

"Elle, I need to hear it. I need to hear this is OK." he asked, grasping for control as she continued to kiss his jawline and neck. Blake arched up in the bed and took a deep breath when she began to roll her hips in small circles against him. "Please—" he begged, more for his own control.

"I want this," she breathed. "I want you." She sat upright and pulled her nightdress up and over her head. Blake studied her in the muted light; the soft and gentle curves of her body and the slight line of ribs that should have more flesh on them. The graceful swell of her hips and the tender softness of her stomach.

"God, Elle—" he sat up and kissed her again. Her hands threaded through his hair as he stripped off his shirt and went quickly back to her body, running the length of her long legs, up her ribs, her neck, into her hair. His strong and calloused fingers came down her back, curved around her bottom and tenderly between her legs, fingers exploring her willing body.

"Blake," she gasped at a loss for words as his fingers caused tears to spring up. Her body began to shake, the power of needing him so much shuddered through her. "Oh God, Blake," she cried. He pulled away.

"Is everything OK? Are you—"

"Don't stop," she huffed and reached for his hand. His hands curved around her backside and spread her legs further apart. His straining cock pressed against her.

"I want you so much," he said. "But I'm gonna take this slow," he whispered, looking up into her face and she moaned softly as she brought his hand to her breast. Blake closed his eyes, as his thumb and finger brought it to a hard peak. She moaned and gasped and arched into him. He sat up, took the other one in his mouth, and teased it with his tongue. The taste of her clean skin, the hard tip against his teeth, made his body shiver and ache to be inside her.

"Please," she whispered. "Please, just love me—"

"God, Elle," he gasped, "you never have to beg me for that," he said and freed himself, hard and straining for her heat.

"Yes," she whispered, "Oh, Blake—" her sharp intake of breath, the cresting of her anticipation as too much. He began, achingly slow, and as he slid inside of her the world was heaven, and shadow, and quiet. He closed his eyes and his head fell back as her warm, tight body took him. Elle sighed deliciously and arched her back.

"God, Elle—I can't—" he stopped to growl, and she pulled tight around him, the ebb and flow of pressure upending his world.

"Yes, you can," she whispered and plunged down, in ever deepening strokes, until she felt the pressure in her body like a tightening knot break open, and she came with a loud cry of release.

"Elle," he said, his voice strangled as he rolled over on top of her and drew out to rush in again. He kissed her face and neck; his hands trailed down to caress her breast, curve around the flesh of her thigh, drawing her closer, pushing deeper. She threw her head back and cried out a second time, and he felt the unmistakable tightness as she rocked beneath him, her fingernails digging into his back. She wept.

"Are you alright?" Blake asked in the soft hush of the night. He slowed his pace, his body dying for more. He resisted, drew away.

"That's only two," she gasped, biting his neck, "I'm sure we can get one more," she wrapped her legs around his waist and urged him on with her strong hand grasping and pressing the muscles of his backside, until the sweat and heat between them was intense and his fervent and ravaging pace made the whole universe spin. Elle clung to him like a sparrow in a gale, and he was her only safety. It built so quickly, so intensely, that nothing could stop the explosion that hit them at once, like a bolt of lightning and he held her to him, biting her neck and grunting in self-satisfied release, while she cried out his name.

He fell into her arms, sobbed into her neck, caressed her hair, her skin, her shoulders. He sat up, kept her close to him, and she wound her legs around his waist. They sat, intertwined in the darkness, and gasped through their tears.

"I can't—I can't—" he gasped, his nose delicately brushing her neck, her chin.

"Can't what?" Elle's voice was satisfied and dreamy.

"Can't let—can't let you go." He held her close enough to feel her heartbeat and her breath as it slowed down against his shoulder. He turned his head and kissed her jaw, her neck, and down her collarbone. She shivered and threaded her hands into his hair as her body shook against his.

"Then don't. Don't let me go," she said and kissed his swollen lips.

He shook his head and their noses gently brushed. He fell back into bed with her wrapped in his arms.

So many questions, so many doubts, and worries, and unspoken fears rushed in and out of her mind. So many concerns about what the light of day would bring. The safety of the dark and the night would only last until the sun rose, and then they'd have to figure it all out. Blake cradled her body against his and pulled the blankets over them both. She fell into a deep sleep against the beat of his heart.

TWENTY-ONE

ELLE WOKE TO SUNLIGHT SPREADING WARMTH ON HER naked leg. She opened her eyes and stretched her arms high above her head. Her body ached in strange and forgotten ways. She sat up, hugged the down comforter to her chest, and looked around the empty room. A very Blake-sized indentation was still pressed into the flowery sheets. She grabbed his pillow, held it to her nose, and burrowed into it.

"Oh, Blake," she said before the sound of her nieces' laughter floated up the stairs. Elle looked out the window. It must have been late morning. She'd slept so hard that she hadn't even woken up in time to do her chores. "Shoot!" She sprung from the bed, got dressed, and hurried down the stairs.

"Well, looky there," Laney said, bemused at the oven where she was getting Elle a plate of biscuits and gravy, bacon and two eggs. "Somebody done laid my sister," she chuckled. Elle's cheeks burned.

"Where's Blake?"

"He's out feeding. He was up before all of us, made breakfast, and told me under no circumstances was I to let anyone wake you up." Laney raised a bemused brow.

Elle looked out the window but didn't see him. The dew on the grass outside was already evaporating in the places where the sun cut its yellow warmth across the lawn. He must be in the barn.

"So?" Laney asked her from behind. Elle looked at her sister, then to the plate of food. He'd burnt the biscuits, and the bacon was underdone, but her heart melted all the same.

"Wow, I'm hungry." Elle said, attempting to dissuade any more questions.

"Uh huh. I bet you are." Her sister handed her the plate and Elle sat down. She wanted to see him. She wanted him to be sitting across the table from her instead of Laney. She was anxious to talk to him. She ate three bites and stood up.

"No. The whole plate, Eleanor," Laney reprimanded and put a hand on her arm to make her sit.

"But I—"

The door banged open and Blake came in. Sylvia came up to him and told him a knock-knock joke so quickly he couldn't respond, while Charlotte reprimanded her for telling it wrong. Blake smiled and nodded; his mind preoccupied. He took off his work gloves and looked at Elle.

"Laney's right. You should eat a little more."

Elle couldn't even swallow, let alone eat, while she looked at him and remembered his lips on her skin, his hands all over her body, his—her eyes fell lower and she blushed. Laney cleared her throat.

"Well, kiddos, I reckon it's about time we head back. Why don't you girls start gathering up all your stuff."

"You're leaving?" Elle's eyes peeled from Blake to look at her sister. "Already?"

"I think things are pretty much handled here," she smiled. "I should get back and start working on my fall class schedule. Then there's the book promo I should have gotten done last Tuesday. My publisher's gonna have a shit fit over that." Laney looked between Elle and Blake. Lost in their own world, unable to take their eyes or thoughts from each other. "Then my hat blew off, and I had to go get it."

"That sounds—I'm, I'm sorry—What did you say?" Elle fumbled and looked at Laney who just snorted a laugh.

"Ladies, I'll help you get your stuff outta the wagon. I'll have to clean all the girl cooties out of it now," Blake teased, and the girls giggled in return as he led them outside. Laney smiled and looked at Elle.

"I'm pretty sure he got some cooties on him last night."

Elle burst out laughing. "What is wrong with you?" She threw her napkin at Laney.

"Just be happy OK? For me? Until I find that." She nodded towards the door. "That kind of sweetness, enjoy it. Let yourself enjoy it. That's the real thing. That's the kind of love you deserve."

Elle watched Blake with love blossoming in her guarded heart. He came back into the kitchen and bee-lined for the coffee. He filled two cups and held his shoulders with nervous energy. She wished she could read his mind.

"We'll be up again next month for Mom's birthday," Laney said, but Elle and Blake weren't listening.

Blake set down a cup of coffee at Elle's place. Milk no sugar. Just like she liked it.

"Eat." He whispered again and his eyes stared into hers hungrily.

"Ok," she whispered back.

"See? Now I can leave, because I know Blake is going to watch out for you, right?" Laney said, and winked at him. Something strange fell over Blake's face, as if a distant thought had dropped over the light in his eyes.

Within an hour after Laney and the kid's left, the order list for that week's baked goods rolled into Elle's email, not even allowing her time for a shower or another quick romp with Blake, who found excuses to come in from the hayfields he was cutting to plant kisses on her neck while she worked and whisper naughty things between bites.

"You smell like cream and sugar and I can't wait to eat you. If only my boss wouldn't make me work so hard." he said in passing, out the door, taking along the lunch she'd made him. She tried to focus on the goals set before her, instead of Blake's tongue between her legs.

"What if your boss made you hard then asked you to work her over?" she quirked an eyebrow at him and he nearly rushed back into the house.

"Don't say stuff like that to me or we'll end up with half-plowed fields." He smiled over his shoulder on his way out to the baler they borrowed from the Collinses down the road. Even with the remaining flock to feed, they knew they could sell the first round and hopefully use the money to pay the property taxes, plus the repairs that had already been done.

The bakery had promise to pull its weight, and if she could keep up with the orders, she would have enough to help her dad and mom with the mortgage on their house. Then she would feel like she'd earned a right to be here. A heavy stone dropped in her stomach.

She didn't have to earn it. This was the life she'd always been meant for. She wasn't afraid of the hard work ahead; she was exhilarated by the challenge. Elle's heart felt strange and open, and the soft breeze that came through the kitchen window, the sound of Blake whistling happily on his way to work he was proud of, and knowing he was anxious to come back to her made her feel like she'd finally found a safe home.

As Elle was coming back from the garden later that afternoon, annoyed that the deer had destroyed so many of the herbs she'd planted for her recipes, Ty pulled into her drive. Blake was still out in the fields and her heart picked up pace at the sight of Ty's beat-up truck coming to a stop outside the fence. She looked around. The guns were in the house. The baseball bat was in her room upstairs. She was nearly defenseless. She picked up a rusty rake from the side of the house and weighed it in her hand.

Ty got out slowly, holding up both hands.

"Easy, Elle. I ain't here for trouble." He swallowed and backed slowly towards the tarp-covered bed of his truck and took out a box that was sealed carefully against the sun. When he stepped around and saw her, rake pointed in his direction, he held up the box and his head sunk down between his shoulders.

"What *do* you want, Ty?" she asked.

"What I did was wrong. I know that. I also know you could have turned me in. You could have made me pay for it. You could have given me a record. Hell, you could have shot my nuts off. But you didn't. Truth is, Elle, you've got a way of pissin' me off."

Elle scowled at him.

"I know you know that," he smiled.

"What is your point?"

"I regret what I did. I'm man enough to admit it. I figure—" he paused to set the box down, and in doing so, a riotous sound erupted from inside. "I figure I'd rather have you as a friend than as an enemy." He backed away two steps towards his truck. "Just, can you tell people around town that I did this 'cause I don't think I can get turned out of another store."

Ty quickly got back in his truck, nodded to Elle, and sped away. Elle put down the rake, knelt down, and carefully pried open the edges of the cardboard box to find twenty-five juvenile chicks bouncing up and down excitedly, peeping over one another in loud and joyous bursts.

"Well, you soft-hearted son-of-a-bitch," she said and picked up the box. She shook her head with a smile and carried the precious cargo to the coop. Henrietta may or may not take well to the new brood, and she didn't want to risk the older hen killing them, so she settled the chicks into a smaller enclosure in the coop and set up a shallow dish with feed. She'd check on them later to ensure they weren't huddled or stressed. She also had some fresh greens from the garden ready for them. She let Henrietta out for the afternoon to free range in the garden. Blake would be back soon, so Elle didn't give herself too much time to dote on the new chicks. She went back into the house, with the old screen door swinging shut behind her.

The silence of the old house gave her ease and Elle's long fingers kneaded the bread dough in a methodical and rhythmic pattern, folding over, pressing down, deep and even. The smell of yeast, the warmth of the firm dough beneath her palms, the soft floating of flour motes in the sunlight called Elle to close her eyes, and she felt everything in the quiet.

Her brain had been so much like an electric fence in these last few years, always on, wired, trembling and seething with the need to act quickly and stay hyperalert. Soaked to the tops of her neurons with fear and anxiety. It was a goddamn wonder she'd made it out alive running on that kind of constant adrenaline. But she did.

She'd made it out alive.

Her hands quieted on the dough; eyes still closed. Her brain flashed back. A soup pot. Beef stew. Carrots, onions, chunks of meat, potatoes, and...parsnips. She hadn't eaten that night, just sipped her tea and watched him devour bowl after bowl.

Oh no, you eat! I'm trying to keep my figure, but please have another bowl. It is good. Maybe the best stew I've made? It was my grandma's recipe. I made a few changes...

Elle inhaled the memory of strange and peppery notes, heard his greedy slurping sounds. Watched the juice drip from his chin.

BLAKE CAME THROUGH THE DOOR BEHIND HER. "I forgot to tell you that I ran into Boss Jasper, he says he could use someone to watch his granddaughter's horses this spring—" the banging of the door startled Elle out of the soft, haze of memory, and she jumped back, defensive.

Blake halted his movement. His hands dropped, cap to his thigh as he studied her.

"Sorry—I didn't mean to startle you."

"I'm—I'm fine."

Blake shook his head. "It's okay that you aren't, Elle." He whispered and took his cap in both hands as if trying to hold on to something real. Elle scowled and went back to kneading. "It's gonna take a—"

"Goddamn it, Blake, please don't tell me it's gonna take a while. I'm sick to death of hearing it. I'm sick to death of thinking I'll never be normal or it'll be years until I'm myself again. Maybe I am myself. Maybe this is my new normal and maybe it's as good as I'll get." She accented her anger with deep folding presses of the dough. Flour puffed out angrily over her shirt. "I'm never gonna be the girl you used to know, Blake, not really." She looked up, past a curl that had fallen across her stormy brown eyes.

"I'm never gonna be the boy you knew, so what?" he argued back. But unlike the instantaneous buzzing-brain feeling of adrenaline and cortisol hitting her at the sound of Aaron's shouting, something else flooded her. Something new and strange.

"Well, I like you even more now." she barked. "I love—how hard you've worked and changed and I'm mad as hell that I—that I—" she stopped, her hands propped on the counter to support the sagging of her body.

"What—"? He croaked and stayed still in her peripheral view.

"Wasted so much time away from you." Blake's brow drew in and he tossed his hat on the bench, crossed the kitchen and took her flour-dusted fingers, warm and soft, in his calloused hand. She looked down and refused to meet his gaze. Blake searched the downcast features of the girl who never left his heart. He tipped her chin up gently, thumb pressed to her chin.

"I'm not sorry. We wouldn't be who we are now if we didn't have to climb back up from rock bottom. And I don't know why you think you need to be better for me. I like you just the way you are."

"You do?" she sniffed and looked into his hazel eyes. "Messy and fashion challenged?" she gestured to her torn jeans and flannel shirt. Blake's mouth quirked up on one side and shook his head.

"Jesus, Elle. I just wiped my nose on my sleeve before I came in, and I haven't showered in three days."

Elle crinkled her nose up. "Ew, gross!" She started to laugh, but he caught her lips in his and stole her breath.

"What was all the fuss about with Jasper?" she said, breathlessly coming up for air.

"Is that what you really want to talk about right now?" he gasped and kissed her again, pressing her body against the counter and encouraging her arms around his neck. She dusted the nape of his neck with floured fingers and swayed against his body.

"Daylight's for business." she smiled between kisses.

"Time is a socially constructed prison," he countered and gently herded her towards the stairs.

"Big fancy words. What about my bread?" She broke the kiss and looked back to the smooth rounded dough sitting happily in the sunshine on the counter.

"I'm sure that needs to rise for an hour."

"An hour? What'll we do for the other 50 minutes?" she chuckled against his lips. Blake laughed deep and full and gently curved his hand around her backside.

"Maybe I'll get fancy."

"You ought to get a shower," she laughed back.

"Let's do both," he nodded and kissed her while shedding his shirt and unbuckling his belt on their way up the stairs. With his hands like strong waves along her body, she pressed and molded into every caress. They fell against the hallway wall, giggled as he upended an old cross-stitch of a rooster her mother had made, and let their heavy breathing trail behind them down the hall. She'd left floured prints all over his clothes and hair, and he loved the smell of fresh bread on her fingers and the warmth of her skin beneath his mouth. He kissed her smiling lips and pushed her back towards the bed.

"Do you want me to shower?" he whispered.

"I'm just going to get you all dirty again."

"I should at least wash my hands," he smiled and kissed her again.

"Where have they been?" Elle laughed.

"I'll tell you where they're gonna be," he bit her bottom lip and dipped his long fingers below her waistline.

"Go quick then," she gasped, and gave him a gentle push. Blake laughed and ducked into the bathroom. As he washed his hands, he noticed he'd left the toilet paper roll empty that morning. Before she got on to him about it, he stooped over to pull out a new roll from the cabinet. His hand knocked over a small box.

Probably one of her feminine things, he thought. He picked it up to put it back and glanced down at the oblong package. An image of a stick with a plus and minus, the silhouette of a baby in the background. Blake dropped it like a match burned too low. He crouched down and stared at it where it lay, on the bathroom rug. Studying it as though it was some ancient artifact that may curse him if he touched it again. The box looked old. Like maybe it was here before her. Why would she have kept something like that? She hadn't been with anyone except him. Maybe it had been there before she'd lived here. Laney used the house for a bit in graduate school.

But Blake's reasoning was cut short as he thought of last night, in her bed, skipping out on working this afternoon. They hadn't exactly been careful and he didn't have any protection on him. Her test or not, he hadn't really thought much about that particular consequence of loving Elle.

"Shit," he whispered, stood up, tugged his hands through his hair and paced the small room from end to end. "Shit," he said

again, put his hands on his hips. Did it really scare him? The idea
of being a dad? He looked at himself in the mirror. A man
recovered from the brink. Having a baby with Elle, he looked into
his own eyes and closed them. His baby. His and Elle's baby. The
girl he'd loved since he was eight. Their family. The sound of small
feet running down the hallway. The squeals of delight on
Christmas morning, the small pairs of cowboy boots by the door,
and curling up to read in bed with a small hand pressed into his.
Giving his child the love and family, he never had himself.

Blake opened his eyes. The bright excitement and hope in
them was like a new and strange wave that took over his whole
body. He smiled. He laughed outright and put his hand to his
chest to feel the strength of his heart. He took a deep breath and
bent down to pick up the box. He placed it carefully back in the
cabinet.

When he opened the door, she was bent over the bed, pulling
the sheets down and straightening the blankets. He wanted to get
started right now. He crossed the room with a hungry growl.

"Were you laughing in there—oh!" Elle burst out with a laugh
when he tackled her back into the half-made bed. "What are you
doing?"

He laughed so deep and full; she wasn't sure if she'd ever heard
him that happy.

"Only thing I wanna do right now, is you."

TWENTY-TWO

ELLE STARTLED AWAKE THE FOLLOWING MORNING, WITH Aaron's hands on her throat, squeezing the life and happiness from her in tiny gasps of hopelessness. He'd found her. He'd found her! She clawed at the strong fingers, saw the light of anger in his eyes, boring holes into the middle of her soul.

"No! Get off!" she croaked, bolted up and out of bed, and landed hard on both knees against the wood floor.

"Elle?"

"Get away. Get away from me!" she yelled, scrambled to her feet, hit the wall, fled into the hallway and wavered precariously at the top of the stairs. Her body felt a weightless pull, the known fear that ripped through her nerve endings and shocked her body awake as one foot slipped, then the other. A strong hand took her wrist and pulled her back. Her hands went instinctively to dislodge him. She'd rather die than go back.

She'd rather die.

"Elle, goddamn it, honey. Wake up!" Blake yelled. She stared, confused, into his face, for longer than it should have taken to recognize him. Aaron's face melted away. The smell of the concrete stairwell faded into the homey smell of wood and morning dew on the grass outside. Elle fell to her knees, and Blake fell with her. She sobbed, her hands flailed uselessly like two birds caught in a new and strange room, trying to brush away the memory and feeling of Aaron's touch still living in her muscles.

"Honey," Blake whispered again. "It's OK."

"It's not—" she shook her head in answer and scrambled away. He reached out to hold her, but she held both hands out. "I can't. I can't right now—" the tears choked her sore throat. She rubbed the unbruised skin and fought with the memory. Blake watched. He sat back on his heels, shirtless in his underwear and a sad sunken curve to his broad shoulders.

"Elle—"

"I'm sorry. I'm sorry I woke you—I—it's almost dawn. I'll— I'm up," she mumbled incoherently, and stumbled to her feet, past him and rushed into the bathroom. She threw up and sat beside the toilet, while her hot skin began to cool. She saw Blake's shadow slide down outside the bathroom door. His head fell gentle against the frame with a soft thud. Elle coughed, flushed the toilet, and stood on shaky legs to rinse her mouth out at the sink. She stared at herself in the mirror. The last time she'd vomited, she'd been pregnant. It was probably just the stress of the panic attack but, what if it wasn't?

What if, after days between the sheets, in a dream-like world of loving Blake, something had taken root? It would be too soon to tell, but it wasn't impossible. Elle took a deep breath in just as Blake gently knocked on the door.

"Elle, baby, are you okay?" The strange simultaneity of hope and dread rose and sunk her guts into undulating waves. She felt her stomach churn again. What if she got pregnant?

Elle opened the door and Blake stepped back to give her space, even though his eyes said he wanted to hold her. She suddenly felt ridiculous.

"I'm sorry."

"Nothing to apologize for. Are you OK?"

"I'm going to be fine." She steadied her voice, and he stepped forward to take her in his arms. "Sometimes, my brain forgets that, Blake." She sniffed into his bare chest and he kissed her temple.

"You can tell me anything, you know." He pulled away and looked in her eyes. She closed hers, planted her forehead in his chest and sighed. There were things about Aaron she definitely could not tell him.

"Some things I'd just rather spare you from."

"Don't spare me," he whispered. "I can take it."

Elle closed her eyes and the tears that sat on her lashes fell against her cheeks. She wiped them away quickly.

"I'll go start some coffee. We've got a lot to do today," she whispered, reached up on her tip toes and kissed his lips. She hoped he couldn't feel the omission behind her lips and did her best to feign normalcy. He didn't follow her right away, and she wondered how many more panic attacks he would be willing to sit with her through.

"Eggs?" she shouted and started the coffee pot. She heard him bumping upstairs. The open and close of a closet door. Getting dressed for a day she had insisted they get started, as though she hadn't almost pitched herself down the stairs.

"Blake?"

"Sure," he called back weakly.

LATER THAT DAY, BLAKE TOLD HER HE WAS GOING WITH Warren on a call. It wasn't a lie. He did need to talk to her father. After the morning, the panic attack, and her throwing up, his mind had been in motion. She would never be free. They would never be free. No matter where they went, where she lived, how many wins she earned, she would always be looking over her shoulder. If she did carry their child someday, she would have even more cause to fear Aaron finding her again.

She was his girl. His whole world. He hadn't fought for her all those years ago. He hadn't saved her when he could have. But things were different now, and he wasn't afraid of loving Elle too much. There was only one way their story could go.

"I need your help," Blake said the uncommon words, with an even more uncommon humility. Warren took off his reading glasses, nodded, and gestured for him to come inside with a hand that still clutched his daily crossword. Blake sighed. The comfort and accepting motions of the man steeled his nerve for what would come.

"What's going on, son?" Warren said. Blake checked around the corner of the living room before following Warren to his office. "Melissa is in town this morning, helping out at the clinic."

"She's having nightmares, bad ones."

Warren didn't have to ask who Blake meant.

"I suppose that's normal, given what she's been through...and the stress of her working so much."

"But these are—" Blake sighed and adjusted his ball cap. "This morning, during one, she almost fell down the stairs trying to run away. It was like she wasn't even in this world. She was back there, with him." Blake settled his hands in his back pockets and sighed. "I—Warren, I love her."

"I know you do, Blake. You always have. And she loves you too. Always has."

Blake's eyes fell. "I can't let her keep living in fear. Fear that he's going to show up someday. Fear that he might come after her."

Warren nodded. "What do you propose we do about it?" He watched Blake hesitate, lifted one eyebrow and added, "within the confines of the law?"

"Well," Blake took in a heavy breath. "I don't know if there's a way to handle it legally."

"Blake, I understand wanting her to be safe, to feel safe, but I won't let you—"

"She was pregnant, Warren."

Warren stopped and looked at Blake before taking his glasses off. He bowed his head. Blake continued.

"When she found out, she tried to leave him and he—he kicked her down a flight of stairs and she miscarried her baby. That's what drove her to finally leave. She ran away from him, and never got any closure to the matter and now, with all of these nightmares suddenly getting worse, I think it's her brain, trying to protect her. We—well, we're—"

"An item?" His wiry eyebrow rose and a small smile played on his lips.

"Well, yes sir, but only just recently, and I'm being as patient and gentle as possible. But I think being close to someone again has opened some things up, and now I think she's even more afraid he'll find her."

"Because she has more to lose now." Warren wiped at his eyes and blew his nose on an old handkerchief. His voice shook when he continued. "What are we going to do, and what do you need?"

SHUFFLING THROUGH HIS OLD BOOKS, HE FOUND THE faded cream envelope wedged between the pages of his largest textbook, along with his acceptance letter and invitation to test for his veterinarian license. Its worn edges surrounded her neat handwriting on the front. His heart seized. She hadn't sent it to rub her perfect new life in his face; it was a cry for help. He swallowed back the bile. The past was the past. He was only thinking about the future now. And he was glad he'd kept it. He traced over the address, stuffed it in his bag along with some clothes, the money he'd borrowed from Warren, and his grandfather's .38 Smith and Wesson. He had a long drive ahead of him. He almost made it out of town but swore the universe had it out for him when, as he filled up the Jeep at the gas station, Katelyn Sullivan pulled up at the pump next to him.

"Shit," he muttered under his breath. Just play it cool. Katelyn won't know a damn thing if I just don't talk.

"Hey, jerk-face," she said lightly, stepping out and grabbing her wallet from the dash. "What the hell are you doing in town this early?"

"Getting gas?" he responded with a scowl. She looked at him from under the brim of her ball cap.

"Yeah, but you have a tank out at Gran's. Why would you come all the way to town for—" she stopped. Blake looked at her. She was staring at his packed bag in the back seat. Katelyn studied him, discerning eyes on the slump of his shoulders, the tension in his jaw. "Where you headed, kid?"

"I'm not a goddamn kid. I'm still two years older than you."

"Answer the question, Blake," Katelyn yelled back, hands on her hips.

"No place you need to worry about, and keep your voice down."

"I'll tell this whole goddamn street you're leaving my sister, you good-for-nothing son-of-a bitch if you don't give me a good reason to keep my mouth shut!" She came through the gas pump island and put a finger to his chest. Blake shuffled back and glowered down at her.

"I'm going to find Aaron," he seethed. "And you can't tell Elle or she'll never let me go." Katelyn's cheeks drained of color.

"Is that the best idea, Blake? The guy's a psychopath."

"I know he's a goddamn psychopath. That's why I'm going to find him before he finds us." The last word felt strangled and beautiful, tender to the ears. "The only way she's ever gonna be free, the only way she'll stop having nightmares is if he—can't come for her."

"Hang on, Blake," Katelyn held out her hand. "That sounds kinda fucking permanent. What exactly are you planning to do once you find him?" Katelyn had lowered her voice. Their initial argument had drawn some attention, but the town was used to them fighting like siblings do. She nonchalantly opened her gas flap, opened the cap, and tried to control the shaking of her hands.

"I don't know." Blake breathed and finished filling his tank. He replaced the nozzle with a resounding thunk. "Let him know someone bigger and stronger is looking out for her now, so he'd better back down," Blake sighed, "and hope that's all it takes. But I—" he took in a steading breath and looked at the duffle bag in the backseat. "I've made a backup plan since it probably won't be that easy."

"Jesus, Blake, you shouldn't be doing this alone. Let me come with you."

"No! Goddamn it, Katie, I'm not going to let you or anyone she loves get in trouble over this."

"Well, what about you, ass hat? She loves you too."

"That's what I hear." He slammed his flap closed and sighed. "All the more reason I need to do this. It shouldn't take me long."

"Unless it fuckin' goes south and then you'll be gone forever." Katelyn crossed her arms over her chest. "She can't lose you, Blake. She just can't," she said, softer, with tears behind her eyes. "She loves you."

"And I love her," he confessed softly. "But I've fucked up a lot in my life, and I need to do this thing for her. I didn't save her the first time, Katelyn."

"None of us did."

"So, let me go. Let me go and do what I can."

Katelyn's eyes filled, and it took her a moment to clear them.

"You'd better come back, you big jerk," she sniffed, and looked up at him. Blake pulled her into his arms for a hug.

"Get out of here before people start thinking we're dating."
She shoved him away. "How long?"

"Week? Maybe two? Think you can keep an eye on her until I
get back?" He swallowed, hoping that would be the case.

"I will." Katelyn nodded. "Until you get back. However long
that takes." She watched as he got in and turned onto the highway.
The direction that led out of town.

TWENTY-THREE

THE SOUND OF JEEP TIRES CRUNCHING IN THE GRAVEL of her driveway made Elle's adrenaline-soaked heart stop. She'd been edgy since he'd gone out that morning. There was something different about Blake since her nightmare. She was wondering if he was reconsidering being with her again. She knew she'd probably rethink it if she were him.

She washed and dried her hands off on the old flour sack dishtowel that hung below the sink. She straightened her hair, checked her face in the glass of the dish cupboard, and took a deep breath before heading out the squeaky screen door.

Blake questioned his sanity as he leaned against his Jeep and listening to the sink stop and the screen door squeak. The Jeep was packed with a bag in the backseat. He should have just gone. He still wasn't sure why he'd even thought to stop on his way out of town. He could have saved them both the awkward hurt, cause he sure as hell couldn't tell her where he was headed, or that he didn't know if he'd make it back alive. But that's what made him turn off on her county road. If this was his last time, he wanted to make one more memory of her before he left.

And what a memory she was making.

He tucked his hands into his pockets as she walked to him with her cut-off blue jeans, hugging her hips just so. Her shirt unbuttoned one button too low for his brain to function. Her hair pinned back from her flushed face. He looked into her eyes and relived every painful memory of their past. He never wanted to see those eyes sad or scared again.

"Where've you been all morning?" she looked behind him to the Jeep, the duffle bag in the back. "What's going on?"

He swallowed painfully and looked away. "I had to gather a few things. I'm headed out of town. For—for a while."

"Out of town where?"

"Elle, I can't—" he sighed and looked away.

"Can't stay or can't tell me where you're headed?"

He swallowed thickly. Goddamn her for knowing him so well. "Both."

Elle untucked her hands from her pockets. She refused to look away even when he did.

"Is this because of—because of the other morning? Because I freaked out?"

"No, please don't think that," he said, too desperately.

"Then, what is it?" she said.

"Elle, I just can't talk to you about it right now. Not yet. But it's got nothing to do with your nightmares." In part, it was a lie. He was going to get rid her of her worst nightmare.

Elle smiled, unexpectedly calm, while he felt like he was falling to pieces in front of her. She leaned in and he leaned back. He was afraid if she threw her arms around him now, he wouldn't go. If he didn't go, she'd never have a chance to be free.

"Not even a hint? Peace Corps? Rodeo? Circus clown?" She paused then, her gears turning. A light lit up in her eyes and excitement bubbled over in a smile. "Is it school? Are you gonna go take your test?"

Blake nearly hit his knees at the way her whole face shone thinking kinder thoughts than he deserved.

"Yeah, something like that."

"What do you mean, something like?"

"It's something I gotta finish, Elle. And I'll tell you about it when I get back. Can you just trust that I know what I'm doing?" he whispered. Trust. Asking the woman he loved to trust him, after so many years of scarring hurt. She stepped away and looked up at him with a strange expression on her face. The gathering thunderheads in the east rumbled and she took a steadying breath.

"I trust you, Blake. And you should know that I'm so—"

"Elle, please don't—"

"Proud," she interrupted him. "I'm so proud of you, Blake. You've worked really hard these last few months and I'm proud of what you've done and whatever it is you're setting your mind to."

Blake's face went pale and he closed his eyes. He grunted and shook his head.

"Elle—"

"All I ever want for you is the world, Blake." She looked up into his eyes lovingly. She was so close he could smell her, feel her warmth. "For you to get out of this town and do right by yourself. I'm so proud of you and if I have to stand here and tell you goodbye—" her voice broke, but she recovered. "Then I'm glad it's for this. For you to be chasing something you love. That's all I've ever wanted for you."

Blake wasn't fooled, and he wasn't convinced she was right. Doing what he loved and having what he wanted had everything to do with staying right here with her. He could see she was holding back tears behind a fine line of stubbornness. She nodded, as if acknowledging the barrier between them, and turned to walk away.

Six years ago, they'd said goodbye when she'd left with the man who'd broken her apart. He had been torn, and achy, and angry. He hadn't wanted her to go, but he thought because he loved her, it was the right thing to do. If Elle loved him even half as much as he had loved her, he knew how her heart was breaking now. Before she could take another step, Blake grabbed her, turned her in his arms, and crushed her to his chest.

Elle clung to him, arms entwining around his back.

"I miss you already. I will miss you until you get back," she said and held him tighter around the strong and healthy muscles. He smoothed his hands over her hair and committed to memory the way her body felt in his arms.

"What am I going to do with you, Sullivan?" he whispered desperately. She looked up at him.

"Well, if you're really asking, I have an idea," she said, and traced his chin with her nose. Blake's face fell into a hard frown, but the way her body trembled against his, stretched his resolve thin.

"Except that, Elle."

"Kiss me," she said. "Unless you really don't want to."

"You know I do."

"Then do," she said and gently bit his jaw. Blake sighed.

"If I kiss you, Elle—"

"Then what?" she asked.

"You know where it'll lead," he said.

"I do. Come on, O'Connor," she whispered and continued kissing his jaw sweetly and slowly. She moved to his neck, the open v of his shirt. It made him dizzy with need. He growled in the back of his throat and held on to her as he turned her mouth to meet his. The kiss was hard, and fast, and hungry. Her breath caught, and he swallowed her surprise.

"I'll miss you too," he grunted between kissing her. She tasted like sweet, and summer, and everything he'd ever wanted. Her soft curves fit deliciously against him until he couldn't think of anything but touching her, tasting, feeling her bare skin on his.

He backed her up towards the house. Frustrated that the rocky ground tripped and tumbled them out of contact, he picked her up, wrapped her legs around his waist, and carried her inside. He banged through the screen door and crossed the kitchen. She gasped as he bit her neck and her shoulders. He set her down and gently led her up the stairs.

Desperation and sadness made him meet every move with eager acceptance. It was more than two scared teenagers on a moonlit night or two love-shy adults bumbling through feelings they were unsure of, keeping their hearts from crossing over into love. The daylight stretched across the bed where Blake laid Elle down and took off the rest of her clothes, his lips never leaving her skin. His hands, rough from hard days of work, trailed up her ribs.

"God, you end me, Elle," he whispered, "in the worst and best of ways." He tossed her shirt to the floor. She lifted his, up and over his broad shoulders, and trailed her fingers over every line and tense muscle, staring with wonder and happiness. "You ogling me?" His scarred eyebrow raised rakishly. Elle blushed and smiled.

"Can't help it. You're beautiful," she said softly and Blake looked as though he might cry. He nudged her down to kiss his way up her stomach. When he reached her mouth, his touch changed. He kissed her more delicately, savoring the slow and sunny moment.

"We both know who's the beautiful one in this bed," he said, and ran his thumb over her bottom lip. His touch softened, and she felt not the angry passion of before, but the loving need in him. He gently pressed her into the bed and memorized her face. His eyes turned sad.

"Blake, you know I lo—"

Blake kissed her quiet. "Shh...I know," he whispered into her lips. He undid her shorts, slid them down her legs, and she shivered in the heat of the afternoon. His touch was halting and tender and she opened her eyes to find his. They were soft and dark blue and his face showed the strange juxtaposition of pain and desire; his denial and his need. The history of hurt and bad choices that had nearly destroyed this moment.

They were both mending, both formerly battered. Once heartbroken, just now learning how to heal. And he shouldn't be here, he should be on the road, heading west, he should be fighting for her future. But the present, in this sunlit bed, with the girl he loved, finally having a purpose and a reason, maybe was the most important memory he could make. She accepted his kiss and his warmth pressing her into the bed like a bandage holding her pieces together.

He was lost in her soft honey skin. She smelled of sweet grass and fresh air, and her curls tickled his neck as she reached to kiss him. Her hands made no apologies or hesitations about undressing him and when, in the heat of that afternoon, he came to her filled with a thousand different reasons to love her and equally as many to leave, Blake let his heart go.

"Elle," he whispered as his hands caressed her face, her neck, took her round breasts gently in his hands. She arched to him, gasped in surrender to everything and anything he offered. Blake kissed her tenderly, felt her heart beating beneath his hands as he caressed her. She nuzzled his neck, breathed in the smell of him, and closed her eyes to seal it into her memory.

When he nudged her legs apart with his knee, she lifted them to grip his waist. He shook from the effort to hold back and he met her eyes with his as he slid gently inside of her, fitting together like two perfectly matched pieces. Elle's eyes turned stormy as she gasped. Her head fell back into his hands and he bit her neck. So tight. So warm. So perfect the fit. He murmured delicately into her neck, incoherent loving words. Her hips rose and fell against his as they moved together, deep and slow, savoring every shiver that rolled through them. Her nails dug into his back when he quickened the pace.

"Blake," she cried, and felt her whole world tumble out of control.

"There," he whispered, knowing. "More there, just there—" he grunted and shook, and she felt him swell inside of her. She cried out in desperate release and clung to him as he crested and crushed her against him and into the bed.

Their bodies rocked together as the storm quieted. He kissed her lips hesitantly, as if she might break in his arms. His Elle. Beautiful, stubborn Elle. He studied her face, glowing with satisfaction. Her eyelashes touched pink cheeks, and only fluttered open when his kisses stopped.

She looked into his tormented eyes and couldn't place what she found there. Love? Fear? Regret and uncertainty? They all mixed in a cocktail in his brain and made him drunk with confusion.

"I love you, Blake," she said.

"Goddamn it, Elle."

"That's what a girl wants to hear." She smiled and kissed him. Her legs pulled him in and he felt her tighten around him from inside. He groaned and shivered.

"Jesus, Elle—I—" He should have said the words...should tell her how much he loved her. But it wouldn't be fair to tell her he loved her and then leave, maybe never to come back. It wouldn't be fair to himself to say those things, with his whole heart behind them, and not be able to stay in this bed with her, in this house, on this land. His thoughts were chaotic and Blake tightened his jaw, dropped his eyes, and pulled away.

He got out of bed and dressed without a word. Elle watched as he slid on his jeans, feeling the change in him like a wall of cold air coming down over the mountains. He walked to the window and stared out at the fading green leaves that would be turning to gold in a few days. He thought of pumpkins, and hot cider, and hayrides and all the things he may miss out on. His heart broke and he closed his eyes. If he really loved her then he had to go. So she could move on. So she could have a life. A new life. Not one tarnished by the past or darkened by the fear that followed her.

"I'm still leaving. I—I have to—"

"I know," she said and got dressed. He looked back and watched her reaching back to hook her bra and the delicate way her shoulder blades stuck out like angel wings.

"I may not—come back." His voice wavered.

"You'll come back."

She said the words, but she didn't know, Blake thought, nearly bursting into tears. He could die. He could be sent to prison. A million things could go wrong just to give her a chance at freedom. And he was scared, and hurt, and he just wanted to stay. But it wouldn't be a life worth living if she was always looking over her shoulder.

"But what if I don't?" His heart tore out of his throat.

"It's pretty clear that you're trying to convince yourself more than me." She came closer, her voice calm and soft.

Blake felt his heart stop in his chest. He couldn't tell her. She would try to stop him. She would worry. She'd blame herself. It had nothing to do with fooling his breaking heart. It had everything to do with trying to save her from any more agony. Elle reached up on her bare feet, kissed his rough cheek, turned and left the room without looking back.

Blake went to the bathroom, splashed cold water on his face, and stared at the man in the mirror. A man he was proud to be. A man who would do anything for the woman he loved, even if it meant leaving her. When he came downstairs, she stood at the kitchen sink, looking out into the yard. He froze the moment in his mind, her sunlit hair golden and soft, pink lips roughened by his kisses. There was a small bite mark on her neck. Jesus, he shouldn't have. Everything had been so clear in his mind before he'd taken her to bed. Now, he was dreamy and euphoric, and she loved him, and he didn't want to leave.

"There's some iced tea and a snack on the table for the trip." He looked to the neat little basket full of his favorite oatmeal raisin cookies and the mason jar of ice-cold tea. She certainly knew how to make leaving harder and loving her all the easier.

"Elle—"

"Drive carefully," she whispered, taking the basket and holding it out to him. He hesitated. "Be safe, wherever you're headed."

"Elle—I—" Blake stepped across the shining kitchen floor and took the basket. He bent his head and gently grazed her lips. She touched his cheek and held his open hand with hers, the fingertips intertwining. She shook her head.

"Please don't go."

"Elle, I have to."

"If you really have to, I won't stop you. Just come back to me, ok? I'll still be here."

"Damn it, Elle," he sobbed and kissed her, biting into her mouth and holding her close.

"Goodbye, Blake," she said breathlessly when he pulled away.

"Bye, Elle." He wiped his eyes and stormed out of the kitchen, down the steps, across the drive and to his Jeep.

He made it to the highway before he broke into tears.

Twenty-Four

ELLE WAS MAKING A PIE. ACTUALLY, SHE'D MADE FOUR. The crabapple orchard started bearing fruit, and she stayed up late into the night to can her first apple butter before starting the pies. She told herself she was staying up to finish the project, and not waiting for him to come back. She still didn't know exactly where he'd gone. Or why he'd left, even before summer was over.

Had she gotten too close? Was he that scared of being with her? He didn't seem scared. Maybe he thought she wanted him to become a vet and felt like she'd backed him into a corner. She'd never meant to make him feel that way. How, in the course of a few days, she had gone from the pinnacle of happiness to this moping sadness was beyond her. But the yo-yo tug of emotion stopped her up short, and she slumped into a kitchen chair and stared at the settling dust for the next few moments before standing back up. She couldn't afford to think about it. She had business that didn't stop for broken hearts.

Elle sighed and started on her grandma's Crabby Pie recipe. Using the best of the apple crop, she'd started the pies in the early dawn and called around town to see if any of the restaurants would be interested in trying them. The Roost had agreed to buy all of the first round.

When she'd called Judy Prym, she'd told her that a reporter from the Casper Tribune had come to town last week and reviewed her baked goods, calling them 'a taste of home and a mouthful of comfort'. Judy suggested she start a website for her business so she could take in orders from around the state. Just the idea of the planning and coordinating she'd need to do consumed her aching heart and worried mind.

She went through the new and old recipes in her mind while she baked. She told herself that caring for the business was centering to her soul and was more necessary than calling Blake's cell phone...again. She told herself that multiple times in the day, all the while keeping one ear on the drive for the sound of his Jeep.

He didn't come home that day.

Or the next.

By Friday, Elle's worry turned to anger. If he was going back to school, why hadn't he just said so? If he was leaving her because he didn't want to be with her anymore, why didn't he just say so? She thought they'd overcome the whole 'not being honest with each other' thing. What if he was drinking again or passed out in some motel room, or worse; in the arms of another woman? Elle gritted her teeth and accidentally peeled her knuckle instead of the apple she held.

He'd gotten scared off by her crazy. The nightmare from her trauma had been too much. Her rational brain couldn't seem to get through to her survival instincts to stop the fear. Elle stopped peeling and looked down at the pristine white flesh of the apple streaked with red. A stain on the pure white of its flesh.

Blake didn't deserve to be haunted by her past too.

KATELYN VISITED THAT FRIDAY, BURSTING INTO THE barn, just like she lived there. Elle was torn between needing the distraction and wanting to be left alone. Katelyn and looked quizzically at her when Elle hauled hay to the horses, alone.

"Where's the punk?" she asked.

"Gone," was all she replied.

"Still?"

"What?"

"I meant, where? *Where* is he?"

"Hell, if I know." Elle pitched a large forkful of hay into the trough and turned for another. "He had living to get on with, I suppose."

Katelyn's brow furrowed, and she kicked dust. "Come on, Elle. Blake wouldn't just leave."

"Well, he did, okay?"

"It's probably nothing." She shuffled her boots and avoided Elle's eyes. "Have you asked Dad?"

"Why would Dad know, and I wouldn't?" Elle grouched back. Katelyn sighed and left without saying goodbye. Elle watched her go. She had too many things to get done today to let herself succumb to the heartache that threatened to drop her to her knees.

She was sure the news was already blowing through town about what had become of Blake O'Connor and Eleanor Sullivan. No one had seen him in the bars. She spent the last few days keeping busy at home in an effort to not give them more to talk about. She was close to setting up contracts with the local stores to carry her baked goods along with catering menus they could collaborate on. She created a website and picked a launch date. She signed a contract with two other restaurants in a neighboring town for her biscuits and baked goods.

In a fit of Pinterest creativity, she'd shadowboxed the first three checks she'd earned after remotely depositing the funds. She hung them above the calendar by the door, where they reminded her, every morning over her coffee cup, how far she'd come. Alone, without Blake, she could hear herself think, feel her resilience steady her brain and allow her to sort through the years of abuse she'd suffered and the losses she'd taken. The time and things she'd lost became less her mistake and more rightly the victim of Aaron's cruelty.

In the new quiet and loneliness, with her heart broken to hell and her future of living one long day at a time, Elle found comfort in walking outside in the darkest part of the night. She stood on the front porch and let her hands dangle at her sides. Even in the thick silence, where only the things that hid, and those that hunted came out, she would make herself close her eyes and hold her breath. At first the fear would hit her, sharp and spiking up the length of her spine, *open your eyes*, her brain would cry.

Open your eyes, you don't know what's out there. He could be behind you. Protect your head! Cower, run, scurry.

"No," she would whisper to the voice inside. The voice of her past. Of the woman who had somehow survived. She held no hatred or blame for that woman. She held no guilt over having been the one, hugging her hands tight across her body, shrinking from the danger. That woman survived. But she was now the woman who lived. She'd more than survived. She'd been reborn.

So, in the darkest part of the night, where the soft silence of owl wings glided somewhere to her left, and the sudden snatching squeal of its prey called out...when the lonesome coyote three miles to the south called to his cohorts in sharp yipping cries and got a holler-back, she kept her eyes closed. She kept breathing; kept living.

The brink of the cliff she'd clambered back from was always an edge in her heart, but she refused to be controlled by it. So, she played the game nearly every night. And every night when she went back inside, poured a cup of tea and went upstairs to bed, she was calm. If she could survive this night, this solitude, and all of the challenges in her day, she would survive—even thrive, for the next fifty years all the same. She would continue working, planning, and carefully going through the motions of making her life her own.

One afternoon, over a week since Blake had gone, she pored over the ledgers, splayed out amongst pies and various other orders. The numbers in black finally outnumbered the ones in the red. She had enough to take a check to her parents the next day. Her heart nearly beat itself out of her chest. Being able to help save her family's land was more than she could have wanted.

"Well, I guess that's one lost cause, no longer lost," she said to the empty kitchen. Only then did she stop to feel the silence. Only then did she stop to think about how she'd lost him because she couldn't stop the deluge of trauma that was bound to resurface in some form or another for the rest of her life. She wiped her nose on her sleeve. Ending six years with Aaron hadn't been nearly as painful as losing Blake O'Connor for the second time. She sighed and shook her head.

"Back to work, sap," she said.

Another round of pies cooled on the tables and sideboards of the house before she boxed them up. The last one in the oven was for her neighbor down the road who had just had a baby. Elle made its top especially pretty, with flower cutouts and brushed egg wash, and sprinkled it with sugar to make it sparkle. She tucked the pie in to a large wicker basket with some fresh eggs and an economy-size pack of diapers. She stepped back to look at the basket, waiting expectantly by the door.

Would she ever have another chance to be a mom? The only man she'd even consider a family with was—somewhere else now. Elle gave in to the flash fantasy of a blue-eyed baby, his perfect pout, and her cheeks. Her heart contracted in her chest. She and Blake hadn't been very careful in their week of rampant love making. Elle's gut tumbled as her mind scrolled through the calendar, trying to remember when she last had a period.

"Probably not," she said to herself. After all the damage the fall had caused to her body, a baby may never be in her future. Since the oven was hot, she made a large batch of cookies for the church bake sale and cleaned the kitchen. Then she piled the pie boxes carefully into totes to be taken into town that evening.

Even though her mind stayed busy during the day with all of the responsibilities of the ranch and her new business, it always found Blake in vivid dreams. Dreams, where he sat across the table from her, but when she reached out, the table grew longer and longer until they were miles apart. Dreams where she stood in the high prairie grass alone against a massive wall of thunderstorms looming in the distance and his voice echoing in every rumble.

I'm not coming back.

One evening she'd fallen asleep while reading about the benefits and drawbacks of alpacas, and found herself in the throes of a vision that caused her heart to beat madly and sweat to drench her body. Storm clouds were again on the horizon and the ferocious wind whipped around her, tearing at her clothing and hair. She felt the electricity of the storm's building pressure, as though it meant to strike her down. Through the wind and the thunderous sound of the storm, she heard a cry come from the other side of the wall of clouds.

Without thought for her own safety, she ran headlong, into the murderous black and towards the small sound. The second she breached the line of clouds, the storm stopped and she found herself in a lush field of sweet hay, high as her waist. Blake, in his weathered flannel shirt and jeans, held a soft white bundle against his chest. Cherub arms reached out from the blanket to touch his face and cooing laughter filled the space.

Elle walked towards them and this time, instead of the field growing between them like the table, keeping them forever out of reach from one another, each step brought her closer to him and the bundle in his arms. Blake handed her the baby and his strong arms went around them both. The warmth of the child, the soft smell of her skin next to Elle made her world spin with elation. A rush of chemicals filled her blood stream and the echoing sound of Blake's voice, his lips near her forehead, whispered.

You did it, Elle...she's perfect.

Elle startled awake, tumbled from bed, and sat on the old wooden floor with her knees tucked tight to her chest. The most intense part of the dream wasn't the baby. It was seeing him so clearly. And how the denial of missing him in the day couldn't compare to the truth her resting mind knew. She dialed his phone. It went straight to voice mail.

"Still here," she said in a sleep roughened voice. "Still missing you." Elle hung up the phone and sobbed into her knees.

TWENTY-FIVE

BLAKE DIDN'T KNOW HOW ELLE COULD HAVE STOOD this place for as long as she had. The smog, the heat, the crush of traffic and people. The noise. Blake had taken his time on the drive. He knew he needed the space to think, to plan out for every possibility. He'd pulled plates off one of the old pickups at the junkyard to switch for his own, and picked up a burner phone at a truck stop in St. George. He drove the speed limit and made no mistakes. The last thing he needed was to get pulled over and a record being made of him on his way to Aaron.

Blake made it into the city limits of L.A. four months after Elle had taken her life into her own hands and run away from there. As soon as she'd been well enough to run; after Aaron had killed her baby and had almost killed her. Fire reignited in Blake's veins. He'd tried not to think about what might happen when he confronted Aaron. He tried not to think about what he might do when he saw his stupid, sharp-chinned face, or what kind of violence would follow if Aaron found out Blake was with his soon-to-be-ex-wife. He didn't know if the guy was over her, and moved on, or would if he'd try to make a stand. What Blake did know, for certain, that the outcome would be the same. Aaron would never bother Elle again.

His gut twisted and burned as he navigated slowly through the five lanes of westbound traffic. It was getting late in the day. He wanted to be rested, ready for whatever was coming. He pulled off and found a hotel three miles from her old apartment. The single bag he took into his room was light; just a change of clothes and his revolver.

Blake didn't know what constituted 'early' in L.A., but he was up at six the next morning, pacing his room, brewing a cup of shitty coffee in the small gurgling pot, and wondering if the last sunrise he saw was going to be shrouded in smog. He wondered, if things went wrong, who'd find Aaron's body? He wondered if things went really wrong, who would find his? Would he get caught? Would he spend the rest of his life in prison so she could be free? Blake rubbed his forehead. He wanted to hear her voice. To know she was all right before his life turned to hell.

He reached for the burner phone, dialed the number, and imagined the melodic tone of the kitchen phone echoing through the house. She was probably already out with the goats; she may not even hear—

"Hello?" Elle's voice sang.

"Elle," he whispered.

"Blake? Where are you? Are you okay?"

"I just—I just wanted to hear your voice."

"Blake, honey, you don't sound well? Are you all right?"

"I'm—I'm going to be fine. I just—I wanted you to know that."

"What do you mean, you're *going* to be fine? What kind of cryptic bullshit is that? Are you in some kind of trouble?"

"Don't worry about me, just promise me you'll take care of yourself."

"Blake, what—"

"I love you, Elle. I always have. I will for the rest of my life," he choked and hung up. He shut the phone off. By calling her, he'd left a trace that the authorities could follow back to find him. At least he got to hear her voice; at least she knew that he loved her.

———

"BLAKE? BLAKE, DAMN YOU! WHAT IN THE HELL DOES that mean?" Elle yelled into the dead line and startled the birds on the feeder outside. She tried redialing the number. Nothing. She grabbed her coat and keys. Someone had to know what was going on and, goddamn it, she was going to find out what.

She drove with her hands clenched tight on the wheel. Her heart couldn't stop skipping beats, and she felt light-headed. He'd sounded scared. Sad but determined. He said he was going to be okay, but she didn't believe it. How could he be okay if he wasn't with her? Where had he gone? Was he drinking again? What kind of trouble was he in? Her jaw began to ache from clenching her teeth and the old wounds of being struck by fists not worthy of her.

Elle turned up at her parents' place. The few quarter horses they still kept grazed in fields on either side of the road, and the sturdy but decades-old stables and modest house with its large front porch greeted her. Melissa had put out her chrysanthemum pots for the season, a sure sign it was now officially fall, even with the still-warm days. Soon there would be hayrides and corn mazes and cold crisp nights. Elle's favorite season and she'd be alone, maybe forever. Her gut contracted and a new nausea hit her. She got out of the truck and bent over, with her hands on her knees until it passed. He'd officially worried her sick. Elle marched up to the door and walked right in.

"Mom? Dad?" she called. No answer came, so she searched through the rooms and went through the back door in the kitchen. The yard was empty and quiet. "Mom?"

"Hullo!" she heard her dad call from the stables, probably in his office working on paperwork. More likely taking a nap. Elle stomped through the yard, through the back gate, and into the building. The cool smell of hay dust and horse, the comforting shade and wood floors helped to calm her in the corner of her heart that still called this place home.

"Dad?"

"In the office, Elle." he said. She came through the door and found him, boots on the desk, looking over a file from the clinic, half-moon specs tipped down on the ball of his nose. "What's up, honey? You alright?" He took his feet down and moved to stand.

"Where is he, Dad?" she said. Warren looked at her, hands on her hips, just like his mother, strong and tall. No longer the cowering woman who had come home, but the daughter who survived.

"Uh—who?" he asked.

"Don't pull that shit with me, you know who."

"Eleanor Augusta," he reprimanded, but rethought his outrage at her unflinching gaze.

"He called me this morning, from a number I didn't recognize, and said he loved me, to not worry that I would be fine. That I needed to know he'd be fine. What the hell is going on? Where did he go?"

"Elle, I don't—"

"I know you know! Katelyn asked if he was still gone, and that I should ask you. So what is it that everyone else can know, but I can't?" Temper rose in her cheeks and she paced closer. Warren looked over the top of his glasses.

"Now, I didn't know that Katelyn knew anything about it."

"Don't change the subject."

"Blake and I both agreed that the less you knew the better, and that's all I'm going to say."

"So, you *do* know! Why would you lie to me? Your own daughter?"

"Elle, he has reasons."

"Well, that's not good enough, Dad. We all have reasons, and if he doesn't want me knowing them, then they must be something bad. What has he gotten himself into?"

Her dad shook his head in a way that meant he was done talking.

"I can't believe either of you. Secrets and lies! Running off, worrying me—"

"He's got something that needs to be done." Warren slapped the file down on the desk, took off his glasses and rubbed his eyes.

"The man I love left, and I don't know if he's ever coming back." Elle willed the tears away and stormed out of the stables, back to her truck, and sped out the drive. She looked in the rearview mirror and saw her dad, growing smaller where he stood by the barn. She took the turn away from town and up the winding mountain road.

In no mood to face the home they once shared, and the now empty spaces that he once filled, Elle meandered up the dirt road, framed with the newly turned leaves of aspen and cottonwoods. She pulled over at one of the smaller trail heads along the river and got out. She stood beside the babbling brook, now much slower that the snow had all but melted off from above and the winter had not yet hit. She stared at the rocks that once were covered by the cold rushing current. Now exposed, thirsty and open to the world.

She'd just gotten back on her feet, and now everything felt like it was falling down around her. Where would Blake go that he couldn't come back from? If he loved her so much, what would be more important than coming back to her? Her phone pinged from her pocket and she scrambled for it.

A message from Judy—asking if she could add to her order. Elle sighed. She could stand beside a drying river all day, pining for the loss of love, or she could get her shit together and do her job. She sighed, closed her eyes, and stowed the pain back into her chest. Worrying about it wasn't going to solve anything. She returned to town and the list that had grown longer.

It was another full day and though she was busy enough to not dwell on Blake, she could still hear his voice ringing through her ears. *I love you. Always have. For the rest of my life.* But he had something to do, without her. Why would he want to be without her if he loved her that much?

"Maybe it's time I let go of that lost cause," she grumbled. She had living to get on with, a business to run, and a whole list of things to do. She didn't want to waste any more time thinking about Blake when she had no power to change the situation. She tapped her finger on the counter and looked out the window to where the sheep wagon sat beside the barn, empty. Reminders of him everywhere. As soon as the biscuits were done, she pulled them out, shut off the oven and put on her boots.

With single-minded determination, she hooked up the wagon to the tractor and pulled it around the other side of the barn, out of her line of sight. But it did nothing to ease how she still missed his smell. His voice. Seeing him from afar, lumbering through the field, broad shoulders and cowboy hat tipped down. She missed the way he stomped his boots on the kitchen rug, hoping it would be enough before she'd insisted that he take them off. The way his white tube socks would pull loose when he tugged the boots off with a curse. She missed his stubble, his smile. His angry insistence that she butt out of his life. His eyes; sometimes dark and seeped in thought, sometimes laughing with a near lavender hue.

She missed all that he was, and all she was with him.

Elle grabbed the keys from the sideboard and slipped on her jacket. She went to the truck and forced her to do list over memories of Blake. The order of business cards, flyers, and pie boxes should be at the post today. The goats were running low on vitamin B so she needed to go to the feed store. The grocery store got its truck in on Tuesday and she wanted to be among the first to get the best produce in the dwindling season.

It sure was easier when Blake was there to divide and conquer the lists. Elle sighed as he fell into her thoughts again. The grocery store was busy. Chuck Hayes caught her in the canned soup aisle and began a long conversation about his wife's knitting group looking forward to local wool in the valley and did she think she'd be shearing her angoras?

When Elle had politely extricated herself, she wandered into the dairy aisle and picked up extra butter for the pies and the homemade rolls she'd promised to bring to the family picnic. Her mouth watered. Warm rolls with heaps of butter, green beans cooked in bacon fat, and tart apple and cherry pie with whipped cream sounded divine. Peanut butter sounded good too. And apples. She needed lots of apples.

Alice O'Connor, Blake's second cousin, surprised her with a loud gasp from behind.

"Well, Elle Sullivan, it's been years!" The bustling older woman forced a hug on Elle. "Why you ain't any bigger than a bean pole. Aren't you eatin' any of that delicious stuff you've been selling? What happened to that no-account cousin of mine?" Alice looked around Elle's shoulder as if Blake had ducked behind her to hide. Elle wouldn't have blamed him.

"He's...uh, he's gone, Alice. He's—moved."

"Moved?"

"Yeah."

"Well, that's the first time I heard it put that way. The rumor mill says he took your money and ran." Elle clenched back the hatred rising in her throat. Goddamn busybodies. No wonder Blake yelled at them after the dance.

"Well, he didn't," she said. "He earned money interning with Dad for a while and then moved on to bigger and better things. I suspect he's gone back to get his license, or found a better job." Elle fished for any reason that would put Blake in a good light and shut the woman up.

Alice eyed her suspiciously. "Really? *My* cousin, Blake O'Connor? Finally getting his license? To be a vet?"

"I—I guess. You probably ought to ask him yourself, next time you see him." Elle's words trailed off. She picked up a carton of cream cheese and looked over the label to avoid Alice's gaze.

"Well, I suppose I should get back to it. You see him, you give him my best."

"Will do," Elle nodded as Alice left to finish her own shopping. Elle wanted to go home. She hadn't thought about how she'd react to anyone asking about him.

Elle spent thirty minutes in the small store, loading up on extra pie-making ingredients for the Labor Day picnic as well as two large jars of peanut butter and a bag of apples. The bright, golden-red skins of the Honeycrisp apples made her think of his favorite pie and wondered if she should make the crumb topped apple, just in case he made it back.

Her fingers dug into the two-pound bag of brown sugar. She couldn't think that way. He'd made it pretty clear he had no intention of coming back to Sweet Valley. Life didn't work in fairytales and she reprimanded herself for thinking that it would be any different for them. She threw in the sugar anyway, resolving to make the pie for herself, and stalked to the checkout line. She left as quickly as possible and stopped at the post office.

Blake was still getting some things. Mostly just junk; credit card applications, student loan offers, and the occasional veterinarian informational brochure from other schools. She ran her finger over his name and then dropped it all in the trash. She picked up the large box of her "Raising Elle's Bakery" marketing materials and sped back home.

Twenty-Six

Blake's hand was steady; his mind clear. The quick knocks were self-assured, and he waited patiently for a response. One hand on the stock of the gun tucked in the back of his jeans, the other in his front pocket nonchalantly. Shuffling on the other side of the door caused his pulse to spike. Here it was...how could he even look at the son-of-a-bitch without knocking every single one of his teeth out? Blake clenched his jaw, knocked crisply twice more, and the door opened.

Blake looked down to meet the small Filipino woman's smiling face.

"Yes?"

"Uh—I think I have the wrong apartment." Blake said and glanced back up at the door's number. The same one on her invitation. He hadn't thought she'd moved in the time they'd been here, but maybe—

The older woman looked up at him appreciatively.

"You're tall. You look like a cowboy." She smiled. Blake, taken aback, took his hand off the gun and took a step back in a flustered, aw-shucks manner.

"I'm sorry to disturb you, ma'am. I was looking for Aaron Lowry? I think he used to live here?"

"Oh, are you with the police?"

"No? Have the police been here?"

"They came by a few days ago. I told them that ugly man hasn't lived here since last spring. You sure you aren't with them? Like—a Texas ranger or something?" Her eyes sparkled.

"No," Blake sighed. "I'm a friend of his—wife—" the word stuck in his throat.

"Oh! You know Elle?"

Blake's heart leapt, and he resisted the urge to grill the older woman for information.

"I do."

"Is she okay? I know the apartment was abandoned and then they broke the locks and cleaned it out. I'd been waiting for a third floor so I was excited. But, I miss that girl! She used to go to the grocery store for me and watch my grandbabies."

"She's certainly a sweetheart," he choked.

"I was worried he killed her! That he killed her and ran away. I'm glad she's ok," she said and turned to walk away. When Blake didn't follow, she turned back. "Well? Come in, I just made sisig!"

"Uh, I don't—" She came back, grabbed him sternly by the wrist, and led him inside to the kitchen. Blake looked around. No sign of Elle remained, but he did see inconsistencies in the wall, places that had been patched over and repaired. Where fists were probably laid. He swallowed.

"Ma'am, do you know where Aaron went?"

She gave a dismissive click of her tongue and made him sit at the oak table where she laid a bowl of pork, onion, and chili peppers in front of him with a spoon.

"This looks amazing but I—"

"No friend of Elle's is going to come to my house and not be fed."

"No wonder you two got along," he smiled.

"But you need to tell me she's OK." The woman shook a wooden spoon at him and her mouth was stern.

"She's fine," he said. "She's safe. She's—" Blake looked around. He had to trust that this woman wasn't somehow in contact with Aaron. "She's back home with family."

"Thank god—and you? Are you looking after her?" Another shake of the spoon and a hard glare.

"Yes ma'am. I'm trying to, at least."

"Eat!" She tapped his arm with the spoon and waited until he took a bite of the tangy and spicy mix. His mouth was on fire and his eyes watered.

"Jumpin' Jesus, that's hot. And good," he sniffed and took another bite. The woman cackled approvingly and sat down beside him.

"I don't know where he went, but I'll tell you what I told the police. Aaron went out late one night and just never came back. She disappeared too. Neither came back. They stopped paying the rent. The landlord emptied out all the stuff they left. Then, I got the apartment after." The woman waved her hand as if brushing away smoke that disappeared into the air.

"Is that all that happened?" Blake said, pausing the fork at his mouth.

"Close enough," her brown eyes met his and a mischievous twinkle lit them.

LATER THAT MORNING, BLAKE CHECKED WITH THE landlord. Aaron had left no forwarding address. Neither had Elle. Though, he suspected, everything had been in Aaron's name anyway. He hadn't wanted Elle to exist outside of him. In all his efforts to control her, erase her as a person, he'd made it easier for her to get away. But now, Blake was at a loss. If he wasn't here, where was he? The neighbors didn't know. Blake had gotten the name of Aaron's employer and was headed there. Maybe they had forwarding information.

A week in L.A. made him hungry for home and every minute he spent in the asphalt-driven heat and grimy streets, was a minute he missed her and felt like space and time were growing between them. What if he did make it back and she wouldn't forgive him for leaving? The car dealership was on the corner of a busy intersection, and Blake had to drive around to find a parking spot. He didn't take the gun.

The dealership itself was shady. Flickering florescent lights and worn, dirty tiles led the path to the lone reception desk. Behind it was a woman angling her phone for the best selfie she could take in the poor lighting. Blake looked around. There were two men in sport coats and slovenly ties already talking to customers. Neither of them was Aaron. He approached the young Instagram star and cleared his throat.

"Hey," he said. She didn't look up until she'd taken at least five more shots of her best pouty face.

"Yes?" Her tone said he was interrupting her launch into stardom. Certainly not the small town greeting he was used to.

"I'm looking for Aaron Lowry?" The woman rolled her eyes and settled her scowl on him.

"You and me both."

"He's not in today?"

"He hasn't been in for months. I should've known that asshole wouldn't stick around long," she grumbled. Blake looked down at her name tag briefly, trying to not linger on the tight t-shirt.

"What do you mean by that, Vicki?" he asked. The woman scratched her bleached-blonde hair and looked around to where the salespeople were still busy.

"Aaron—" she paused to sigh, "promised he was going to leave his wife for me. We were in a relationship. But then, a week before it was supposed to be done, he just didn't show up. Figures, right?"

"You were having an affair with him?" Blake wasn't surprised at the affair, but that Vicki would be so open about it.

"Why wouldn't I? Aaron said his wife was a lazy, no-good, dead weight in his life. Some small-town yokel that he had to support," she scoffed and adjusted her fake breasts. Blake clenched his fists on the desk. "What do you want with Aaron?"

"I'm just—an old college buddy and heard he worked here. Do you know where his wife is?" Vicki studied him, a lingering caress of eyes that said she was already past Aaron.

"Wherever Aaron is, I guess? I should have known he'd never leave her. It was almost sick how he kept her so close all the time... maybe I dodged a bullet, huh? Listen, if you're not busy, it's almost my lunch break." she added with a smile. Blake leaned back.

"I really ought to go," he said.

Blake left the dealership quickly. One thing stuck in his mind; wherever Elle was, Aaron would be. She'd only been gone a few months. Maybe it had taken him that long to figure out where she'd run. Maybe it had taken him that long to plan his revenge. Maybe while Blake had been out looking for him, Aaron was already on his way to Elle.

Blake had the sickening thought that Aaron could have been already watching her, waiting for the right moment. When Elle was broken hearted, vulnerable; alone. Blake tried not to let the thoughts get ahead of themselves, but they piggy-backed on one another until he was rushing out into the boulevard and headed for his Jeep. He had to get back to Elle before Aaron found her. Blake kicked himself for thinking he could have protected her by leaving her. His chest filled with anxiety and he got back into the Jeep and sped away, hell-bent for home.

TWENTY-SEVEN

ELLE SWORE SHE'D HEARD SOMETHING IN THE NIGHT. But her body was so tired from working over sixteen-hour days that she didn't have the energy to get up in the dark to see what it was. Who knew what wild critter was out there? Probably deer or maybe even a wayward moose or elk. When she rose the next morning, she looked out her window in early dawn to see a horse, quietly pulling up and munching the carrots from her garden.

"Lottie?" Elle said and ran through the house and out the kitchen door in her bare feet. Ignoring the prickly weeds and rocks, she jetted across the lawn and slowed as she approached the mare. "Where have you been?" Elle breathed as Lottie looked up and grunted. She was coated in mud from the river, and her hooves were worn. Elle wondered how many miles she'd ran and what kind of company she'd kept in the last few weeks.

"Doesn't matter," Elle whispered. "You're home now." Elle's eyes filled with tears and she ran her hands up Lottie's withers and to her neck. The mare leaned into the affection and offered Elle an appeased grunt. From across the gravel drive, Goliath's echoing cry caused her to perk up her ears and nicker.

"He's been missing you something awful."

Lottie huffed in agreement and took off towards the paddock behind the barn. Elle walked alongside her and opened the gate to let her in. Goliath greeted her with a trumpeting whinny, and they touched noses before winding their necks together and walking off towards the watering trough. Elle smiled to watch them and quickly went to fill the feeder with fresh hay and put out a new salt lick. She let the goats out in the adjacent paddock and Lottie greeted them at the fence, like a big sister coming home.

For a moment, in that peaceful morning, Elle's world and heart were almost full again. She called her dad and mom to tell them the good news and Warren agreed to come over later that morning and check the mare out to make sure she hadn't suffered any injuries. Katelyn said she'd come too. Life without Blake was rough, but it seemed the world was filling in his space with love just the same.

DETECTIVE MARIA BARBOZA TOOK THE SHAKY STAIRS off the small jet carefully and nearly kissed the cracked and aging tarmac at the bottom. It was barren, and dry, and windy. She tightened her blazer close to her body, fighting back the nausea from the horrific turbulence and the noisy, reeking old plane that may have been held together with duct tape. She knew she had no real jurisdiction here. She knew she could have just called the number listed for Eleanor Sullivan's family and hope they would tell her.

But after questioning witnesses, learning of Eleanor's story, so much like her own, she needed the closure of finding the woman and making sure her body wasn't somewhere, unfound, unmarked in L.A. County. Barboza hated loose ends. The only way she could sleep at night was to make sure justice was served, and that no one had gotten away with a crime. She was going to find Aaron Lowry's wife, and put the case to rest.

Mid-afternoon, three pies, and six dozen biscuits covering the kitchen counters later, Elle was packaging up the last pie for Prym's when a car pulled in front of the house. The driver parked in front of the 'official' front door. The door only a stranger would use, driving a rental without of state plates. A short, dark-haired Latina woman got out, stretched as if she'd been in the car for a while, and reached into the back seat for her suit jacket. As she turned to sling it on, Elle saw the flash of a badge and a gun at her belt.

The sun darkened, and Elle couldn't seem to find air for breathing. That wasn't a small-town sheriff. She looked like L.A.

Elle looked around to the bright and clean kitchen, the smell of baking and warmth, the beautiful little world she'd worked so hard to build. The life she'd fought to get back to. The strength she had earned. The world inside of herself she was building. She didn't know how the conversation was going to go, but she knew she wasn't going to lose her new life.

"Gran—I sure wish you were here," she said as she sat down at the kitchen table and waited.

When the knock came on her door, Elle took a deep breath and waited until the count of five. She picked up a stack of mail and flung a dishcloth over her shoulder as if to reinforce the idea of a busy woman in the middle of her day, not a paralyzed one waiting for her whole world to change. She swung open the living room door with a bright smile.

"Yes?" Her eyes landed on Barboza.

"Mrs. Eleanor Lowry?"

Elle stared at her for a half second, the name making her shudder with disgust.

"It's Sullivan now," Elle corrected.

"Ah—OK. Formerly, Mrs. Lowry?" Barboza asked, flipping through her notes.

"Yes. Formerly."

"I'm a detective with the L.A.P.D. I have a few questions about your husband, Aaron." Barboza flashed her ID and watched Elle's reaction. Elle looked down at the badge and back up into Barboza's face, unflinching.

"Ex-husband. Or soon to be, as soon as he signs the papers. Is this about the papers?"

"No, Miss Sullivan. I'm sorry to inform you that your husband's remains were recently found in the Angeles National Forest."

"Remains? What do you mean 'remains'?" Elle searched the detective's eyes.

"A fire clean-up crew discovered them a few months back. We were only just recently able to get the dental records to confirm."

"I—I don't understand—" Elle's brow dropped.

"I was hoping you could tell me what he was doing up there. You didn't report him missing?"

"I left Aaron in April. He and I—" she swallowed back the bile in her throat. "Would you like to come in, Detective—"

"Barboza."

"Detective Barboza—please, come in." Elle led the athletic and commanding woman through the house and into the kitchen. Elle gestured towards a seat at the table. "Coffee?" she asked, and reached into the cupboard for a mug. The detective watched her with hawk eyes and studied the way her hands shook around the cups, causing them to knock together.

"Sure, so tell me, Miss Sullivan—"

"You can call me Elle."

"Elle—when did you last see Aaron?"

Elle poured coffee into the cups and set them down on the table. She pushed the cream and sugar towards Barboza.

"Ah—just before I left? Mid-April?"

"Witnesses at your apartment complex say you two had a little trouble sometimes."

"He beat the hell out of me, if that's what you mean." Elle said and her eyes locked with the detective's. Something changed in Barboza's hard-ass demeanor.

"Pretty bad, huh?" Her voice was softer.

"Sometimes. I told him I wanted to leave, that I—I wanted a divorce, and he threw me down the stairwell of our apartment building. I cracked open my skull—" she touched the scar subconsciously. She took in a shaky breath, "and miscarried my baby."

Barboza was quiet for a moment.

"That aligns with what I've heard from your neighbors," she said quietly. Barboza looked down at the Rawlins Bank and Trust coffee mug and added three sugar cubes. The bitterness of the circumstances couldn't be cut with enough sweet. "I'm sorry for your loss."

Elle shrugged, wiped away an errant tear. "I started thinking I'd never get free."

"So—how did you get free, Elle? How did you get away from Aaron?" Her sympathetic brown eyes held Elle's. Woman to woman. Tough cookie to hard ass.

"A few months after the miscarriage, he went up to the mountains for the weekend. I took the opportunity and ran away."

"And what was he doing up there? Camping?"

"Hunting."

"Hunting? In April?"

"He doesn't always do it legally, and he likes going early in the season for wild turkey. Mostly it's an excuse for him to go get drunk and shoot whatever he can focus on." Elle said with an air of disgust. When Barboza quirked her head, she went on. "I was raised in Sweet Valley. Out here it's a matter of putting food on the table. We respect the laws and the animals. Aaron hunts for trophy. That's actually how we met. He and his dad came here to hunt at the Bar Nunn. Anyway—he just enjoys killing things."

"I see. So—he went hunting?"

Elle nodded and swallowed a sip of coffee, nerves on fire. "Normally he'd make me go, but I told him I was on my period and he—" she stopped to roll her eyes, "he said the smell might scare away the game, so he let me stay home. I didn't have a car or anything, or my own credit cards, so I think he thought I wouldn't go anywhere over the weekend."

"So, you didn't go with him, up to the mountains?"

"No," Elle shook her head.

"And he went alone?"

"As far as I know."

"So, then—you waited until he was gone, and you just left?"

Elle looked at her and scowled. "You make it sound like it was easy. Nothing was easy about leaving Aaron. He never left me alone, except when he went to work, and even then, he'd call me every hour."

"Did he call you when he went hunting? To see if you were home?"

"At least not for the first hour. I think the reception is spotty up there so I left as soon as I could gather my things. I don't know if he tried calling after that. When I left, I left everything; my phone and most of my things. I figured once he couldn't call me, he'd come looking—so I wanted to get miles between us, as quick as I could."

Barboza studied her. "But what did you do about money?" The conversation eased into an interrogation, and yet, still like two friends talking over a cup of coffee. This was Barboza's talent. Elle understood that.

"Well—" she took a deep sigh. "After I lost the baby, I knew I had to leave. I had to find a way out. I didn't know anybody there; I had no family and no friends. He made sure of that. So, while he was at work, I would do little jobs around the apartment complex —you can ask my neighbors. Babysitting, repairs, cooking, that kind of thing. I even baked a few cakes for birthdays and cooked for one of the older tenants below us. I tried to get paid in cash and saved up what I could. Then I just waited. When he went hunting that evening, and didn't make me go with him—I think it was a Friday? I bought a bus ticket to Vegas and got the hell out of town."

"Did you come by bus all the way here?"

"I stopped in Vegas to hock my wedding rings and used that money to get a truck. Then I just—" she drifted back to the journey that seemed at once too fresh and still a lifetime ago. "I just kept driving until I got here."

"You say you grew up in Sweet Valley?"

"Yes, that's right. This is my grandmother's ranch. I'm helping my parents run it."

"I heard from people in town that you're quite the baker."

"It's all my grandma's recipes really. She was amazing at filling people up. Oh here! I think I have a few extra biscuits from this morning." Elle jumped up suddenly and startled Barboza. "I'm so sorry I didn't offer before. My mind's a little off with—well, with the—news." Before Barboza could protest, Elle set the warmed cloud of buttery divinity in front of her with homemade jam and butter. "Please, have one. I'm sure it's been a long trip for you."

"Thank you, Elle." Barboza said and grunted after the first bite. "That's amazing." Elle watched her slathered the next bite with the tart and bright strawberry rhubarb jam.

"Do you have anything to prove you left town that April?"

Elle paused and then rummaged through her stuffed planner on the side table. In the back pocket, next to a meadowlark feather she'd found, and an old black-and-white photo of her grandparents, was a fading slip of paper. She took it out. "Here's the receipt from the pawn shop in Vegas. The paperwork for the truck is in the glove box. I can get it if—"

"That won't be necessary." Barboza looked over the receipts and tapped the April sixteenth date with her finger. "Did you think it was strange that he hadn't contacted you? Or tried to come after you?" Barboza asked over another big bite.

Elle stared at her; hands trembling around the planner.

"I did think it was strange. I mean, I really didn't have anywhere else to go but here and he knew that. To be honest, Detective, I've sort of been living on edge the last few months. I kept wondering when he'd come and get me, and—" she swallowed and her voice shook "And I knew he'd probably kill me when he did. I just thought at least I wouldn't be alone here. I have my family." She started crying. "You must think I'm awful to—to feel relieved that he's—is he really dead?"

Barboza reached across the table, gave her hand a squeeze. "He is. And I don't think you're awful, Elle. I think you're a resourceful woman who saved herself with limited opportunity and means."

"I guess that explains why he hasn't signed the paperwork I left him."

"Well, you won't have to worry about the divorce. You're a widow now."

Elle sniffed and shook her head. "How did he—I mean—was it the fire?"

"We're not exactly certain of the time or manner of his death. It appears that he had been drinking and passed out. We think either it was exposure, or some other—" Barboza paused, "Trauma. That early in the season, that high up, he might have gotten hypothermia, especially if, like you said, he liked to drink. When the Angeles fire burned through, it destroyed most of the camp site."

"That's—" Elle swallowed and her hands clutched the cup. "That's awful."

Barboza shrugged, a little too hardened. "Sometimes Karma is a bitch."

"What can I do? I mean, what do I need to do? I'm sure there are things left to take care of?"

"I'll have to get an official statement from you. If you have anything else you can think of, about the time he left or if you knew where he was going, or if he went with anyone else, let us know."

"Do I have to go back to L.A. for anything?"

"Not regarding his death," Barboza shifted, as though there was something else on her mind. "Are you close to his family at all?"

Elle shook her head. "They weren't like my family." Her heart warmed and she felt her sisters' hands on her back, her grandmother's fingers in her hair. "They didn't come to the wedding or visit us. I think I met them once. I know his dad was a real estate broker and his mom was—wasn't she an actress?"

Barboza chuckled. "His mom was an...adult film star. They divorced ten years ago."

"Jesus, I guess I really didn't know them," Elle shook her head.

Blake burst through the door, and startled both women. Barboza rose swiftly and spun to face him with authority. Blake's eyes took in the sight of the woman's steady hand hovering near her gun. He put his hands up and looked at Elle.

"Heya, boss. Everything OK?"

Elle looked at him and smothered the leaping joy of her rapid heartbeats. Had it been weeks or years? She ached to both throw herself into his arms and throw him out of the house. His stubble had grown long and dark. His blue eyes were sharp and wild. Fearing he might say something to the detective about where he'd been, as she had a pretty good idea now where he must have gone, Elle put on her best, annoyed face.

"Did you get the udder cream?"

"I—uh, I forgot my hat halfway to town." Blake stammered.

"Your hat?" Elle scowled. Blake looked at the detective and back at her. Elle sighed. "Detective Barboza, this is Blake O'Connor. He works for me and trains with my dad at his vet clinic. Blake, this is Detective Barboza, from the L.A.P.D."

"Is this about Aaron? Is he here? Should we get Elle someplace safe? Are you gonna arrest him?"

"Blake—"

"Detective, you should have seen her face when she got into town—" he started, and the memory made his stomach tumble. Barboza watched him carefully.

"Did you know Aaron Lowry, Mr. O'Connor?"

"Not really. I met him and his dad years ago when they came to trophy hunt. What I did know of him, I didn't like."

"Blake—"

"That seems to be the general consensus amongst his co-workers and neighbors. Aaron's remains were found by fire crews in the Angeles National Forest. It took us a while to identify his body as not much was left."

Blake stared at Barboza as if she'd just told him that the moon was, in fact, made of cheese.

"Remains? What do you mean? His—his body?" Blake's fear turned into confusion. "Shit—holy shit—" he stepped back a pace and looked to Elle. She shrugged her shoulders, as if she had nothing more to add.

Barboza sighed, took out her notebook, jotted down a few things. She turned back to Elle.

"Well, I can't think of anything else. Thanks to you, at least we know why he was up there." She tapped her pen on the table, picked up her biscuit and took a bite, then snapped her fingers. "Oh, what I was saying before Blake forgot his hat—" she said mid-bite and turned to Elle. "Were you aware of Aaron's financial situation?"

"I don't know what you mean. He controlled all of the money. He never let me know what was in our bank account. Only what I was allowed to spend—groceries and that sort of thing."

"I see. So, you never questioned the car he drove or what the rent was?"

"It—" Elle stuttered and felt tears form. "He always said it wasn't any of my business what he made. He wouldn't let me have a job, so it was always his decision where the money went." Blake's brow fell and he looked at the framed checks above the wall. He looked back to the detective with softer eyes.

"Did he owe a lot of money? Is she responsible for that? We'll figure out a way to pay off the debt, Detective. It might take some time, but Elle is a hard worker; she wouldn't shirk on bills." His voice died away as Barboza studied him.

"He had no outstanding bills," she said.

"Oh—" Elle was somewhat surprised. "Well, then what was his financial situation?"

"Aaron was the beneficiary of a long-standing family trust." The room spread with silence.

"He never mentioned a trust," Elle said.

"Well, that's something that I'm sure the lawyers will have to discuss with you. But I believe, as his wife, that you stand to inherit it."

Blake's eyes swung to Elle.

"He wouldn't do that," Elle said to Barboza. "He hated me. He wouldn't even give me ten dollars for new underwear."

Barboza shot her a quizzical look, and then one that said she would have liked to kick Aaron down some stairs.

"Without a will, and per California law, I believe it all goes to you, just the same."

Elle's eyes snapped away from her to Blake, whose hand twitched, agitated, at his side.

"I don't want it," Elle shook her head. "I don't want his money. I wish I could have all of those years back. The baby I lost. If I could ask for anything, it wouldn't be the money." She looked at Blake, who looked down at his feet. "I have everything I need here." She looked out the window at the old fenceposts and run-down pick up. "I know it's not shiny and new, but it's mine and I've worked for it, and it's worth so much more than anything he ever gave me." Elle wiped her eyes again. Blake cleared his throat.

Barboza sighed and looked around the quaint and clean kitchen. Somewhere, a horse neighed outside. She studied Elle's face, the scar on her forehead, more on her arms. Her face lost its hardened mask.

"Well," she sighed, "I hope you can do something good with the money. If you wanted, you could give it to a local charity, if it makes you feel better." She wiped her mouth, having demolished the whole biscuit. "I'll have the local officer...Stan is it?"

"Yes, ma'am," they said in tandem.

"I'll have him take your official statement and send it in to me. That'll give him something to do when he runs out of speeding tickets to write," she chuckled. "The Lowry's estate lawyer will probably be contacting you within a few weeks. I've got a flight to catch out of Laramie this afternoon."

"Ugh, the vomit comet. I'm sorry." Elle sympathized.

"Yeah, it was pretty bad coming in."

"Here—" Elle rose and wrapped up the last biscuit in a box with a side of jam. "Take this with you. In case there's nothing worth eating at the airport."

"Thank you, Elle." Barboza took the biscuit, and handed Elle her card. "If there's anything else you can think of, or if you need help in the process of settling Aaron's affairs, let me know. I know some good people in L.A. who can help."

"I appreciate that, Detective." Elle said and meant it. If there were good people in L.A., she believed that Detective Barboza was one of them. "Take care and drive safe." she said.

"I should probably go get that udder cream," Blake stuttered, having the sense to grab his hat, still hanging on the hook, like he'd never left. He stepped up to Barboza and extended his hand. "Detective, sorry I barged in like that," he said. She returned his firm grip.

"Don't worry about it, Blake. I understand your concern." She winked, barely noticeable. Blake cleared his throat and muttered a goodbye before walking determinedly to his Jeep and pulling out of the driveway. Barboza watched him, all the way until he'd disappeared out of the gate.

"Hmm—a hired hand, huh?" she quirked an eyebrow at Elle with a sly smile. Elle shrugged.

"I guess you could probably see through that, huh?"

"You two are oozing all those thirsty looks."

Elle covered her face. "It's kind of new, and—well, old too. It's a little complicated and—tender," she confessed, the least of the truth.

"Then best you take care of it." Barboza nodded, and Elle led her to the door.

Twenty-Eight

Blake found Elle in the barn, where she'd been sitting, next to Lottie's stall, crying with her arms wrapped around her belly. He dropped the bag with a tub of udder cream at her feet, and she looked up without startling.

"You just show up?" she growled, wiping at the tears and rising to her feet. "Like you hadn't been gone for weeks. Like you hadn't told me that you weren't coming back! Made me think you were going off to go die—"

"I thought I was!" he yelled; his jaw clenched beneath the stubble. "I thought I was going to die, or end up in prison."

"And where in the hell did you go? What in the hell did you think you were gonna do?" she yelled back, though her brain had already sorted out the where and what.

"To kill that son-of-a-bitch."

Elle stopped and looked at him for half a heartbeat. "You idiot."

"I'm an idiot? You want to tell me how Aaron ended up in the woods? Dead?"

"How should I know? He went hunting," she argued and

snatched up the udder cream to take it to the storage cabinets in the office. The office he'd built with bare hands and scraped knuckles.

"Elle—" he yelled and followed her.

"Save it, O'Connor. You left." She slammed the cabinet shut and spun on him.

"Because I didn't know he was dead, and I didn't want you looking over your shoulder for the rest of our lives, or to have you worry about our babies."

"Well, he is dead, and I'm not scared of him any—" she stopped. "Whatta ya mean, 'our babies'?"

Blake looked at her, a small smile tugging beneath his lip. "Just what I said, Sullivan."

"You don't want to stay in this stupid little town. You don't want to settle down, raising a pack of kids."

"I do."

"You don't want to tie yourself to a basket case like me," she argued.

"I do—both hands, behind my back," he smiled.

"Blake, I've done some horrible th—" she sighed, her shoulders dropped and her head hung. Blake walked closer and she could smell the flannel of his shirt, his cologne and truck-stop coffee.

"Elle, and the horrible things she's done." He shook his head. "Parsnips taste funny," he whispered.

"What?" Elle looked up from her boots to him.

"You said it in your sleep the night you told me about the baby. I didn't think about it until Barboza was talking about how the fire had destroyed Aaron's remains."

"He went hunting and got drunk. Passed out."

"Parsnips get confused with another plant, Elle." Blake lowered his eyes to hers.

"Oh?"

"Hemlock."

"I don't know what you're talking about."

"I'm not mad that you killed that son-of-a-bitch," he whispered. She looked up and started to protest. "I'm mad that you had to. I'm mad at myself. That I wasn't the one saving you." Elle looked away, to the window and the glaring light of the day contrasting the dark barn.

"Then again, my Elle is the patron saint of lost causes...even when it's her own." He stepped closer, but she backed away. Something deeper on her mind now, that he was back, standing in front of her. The shuddering truth she didn't want to burden him with. What if he left all over again?

"What are you thinking?"

"I don't know what I'm thinking," she shook her head.

"You said, you'd wait—"

"You said you weren't coming back—"

"So, which one of us was lying?" he said, and studied her face. "I hope it was only me."

"Blake, there's things you need to know before you—before you—"

"Before I what, take you back to the house?"

"—before you decide what you really want." She stepped away, but the rough wall of the barn pressed into her back while his blue eyes searched hers.

"So, tell me."

"Well, first, you should know you don't need to worry about me anymore. What Barboza said—knowing for sure he's gone—well, you don't have to worry over me. I won't get in the way of you getting on with your own life."

"My own—" he paused. "My *life*, Elle? What in the hell is that supposed to mean?"

"I didn't spend all these months nagging you, and put in all that time getting you back on your feet for you to stay in this little town." She side-stepped. "When you left, for the first few days, I was sad, but then I realized you deserved better. You deserved to take your test, to go find some swanky clinic to set up shop, to do and be whatever you want."

Blake stared at her, bewildered. "Is there anything else?" His intensity broke through her walls. Elle took in a deep breath; her eyes filled with fresh tears.

"Yes."

"Tell me," he said softly.

"You need to know that I believe in you. You need to know that I want more for you than to be stuck in Sweet Valley your whole life," her voice shook, but she continued. "You need to know that I'll be madder than hell if you don't get out there and find a job that feeds your soul. You need to know that I love you, always, but I'm not going to hold you to something you never promised."

Blake's eyes fell to where her teeth bit her lips, nervously.

"Is that all?" he whispered, coming closer, her words not altering the decisions he'd already made in his mind. "Elle?"

The silence sat heavy between. She was scared of what he might think; what he might do. She was afraid of the destructive history that plagued her. She sniffed.

"I might be—well, I might be pregnant, and if I am—I want to keep it," she said and dropped her arms. He came to her tenderly and knelt down, slipped his strong fingers beneath her shirt, and felt her shiver. The gentle curves of her body were warm beneath his hand, and Blake wondered if he'd died and gone to heaven.

He collapsed into her. His arms went around her and he pressed his cheek to her bare middle, his stubble scratching against the delicate skin. Elle would have been knocked back if he hadn't been holding on so tight. She stiffened at first, but the warmth of his protective hold softened her and she threaded her hands into his hair.

"God, Elle," he whispered, and kissed her belly over and over, nuzzling and touching the soft and sweet-smelling skin of her. His body followed his heart, reacting with such desire and love that all he wanted was to take her inside and cement the new-found devotion that filled him. The possibility of his baby, his very own child, carried by the woman he loved for so long, made him dizzy and full in heart.

"Blake, if I am, you don't have any obligation—"

"We're not eight anymore and you don't get to tell me what to do." He sniffed, emotionally shaken as he looked up at her. "I love you so goddamn much. If you aren't pregnant—then I want to keep trying. If you are—well, shit, I still want to keep trying," he looked up at her with a mischievous grin. She had a hard time not laughing out loud. She screwed her face up into a frown.

"Blake Lee O'Connor, it doesn't matter what I'm gonna do. I will not let you waste your life here!" She pulled against his arms, but he held fast, and rose from his knees.

"Why would I want to leave everything I've ever loved or will love?" He bent his head to kiss her. His lips were warm and soft. "And why can't I have both? Why can't we have it all?" He framed her face with his hands, smoothed her hair from her forehead. "Haven't we suffered enough? Haven't we paid for our sins? I know you sure as hell have. So why can't we have all the happiness we can get our hands on?"

Elle stared at him with her down-to-earth smirk.

"Blake," she sighed. "What in the hell will you do? Just keep running errands and fixing fence all your life? You went to school to be a vet and I'll be damned if I let you give that up."

He thought about the options for his clinical year, the off-handed way Warren had mentioned it more than once. Even offering to pay for Blake's testing fees as payment for the work. The old veterinarian was pretty cunning. Blake chuckled and Elle scowled at the sound, so much more her best friend than before.

"What?"

"Yeah, well, it won't be easy, but I'll do what I have to."

"What do you mean? Why are you laughing?"

"Well, I've been asked to work for Dr. Sullivan, to get ready to take over for him when he retires. Maybe even take on his family business and all, but he has this super-demanding, pliers-wielding daughter who I'd have to put up with. That woman is *so* pushy." Blake rolled his eyes.

"Dr. Sulliv—"

"Though truth be told, I kind of like it when she bosses me around," he whispered with a wink.

"I don't understand—" Elle's voice shook and confusion drove her breath in gasps.

"She's got this whole, lost-causes habit and needs someone to keep her from shooting her neighbors and fainting on trails. They gotta be able to make her laugh and kick her ass at Scrabble. It's really a full-time, kind of gig. I'm not sure how much time I'll get to spend actually being a veterinarian—"

"You do not kick my ass at Scra—"

"I've been around enough to know what I want," he interrupted. "I've seen enough to know what I need. I've lived long enough to know what's best for me, and that's you. Living here with you. Working with you. Being in your life." Elle's heart sang, but her brain feared.

"What if I don't want to get married again? What will you do?"

"I don't want to own you, Elle." His gaze narrowed. "I'm not asking to be your husband, if that's not what you want. I'm just asking to be a part of your life. A place for you to land, a person you can trust in. I can't be anything else, because you're my heart, Elle," he clutched at his chest. "Whether you want me or not, I love you. I always have. I'm always gonna. Even if I have to live in a crappy apartment in town or out in the wagon for the next fifty years. I'm your 'count on it'; whether you count on me or not."

Elle's eyes filled with tears.

"Goddamn it," she laughed suddenly.

"Well, now, I don't take kindly to a filthy mouth," he teased and looked down at her.

"Shut up and kiss me."

"Yes, boss," he said and did. Slowly, remembering every note of the moment. The way her eyes shone up at him with laughter and smiles. The way she glowed to light the day. The way Elle, his best friend, had finally come home.

TWENTY-NINE

THE EARLY SUMMER HEAT BURGEONED FROM THE hayfields. With luck, this would be the first hay of two rounds this summer. But Elle had a feeling the days were short when she'd be able to work with both hands free. She rubbed her swollen belly and felt hot and itchy beneath the afternoon sun's onslaught. She pulled to a stop at the end of the row and stepped off the tractor just as she heard Blake yelling from the gate. He stomped angrily through the field; hell bent on her.

"Hey, goddamn it! You know you're not supposed to be up there, and not anywhere out too far by yourself." She smiled and crinkled her nose beneath her straw hat. His frown faded as he came closer.

"You don't get to tell me what to do, Blake O'Connor."

"The hell I don't," he said, less anger and more sweetness. He came close, his hands circling around her waist, pausing to caress the perfect swell of her belly.

A foot jabbed out to meet his touch, and Elle buckled with the strength of it.

"She says you can't boss me around either. She's kicking you."

"*He* is agreeing with me. He says Mom's hot, and she needs to go put her feet up and drink something cold."

"Mom's got work to do," Elle said. "I thought you were at the clinic today."

"I was, until Ty called me and said he saw you out on the tractor."

"Now you've got spies on me?"

"You are not an easy woman to keep safe. I gotta use all the resources I have." he said.

"Worrying over me?" she said and reached up to thread her fingers through his curly hair, pushing his cowboy hat off.

"I'll never stop," he whispered and bent to kiss her. She pressed her body into his and he groaned. The warmth between them blossomed. He wanted her. The baby kicked and pushed against the warmth of Blake's stomach and he smiled into Elle's lips.

"He's not gonna like the things I wanna do to his mom," he chuckled. A contraction crested suddenly, and Elle doubled over.

"Oof, I guess not." Her muscles trembled and clenched. Blake gripped her arms and looked down at her.

"You OK? What is it?"

She shook her head. "Nothing, just Braxton Hicks."

"Come on, let's get you to the house so you can put your feet up."

"I don't put my feet up, you know that. It's nothing. I've got three more rows to get through."

"Not today you don't."

"Oh, for cryin' out loud—" she gave an exasperated sigh and sat up between the waves. "Will you just calm down. Women have been birthing babies in fields for hundreds of years."

Blake's eyes widened. "That shit is not funny, Elle. You're not giving birth to our baby in the middle of a hayfield." She smiled up at him from her crouch and chuckled before another contraction hit her and she had to stop to breathe. Blake bent down and scooped her up, lifting her into his arms without so much as a grunt.

"What in the hell?"

"Goddamn it, you're the most stubborn woman I've ever met," he grumbled as he took her back towards the house. Elle put her arms around his neck and nuzzled him beneath the ear.

"You're no picnic either," she whispered as another wave swept over her and she curled into his arms. "I'm not sure if it's Braxton —I—oof!" She buckled into him and he set her down on the ground near the house. "Call Katie, call Laney, and Mom. Call Dad—" The laughter was gone and Blake looked fear-stricken.

"I'll go get the Jeep; you stay here."

"I don't think there's gonna be time, Blake," she gasped and held on to her belly. She could feel the pulling in her hips, pelvis, and low back. The vibrations of the tractor and the distraction of work had kept her from noticing their progression. She cried out behind her clenched jaw as another wave pushed over her. Blake rushed to her side, took his phone out of his pocket, and dialed Katelyn. She was working with Warren today and they weren't far away. Laney was home with their mother and her girls.

"Take me into the house. Can you take me in?" Elle breathed between contractions. Sweat beaded on her brow. Blake nodded, scooped her up, and rushed her into the clean, sunlit kitchen. "Here, here is fine—" Blake set her down on her feet and Elle leaned against a chair. She felt the strangest urge, undeniable and ancient.

"I think I gotta push..."

"You gotta what? No! Elle, honey, just hang on a minute." Blake dialed the emergency services number, but the line was busy. He tried again, while rubbing Elle's back in long, even strokes. Tires on gravel heralded the family's arrival and Katelyn nearly skidded into the fence in her hurried park of the old rusted two-ton.

"I'm here!" Katelyn shouted. "We're here!" Her breathless yell came closer as they both ran through the door. "Mom's on her way too." Katelyn, Laney, and Warren barged in to see the pain and relief in Elle's eyes.

"She says she wants to push; I say she should wait until the ambulance gets here." Blake said, desperate to get them on his side. Laney shook her head.

"If she already wants to push, that ambulance won't get here in time."

"But that can't be right. How'd it happen so fast?" Blake asked, bewildered. Warren put a soothing hand on his shoulder.

"Son, every baby's different. Laney came right as expected, like she'd scheduled it in. Elle was born in Doc Johnston's office." He smiled at his daughter and pushed a sweaty blonde curl off of her forehead. "Katelyn, bless her pointed head, was born in the hay loft."

"My excuse for the way I am. Literally born in a barn," Katelyn said. Elle half laughed and half groaned. Katelyn smiled and kissed her forehead. Laney moved the table out of the way and took Elle by the shoulders.

"OK, honey, let's get you comfortable. Blake, I'm gonna need some towels, and boil some water, and—"

"What the hell are you talking about!"

"Oh? How many babies have you had, Blake?" Laney grouched back.

"Well, okay—but—Katelyn, you think we should wait for the ambulance, right?" Blake argued hotly as he dialed the number again.

"I've helped a lot of mares—" Katelyn shrugged

"Elle isn't a goddamn horse!" Blake yelled.

"Not so different...the legs are shorter—"

"Right, so the baby won't have as far to fall," Laney joked along with Katelyn, keeping the mood light. "Relax, O'Connor, we're in this together."

Blake held Laney's eyes for the first time since they were young. She was his big sister too.

"She's my whole world, Laney." His voice wavered, and his eyes teared up.

"I know—we won't let anything happen to her, will we?" She nodded to him and squeezed his shoulder.

"What in the hell is the boiled water for in movies?" Katelyn asked.

"Sterilizing things. Let's just start with some clean towels, but not the good ones unless you want Elle to tan your hide— "Laney said between sweet and soft coos to her sister as she groaned and buckled against the chair.

"I don't care what you do, just make it stop!" Elle yelled with her brow beaded in sweat and red from the exertion.

"Only one sure fire way for it to stop," Laney smiled at Elle. "Let's have this baby."

Blake ran for towels. Warren smoothed Elle's hair from her face.

"You're gonna be alright, Slim. You're a strong woman, and I'm so proud of you. You can do this thing. You can do anything," Warren said with an air of calm, but even his steady blue eyes were clouded with worry.

"Let's get you outta these," Katelyn said and helped Elle shimmy out of her pants. Katelyn wrapped the flowery tablecloth around her waist just as Blake brought in an armful of towels. They spread them out on the floor.

"Lay down, honey," Blake said, pushing back the table and chairs. Elle held on to his arms and shook her head.

"No, you hold on to me, Blake," she said. "Please, don't leave." Her voice shook with fear as the next demand to push hit her.

"I won't, I won't," he whispered. "I'm here, I won't be going anywhere," he held her elbows in his hands, took her weight as she gripped his shoulders. Bearing down, her knees threatened to buckle, but Blake held her up as he whispered sweet and soothing words into her ear and kissed her temple.

"That's it, baby, that's it. You're doing so good, Elle."

Elle screamed and tears soaked into Blake's shirt as she clung to him.

"I see the head. It's got a head!" Katelyn exclaimed joyously from below the tablecloth.

"Well, of course it's got a head." Laney pinched Katelyn hard and Elle, in the midst of the excruciating pressure, laughed.

"Our baby has a head," Elle gasped, elated. "Our baby." The need hit her anew, to meet their baby.

"Ok, Elle, give me a push—" Laney said and Elle bore down with a yell.

"Holy shit!" Katelyn shouted, as the burst of fluid and life spread across the towels, the floor, and her legs. A shrill and beautiful cry filled the air.

"Sh—she's a girl! It's a girl!" Laney yelled and cried at once. Elle crumpled to the ground with Blake while Katelyn and Laney helped their dad wipe the tiny, pink wailer clean. He wrapped the baby up in a soft blanket and placed her gently into Elle's arms. With a face scrunched against the light and cold world, she bawled; open mouth and clenched fists. Elle's heart was completely outside of her body and vulnerable.

"Oh, sweet girl," She breathed, kissing the baby's head and holding her close to her chest. She unbuttoned her shirt and moved her bra away, offering the baby her warmth and smell. The baby nuzzled in.

"Elle," Blake whispered, his voice strangled and choked with tears and laughter. "Oh, God, she's just so perfect."

"Look at her go." Katelyn said as the baby latched on. Elle's belly contracted and Laney directed her to push, helping to finish the birth. Blake held her, cradling her against his chest and staring lovingly down at the baby whose hair had already begun to curl as it dried.

"She's as strong as her momma," he whispered, kissing Elle. Elle looked up at him.

"Pretty as her daddy," she said.

"Whatcha gonna name her? Something kitchen-y? Kenmore or Whirlpool? G.E-lle? Ha!" Katelyn teased. Elle smiled up at her sisters.

"I don't know," she shook her head, exhausted and in awe. The feeling of finally coming home; of coming into herself made the world anew. "I thought of Emma after Gran, or Lee after Blake's middle name," she said. Blake squeezed her shoulders.

"Emilee," he said softly.

"Emilee." Elle's heart sped up and she nodded. "That's perfect, that's it. That's our girl," Elle said, her eyes teary and her heart filled. Blake kissed her and ran his thumb over the sweet brow of his daughter.

"Welcome home, Emilee," he whispered.

THIRTY

THE L.A. TIMES ARTICLE READ:

THE REMAINS OF A MAN FOUND IN THE ANGELES National Park, by fire crews scouting the burn area of the Mount Rose fire, have been identified as Aaron Lowry. Authorities say that Lowry died before the fires, possibly of exposure, sometime in the spring of last year. Family members have been notified.

AUTHORITIES ARE REMINDING CAMPERS, HIKERS, AND hunters to take precautions against the dangers of exposure, limit their alcohol use, and be wary of forest fires, especially in years of drought.

"HUH...MAYBE AUTHORITIES SHOULD REMIND ASSHOLES not to abuse their wives." Blake glanced past his phone at Elle, who sipped her tea while rubbing Emilee's back and patting out tiny, perfect burps. "Might make an interesting plot for one of Laney's novels." He shot Elle a raised eyebrow. There was no flash of fear. No shudder or curling up in the corner. Elle simply smiled.

"Not too interesting. Unless you could think of a good cause of death. Like—maybe he accidentally ate hemlock stew and died while choking on his own vomit in the cold wilderness by himself, where sharp toothed beasties found his body and made good use of him."

Blake smiled over his cup.

"That would make it more interesting, hypothetically."

"Purely hypothetical." Elle nodded.

"Remind me not to eat at home when I piss you off." Blake said and turned back to his textbook with a grin. Elle marked the week's paychecks into her ledger with one hand and bounced Emilee in her other arm.

"Best you just not piss me off, I guess." Elle said, and they both smiled at each other. The past burned and buried behind them, a world away.

It wasn't much long after, on Emilee's first birthday, that a small present was tucked among the teddy bears and gifts from well-wishers. The tiny cardboard box was addressed to the proprietor of Raising Elle's Bakery. Elle looked suspiciously at Blake when he handed it to her quietly amongst the merry sounds around them. Melissa sat with Laney's girls on the couch, each of them doting over their baby cousin and reading stories aloud. Warren was talking to Katelyn about her newest offer for employment on the East Coast, helping to rehabilitate an injured thoroughbred. Laney was watching Elle and Blake, starry-eyed and taking mental notes.

"What's this?" Elle asked.

"A box," he said.

"Okay, smart ass, what's in the box?"

Blake shook his head and smiled mischievously. "Only one way to find out."

Elle slid her fingers under the tape and popped the top off. On a bed of soft cotton fluff sat a ring, shaped like a circular twig. Small, golden leaves flanked a rough-cut diamond.

"Blake—"

"It's a diamond in the rough," he said and his eyes nervously shot up to hers. "Like me." When she didn't respond, and her downcast eyes offered no clue as to what her heart might be feeling, he went on. "It doesn't have to be anything, Elle. It's just a thank you. Thank you for saving my life. Thank you for saving your own so I could be with you. Thank you for our daughter and being the mother you are to her, just a—I—" he paused and swallowed at her silence.

"A thank you?" she scowled.

"Yes?"

"Well, don't you want to marry me?"

"Well, of course I do! But you said that you—that I—"

Elle laughed, beautiful and full.

"My God, O'Connor, you gotta learn to take a joke."

"This isn't a joke, Eleanor. It's my life. You're my life!"

"So then?"

"What?" he said, perturbed.

"Well, then ask me!"

"What if you say no?" he yelled back.

She smiled mischievously. "There's only one way to find out."

"Eleanor Augusta Sullivan—"

"Yes, Blake?"

"Will you make me the happiest idiot on the face of the earth?"

She sighed, put her hand on his cheek and leaned in. "No," she said. Blake's brow wrinkled. "But I will marry you."

He smiled then and pulled her into his lap for a kiss.

"Fair enough." The whole family cheered and whistled. Laney sniffed, wiped her eyes, and came over to plant a kiss on Blake's forehead.

"Way to lean in, O'Connor."

GRANTING KATELYN
THE SWEET VALLEY SERIES - BOOK TWO

We hope you have enjoyed *Raising Elle - Book One in The Sweet Valley Series*. Here is an excerpt from *Granting Katelyn - Book Two in The Sweet Valley Series*. Please visit 5 Prince Publishing for release information.

GRANTING KATELYN
CHAPTER ONE

The sun was hotter than hellfire on her dust and sweat-covered skin. Muscles in her shoulders tensed as she tightened her core and narrowed her eyes on the target ahead. The angry bull charged the group of riders and Katelyn Sullivan dug her heels into Dakota's sides, her hips nudging effortlessly and thighs contracting as they flew, one being, over the expansive field. Dakota's nimble and honed muscles responded to Katelyn as if the same neurological impulses were shared between them. The bull dodged right, Dakota anticipated, and responded. It swerved left and tripped in the rush to evade horse and rider, then turned a semicircle around a clump of sagebrush.

"Son-of-a-bitch," Katelyn growled. "Go get 'im!" She took the rope into her calloused right hand. The thunder of the bull's hoofs against the clay-packed ground shook through and across the field, and Katelyn leaned into the chase, raising her hand above her head while guiding Dakota with the other. The loop began large and easy, as Katelyn slowed her breathing and focused on the twin tips of the horns ahead. While the world sped by at a breakneck pace, it faded in Katelyn's brain, and her focus narrowed.

"Ease up, babe," she spoke softly in the palomino's ears. The mare was attuned to her voice. The bull cantered to the right, as Katelyn anticipated it might, to avoid the approaching fence line, and her nimble fingers tightened the loop and sent it through the dusty air with a whispering hiss. It ringed around the bull's right horn, and before the slack could disappear and cost her a finger, Katelyn wrapped the end around her saddle horn and pulled Dakota up with a lean back and a soft "Whoa." Without taking the bull to the ground, and gently turning its head in the direction she wanted it to go, she safely secured it to Dakota and led it back to the open fence, where it had come over to romance the heifers of Bar Nunn's only-for-show herd.

"Wow!" one of Bar Nunn's guests gasped, mouth hanging open. "Does she work for you?"

The hired hand being asked could barely keep his own horse from bolting at the excitement.

"Uh, no."

"Make that, *hell* no," Katelyn said as she passed by and tipped up the bill of her ball cap to the yaw-mouthed male guides as she passed. "Ladies."

"Who is that?" a man at the back asked tersely.

Another guide at the back of the group chimed in. "Katelyn Sullivan. All-state barrel racing champ."

"Sullivan? Like the baked goods they deliver to the resort?"

"That would be her sister, Elle."

"Quite the horsewoman," the terse man said and watched her pass by the group, spine straight and riding just as effortlessly as if she'd been born on the horse's back. He hadn't been able to keep his eyes off of her from the minute she'd jumped the palomino over the fence and taken after the bull upon hearing the guest's screams from one field over. She certainly was a take-charge type.

"She's also an equine therapist. She's worked with a couple of our own," the guide remarked as his agitated horse tried to follow Katelyn. "Including this one," he grunted.

"His name's Otis, Joey, and if you'd take a minute to actually get to know your horse, he might do what you want him to," Katelyn grouched as she passed by. "I'll send you a bill for my services," she called over her shoulder and escorted the bull back to Garrett's ranch down the road.

"Therapist, huh?" The interested older man watched her go and committed her name to his sharp memory.

"She's good with horses, but a bit crass," the first guide sneered.

"You mean she doesn't put up with bullshit?" the man said. "I need to speak to that young lady," he whispered to his wife. "I think a mutual friend of ours could use her help."

"Maybe even help his horse, too." His wife wiggled her eyebrows.

Katelyn May Sullivan hoisted the western saddle up and onto the fence with little difficulty. She wiped the sweat from her neck, just below her ponytail, and looked out over the cottonwoods into the setting sun. It grazed the bright green shuddering of leaves and left semicircles of shadows at her feet.

"That was some decent riding," came an older man's voice from behind.

Katelyn turned to the couple approaching the small paddock at the back of her parents' house. She recognized them from the Bar Nunn group this afternoon and eyed them with caution.

"It was all right. Nothing that any decent rider couldn't have been able to handle. Sorry you didn't have better examples with your 'dudes'." She turned to wipe the saddle down.

"I'm Jim Parsons and this is my wife, Sharon."

Sharon nudged in front of him. "That was the best thing I've seen all week," she said and held out her hand. "Should have seen their chins hit the dirt when you roped it in a single throw. Serves them right." Katelyn took her hand with renewed interest and a warmer smile. "Many moons ago, I won Sheridan County Fair in calf roping."

"I bet you did, Sharon," Katelyn said. Jim cleared his throat and Katelyn turned to shake his as well.

"What can I do for you two? I assume you don't need real riding lessons." She smiled. Jim put his hands on his hips and Katelyn felt like she was about to get roped into something herself.

"I hear you're an excellent equine therapist as well as a helluva barrel racer."

"My reputation might have been exaggerated."

"Humble is fine too," he said, and nodded. "I have a proposition for you."

Katelyn looked across the paddock to the small stables where Dakota had finished her dirt bath and was now swishing her long blonde tail at the water trough. When Jim didn't go on, she turned back to look at him.

"I'm afraid to ask what that might be," Katelyn said, disliking the hanging question in his voice. Sharon sighed, threaded her fingers together, and leveled her eyes on Katelyn.

"Have you ever heard of Tennyson Stables? The horse racing facility in North Carolina? Ian Tennyson owns one of the most promising bloodlines of thoroughbreds in America."

Katelyn leaned back on the fence, took off her gloves, and tucked them in her back pocket. She looked back to the burly and hardworking quarters her family had bred. A long way from the best thoroughbreds in America.

"Can't say as I've heard of them." Truth be told, that world clashed with the ideals of her heart. She'd seen too many case studies of racehorses and the damage done to their bodies for the sake of a payout.

"Grant Tennyson, Ian's son, is a friend of mine. When he came over from the UK about ten years ago, it was his first experience with that kind of work. I helped him get Tennyson Stables up and running. He's managing the facility himself now." Katelyn could read the slight change of tension in Jim's voice.

"Okay?"

"But he's had a rough go of it lately, especially with their breeding program."

"So—what's the problem, exactly?"

Jim smiled and leaned on the pole fence next to her, studying Dakota. "Well, it's their prize stallion, Hugh Dancy McFinnegan O'Shea."

Katelyn snorted. "Jesus, that's a hell of a name."

"Yeah, pompous, I know," Jim said.

"So? What happened to McFinnegan Sir Prance-A-Lot?"

Sharon stifled a chuckle. "Hugh was in an accident last fall and he's not performing as he should be."

"Well, that I'm sorry to hear," Katelyn said. "Surgery?"

"They flew in the finest equine surgeons they could find and, initially, it went well, but he's not responding to the recovery program." Katelyn watched Jim's body language. He seemed reserved, holding back the whole truth.

"Surely Tennyson can find a closer and more experienced therapist—"

"Well," Sharon interjected, "Grant is a—" She cleared her throat and looked out into the red-soil paddock.

"What?" Katelyn scowled.

"Grant isn't good with people. He's fired most of the therapists assigned to Hugh."

"Uh...golly, that sure sounds like a fun job. I don't think I'd be a good fit."

"That's just it," Sharon interrupted. "Jim and I, after seeing you ride and deal with the ranch hands this afternoon? Well, we both think you might be exactly the right person for the job."

Katelyn looked at Sharon sideways. "On account of my charming personality?"

"On account of you seem like someone who doesn't put up with bullshit, and this job requires a bit of fearlessness."

Katelyn didn't respond. She sighed with a troubled scowl set between her brows. Her brain turned the idea around and around in her head. She liked a challenge. She didn't put up with bullshit. And lost causes *were* a specialty of the Sullivan clan, her father had always said.

"What kind of injury?" she asked.

"He took a bad fall. Down an embankment. He was being pushed too hard over rocky terrain. Pulled a tendon in his chest, tore ligaments in his forefoot."

Katelyn nodded and thought. "I've seen something like that before, when I was younger. We had a gelding, Sal, who fell down a creek embankment. My grandma Em was able to help him recuperate nearly altogether."

"So, you think there's a chance Hugh could make a full recovery?" Jim asked.

Katelyn sighed. Thoughts of helping her dad bring in the summer hay and working with this year's foals fell away while the chance to work with a thoroughbred and help free it from pain and immobility pushed them aside. The added bonus of working in a new place, with high-end stables, no doubt a beautiful arena, and getting out of Sweet Valley for a spell, did its own work on her stir-crazy brain.

"Could be," she whispered.

"Great! I'll make a few calls this evening and have it arranged," Sharon said resolutely and shook Katelyn's hand again.

"Uh, oh—okay?" Katelyn stuttered. "Is this Grant guy gonna be upset if I just show up?" Katelyn asked. Jim smiled a charming grin and winked.

"Don't worry, Miss Sullivan. I don't think he'll stand a chance."

"Well, I don't know what that means."

Sharon smiled, and a slight blush rose in her cheeks, flashing her mischievous blue eyes. "I'm sure he'll love you."

"Uh—I'm not very—loveable," Katelyn said awkwardly.

Jim and Sharon laughed together, and Jim gave her one of his cards.

"We'll be in touch."

They walked away, hand in hand, and whispering excitedly to one another. Katelyn sighed. It wouldn't hurt to take a look.

PLEASE REVIEW

We hope you enjoyed *Raising Elle* by S.E. Reichert. If you did, we would ask that you please rate and review this title. Every review helps our authors.

Rate and Review: Raising Elle

MEET THE AUTHOR

Sarah Reichert (S.E. Reichert) is a novelist, poet, and blogger. She owns and operates The Beautiful Stuff Blog, a website for writing advice, poetry, and inspiration for living a more balanced, realistic life.

Currently, she is a full-time mom of two creative and talented teenage girls, and a full-time writer of both fiction and poetry. She is a terrible cat wrangler and her rescue pit bull steals all her cookies. Her garden is passionately planted every spring, and quietly neglected for most of the summer, in favor of getting lost in the wild gardens of the Rocky Mountains.

Acknowledgments

Good books aren't written in solitude. It may be where ideas blossom, words get put onto paper, and drafts are made. But a *good* book happens because a writer has a support system to help them along each step of the way. For all the hours at my computer I spend, there are equal hours of time spent by other people giving me a hand.

To my husband: thanks for supporting me while I write. I could get a real job. I *should* probably get a real job. But you've helped to make this endeavor easier with all of your support and that is a beautiful, loving thing. I can't ever repay you for what you've given me and our family while I traverse this minefield between dream and reality. I love you. More than I can ever tell you, and that's saying a lot because words are kinda my thing.

To my children, my daughters, Madelyn and Delaney. You are the brightest, funniest, strongest people I know. You've battled a lot of terrifying demons these last two years while the world crumbled around you and so many horrific events took place, outside of our control. The only sure hope I have for the future is knowing **you** will be leaders in it. You are more compassionate and kinder than I have been, stronger than I will ever hope to be, smarter than you give yourself adequate credit for, and I write for you. Because I hope that by following my dreams, you will also follow yours. I hope that by believing in myself, you'll believe in yourselves. Like I believe in you.

The Northern Colorado Writers has provided so much inspiration, instruction, support and laughter. In your writing retreats I find the solitude and focus as well as a sense of belonging to a wonderful community. I wouldn't be the writer I am today without your help. Because of your conferences I've improved my technique, learned all the ways I've done things wrong, and met some incredible human beings who also happen to write.

Thank you to Kerrie Flanagan who is THE best retreat roommate ever, my go-to martini and 80's pop-culture gal, and the mentor every writer should have. You are a dear friend and I am lucky to have you. Your belief in me and what we can accomplish together has driven me further than I ever could have made it on my own.

To Rebecca Schwab-Cuthbert, my absolute favorite writing buddy and gardening phenom. You've encouraged me through some of the darkest nights of my soul and I wouldn't be able to do this writing thing, or this living thing, without having you at my side. Here's to 100 more rejections.

To my beta readers, Misty, Kristine, Heather, Lucinda, Jean, Heidi, and Jessie; thank you for taking the time to read and give me feedback. You make a better book and you help make me a better writer.

To my Ohana at Kaizen IBBA. At first glance, there's not much in common between stepping onto the mats to get thumped on, repeating techniques over and over until I find the right movement, or imparting my knowledge to all those little ninjas out there and writing a novel; but first glances are deceiving. My martial arts mentors and family have encouraged my perseverance, uplifted my self-worth, and supported me through many hard times. Every kid that shows up with smiles and enthusiasm, every instructor that gives their time and help, every fellow student who stands beside me, makes me a better person and a better writer. They help me remember that I can do hard things with grace, humility, and resilience.

Thank you to the fantastic team at 5 Prince Publishing. To Bernadette Soehner who has given me warmth, laughter, opportunities and encouragement since the first day I met her. To

Cate Byers who takes my rough work and makes it so much better, with a level of talent and kindness that is unparalleled. I am so grateful for your support and help.

Also—thanks Google. I can't think of when I've needed so much help, from what the going rate of mohair is, to whether or not skunks kill chickens. From common muscle injuries in thoroughbred racing horses to if St. Croix has bioluminescent bays...you're the little search engine that could...make my books a little more accurate.

To all my readers, thanks for continually picking up these books. Thank you for sticking with the characters and for believing in their happily ever afters. May we all find a little of the same for ourselves.